CLOS[E]

Whatever they were, they were definitely not human.

Revna watched for another half minute. What were they doing here? What *were* they? A hundred questions formed and tried to rise all at once. Incredible.

He licked his lips and focused on one of the alien faces. Some kind of mask it wore, like the others. Breathing gear?

He would go back to town, get some of the ranchers, some photo equipment—

Revna blinked. One of the creatures turned and looked at him. It threw back its head; its long, odd braids fell back. A long, crazy howl filled the canyon, echoed off the cliffs and beat at his ears, joined by others.

Impossible; he was mostly hidden from view, and he could hardly see them with the scope. They couldn't see him.

But they did. He knew for sure in a second:

When they ran toward him, waving those spears, screaming.

Also available in the same series

Aliens: Earth Hive
Aliens: Nightmare Asylum
Aliens: The Female War
Aliens: Genocide
Aliens: Alien Harvest
Aliens: Rogue
Predator: Concrete Jungle

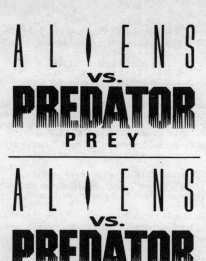

ALIENS vs. PREDATOR
PREY

ALIENS vs. PREDATOR
HUNTER'S PLANET

Omnibus edition

Steve Perry and Stephani Perry
David Bischoff

(Based on the Twentieth Century Fox motion pictures, the designs of H. R. Giger, and the graphic novels by Randy Stradley and Chris Warner)

A DARK HORSE SCIENCE FICTION NOVEL

MILLENNIUM

This edition first published in 1995 by
Millennium
The Orion Publishing Group
5 Upper St Martin's Lane,
London WC2H 9EA

ISBN: 1 85798 419 6

Printed in England by Clays Ltd, St Ives plc

ALIENS™

VS.

PREDATOR™

PREY

Thanks this time go to Kij Johnson, for giving us the work—despite all that ugly money stuff that came later. Or didn't come later ...

Fiend behind the fiend behind the fiend behind the
fiend.
Mastodon with mastery, monster
with an ache at the tooth of the ego,
the dead drunk judge:
Wheresoever Thou art our agony will find Thee
enthroned on the darkest altar of our heartbreak
perfect.
Beast, brute, bastard. O dog my God!

George Barker

1

Well, not to put too fine a point on it, I still think you're full of crap."

Scott smiled to take a little of the sting out, but not that much. They'd dropped out of hyperspace a week back, were running on the new and improved gravity drives, and the old argument had been lit and burning almost since the crew left the sleep chambers. The others were working the plant or attending to ship routine and the two pilots were alone in the control module, staring into the blackness of the Big Deep. Still a few weeks out from their next port, but it was starting to look like a few years.

Tom, whose still-short dark hair had been cropped to his skull before he'd gone into the sleep chamber, was up on his soapbox again, looking kind of like a military-college freshman in free-speak alley.

Scott stroked his blond beard and waited for the reply he knew was coming. Around them, the stale ship air smelled like a gym locker.

Tom didn't miss a beat. "Sure, I'm full of crap. Me and everybody else. But I'm telling you, the bill is gonna come due sooner or later. You can't just keep raping virgin planets, stripping them of everything valuable, and leaving the hulks behind."

"I don't recall that I stuck my dick into the dirt anywhere lately," Scott said.

"You know what I mean."

"No, I don't. *The Lector*, in case you fell asleep during the orientation session, is a tug. We're towing a half-full barge with about fifteen million tons of rendered fish and animal products and the processor that did it to collect *more* meat on the hoof from the poor suckers on Ryushi, a bunch of shit-kicker cowboys—no, not even cows, they're *rhynth*boys—living on a middle-of-nowhere planet."

"Scott—"

"And," he continued, ignoring Tom, "*and* the barge, this ship, the cowboys, *and* you and me are all owned body and soul by the Corp. Talk to old man Chigusa with your raping-the-environment complaints."

"Jesus, you are so damned close-minded—whoa!"

Scott waved his hands over the controls, trying to get a fix on the blip. Here in the middle of the Big Deep, where there was nothing but their vessel and occasional hydrogen atoms to bounce off it, something had just shot past them so fast it wasn't even a blur. And gaining speed like a bitch, too. Okay, yeah, it was a couple hundred klicks away, but out here, that was almost a sideswipe.

"Goddamned cheap fucking doppler!" Tom said,

trying to get the computer, to adjust its scan. "What the hell was that? A ship?"

"Not hardly. That acceleration would probably turn people into seat pancakes. Nova debris, maybe, old rock spat out by a real big planet-buster blast."

"Yeah? Maybe it's God on His way to the Final Reckoning. Better scrub your conscience clean, Scotty."

"I'm just a grunt, pal, don't blame me for the way the universe gets run."

"Fucking spectrograph missed it altogether." He slammed the heel of his hand against the console. Nobody wasted any money on these ships for such things as decent hardware.

"Like we were going to chase and catch it even if it was solid platinum, right?" Scott smiled. "It's not our job, buddy. One more rock in the dark, who cares?"

Seated in front of the sensor array on *Ne'dtesei*, Yeyinde watched the alien ship dwindle in their wake. He was Leader; his very name meant "brave one" but he knew the warriors called him "Dachande" when they thought his ears too dull to hear them. That name meant "different knife," and it referred to his left lower tusk, broken in a bare-handed fight against the Hard Meat, the *kainde amedha*, they of the black armored exoskeletons and acid blood. He smiled inwardly at the name. It could be considered an insult, but he was proud of it. The Hard Meat, save for the queens, were no smarter than dogs, but they were fierce and deadly game. Good prey upon which to train the young warriors. He could have had the tusk capped and reground, but he had left the broken fang a dull stump to remind himself—and any warriors who felt brave or particularly stupid—that only one yautja of all had ever faced the Hard Meat unarmed and walked away. As befitted a true warrior, Dachande himself never spoke of the battle, but let others tell the tale, holding a serious mandible at the embellishments they added in the singing of it. He was Leader of the *Ne'dtesei*, son and grandson of ship leaders and warrior trainers, and he bowed to no one in his skill with blade or burner. He had taken hundreds of young males out to learn the Hunt and had lost but a dozen, most of whom would still be among the living had they obeyed his orders.

But he sighed at the ship now so far behind him as to be invisible to even the sensors' keen eyes. Oomans flew in that vessel. He knew of them, the oomans, though he himself had never Hunted them. They were toolfolk, had weapons equal to those of the yautja, and were, if the stories could be believed, the ultimate *pyode amedha*. Soft Meat. But with deadly stingers, the oomans. A true test of skill. What were they doing out here? Where were they bound? A pity he was locked into this Hunt, responsible for a score of itchy would-be warriors full of themselves and ready to show off their prowess.

Well. Someday he would Hunt them, the oomans.

For now, he had a ship to fly, Hunts to prepare.

He switched to the electronic eyes that watched the Hard Meat queen in the nest they had made for her deep in the belly of the ship.

The image blossomed on the plate in front of him.

Tall she was, the queen, twice his own height, massive even in the reduced gen-pull of the ship, probably four times his weight. Black as a nestcleaner's hands, gleaming dully under the lights, the queen looked like a giant *zabin* bug, with the addition of a long segmented tail and smaller supplemental arms jutting from her torso. Her comb rose high like antlers, flat and flaring, and she had two sets of needle-toothed jaws, one nesting inside the other and able to extrude a span from her mouth to grab like pincers. Freed, she would be a formidable opponent, fast, powerful, intelligent. But she was not free, the queen. She was bound in bands of dlex, wound in restraints that could resist the sharpest blades, the hottest fires, the strongest acids. Bound and made into nothing more than an egg-laying captive, subject to the will of the ship's Leader. A conveyer ran beneath her massive ovipositor, catching the precious eggs and carrying them to the packing compartment. There, they were fed into the robot crawler in the sucker ships connected to the *Ne'dtesei* like leeches on either side. Inside the suckers the robots—treaded machines designed for one purpose—prepared themselves to transport and place the eggs on fertile ground. Like a mechanical mother, the robots would leave the eggs where they could open and the crablike first-stage Hard Meat could find game to infect with the next stage. Those embryos would eventually chew their way free of the hapless host to become drones, the final stage for most of the Hard Meat. Prey, to the warriors he had brought to learn the rules of the Hunt. Stupid but deadly, the Hard Meat would teach the main lesson the young ones needed to know: move well or die. There was no room for error in the Hunt.

Dachande looked at the fettered queen, the fleshy eggs she laid. His own trophy wall on the homeworld held half a dozen of the Hard Meat skulls, bleached and clean, including the one he had killed with his bare hands, as well as a queen, taken during a hellish hunt in which nine already-Blooded warriors had died. He had killed fifty others, but had kept, as was proper, only those he had thought worthy of his wall. They were fierce, but usually no challenge to one such as himself. If he had occasion to face one on these Hunts, he would limit himself to spear or wrist knife. After all, any yautja could *burn* the Hard Meat; a Leader had to handicap himself. The females smiled upon a brave male more often than they did others; Dachande had never lacked for female attention before, nor did he intend to begin now. He had sired seventy-three suckers over the years since first he had become a Blooded warrior and he was planning on reaching eighty by the end of the next breeding season. A yautja did what a yautja had to do to bolster his line and when his Final Hunt took place, he intended to leave behind a legion of younglings.

He grinned. Any Hunt could be the Final Hunt, that was the Path, but he did not think this would be the one. This was routine; he had led a score of missions such as this one, and he could do it blindfolded, with dull blades and a dead burner in his sleep. An easy run, *gkei'moun* simple.

He switched off the eyes watching the queen. He should go and release some of the pressure that had built up among the young males. A couple of them in particular were showing signs of preparing to do something stupid, such as challenging a Blooded warrior or even the Leader himself. Young males were not a whole lot brighter than the Hard Meat, Dachande sometimes thought. He could still recall his prewarrior days when he had known everything, was the bravest yautja ever born and ready to prove it at the slightest provocation. Ah, the days of his invincible youth. Surely there could have been no male who had swaggered more, thought more highly of himself, acted as if he were the linchpin around which the galaxy would someday turn. A creature of destiny, he had thought, different from the other obnoxious would-be heroes who strutted and stood ready to be offended at the hint of disrespect.

He recalled an instance when a younger male had glanced at him with what he thought an inappropriate demeanor, had allowed his gaze to linger a quarter second longer than the galaxy's would-be linchpin had deemed respectful. How he had puffed up like a poison-toad and stepped forward to issue a claw-challenge, and that only because death-challenges were forbidden to the un-Blooded. How when crossing the empty space between himself and the insolent pup who had offended him, he had been knocked sprawling by a female going about her business. By the time he had recovered, the disrespectful one had gone and the female, if she had even noticed, had also continued on her way.

He grinned, tusks going wide. Such a long time ago that had been, before most of the current class of pups had been sap in their fathers' rods. They would learn, just as he had learned. They were not the gods' gift to the universe. He would see to it. Or he would see them dead. Either way was the Path.

2

Dachande walked slowly down the dim corridor toward the *kehrite*, the room where the training yautja learned blade and simple unarmed combat. Many Leaders focused on the importance of shiftsuit mechanics and burners in the teaching of the Hunt, but not he; from long experience Dachande knew that sometimes there was nothing to rely on outside of one's own prowess. To teach anything else would be to risk the death of future warriors, and a good Leader had many students still Hunting.

The measure of a teacher was the life span of those he taught. The longer they lived, the better the instructor.

Dachande inhaled deeply as he neared the *kehrite*. The musk of aggression was strong in the air, an oily, bitter smell that promised confrontation, but he did not hurry. Being the eldest Blooded on a Hunt had its privileges; no fight would begin without the Leader to witness it.

The winding passageway narrowed to an arched entry in front of Dachande, the walls lined with Hard Meat armor. Already he could hear the clatter of taloned feet and the mumblings of expectation. He stepped through the arch and waited for acknowledgment. Quickly, he located the few students he had picked to cause trouble early on and marked them; Mahnde, the short one; Ghardeh, with the long tress; and Tichinde, who talked louder than any other. Of the three, Ghardeh would be the least trouble; he was but a follower. But the other two . . .

Within a short span, all yautja had turned their attention to him. There were fourteen in all who wore the plain dlex headband of student, plus two Blooded warriors who helped supervise; these two, Skemte and Warkha, were also the navigator and flyer. The ship was fully automated, a single trained yautja could handle it—but it did not hurt to take precautions. Both warriors carried Dachande's signature mark upon their foreheads like a third eye, the etch of Hard Meat blood from their first kill, and they watched him carefully for direction; each sought their own Leaderships; both were wise enough to know such achievement would not be through Challenge against him.

One by one, all heads bowed to him. Dachande nodded curtly, never taking his sharp yellow gaze from the group—Tichinde in particular. What he saw did not surprise him. Tichinde had lowered his head but kept his own gaze on Dachande. When he saw that his Leader watched in return, he flared his lower

mandibles and raised his head to face him—a sure
sign of aggression. It was insolent, but forgivable,
were his Leader a patient one; had Tichinde begun the
low growl of confrontation, it would not be so easy to
allow him to remain unmolested. As it stood, this was
a prime opportunity to let the cooped-up young males
practice.

"Tichinde!" Dachande made his voice angrier than
he was. The yautja surrounding the arrogant youth
stepped away from him, tusks opened wide.

"You may show your 'skills,'" Dachande continued,
his voice threaded with sarcasm, "by a *jehdin/jehdin*
spar with . . . Mahnde. First fall determines the win-
ner."

There were rumblings of disappointment as the
young males moved from the match area to line the
scarred *kehrite* walls; with no weapons to be used,
both combatants would probably still be alive after
the match. Still, the energy was high. Several yautja
had seen the look between Tichinde and the Leader,
and all could see the disrespectful face of the student
now. What would the Leader do about this? How
would he respond? Was he weak enough to allow a
Challenge to pass, even one so veiled?

Dachande paused until all were in place before giving the command.

"Begin!"

As one, the yautja began to howl and chant as the
two young males circled. Dachande watched carefully
as Mahnde lunged forward for the first blow, arms
raised.

Tichinde blocked easily and countered with a jab
to the throat.

Mahnde moved aside, not fast enough to avoid the
shot completely. A chorus of guttural hisses filled the

room as he stumbled and pulled back. A clumsy response. No one was impressed.

Tichinde shrieked and ran at Mahnde, talons extended for a stab to the abdomen.

The defender, already off-balance, blocked too high. Tichinde hit full on and knocked Mahnde to the padded floor. The victorious youth threw back his head and screamed in triumph. The *kehrite* pounded with the cries of the agitated students. The match was over.

Too soon. Blood was still too warm; none would be satisfied with such a quick bout.

Dachande looked for a challenger amidst the yowls and clicks of the clamoring spectators, displeased with Mahnde's performance. Perhaps Chulonte, he showed promise . . .

A score of new sounds filled the room as the yautja began to scream in surprise and renewed excitement. Dachande's gaze flickered back to the match area—and he watched in amazement as Tichinde kicked his fallen opponent in the head.

"*Ki'cte!*" Dachande had to shriek to be heard. "Enough!"

Tichinde kicked again. Mahnde rolled over, tried to cover his face and grab at Tichinde's foot at the same time. The yautja were going wild. Blood was molten; spittle flew as they shook their heads in excitement.

"Tichinde!" Rarely had Dachande seen such disobedience. He stalked onto the match floor and shouted again.

Tichinde turned to face the Leader. He snarled. The young male extended one hand and shoved at Dachande's left shoulder.

Dachande avoided the push automatically.

The clawed hand fell short.

The watching yautja suddenly fell silent, only a few dying clicks and cries of wonder. Tichinde's movement was unmistakable, and since Dachande had attained Leadership, a move that he had not seen. The sign of direct challenge.

Dachande sighed to himself silently. What an idiot this one was. How had he survived this long?

The baked dirt that covered the valley floor appeared nearly lifeless under the searing heat of the dual suns. What vegetation there was appeared stunted, twisted, cooked. The twin stars were hardly an exact match; the secondary's shadows were barely visible, a frail blur next to the deeper charcoal hues cast by the primary. The towering plateaus of dirty tan rock—there had once been water here to cut them so—ran in corridors throughout the basin and offered no comfort unless you crawled among the stones—which no sane human would want to do for all of the venomous forms of hidden life there. Besides the stinging flies and poisonous snakes, there was a particularly lethal form of scorpion that nested amidst the boulders during Ryushi's nineteen-hour day. Even after sundown, the heat rarely fell below body temperature, and without the relief of the cool breezes that sometimes came with desert climate after dark. The air was always bone-dry and the feverish winds that occasionally blew were sharp and unpleasant, the crack of a hot whip. Maybe it was somebody's idea of paradise—

But not mine.

Machiko Noguchi ran a delicate hand through her short black hair and punched the scan button. The portable eye panned across the barren wasteland, showing her more of the same. It was identical to almost everywhere else on Ryushi. Besides the few artificial watering holes and the settlement itself, the whole planet looked like a desert prospector's version of hell—rocks, dirt and heat, and no precious metals hidden there, either.

Noguchi sighed and tapped a few keys. As the small screen faded to black, she leaned back in her form-chair and closed her eyes. She took a deep breath and growled softly through clenched teeth. When the opportunity had presented itself, she had not hesitated. Only twenty-nine years old and already offered an overseer's post for the Chigusa Corporation. Prosperity Wells, at the far edge of the Beta Cygni system, very quiet; "Sounds exhilarating," she'd said.

Right. Only her six months of phase-in was almost up and she was so sick of this rock she could vomit. A necessary career move, she kept telling herself.

Well, at least there's air-conditioning . . .

Noguchi stretched her arms over her head and arched her back. Her lunch break was almost over, time to get back to the office. She usually ate with Hiroki, but he'd had a meeting with a few of the ranchers and she had decided to slip back to her apartment and go over a stat report for the company. Might as well let him keep the reins for the last few weeks of his stay. Besides, only in her private chamber did she feel free to relax; to let her feelings show anywhere else was—it was not an option. There was too much at stake for her to be anything but completely professional.

She glanced at the holomirror by her door on the way out and nodded at what she saw—cool, composed, detached. Attractive in a typical Japanese way, although that was not important to her. She looked

... *authoritative*. The ranchers didn't seem to like her very much, but they *would* respect her—her honor would accept nothing less.

Dachande felt his anger flare and then, almost regretfully, he let it pass. Half a lifetime ago, such a display of brash audacity would have meant a quick death for the young male; the yautja who would dare to challenge him? Certain *thei-de*. And grinning all the while he delivered it, too.

But he was Leader now. Not a kind Leader, but a just one. There were others who would kill for such an offense—but these days, he would teach. There was no point in a match you knew you would win. Doubt was necessary or it was but an exercise.

All of this flitted through his mind in less than a second.

Tichinde pushed at him again.

Again Dachande slipped the move unthinkingly. He saw the surprise on the young one's face. And perhaps, too late, a touch of realization that he had made an error. A very bad error.

The juvenile yautja gave up their stunned hush at this new transgression and roared for blood. It did not matter whose.

Dachande reflected no longer. He grabbed Tichinde's hands and held them high with his own.

Tichinde screamed into his face, the shrill sound blended with the cries of the spectators.

Dachande did not pause.

The Leader jerked his head forward. Their skulls met with a dull *crack* that sent a peal of renewed clatterings and hisses through the assemblage.

Tichinde pulled his hands loose and staggered back, arms still held high, but dazed.

They circled.

A tiny trickle of pale blood ran down Tichinde's face from beneath his dlex band. Without taking his gaze from Dachande, the student reached up and touched the flow, rubbed it between his fingers for confirmation; he did not seem to like the feel.

Too bad.

Tichinde spread his arms wide, back hunched, and screamed. The sounds were garbled with fury, but the inflections unmistakable—*Nan-deThan-gaun*. The Kiss of Midnight.

Tichinde's intentions were crystal: he would kill his Leader, if he could.

Enough was enough. Dachande locked his fingers together and leapt. He landed beside the impudent yautja and brought his double-fist down, hard, into the small of the still-screaming Tichinde's back. Tichinde fell to the floor. His lower jaw smacked the mat quite audibly.

Dachande jumped back quickly as Tichinde slowly regained his feet. Aware of his audience, the Leader moved with all the grace and skill he could muster. The motion was nearly perfect and any of the watchers who could recall even a bit of training would be impressed by the flow of it. Which was the point.

New blood oozed from the young male's lower mandibles. The watching students sang out calls of victory for their Leader as Tichinde turned to face Dachande. The cries of derision from his peers were perhaps what spurred the young male into action. With a strangled hiss, the bleeding yautja ran at Dachande, fists extended.

Give him credit for spirit. Credit for brains, no. For skill, hardly. But he was no coward.

Still, it was poor form. Dachande fell to his knees before Tichinde reached him and grasped the student's overstretched upper body with one hand, his nearer leg with the other. Suppressing a grunt, he strove to make the move appear effortless.

As if the youth weighed no more than a suckling, Dachande stood and thrust Tichinde high over his head.

The howling yautja tried to escape and regain the floor, but his writhings were to no avail. Dachande held the young male high, let out a growl of conquest—then threw Tichinde across the room.

The mob of howling young males split, narrowly avoided the flung body before it smacked into the wall. They chanted triumph for Dachande, harsh sounds of *nain-desintje-de;* pure win.

Dachande made no chant himself and none was needed. The fallen Tichinde spoke for him.

For a short time, nobody moved.

Finally, Tichinde staggered upright and walked slowly toward his Leader, head bowed. The outcome was obvious, and a further display of aggression would be dishonorable, not to mention stupid. Tichinde stopped in front of him and raised only his eyes to see what Dachande would decide; in such a Challenge, death was not an unreasonable punishment.

Dachande pretended to consider his options as the chants fell to a breath-held stillness and overstretched tension. There was really no question for him; a good Leader did not have to kill one of his own to prove anything—and to embarrass the young male would tell later in Tichinde's Hunts. He waited because all eyes watched and the hesitation was penalty enough.

After a few breaths-time Dachande tilted his head to one side and spoke. *"Payas leitjin-de."* He paused. *"Hma'mi-de."*

Tichinde hung his head lower and stepped back, his relief visible. Several young males came forward to touch Tichinde's hair in appreciation of the Leader's compliment. The precise tip of Dachande's head combined with the words indicated both acknowledgment of the student's submission and a respect for his bravery—"Remember God's practice." Tichinde was allowed his life and his name, but with the ritual warning a slap to his embarrassed face. Still, there was no real shame in losing to one who had faced the Hard Meat with nothing but talons and blade.

Dachande almost allowed himself a grin, but did not want to lighten the effect of his pronouncement; he raised his hand and gestured for the students to fall in line for training. Tichinde knew who was Leader, and would not forget it. And if another yautja strayed from obedience . . . ?

After this, it would not likely happen. If it did, there would be more than one "dachande" on ship. His honor would accept nothing less.

3

They were still in space, but it wasn't nearly so deep now. The ship's drone had mellowed as the gravity drives slowed them to intersystem speeds.

"Eleven days, buddy boy, and then no more of your dick in my ear for what, seventy-two hours?"

Tom grinned and shook his head. "You wish."

Scott raised his coffee cup in a mock toast. "Here's to pretty girls and sunny days, Tommy." He sipped the watery liquid and grimaced. "Nothing like a nice mug of shit to put a shine on the morning, hey?"

"It's . . ." Tom glanced at his terminal. "Four in the afternoon, you pig. Happy hour."

"Right," said Scott. "Whatever."

They sat in silence for a few moments. Tom worked studiously at one of his crosswords, tapping in words and erasing them at the same rate. Scott gazed into the darkness and tried to remember the words of a poem he used to know. He could probably just look it up in the ship's library, same as Tom and his puzzle, but learning how to kill time was a good trick in their line of work. Nothing to do and plenty of hours to do it.

'Twas brillig and the slithy toves, did gyre and— something-something wabe—all mimsy were the borogoves and the something-hath outgrabe—

"Six-letter word for 'saint'?"

Scott thought for a second and then smiled. "Thomas."

"Funny. Like not wanting to fuck over all things great and small makes me some kinda prince. I mean, really—" Tom paused. "Hey, that's it. Prince. You're good for something after all, you pagan asshole."

"You still pissed about last night?" Scott shook his head. It seemed that this debate would never die—but eleven days *was* eleven days. "Like I said, survival of the fittest. The fact remains that if the human race needs to do something to survive—and the lower orders don't have the power to stop us—we'll prevail. It's not right or wrong, it's just the way things are."

Tom looked up from the monitor, jaw set. "So it's all right to do whatever we want, exploit any ecosystem, as long as we don't run into anything big enough to kick our butts—that's basically it, right?"

"Couldn't have put it better myself."

"That's opportunistic rationalization, Scott. Where's your sense of social responsibility? Didn't your mama raise you right?"

"I was a tube child, thank you very much."

"That must be it." Tom hit the store button on his keyboard and stood. "Now, if you'll excuse me a moment, I have this sudden overwhelming urge to take a dump."

Scott chuckled. "I'm not even gonna *touch* that one."

Tom slapped him on the shoulder and exited the control module. Tom was all right, he didn't take himself too seriously at least. Scott had been paired up with worse. He felt his grin slowly melt as he turned his gaze back to the deep. Killing time, that was all.

Beware the jabberwock, my son, the jaws that bite the claws that catch—beware the jub-jub bird and shun the frumious bandersnatch.

Yeah, that was it. What, he wondered, did it mean? And why was he thinking about it now?

Hiroki's face remained expressionless as Noguchi lit a cigarette at her desk and exhaled a haze of gray smoke. She knew he disapproved, but she also knew that it was not appropriate for him to speak of it; it was, after all, her office now. It was not even a habit that she was particularly attached to—

But wouldn't your father *be displeased, Machiko?*

Noguchi inhaled deeply.

Hiroki uncrossed his legs on the couch and smoothed his small mustache carefully with one finger. "As I was saying, Ackland expressed some concerns with the agreement. He says that he has the support of the other ranchers, or at least Harrison and Marianetti."

"Well, that's three of the big four," Noguchi began. "Perhaps we should contact the company—"

A small green light flashed from the control panel set into her desk, accompanied by a low tone.

"Excuse me, Hiroki."

"Of course." He picked up a sheaf of hard copy and settled back into a plush cushion.

Noguchi punched up visual and hit receive.

"Mr. Shimura, we have an unidentified incoming at—oh, Ms. Noguchi."

Noguchi smiled slightly at the young man's visible discomfort and waited. He was one of the scan watchers, a low-level company worker.

"I, uh, I have a message for Mr. Shimura. Is he there?"

Noguchi frowned. "Yes, he's here. But you can give *me* the message, Mason." She glanced at Hiroki, who made a point of being deeply engrossed in the rhynth count report he was reading.

Mason swallowed. "Uh, yes, ma'am. Long range is showing a UFO. It's probably just a meteor, but it's not breaking up, it is going to hit—if it stays on its present course, it'll make planetfall about thirty klicks north of here—open pasture. Make a boom when it lands."

"Any damage likely?"

"No, it's not that big."

"Then don't worry about it." Noguchi stubbed her cigarette out into the pewter tray on the desk. "We can investigate after the roundup. Noguchi out."

The screen went blank. She took a deep breath and then looked at Hiroki. He had set down the file and was watching her, face impassive as usual. At least there was no sympathy. She opened her mouth, uncertain as to what she was going to say; their relationship had progressed to a first-name basis, but that didn't make them friends.

"I—" She forced herself not to look away. "I've been here nearly six months, Hiroki—and still they report to you. The ranchers, even the staff treat me like a stranger. I have done all I can think of to make this job mine—"

Noguchi fell silent and waited. Hiroki watched her for a few seconds and then stood and faced her, hands clasped behind his back.

"Maybe that is your problem, Machiko. You're trying to adapt the job to you, rather than adapting yourself to it. You can't run an operation like this and hide from it at the same time, no matter how nice the office."

Noguchi nodded slightly, thoughtful. This sounded like something he had been waiting to say until asked, which made her wonder how long he had been holding his tongue. Still, she needed an informed opinion. The ranchers respected Shimura—no, even further, they *trusted* him. She had not thought to find out how he had achieved their loyalty.

"There are only one hundred and thirteen civilians on Ryushi," he continued, "and besides the thirty or so company staff, we are dealing with freelancers here—not men and women who jump when the voice of the corporation speaks. They are not drones looking for advancement; they are people with children and homes. Quoting regulations will not get you very far."

Noguchi felt a flash of anger, but she fought to keep it under control. "What would you suggest, Hiroki? That I bake cookies and invite them on picnics?"

"I suggest that when you ask for an opinion, you should consider the advice you receive." Hiroki picked up his sun helmet from the synth-marble coffee table and walked to the door. He paused with his hand on the entry controls and looked back at her.

"Look, I'll be around for another two weeks, and

then you're on your own. I will do what I can to help in the meantime." He smiled a little. "I think you will do fine, Machiko."

She stood and nodded at him. "Thank you for your ... assistance, Hiroki."

"It is nothing. Get out of the office once in a while, get your hands dirty." He opened the door and then grinned easily. "Get some rhynth shit between your toes."

Noguchi sat back down and rested her hands lightly on the black-lacquered surface of her desk. Hiroki's words had stung a bit, but perhaps because there was some truth there; it deserved consideration. Hiroki was, after all, being promoted off of Ryushi. The ones who went up the ladder were generally not those that kept a low profile, as she had been doing.

Perhaps it's time to make some of my own moves ... Noguchi took another cigarette from the small silver case in her desk drawer and rolled it thoughtfully between her thumb and forefinger. What was the saying?

The journey of a thousand kilometers begins with one step ...

At first there was only the vision of dark, cracked matter all around, seen through a thick cloud of oily smoke. The electronic eye scanned the pit and then looked up. With a sudden lurch, the *lou-dte kalei* moved forward, using its segmented pincers to pull itself out of the crater.

It was a large, armored mechanism, the *lou-dte kalei*, designed to withstand almost any type of environment so far encountered; it was actually modeled after a kind of predator discovered on Thän, a world of dense metals and poisonous weather. Something like the Hard Meat, but more efficiently built—it could climb, walk, run, or dive into liquid. And while the robot crawler did not Hunt as the real creature could, it served a purpose that was more important than simple survival; it was the bearer of life.

Dachande switched to the rear *gkinmara*, another of the rounded eyes that transmitted sensory information. "*Lou-dte kalei*" was a joke, really, a derogatory term that was sometimes used for a female—literally, "child-maker." Not that Dachande had ever heard the name spoken to a female's face. A warrior who would dare such would not be wise, for an insulted and angry yautja female was not something even a not-too-wise male wanted to create. Assuming the warrior was armed and expert, it might almost be an even match, but Dachande would put his wager on the female. His most recent partner had tossed him across a room during the heat of their mating and that had been an accident.

Mating. Ah, now there was a pleasant thought.

As if in accordance with Dachande's thoughts, the heavy dlex ramp in the tail of the crawler lowered and the machine began its function. An egg, the beginning of the Hunt, made its way gently down the plated ramp to be deposited on the dusty ground.

The crawler moved slowly forward to lay another.

Dachande rolled the control bar on the table in his private chamber. The front view appeared again in the oval monitor's screen; the crawler went toward a high mountain of some unknown material, perhaps the cliff was of *tjau'ke* or compressed dust. This world was a warm place, but not as humid as some. Twin suns and no freestanding liquid in sensory range. The read on the crawler showed that there were still dozens of eggs to be set; the red lines and smudges of the counter changed with each placement. Each egg was coded and tuned to a reader that would maintain the connection even after the egg hatched and became Hard Meat. They would not leave the Hunt until all the prey had been taken. To leave even a single one behind was criminal.

Dachande had not visited this place before, although the records showed that there had been Hunts here, many seasons earlier. It was listed as wide and spacious, with no antagonists and many hiding places; large, four legged creatures dwelled there naturally, ideal hosts—perfect for training. They would go in fast and dark, that was standard, but there could hardly be anything on the planet to cause them problems. It was but another dry world with little to offer save a place to Hunt. The galaxy was full of such places.

A small *tarei'hsan* ran in front of the egg-layer, dark in color and spined like an insect of some sort. Its tail curved over its body and ended in a point, and its arms were much like the arms of the *lou-dte kalei*. The crawler rolled over it, the treads crushing the tiny bug into the mottled ground. Dachande shook his head. Better it should die thus, for stupidity did not further any race and running under tank treads was not high up the scale of cleverness.

He watched as the counter ran slowly backward. They were close to this place, this dust world, but there was still plenty of time for the Hard Meat children to find hosts. The tagged babes should be drones by the ship's arrival, but there was not so much slack that they would have time to colonize. Timing was all.

Dachande smiled. Part of being a Leader was not to seem excited by the prospect of a training Hunt, but in the privacy of his chamber, he allowed himself to feel the warmth of things to come. And somehow, this one felt different—there was an air of ... something.

He switched the monitor off and stroked his broken tusk absently. He was too old to muddle himself with cosmic questions, but he knew the words of his ancestors: *Thin-de le'hsaun 'aloun'myin-de/bpi-de gka-de hsou-depaya*—Learn the gift of all sights or finish in the dance of fallen gods.

Dachande cackled and stood up. Philosophy was not his bent. He was a warrior. Let the old ones worry about such things. He was a doer, not a thinker. It was better that way. Almost always.

4

Machiko Noguchi couldn't find the green crayon. There was the jade one and the blue-green, but the emerald-green was missing, and it was the only color that would work for the dragon's eyes.

She sighed and carefully dumped out the crayon pack. Things had been going so *well* until now, it wasn't fair. It was her day off from school and she had received permission to play quietly in her room for two whole hours before dinnertime. The picture of the dragon was going to be a gift for her father; she knew that he had been talking about a promotion for a long time, and that today he had an important meeting with his supervisor.

And the green was misplaced. Her parents had taught her to put things in their place because order was a very important rule; knowing where things were was a crucial ingredient to a successful life. She felt vaguely anxious as she sorted through the different shades—what if it wasn't there? What then?

Machiko spotted the crayon and nodded to herself. She had put it in with the blues by mistake, that was all. It was understandable; she would just have to be more careful . . .

She heard the front door open and close downstairs as she meticulously shaded in the dragon's eyes—emerald with gold rims. A cool spring breeze wafted in through her open window with the sounds of small children playing down the street. A good day. And it was going to be a beautiful picture, a longtailed, proud dragon with green and lavender scales and red taloned feet—

Machiko frowned and looked up. Her mother had not called out to her. Mother had gone to the store to buy things for a special dinner, her father's favorite dishes. But Mother *always* called to her when she returned from an errand. Perhaps she had gone back outside to carry in more things . . .

Machiko stood and walked to the door of her tidy room where she paused and listened. Maybe she had not heard her mother come in after all; the house was very still. She was about to go back to her picture when she heard a noise.

"Mother?" Nothing.

It had been like a heavy sigh, that noise. From down the hall—her father's study or perhaps her parents' room. Machiko was suddenly not sure if it was a good day at all. The silent house was not peaceful anymore, it was—empty.

Bad.

She walked very slowly down the hallway, staying

close to one wall. Her feet seemed like lead; with each step, her fear increased. Her mother would have surely answered, wouldn't she? Who was in their house? Should she leave?

Yes. Machiko decided that it would be good to wait outside for her mother to return. She would say that she had heard a noise and her mother would know what to do.

Except the front door . . .

Was past the study. Past her parents' room.

Machiko felt her legs trembling. The back of her neck was damp and sticky, and her stomach felt as if it were made of stone. She took another tentative step and hesitated. And she heard another noise.

All at once, Machiko relaxed. It was her father! That was the sound of his chair creaking back, as familiar a sound as his voice or the clatter of his key cards. She straightened up and started toward his door, smiling in relief. He had come home early, that was all.

"Father," she began, and reached out to knock. "I thought—"

Her words faltered as the door to his study swung inward. She had time to register surprise that he had left it unlatched before she saw him. Before she saw the knife.

And the blood.

Machiko screamed and ran to her father's side, where she pleaded and cried for him to get up, to speak, to stop pretending. She pulled at him for a long time. When he finally fell to the floor, she was drenched in his blood. He opened his eyes and sat up, smiling gently at her, arms spread.

"This is for you, Machiko," he said, and embraced her. Except that now his arms were claws and his head was a dragon's. His forked tongue flickered out as his gold-rimmed eyes began to bleed emerald tears. He pulled back to look at her as she began to wail in terror.

"You are my child," the words rasped from his dragon-face. "Redeem me . . ."

Noguchi sat up quickly, her breath coming in short gasps. She almost screamed before she realized where she was.

"Lights," she called out shakily. Her room glowed gently to life. Noguchi hugged her knees to her chest and tried to breathe deeply. Always the same dream— except she had not had it for a long time.

She *had* been covered in her father's blood when her mother had found her. There had been no note, only the Death Poem that her mother would not let her read until years later, but the reason had come to light that same night: the esteemed Akira Noguchi, an accountant for the Yashido Company, had been fired for embezzlement. The same man who had scolded her when she had lied about stealing a piece of candy at the age of five, the man who had taught her the value of order. The father who had taught her honor . . .

"Bastard," she murmured, angry. Except her voice didn't sound angry at all. The memories came back so easily when she let them, and now she was helpless to stop them. She had ripped up the dragon picture after the funeral; it had never been finished. The stain on their family's name had eventually faded, and when she was in college, her mother had remarried. She had met her stepfather once. He had seemed like a pleasant man, but she never got past the feeling that her mother had married him so that she would no longer be a Noguchi.

She and her mother spoke occasionally, but any closeness they had once shared was gone. Keiko Noguchi Ueda had never understood how her daughter had really felt. When she had called her mother with the news of her move to Ryushi, her mother had been so proud. "Your father would have been pleased," she had said. Her father.

Noguchi took in a deep breath and closed her eyes. None of that mattered anymore, she did not need to think of it. She was a corporate overseer for a major corporation on a planet far from Earth, and she was good at her job. She would become better in time; she would earn the ranchers' trust and would carry out her position with—with—

"Honor," she whispered. And try as she might, she could not hold back the single tear that coursed down her cheek.

The Lector had made it to Ryushi a little before local nightfall. Scott knew there would be some hard workdays ahead for the ranchers and *The Lector* crew, but as pilot, he had minimal responsibilities for a few days. About damned time for a break.

He and Tom stepped off the ramp and into the deepening twilight of the desert world. They were at the edge of a small, dingy town that smelled like manure, straight out of an old Western vid. There was no one to greet them. In fact, the place looked uninhabited.

Scott grinned. "Looks like somebody forgot to organize the parade," he said. He turned to look at Tom—and Tom wasn't there.

Scott spun and looked around. *The Lector*, too, was gone. Behind him lay only a vast, dusty plain, with mountains far in the distance.

"Tom!" he shouted. No reply.

Scott turned to look at the deserted town. It was almost full dark now, but there were no lights in any of the empty windows. There were only a few faded, almost nondescript buildings, their doors latched against the hot, sandy winds that blew mournfully through the lonely settlement.

Scott cupped his hands around his mouth and shouted.

"Hello! Is anyone here?"

Nothing. In spite of the weather, Scott was suddenly cold. He took a few steps toward the nearest structure and then stopped.

A high, piercing cry came from inside the building. It had the same shrill tone of an animal in pain— except it was angry. The keening wail rose to a fevered pitch, the sound of insanity and hatred. There was nothing human about it.

Scott stumbled backward and fell. He scrambled at the ground, tried desperately to pull himself back to his feet, but he couldn't seem to manage it. He tried to crawl away from the horrible sound but it filled his ears and surrounded him. From behind, he heard the door swing open and the shriek of the creature got impossibly louder.

There was no escape. Scott began to scream. He screamed because he knew what it was, the thing, and he knew that to look at it meant death.

—*the Jabberwocky*—!

* * *

Scott woke up in a cold sweat in a dark room on *The Lector*, still over a week out from Ryushi. He did not get back to sleep that night.

Under the pouring rain, Yeyinde aimed at the Hard Meat drone with his burner and depressed the control. The running bug howled and fell back in a gout of *thwei*, limbs clattering.

Behind him the Leader shouted commands to the other students as the hot, harsh liquid splashed down from the sky, obscuring suit vision.

Another drone ran toward him and Yeyinde fired again, excited and anxious all at once. He felt fear clench his bowels briefly, but the cold twist was quickly overriden by heat. The beast in him snarled and grew proud: *Two!* His first Hunt and there were *two* in his name!

The threat seemed to fall away as the bugs stopped their assault. Yeyinde spun around, looked for more to kill. Between the burning rain and the hanging trees of the *dto*, it was hard to see.

The Leader, 'A'ni-de, called out. The Hunt was completed. The yautja cheered and hissed their triumph, Yeyinde's voice among them. He looked through the dancing young warriors for Nei'hman-de, whose blood he shared by the same father. Nei'hman-de was a strong yautja and fast fighter, but he surely did not kill *two*. Nei'hma-de and he had grown together, play-Hunting as growing suckers—and now they would share their first kill, share the victory of the Blooding. How could life get any better than this?

"Nei'hman-de!" Yeyinde moved through the rain and called for his *mei'hswei*. "Nei'hman-de!"

A talon fell hard on his shoulder. 'A'ni-de.

"Nei'hman-de is dead," the Leader said coldly. "He did not move properly. Now go stand at your kill for approval."

Yeyinde widened his eyes. "But Nei'hman-de is—"

'A'ni-de backhanded him roughly, sent Yeyinde to his knees in the mud. "You question?" The Leader glowered over him, tusks flared.

Yeyinde bowed his head in submission. After a tense moment, 'A'ni-de stalked away.

The young warrior stood and trudged through the downpour back to the fallen drones. That a warrior's life was hard, he knew. That yautja sometimes died, he knew as well. Nei'hman-de, gone. It did not seem real that it could be.

Unbidden came a memory. Of a time when he and his brother had sat drinking *c'ntlip*, the fiery brew that fogged mind and body with pleasure. Someday they would be Leaders, not only of ships but of other Leaders. Great would be their fame. Stories would be sung of their Hunts for a thousand years, each of them was certain. It had been as clear as the high mountain air to them. Warriors together, they would Hunt, they would make the females howl in ecstasy, they would father each two hundred sucklings. Much could be laid to the liquor, of course, but he and his brother had truly believed the core of their fantasy. They would be the ones to survive and rise; it would be the other un-Blooded who would fall. Of that there had been no doubt, none.

Only now, it was his brother who had fallen and his own head was hung low after his first Hunt . . .

Yeyinde raised his eyes and saw the results of his prowess. Two bugs lay on the watery ground because of him. And at that moment, he saw the Path; there would no longer be a place for the dreams of youth in him. Nei'hman-de was gone, but *he* was alive—and

now a warrior. And a warrior did not waste his time
looking over his shoulder at the past. Done was done.
Regret would not bring back the dead.

Yeyinde held his head high as 'A'ni-de traced a claw
wet with Hard Meat *thwei* in the space between his
eyes. He ignored the sharp sting as the acid *thwei* cut
into his flesh to mingle with his own blood, blood that
neutralized much of the Hard Meat's power. The burning mark was proof of his skill and his adulthood, a
jagged etched badge for all to see. Of all the yautja on
this Hunt, only *he* had killed two. Never again would
he bow to the kinship of other males; aligning oneself
with a loser was not the Path, and any yautja could
lose . . .

Dachande awoke warm with pride of the memory. It
was long ago and there had been many Hunts since,
many of them harder and bloodier than the first. But
the first had been where he discovered the truth of
the warrior; it was a truth that had served him well.
Now it was his turn to pass the knowledge on, to
teach it to the young ones who had yet to feel the
power of the Hunt, to know the joy of the first kill. It
had been a long time since he had felt that newness
but the dream brought it back as if it had been only
moments past. The Hunt was what a warrior lived for;
all else was nothing compared to it. Honor. Skill. Victory. Those were the things of life.

5

Noguchi left her apartment early so she could catch Hiroki before he made rounds. The corporation employees' living quarters were all in the same building as the offices and mess hall, along with the community center and central operations; narrow passageways connected this building to the equipment storage and the main garage. To the east and south was open range; the north, mountains, and west was Iwa Gorge, a canyon too deep and long to herd the rhynth—although it certainly kept them from wandering too far in that direction. One less fence to build.

Noguchi walked through the connecting hall and saw one of the geotechs headed toward her, a thin older man with brown skin and very little hair. His name was . . . Hein? Hinn?

As they passed she made a conscious effort to
smile and nod at the man. He seemed vaguely surprised, but returned the courtesy, his teeth a sharp
contrast to his dark face.

A condescending voice spoke in her head. *That
wasn't too hard, now was it?*

Noguchi made a mental note to check the personnel files that evening. She felt almost embarrassed; six
months and she didn't even know the people she was
supposed to be working with.

All of that was going to change. Noguchi had
started to realize just how little she had seen of Prosperity Wells. She had, of course, spent time learning
the layout of the complex when she'd first arrived; it
was an efficient setup. A med center with helipad;
there were quarantine and holding pens for the
rhynth, a transmitter/communications control shack,
and a school connected to a rec center. There was
also a fairly decent, if very small, shopping mall, complete with two tiny restaurants and a bar. Not that any
of these got much use. Only the company people lived
in the Wells, although most of the ranchers were in
walking distance—if you didn't mind a long and hot
hike. If it wasn't Earth, at least an attempt had been
made to try to make it look like a town. There were
hardly enough people in the gene pool to turn the
planet into anything civilized, and even with more set-
tlers, it wasn't likely to ever be a major population
center; still, the company had made a token effort to
make it look like home.

But besides seeing an occasional holovid at the
rec's theater, she hadn't really been a member of the
community. It wasn't her home and she wasn't going
to stay here any longer than it took to show a profit
and shine in the company's eyes enough to earn a

transfer to the next rung on the ladder. But Hiroki was right, she would have to do what was necessary to earn the spot and so far she had remained as insulated as a thermetic bottle.

And *The Lector* would be arriving in less than seventy-two hours . . .

So I imagine everyone will welcome me with open arms and songs of greeting now that I'm finally ready, hai?

Right.

As she walked between shelves piled high with bike and copter parts, she heard voices from the direction of the open entryway into the yard. She could make out the distinct soft tone of Hiroki's voice among the others; he sounded irritated.

Noguchi slowed her pace to catch the gist of the conversation she was about to walk into.

". . . not the point, Hiroki! The company's making a killing from our sweat and we're getting screwed—right, Ackland?"

"That's the way the Ranchers Association sees it."

Noguchi waited just inside the door to listen for another moment; several ranchers and Hiroki stood in a loose circle several meters away. She could just see the edge of Ackland's heavy rhynth-hide coat, which he wore even on the hottest day. He was a large, opinionated man who had an amazing ability to cause friction.

"I don't even know why I'm discussing this with you," said Hiroki. "Ms. Noguchi is in charge now. You should be talking to her."

A perfect cue. Noguchi stepped forward and through the entry.

"That bitch? She doesn't give a shit about us," said Ackland.

"Maybe if she got laid once in a while—" started one of the other ranchers, Rick Harrison.

"Anybody who tried would freeze his dick off," said one of Ackland's men.

The group chuckled, all except for Hiroki.

Harrison broke off abruptly when he spotted her striding toward them. He coughed suddenly into his hand.

"Ms. Noguchi," he said. His voice was loud.

She held her head high and stared at him. He dropped his gaze, as did the other men. Only Ackland had the nerve to meet her eyes.

"I thought we were in the middle of a roundup, gentlemen," she said, voice cool.

Hiroki stepped in. "We were just discussing the agreement their association has already signed."

Ackland tapped his pipe with the heel of one hand. "That was before we saw what the market was doing back on Earth. If we'd known the price of meat was going to jump like this, we'd have asked for more."

"And if the bottom had fallen out of the market, would you have offered to take less?" said Hiroki.

All eyes turned to Noguchi. She faced Ackland, obviously the man to negotiate with.

"I'll talk to the company and see if I can swing a larger cut for your ranchers," she said. "We want to be fair."

Ackland nodded and tugged at his dirty red beard. He opened his mouth to speak, but Noguchi cut him off.

"But there won't be anything for anyone if your rhynth aren't ready for shipment when *The Lector* arrives." She noted his flash of annoyance with smug satisfaction. No matter what she changed, Ackland

was never going to be a man she enjoyed working
with. "I suggest you get back to your jobs."

She smiled at the others as they followed Ackland
across the yard.

Hiroki raised his eyebrows at her after the ranchers had reached a safe distance.

"Pleasant man, Ackland," he said blandly.

"Perhaps someday we'll marry," she said, keeping a
straight face.

Hiroki grinned.

"Let's saddle up," said Noguchi. She shaded her
eyes against the suns and looked out at the open
plain. "I'm ready to get some rhynth shit between my
toes."

"Words of wisdom," said Hiroki.

Noguchi nodded and then walked with Hiroki toward the hover bikes. Already she felt as if she'd set
wheels in motion; and once started, there would be
no turning back.

The young males stood in standard formation and
watched Dachande expectantly. The *kehrite* stank of
musk and the air was alive with tension. He had made
them wait long enough; it was time.

Dachande looked at the heaps of armor and weaponry that Skemte and Warkha had lined up against the
wall. "You may collect your *'awu'asa'*," he said, waving at the armor. "Now."

With passionate cries of excitement, the yautja ran
to the piles of equipment and Hard Meat shell, shov-
ing and kicking to get there first. There was enough to
suit all of them, of course, but they would fight for
the better trappings; the stronger males would get the
prime supplies. That was always the way.

Dachande watched as the yautja strapped on the scarred platings and struggled for arm sheaths and masks. Shafted knives were weighed and measured, burners' sights checked. Med kits and multiple eyes weren't standard for young males' armor, nor were *tarei'hsan* loops; only the warriors used such additions. There was shift capacity in a few of the suits, but the young males would not need such things anyway; the first Hunt was more a matter of point-and-kill than tracking and hiding. Invisibility was generally reserved for prey that shot back. You had to earn the right to use the better gear, and the prey for which it was necessary.

It was still two nights until landing on the seeded world, but the yautja would need to become accustomed to their *'awu'asa'*, to feel comfortable with movement and weight. Dachande himself had slept in his armor the first night he had donned it. They had worn the gear only briefly during their training and under strict supervision. For this there were reasons—the main being that a young male given too much power too early was a hazard to himself and others. Turn some of the wet-behind-the-knees younglings loose with a burner even a few weeks ago and there would have been the risk of holes in the ship's hull or bodies piled in the corridors. The ceiling of the firing range had more scars than a ceremonial blood-pig.

Dachande watched Tichinde backhand a smaller male for the mask he held and hiss triumphantly at the gain. The Leader nodded thoughtfully; Tichinde was strong but reckless. Such recklessness could get him killed. Did he survive, however, he could be a great warrior and a credit to his teacher. It was far better to be brave and die than to be cowardly and survive by hiding from the Black Warrior. Songs were not sung about those who showed their back to an attack.

One by one, the dressed yautja held up their shafted knives and howled to each other, pointing their burners to the floor and pretending to fire in mock battle. Skemte caught Dachande's gaze and growled amusement at their fervor. Dachande nodded and echoed the growl. Doubtless each of the would-be warriors thought himself the bravest to have ever picked up a spear and waved it.

The young males were as ready as he could make them. He hoped they were ready enough. If they were not, it was too late. And too bad—their successes or failures would start soon on the planet now speeding toward them.

Dtai'kai'-dte sa-de nau'gkon dtain'aun bpi-de. The fight begun would not end until the end; a tired saying but a true one.

The Hunt was about to begin.

6

Noguchi rode slightly behind Hiroki through the midafternoon light, their hover bikes setting up whirls of baked tan dust and hot pebbles in their wake. Earlier they had skimmed the inner ridges of the gorge and then circled back to town for a light lunch. Now they were headed out again, toward Beriki canyon, one of the primary runs for the majority of the herds.

Noguchi had spent most of the morning getting used to the flier's controls; fortunately, they weren't too hard to figure out—stop, go, height and speed adjustments. The trick was to watch for obstacles that might cause problems; jump a big rock too fast and you could find yourself on your back, your scooter flying merrily along without you, at least until the deadhand control shut it down. Besides basic instructions and a few landscape remarks through the comsets, Hiroki had kept quiet during their ride.

It was the longest she'd spent outdoors since arriving on Ryushi. The heat was incredible, the rays from two suns slapping at them with tangible force. Fiery winds ruffled the tips of her black hair at the base of her visor, and particles of sandy dirt kicked up by Hiroki's bike pelted her goggles and dusted her cheeks. Ahead and all around, huge cliffs encircled them.

Initially, it had all looked the same, harsh and unforgiving. But she had to admit there was a sparse beauty to the plains as well. It recalled images of sand gardens that Noguchi had visited in her youth at Kyoto. Here the sand was unchanneled and pocked with planets and rocks. Knee-high stands of beige reeds grew randomly near the edges of the valleys. Stones jutted from the earth in layers of shaded browns and grays. The fractured topsoil was a huge jigsaw puzzle with no end. There was plenty of sand, to be sure, but no order here, no simple zen lines. It was raw chaos. Billions of years in the making, this world, and she and a handful of men and women now held sway over it, masters of all the dry land. It was not hard to believe in manifest destiny out here in the far reaches of the galaxy, that mankind's true role was to minister to and control all things.

Their revving motors had surprised a goodly number of small animals out of hiding. A family of jack-lizards hopped in front of Noguchi's bike near the gorge, headed for cover in the grasses. And Hiroki had pointed out an armored fire-walker and her mate as they slipped through a pile of rocks earlier in the morning. The female was a rosy brown, her smaller mate a faded gray. They had been poking at gravel with their short, pointed snouts, probably searching for snake eggs or beetles.

Noguchi could understand, at least intellectually, why the ranchers had left Earth to make Ryushi their home. There was a kind of freedom to the prairies, a calm serenity to the stark lands. A certain beauty in it all. On Earth, a single living plex could house fifty thousand people in tight, tiny cubicles. On Earth, open land still existed but under so many regulations that just to walk upon it without a proper license might be worth a year in prison. Nowhere on the homeworld was there such vast *emptiness* as was all around her here. She found herself even enjoying the weather as they neared the southern end of Beriki canyon, the simplicity of a dry wind in her face. She wondered if it was too late for this new understanding to change her standing with the ranchers. Perhaps with time . . .

"We're coming up on one of Ackland's camps," Hiroki crackled in her ear.

"Right." She slowed as they rounded a bend in the gully. There were several dozen rhynth grazing on weeds a couple of hundred meters ahead, and beyond, the large treaded vehicle that Ackland used to check on his herds. The crawler could hold twenty people comfortably and was equipped with a full kitchen and sleeping accommodations for at least six; most of the ranchers had automatic vehicles—AVs— but Ackland's was the biggest.

Of course.

The rhynth themselves seemed to be unlikely meat animals. They looked to Noguchi much like a beast she had seen in a zoo as a child, a rhinoceros. The rhynth were slightly bigger than her memory of the gray-brown Terran creature, and they had a mottled purple and ochre skin. They walked on stumpy, oddly jointed legs that ended in nailed pads, and they had a hooked, beaklike mouth above which were a pair of in-line horns, the greater horn a wrist-thick and sharp cone that jutted straight up in front, the lesser horn smaller and angled slightly backward toward the animal's rear. Ugly brutes, no brighter than cattle, but very tasty when cooked properly.

Noguchi came to a stop next to Hiroki's bike and dismounted, legs still throbbing with the feel of the engine. Ackland and several of his people stood grouped near the AV and watched them approach. Noguchi set her eye protectors up on her cap and patted dust from her clothing as they neared Ackland.

The big man gazed at them with a sneer. "What's the problem, Hiroki? You and the boss lady get lost?"

"We're just making the rounds—" began Hiroki.

"Yeah, right." Ackland grinned without humor. "What's the real reason? The company shoot down the price increase?"

Noguchi cleared her throat. "You know we can't get through the magnetic interference during the day. I'll contact them this evening."

Ackland scoffed and started to turn away.

"*And*," she continued, "I'll do all I can to get you a bigger cut."

She wouldn't be talking to Earth, of course, the newly invented subspace radio wouldn't stretch that far, but she could get a response from the corporate sub HQ on Kijita's World. Even though it was light-years away, the new equipment could shrink that to a few light-hours, effectively only a few billion kilometers. They could get an answer by morning and the sub HQ was empowered to make such niggling decisions.

Ackland raised an eyebrow. "So what are you doing here?" He made no effort to keep irritation out of his voice.

Hiroki remained silent. "We're checking on everyone's progress—seeing if there's anything we can do to help," she said.

The late-afternoon light glinted off of the AV's pitted hull behind him as Ackland looked her up and down. Finally, he nodded.

"Yeah, you can help. You can stay out of our way. The last thing we need is 'help' from corporate paperpushers."

He faced the young woman next to him and pointed to the shaded monitor built into the AV. "Roth, take some of the boys and run these three gullies. Drive 'em down into the canyon and hook up with Cho's group."

Roth nodded and motioned to two of the men in Ackland's company. Ackland presented his back to Noguchi and Hiroki and punched at the controls set into the monitor's rim. Apparently, they had been dismissed.

They walked back to their bikes slowly. Hiroki placed a hand on her forearm gently as they reached the flyers.

"I'm sorry about the way Ackland treated you," he said.

Noguchi shrugged. "Actually, it's okay. I know how—" she paused, searched for the right word. "I know what kind of an uncaring bitch I've been. I would have been surprised if he had had any other reaction. It is as if I have been in some kind of suspended animation for the last few months. I cannot explain it."

She pulled her visor down firmly and looked to-

ward Prosperity Wells, about to say something else—
except all thoughts disappeared.

"Wow," she whispered.

"What—?" Hiroki looked past her. "Oh, yes. You
haven't gotten out much since you arrived, have you?"

Noguchi barely heard him. The suns were setting,
the desert was bathed now in golds and reds. Long
shadows stretched from the mountains toward them,
and in the cloudless sky, the arrangement of shade
and light left her breathless. It was actually the first
time she had ever seen the sunset outside.

Her mind couldn't pair the stunning sight with the
thoughts she'd had of Ryushi for the past six months;
she would have to let one or the other go.

Ryushi was, in its way, a beautiful place, at least
here and in this moment it was. Noguchi sighed and
watched the sunset, Hiroki quiet beside her. When
they finally mounted their bikes to head home, she
felt as if a heavy weight had been lifted from her
shoulders, one she had not been aware of until it was
gone.

Tom scanned the console and spoke without looking
up.

"Geosynch orbit in twenty hours, and check on tur-
bulence."

Scott's hands fluttered over the controls. "Some
fluctuation, but we can compensate no prob—we can
decouple anytime after orbit is achieved, then it's—"

The magnified Ryushi holo had appeared on the
screen.

"Hel-lo Ryushi! Jesus, what a dust ball!"

Tom looked up and nodded. "So it's a tad dry, big
deal."

Scott leaned back in his form-chair and cracked his knuckles behind his head. "Yeah, but we're not talking vague thirst here—this is just one big parched hell-hole." He watched the vid as it panned the ranges and cliffs of Ryushi. "What kind of mouth-breather would want to move way the fuck out here? Especially when there's still plenty of land available on Nova Terra?"

Tom glanced at the screen and then went back to plugging in data. "Who the hell knows? One man's poison and all like that."

"Yeah, but lookit the reads on the native life. This place *is* poison."

"Ah, I'm sure Ryushi is the perfect home for somebody *somewhere*."

"Not me," Scott mumbled under his breath. Great place for a nice vacation from the tug, sure. If you were a fucking lizard. Oh, well. He could spend his time in the local bar talking to the women, he didn't have to go hiking around in the sunshine now, did he?

Dachande studied the file picture of the desert world less than a half cycle away. Behind him, the yautja sparred under Skemte's supervision and screamed in blood lust. Soon they would have real targets.

He watched the *gkinmara* record and hissed in anticipation.

Perfect.

7

At a quarter past three in the morning, Jame Roth leaned against her flyer and watched for Ackland's headlights. The night was hot and free of wind, and stars twinkled faintly over the mountains. Her dog, Creep, lay panting at her feet, occasionally whining at the bulging sack hooked to the scooter's seat. Behind her a hundred meters or so, Travis and Adam watched over a small herd of rhynth, most of them on the ground asleep.

"Except rhynth sleep standing, eh, Creep?"

The mutt raised his head and whined again.

Roth considered herself a practical woman, but something about all of this gave her the shivers. The things she had found in the canyon were, well, odd. Unnatural to say the least. And now the rhynth were acting funny and Ackland's vet had found no cause for the symptoms. She didn't like it, not one bit.

She heard Ackland's AV long before it came into view. The desert was like that at night; it was one of the reasons that she and her spouse, Cathie Dowes, had moved to Ryushi. Calm and quiet, far away from crowds and the tame ugliness of Earth. Out here was freedom, and for almost three years, she and Cathie had been happy working for the ranchers. They were even discussing having a child together . . .

She cast an uneasy glance at the bundle and waited for Ackland. He was an asshole, sure, but he was the biggest herd-runner on the planet and it was his money that was going to set her and Cathie up after the sale. This was his responsibility.

The AV came rumbling around the bend up ahead and squealed to a halt in front of her, the headlights almost blinding to her dark-adjusted eyes. Ackland climbed down from the cab almost before the transport had stopped moving. Roth unhooked the sack and started toward him, Creep at her heels. He looked at the rhynth beyond her and walked quickly to meet them halfway.

"I got your message, Roth." He sounded out of breath. "What's the problem?"

"Take a look," she said, and crouched down to empty her find onto the dusty ground. Creep growled at the lifeless things and backed away. Roth speared one of the three creatures with a rhynth-stick and held it up for Ackland to see.

It looked like nothing so much as a huge spider with a spiny tail, a little smaller than a male fire-walker, perhaps two hand-spans. Its long, segmented legs curved under its plated body and its half-meter tail looked prehensile. There were no eyes as far as

Roth could tell, but there was a short fleshy tube that perhaps served as a mouth; it hung limply at the head of the creature. The thing was a mottled slate-gray all over.

Ackland took the stick from her and studied it carefully. "What the hell *is* it?" His voice was thick with disgust.

"Besides uglier than shit? I was hoping you could tell me," she said.

Ackland frowned and set the spider down next to the other two. "I've never seen anything like these things. Where'd you find them?"

"Up at the head of Beriki canyon. There were a couple dozen of them lying around dead." She brushed a long strand of sun-bleached hair out of her eyes and looked over at the rhynth. A few of them lowed mournfully, the sounds quiet in the still air. "That's where we scared up these poke-snoots. They were stumbling around and bumping into each other like they were half-asleep." She rose to her feet and faced Ackland, who had also stood.

"I think maybe they're sick, Mr. Ackland. I thought you should know."

"What did T. Stone say?"

"Tests all clean so far."

Ackland tipped his wide-brimmed hat back on his head and then nodded at her. "You did the right thing, Roth." He looked at the herd and then down at the alien things thoughtfully. Roth waited.

"We don't *know* that there's anything wrong with the rhynth," he said carefully. "And we wouldn't want some dickhead from the company to panic and set up a quarantine, right?" Ackland's speculative gaze turned to her face. "I mean, we've invested a lot of time here—and something like that, well, that would mean that some of us wouldn't get the payoffs that we deserve . . ."

He trailed off, leaving the obvious unstated. Roth chewed at her lower lip and nudged one of the creatures with one boot. Ackland was a greedy man, but he would be a *rich* greedy man within the week. And she had checked the main herd before she had called him; the only affected rhynth were the thirty-plus head behind her. Something like this could ruin all that she and Cathie had worked for . . .

Roth shrugged mentally, her decision made. This was Ackland's problem now. "I understand."

Ackland grinned and rocked back on his heels, nodding.

"But what do I do with these things?" she said.

"Take 'em to Dr. Revna—but tell him you found them in Iwa Gorge, okay?" He put one hand on her shoulder and squeezed lightly. "You're doing a great job, Roth. There will be a bonus for you when this roundup is over."

As he walked back to the AV, Roth brushed at the place his hand had touched her shoulder. Asshole.

She shoved the creatures back into the bag with the rhynth-stick and loaded it onto the bike for the trip into town. "C'mon Creep." She patted her thigh and the herd dog followed her back to the watch; the rhynth that weren't asleep lay on their sides, panting heavily. Wet ropes of mucus hung from their mouths and trembled with each gasp. Poke-snoots were stupid beasts, but she didn't like to see them this way— like they had swallowed something poison . . .

Noguchi sat *seiza* on the rounded mat in her apartment and breathed deeply, head down. It was just after dawn, and today *The Lector* came. She had awakened nervous and wanted to try to relax before starting the final roundup—but it had been almost a month since her last real practice and she could feel the muscles in her legs groaning from the stretch.

She had gotten her brown belt in karate before she'd left Earth for Ryushi, and had not been far away from black. While there were holo teaching devices that she could train to at the rec center, she had decided to put her lessons aside for a while—at least until she had found a human sparring partner. Holos weren't a bad way to go, but they lacked something. Dignity, perhaps.

But she hadn't made any close enough friends to work out with . . .

No friends, Machiko, close or otherwise. Don't kid yourself.

Right. Most ranchers probably weren't into martial arts anyway.

Her thighs trembled when she stood to form riding-horse stance; her old sensei, Master Ko, would have put her on the floor for letting herself go like this. She ran through blocks and kicks to loosen up a little, and was surprised at the vague sadness she felt at the familiarity of the moves. Homesickness? No, she had left little behind on Earth worth missing. It was . . .

Loneliness. The thought struck a chord within her that she hadn't felt for a very long time. It was the sense of—not belonging. At least on Earth she had worked in an office building with thousands of other employees, had walked through streets full of people; she had been in a karate class. Noguchi hadn't been very close to anyone, but at least there had been that option. And here there was only Hiroki, who seemed to disapprove of her somehow in spite of his smiling facade. Hiroki and a group of ranchers who didn't give a shit if she came or went.

She stopped midway through the fourth form and frowned, sweat light on her brow. What was next? Block-claw or drop to her right knee and clutch—?

She started the form over and went slowly, concentrating this time.

Chop to throat, that was it. For some reason, she felt near tears for having forgotten. Had it been so long?

She ran through the rest of her workout quickly and then kneeled into *seiza* again, bangs plastered to her forehead. Today would be a nonstop panic, supervising roundup and then preparations for the arrival of *The Lector*. There were responsibilities to delegate and papers to shuffle. She wished there was someone to talk to, someone to commiserate with over the busy day to come . . .

Well. There was no time to regret her choices now, there was too much to be done. She had practiced smiling and nodding and tonight would be her first gesture of goodwill toward the ranchers, the company approved price increase. She hoped that it would be the start of a new relationship of mutual respect.

It has to be; Hiroki leaves in a few days with the rhynth shipment.

Right. Time to get ready.

Noguchi tripped on the step into the bathroom and knocked her head solidly into the door frame. She cursed and placed a hand on the swelling lump, eyes squeezed shut. Great. The bruise would match her lavender blouse for the party. A terrific start to the day, O master martial artist.

She hoped any other disasters would wait until tomorrow.

* * *

Kesar Revna was fascinated. Alien biology was supposedly his forte, but he hadn't seen anything quite like it. He tried to keep up with the UMA reports from Earth, and Chigusa had a monthly online biomed journal that was one of the best; new species were being discovered every day, it seemed. But besides a mutant form of crab that had turned up on Terra Nova a few years back after a radioactive waste mishap, he found nothing in the literature that looked quite like this . . .

"I have to get back to work, Dr. Revna, if that's okay—"

He reluctantly looked up from the examination table at the young woman who had brought in the amazing creatures. She seemed nervous, anxious to be gone; she certainly looked out of place in the lab. Her dusty range clothes and darkly tanned skin didn't seem to agree with indoor lighting.

"Of course," he said. "It's the big day, isn't it?"

"Yeah."

"And you say you found these in Iwa Gorge?"

"Uh, yeah. Right." She dropped her gaze to the table and shuddered slightly. "Mr. Ackland said you might want to take a look at them."

"Give Mr. Ackland my thanks. And I appreciate you coming in, I know how busy you must be."

"Sure, no problem. Let us know how things turn out when you get a chance." She turned to walk out and nearly collided with Miriam, the town's human doctor and Kesar's wife, which made her Dr. Revna, too.

"Excuse me, Dr. Revna."

Miriam smiled. Her tanned skin crinkled at the corners of her eyes. She had her long and dark hair pulled back into a ponytail and she always seemed so tiny and petite she made Roth feel like a rhynth. "Hello, Jame. How's Cathie's knee?"

"Great. Good as new. I'm sorry, I really have to run—"

"That's all right. We'll hopefully see you both tonight."

Kesar had already turned his attention back to the specimen. "What do you make of this, Doc?"

Miriam laughed. "Oh, thank you. No 'good morning, my love, how did you sleep'?"

Kesar looked at his wife and grinned. "Good morning, my love, how did you sleep? Now take a look at what Roth brought in. I could use a second opinion."

Miriam bent over the table and raised her eyebrows. "She found this on *Ryushi*?"

"Iwa Gorge, she says. And she also said that there were at least twenty more, dead. I've already tried to cut one of the legs with the Killian, and nothing. Not a scratch."

"You're kidding." Miriam searched his face for the joke. "Any carbon-based animal . . ." she trailed off. "Silicon? Couldn't be and even if it was, that would at least have been marked—" She gazed at the specimen in wonder. "What is it, Kesar? You're the DVM."

He shook his head. "I don't know. There was that Terra Nova mutation, and I heard some rumors about a weird life form found in a mining colony somewhere, but somebody clamped down on that, nothing substantiated. We're going to need to run some tests; and I think afterward, I'm going to take a little ride up to the gorge and poke around."

Miriam frowned. "Alone?"

Kesar nodded. He felt wired. This was a totally new species . . .

"One of us should stay in case of any problems with the herding. Anyway, like you just said, I'm the vet, right? If I can find one of these alive—"

"—it could bite you, Kesar. Perhaps you should wait for a few days. Until someone can come with you."

"Right. I need a guard to protect me from this little fist-sized spider. Don't worry, I'll be fine, Miriam." He patted her hand and smiled. "I'll take a net and watch where I put my feet."

He turned his attention back to the specimen even though he was aware she was hovering there, concerned.

"Hmm. The belly looks a lot softer than the legs. I bet I can incise along this plate line. Could you please fetch me the scalpel kit? Oh, and the Menashe saw? I'll peel this critter, one way or another."

She pursed her lips doubtfully but went to get the equipment from storage. He stooped over the alien again, already lost in thought. Miriam was a good doctor and a good spouse, but she worried too much. This creature was the most intriguing thing he'd come across on this planet so far. Hell, that's why he'd gotten into offworld medicine, stuff like this. To have some new and fascinating creature with his own Latinized name hung on it and then studied in biology classes at prestigious universities was perhaps an egotistical wish, but not an immoral one, was it? *Why, yes, this is the first of the many unique life forms discovered by the galactically famous Dr. Kesar Revna. A minor find compared to his later work, of course, but even great men must*

*have beginnings. Let him stand as an example to
you all . . .*

He smiled at the fantasy.

How could anyone fear such a unique find?

Besides, the creature was probably as harmless as
his fantasy of academic greatness.

8

They landed on the parched world in the bottom of a vast ravine, far from where the *lou-dte kalei* had sown the Hard Meat eggs; they came in cloaked and during light hours, although the Hunt would not begin until after dark. It was all standard procedure; there were some worlds upon which the natives had developed weaponry and would fight for their skins, infected or not. Dachande had not lived long by being careless on strange terrain, and the planet had not been used for a Hunt so recently that precautions could be discarded. Especially now, because since the yautja's last visit to Hunt here, others had come.

The Soft Meat, bleeding all over the radio bands for all to hear.

It was a shock to find them here. Given his choice,

he would hunt the Soft Meat, a thing he had long desired. They were cunning and they shot back. Soft Meat skulls were highly prized, the centerpiece of a warrior's trophy wall. He would challenge them, were it at all possible. But not with a handful of raw and unseasoned would-be warriors. Not only would it be foolish, it was also against the rules of the Hunt. Dachande could almost smell them, the Soft Meat, and he would like nothing better than to test his mettle against them, but he would not, not this time. He had responsibilities, duties, and to cast them aside for his personal satisfaction would be to dishonor his name. So the ship would remain cloaked, any of his party who might venture even remotely close to the oomans would do so in a shiftsuit, and the Soft Meat would never now how lucky they had been. Reluctantly and without explanation, Dachande caused shiftsuit electronics to be issued to the students. Let them wonder what his motivations were—they knew enough not to ask. He would tell the other Blooded of the danger, but there would be no contact with the oomans on this trip. Was an ooman sighted, the Blooded would order the students to shift into camouflage and to avoid contact. A pity, but that was the way of it. After he finished this training Hunt, his dues would be paid and his application to a Blooded Warrior Only ship would be accepted. Then he would at last get his chance at the oomans. Not here, not now.

In the staging area, the younglings were so *ch'hkt-a* that they would burn each other if they didn't calm down.

Dachande watched the young males hurriedly don their suits. He stood in the entry and felt the thick anticipation that radiated from them in their frenzied movements. It never failed to please him, to see the young so eager to spill first *thwei*.

There would be a short practice outside of the ship to test the world's gravity while Warkha scanned for anything unexpected—it was killing nothing other than time, a chance to wear the edge off of the young males' hyper-enthusiasm. Too, the Hard Meat would also be more active after the suns dropped. It was hardly sport to shoot a target curled up asleep.

Dachande turned and walked through the corridor toward the front of the ship. As Leader, he would be the first to set foot on the Hunting grounds, a pleasure that rumbled deep in his gut.

This would be a good Hunt, oomans notwithstanding.

Noguchi took her second shower of the day in the early evening, as twilight fell over Prosperity Wells. It had been a hard day but a good one; all of the herds had been penned except for one of Cho's and that one was on its way.

She stood in front of the holomirror in the green linen suit she had worn on her first day in Ryushi and smiled at her wind-burned complexion. After only a few days outside, her face had begun to take on the look of a rancher's. She liked it; it was the appearance of a person who didn't mind hard work, even though she had to innoculate herself against skin cancers and had run a small fever from the vaccine for most of a day.

The Chigusa staff had been setting up tables and portable roasting pits near the shield wall when she had gone to shower and change, but she was surprised at the crowd that had gathered in her short absence. She stepped out of her building and was nearly run over by a group of giggling children. Not many of those here, children, but some.

The scent of grilled rhynth steaks carried to her along with the sounds of people talking and laughing. Ranchers and their spouses walked past, hand in hand, all headed toward the landing pad. Noguchi joined them.

Hiroki was easy to spot amid the ranchers in his dark dress suit; he stood near the loading ramp, drink in hand. He returned her wave and wove his way through the crowd to meet her.

"You look lovely, Machiko-*san*."

"Thank you. You look very nice yourself." She gazed wonderingly at the mass of people all around. "Is every person on the planet here?"

"Just about. A few of the staff are watching screens in ops, but other than that . . ."

Noguchi smiled. "A hundred people in one place is now a mob to me. Funny, how perspectives change."

Hiroki nodded. "It is. And I'm glad to see them enjoying themselves. This is their first roundup, everything they've worked for, for three years."

Noguchi looked around at the ranchers, relaxed and mingling in the open compound. It was impossible not to pick up on the mood of excitement and accomplishment. Someone had even fed music over the public address system; couples danced in the deepening dusk while their children ran and played through the streets.

"Come on, let's go greet the ship," said Hiroki. "It's due any minute."

She followed him through the dancing crowd toward the antenna tower. "The home office called," she said mildly. "They've approved the price hike for the ranchers."

Hiroki raised his eyebrows and smiled at her. "Good work, boss."

"Where are we headed, anyway? Wouldn't the best place be—"

"The tower is the only place to watch a landing." Hiroki stopped in front of the runged ladder that ran up one side of the transmitting structure and rested one hand on the lowest step.

"Can that thing support both of us?" Noguchi looked at the ladder doubtfully.

"Let's find out, shall we?"

They scaled one story and hit the first landing, then slowly climbed the stairs to the top, five floors up. There was a moderate, warm breeze blowing, and Noguchi looked down to see the miniature people milling about in the night air.

It was easy to forget the pressures of work on such an occasion. Pleasant memories from long ago ran through her head, Nakama festivals with her parents, walks through bonsai forests that made her feel like a giant.

A low rumbling began, somewhere in the sky. The people below watched the clouds for movement.

Noguchi looked up to see the ship, and even so far away, she could tell it was big. Huge. It was hard for her mind to grasp such a gigantic object in the air. She had seen craft like it before, of course—but this one was bigger than the entire rec center and op building combined. It had pusher vents easily twenty meters long and half as wide on either side; there were three loading docks in front, each big enough to admit four rhynth side by side; giant air-pushers swept a benign wind over the crowd as the ship rumbled toward the landing pad.

With a roar that drowned out all other sound, *The Lector* settled gently. It was quite a trick to land such a tub in atmosphere; the aerodynamics were hardly conducive to such things. The shield wall protected the complex from most of the engine wash, but the sudden gale that hit all of them was enough to whip up dresses and hair and a considerable haze of dust. As the thunder dwindled slowly, Noguchi heard a chorus of laughter and hand clapping.

It was a magnificent spectacle, *The Lector* come to roost. Well, part of the ship anyway. The rest was still in orbit.

A hand landed on her shoulder. Hiroki. He grinned at her.

"Down to the final klick, eh? Let's go introduce ourselves to the crew."

They started toward the stairs, Hiroki leading. Noguchi cast one last look at the ship and thought about what he had said, the final kilometer. In spite of the mood of the evening, she had felt a chill at his words. Odd.

She brushed the ominous speculation aside and went to join the party.

Scott and Tom stepped off the ramp together into Prosperity Wells. For some reason, the mass of people assembled to greet them was a relief to Scott, although he wasn't sure why. Other crew members filed out past them to shake hands and chat with the ranchers and their families.

"Hey, we're celebrities, man, check it out," Tom mumbled.

Scott smirked. It was true; the locals had gathered around each of *The Lector*'s crew with smiles and backslaps.

"Guess they don't get out much," Scott whispered.

A tall, husky man, about forty TS, with a red beard and a grin stepped toward them. He held out two cups of beer to the pilots. "Ackland's the name," he said, extending his large hand. Tom shook it, then Scott. "I'm head of the local ranchers association. How was your trip, Captains—?"

"Strandberg," said Tom. "But just call me Tom. This is my copilot, Scott Conover. The trip was fine."

"Nice to meet you, sirs. Hope you and your crew are ready to party; we got some nice steaks on the grill—" Ackland leaned closer and lowered his voice. "And we got some fine young ladies looking for dance partners, I'll bet. That is, if you're inclined that way—"

Scott grinned. "You bet. Tom here was starting to look pretty good near the last leg of the trip, if you know what I mean."

Ackland chuckled, a forced and overly jovial sound, and clapped Scott on the back. "I thought so," he started. "You know, I was—"

"Can I have your attention, please?" A short Japanese woman in a green suit stood on a chair a few meters away, a dinner tray in hand. "Can I have everyone's attention, please?"

She was pretty, that one. Scott looked her up and down. Nice legs, nice butt. A little shy in the breast department, but Scott had seen worse.

"Who's the babe?" he said quietly to Ackland. Tom elbowed him in the gut. Damn feminist.

"You mean bitch," Ackland replied. "Nitrogen queen. That's the boss."

"I know you're all anxious for the festivities to begin, but first I have an important announcement." The crowd calmed as everyone turned to look at her.

"Loading will proceed as follows—Ackland, you're first on deck. Harrison's next, followed by Luccini and Marianetti. The rest of the assignments will be handed out tomorrow at dusk." She paused, then smiled.

"One more thing. The company gave their answer on the price adjustment—you'll be getting the increase you requested. Enjoy the party, everyone."

She stepped off the chair to the sounds of scattered clapping and hoots of excitement.

"Go figure," said Ackland. "Maybe she's good for something after all."

Scott took a long gulp of beer and then laughed. "I could think of a few other things she might be good at."

Tom rolled his eyes, and Ackland shook his head. "I wouldn't try it. Noguchi probably doesn't uncross her legs to take a shit, you know?"

"Too bad," mumbled Tom. He wandered off.

Scott took another slug and belched softly. "Takes all kinds, right?" he said, and looked into his cup. Not bad for a local brew. He picked out the Japanese woman again and studied her smile as she talked to some rancher woman. Ackland was babbling something about the weather, but Scott watched Noguchi.

Dust ball it was, but the place wasn't a lost cause. He swigged more beer and turned his attention back to Ackland. Anything could happen in three days, no matter what the rancher said. Hell, nitrogen was his specialty . . .

Noguchi walked toward the ops center, the party in full swing behind her. It was definitely a success, in

more ways than one. A few of the ranchers had
warmed toward her after the announcement, and she
had kept up a steady patter of innocuous conversation for at least two hours. Nice people. And she had
been doing a good job of nodding and smiling—

*Although one day doesn't undo six months of stu-
pidity, Machiko.*

Right. But it was a start. It had finally hit home that
Hiroki would be leaving with *The Lector*. A vague sadness had come over her, along with a desire to be
alone for a little while. He was perhaps her only
friend . . .

She walked into operations to see only one person
manning the screens.

"Collins, right?" she said hopefully.

The young man nodded and stood up.

"Go join the party, okay? I'll watch things here for
a while."

Collins's eyes widened. "Really? Thanks, Ms.
Noguchi."

"It's just Machiko from now on." She smiled at him
and moved by so that he could pass.

"Uh, okay," he said. "Machiko." He sounded uncomfortable with her first name but he smiled back. He
started to walk out and then turned.

"Oh, listen—when Doc Revna gets back, tell him
the home office received his report. It's in the tray
with his notes."

Noguchi frowned. She had seen Fem Doc at the
party, but Revna hadn't been around, had he?

"Gets back from where?" she said.

"Said he was going up to Iwa Gorge to look for
something," he said. "He signed out a hover bike a
couple of hours ago."

"Today? Bad timing," she said.

"Yeah, that's what *I* said." Collins shrugged. "But he said it was important. Listen, thanks again."

After he had left, Noguchi sat at the console and gazed at the radar, lost in thought. She hadn't expected much from Hiroki at the beginning, but he had been unfailingly patient with her. His professionalism was top-notch; it would be sad to see him leave . . .

She shook her head and glanced around for something to take her mind off of Hiroki. Doc Revna's report lay in a basket nearby, but she hesitated picking it up. What if it were private information—?

Then he wouldn't have let Collins send it, he would've done it himself.

Brilliant. She picked up the stack of hard copy and leaned back in her chair. What the hell was in Iwa Gorge, anyway? She liked the doc, he was a smart man. She leafed through the papers and settled down to read, with a silent wish for Revna to find whatever it was he was looking for . . .

Kesar trained his binoculars on the sight at the bottom of the gorge and inhaled sharply. His heart hammered in his chest and his hands shook. It was incredible. It was unbelievable.

A dozen or so humanoids stood surrounding a large craft, the likes of which he had never seen. The ship looked like a cross between a fish and a huge engine tube, it was tinted a strange greenish hue, with a broad ramp set into the ground.

The humanoids were tall; he couldn't be sure because of nothing to show relative size, and the scaler in his scope was malfunctioning, but he would guess two and a half meters, maybe a little more. More amazing, they appeared to be carrying . . . spears.

Revna had stopped halfway down into the gorge, had parked his bike near some rocks twenty meters behind him or so. The adrenaline in his system was screaming at him to go back to the flyer, now. Big aliens with spears did not seem like the kind of folks you wanted to meet by yourself in the middle of the desert. But he couldn't stop looking at the amazing sight.

He hit the full magnification button and the creatures zoomed closer. Tall, muscular, definitely armed. Still too far away to get a good view and it was also too bad the scope's scaler was out of whack, he wanted to get a size on them.

Whatever they were, they were definitely not human. Now here was a discovery that would get his name in the books. Not just a new species of spider or crab, but sentient aliens!

He watched for another half minute. What were they doing here? What *were* they? A hundred questions formed and tried to rise all at once. Incredible.

He licked his lips and focused on one of the alien faces. Some kind of mask it wore, like the others. Breathing gear?

He would go back to town, get some of the ranchers, some photo equipment—

Kesar blinked. One of the creatures turned and looked at him. It threw back its head, its long, odd braids fell back. A long, crazy howl filled the canyon, echoed off of the cliffs, and beat at his ears, joined by others.

Impossible, he was mostly hidden from view, and he could hardly see them with the scope. They *couldn't* see him.

But they did. He knew for sure in a second.

When they ran toward him, waving their spears, screaming.

9

Dachande spun, tusks flared, as the cries of his brood vibrated through the gorge. Sounds of challenge, of aggression. His gaze followed the path of the running yautja to a place in the rocks where—

Ooman!

Warkha spoke behind him, but the words were swallowed in the frenzy.

Dachande gave orders without looking.

"Tell Skemte to prepare flight and gather those you can! *Ki'cte!*"

He ran, blade in hand. The Hunt would have to be aborted, but the ooman would die first. There was no other way. Dachande cursed mentally and ran faster.

He was almost to the rocks when the noise of a craft starting hit him.

Damn! If the ooman got away, it would bring others!

He saw that at least two of the students had already made it to the place he was headed, Chulonte and another, he couldn't tell—

The small flying craft came over the rise and struck Chulonte at chest level.

A single ooman manned the ship, was balanced clumsily at the controls, hair swept back from an ugly, pale face.

Chulonte scrabbled at the craft to hold on, but the ooman ran the flyer close to a rock face. Chulonte's skull cracked against the cliff and he fell suddenly boneless to the ground, the mint gray-green of his brain tissue mixed with the darker phosphor-green of his blood splattered on the stone.

Cjit! The Hunt had not even begun and already he had lost a student. Damn!

The ooman's craft was turned by the collision. It roared and swerved past Dachande and headed straight for their ship, the ooman's intentions unknown.

The Leader ran back toward the ship. He screamed the death cry to all: kill the ooman!

It would pay with its life for the death of Chulonte.

Revna ran to his bike, his stomach an empty hole. Stark terror made him fumble the starter. His hands shook uncontrollably.

"Start, please, oh, please, start, start—" He heard his own voice and for a moment it sounded as if it belonged to someone else.

The cycle roared to life. Relief rushed through him,

cool and welcome. He stepped on the accelerator, hard, thinking only of escape.

And he flew directly into them. He topped the rock formation, his thoughts clouded with panic; turn, turn, *turn*, fool—

One of the creatures leapt up in front of him. He tried to swerve, but it was too late. The impact jarred him from his seat; he would have fallen except for the reflexive grab at the handles. The alien was huge; Revna caught a whiff of some musky, bitter oil. Its screech was one of pain and fury. It grabbed for him.

Without thinking, Revna veered toward a cliff wall. The screaming thing smacked into the rocks, hard, and then was gone. He tried to regain control of the scooter but the impact had thrown him into a turn. And the controls were damaged, he couldn't turn, the flier responded sluggishly.

All right, don't panic, it's okay. He would have to use speed to get past them, have to go so fast they couldn't catch him, couldn't *spear* him—

Another of the creatures reached for him, but he passed it. Revna smashed on the accelerator all the way forward as a blast of incredible heat blew by him. He ducked, felt his facial hair singe.

The craft didn't want to alter its course. He was going to pass right next to the ship.

Altitude, he had to get high enough so they couldn't grab him!

The repellors still worked, he managed to trim the elevators and start to climb. Five meters, seven, still heading right at the ship but he would clear it—

Another blast of heat, this one splashed the underside of the flier, cooked plastic and metal. The repellors coughed and the craft dropped a meter, sputtered.

That was no spear! They've got guns! Lasers, plasma rifles, Jesus!

He raised his watering eyes just in time to see that he was headed for the alien craft at high speed and that he wasn't going to clear it.

He was going to hit it dead center—

Miriam—

It was his last thought before the world turned to fire.

Dachande saw the ooman fly at the ship and he ran faster. Most of the students were clear, but at that speed, an impact could cause damage, big damage—

The tiny flier smashed into the ship and blew apart in a fireball that shattered both craft. A second later came another blast, bigger than the first. Flame and debris sprayed, scorched rocks, moved boulders, knocked over delicate formations that had stood undisturbed for millions of years. Huge chunks of burning ship flew through the gully as the hunters were blown to the ground by the blast.

After a moment Tichinde stood and looked around at his fallen peers. He waited to hear direction from the Leader, but there were no instructive cries.

Other yautja rose to their feet, dazed. Small pools of *mi* burned, their flickerings reaching into the dusk, carrying in their fumes the smells of ash and soil and oily death.

The Leader had fallen not far from Tichinde. Several of the others stumbled with him to where Dachande lay.

The Leader was barely alive, his mandibles caked

with *thwei*. Wreckage had hit him, knocked him into *dhi'ki-de*, the sleep near death.

A quick survey showed them that Warkha, too, was dead, and the other Blooded had been on the ship that still burned and smoked and looked now like nothing so much as a gutted crab. No one would be leaving this world on that vessel. And it would be weeks, months, years perhaps, before anybody came to look for them. Not good.

When all of the students alive had gathered around Dachande, Tichinde counted. Ten of them. No transport and no elder to tell them what would happen—

"What will we do?" From 'Aseigan.

"Dachande still breathes," said Gkyaun. "We could—"

"You are a medic?" Tichinde snorted. "He is beyond the aid kits, look at him. Let him die honorably of his wounds, wounds sustained in battle." He waved at the smoking ship. "The ooman deliberately attacked us and killed our ship. Therefore, we will kill the oomans, that is what we will do. Dachande lives but his time is short."

'Aseigan growled. "Who proclaimed you Leader?" His voice was thick with contempt. "You will not lead me. And Hunting Soft Meat is forbidden to un-Blooded, even a fool such as you knows this."

Tichinde grinned and pointed his burner at the yautja. 'Aseigan took a step toward him, arms high.

Tichinde fired.

The blast blew 'Aseigan against a pile of smoking rock. The others leapt back in surprise.

"Others dispute?" Tichinde swung the burner in a circle. "I will spill your *thwei* as easily as I do that of the ooman dogs later! This is not a Hunt, as that dead slave-to-rules thought, but self-defense. We are al-

lowed to defend ourselves from attack, are we not?"
Once again he waved at the ruins of their ship.

None of the nine disagreed. They watched him warily, hands close to their own burners. There was a
long moment when a Challenge might have come,
when one of the nine might have taken it upon himself to raise his burner and try him, but that moment
passed. If another would be Leader, he would have
made his move and none did.

Tichinde smiled. They would follow him, reluctantly or not.

He raised his staff to the sky and screamed of revenge. When Gkyaun returned from the wreck and
handed him the smoldering ooman skull a moment
later, Tichinde crushed it with bare claw to the ap-
proving hisses of the others. It had killed itself and
bravely in the doing, so it could not be a proper trophy. But there would be others to be earned.

The yautja chanted and howled their approval into
the night. Tichinde sent them to scavenge for whole
weapons and armor.

They were stuck here. So be it. The oomans would
be sorry they dared attack the yautja. Sorry they
dared to cross blades with Tichinde.

Very sorry.

10

he disparity in ratio between the smooth-backed specimens and the single carcass with dorsal spines notwithstanding, I believe the differences between the two types represent sexual indicators—not of the specimens themselves, but of the zygote or "egg" that each carries. As stated above, none of the specimens is equipped for independent life, their sole purpose seems to be nothing more than that of a living delivery vehicle—an ambulatory penis, if you will.

Noguchi tapped her cigarette without looking at the tray and skimmed back to the top of the page, totally absorbed. *This* is what Revna had gone after? Why hadn't he told anyone? Why hadn't he told *her?*

While it is risky to postulate so much from such a tiny sample, we need to know as much as possible

about these specimens as quickly as possible. If my
assumptions are correct, or even near the mark,
we're dealing with only one stage of this organism.
The hybrid silicon-carbon cell construction would
lead—

" 'Ambulatory penis,' huh? Conjures quite an image,
don't it?"

Noguchi jumped in her chair and turned quickly,
heart pounding. A tall man with blond hair and beard
stood there, grinning. He swayed slightly on his feet;
from the smell of him, he had been drinking. A lot.

She stood and backed away a step. "You're from
The Lector, right?"

The stranger took a step closer. "Hell, I *fly* that
bucket!" He belched softly. " 'Scuse me. Scott Conover
atcher service."

Noguchi smiled but inched back a little more. His
intentions weren't exactly clear but one thing was . . .

"You're drunk, Mr. Conover."

"Yeah, but not *too* drunk, if you know what I mean.
You're Ms. Nogooshi. I've been watching you—"

"It's Noguchi," she said coolly. "And you can call
me ma'am."

Conover laughed and reached out to take her hand.
Noguchi tried to pull away, but the pilot gripped her
wrist tightly. He leaned close, his alcohol breath moist
and pungent. "I heard about what a tough lady you
were, the company ramrod, right?" His words slurred
together slightly.

The drunken pilot tried to pull her hand down to
his crotch. "I got your ramrod right here, ma'am," he
stage-whispered.

Noguchi narrowed her eyes and took a deep
breath.

* * *

Scott couldn't find the Jap girl anywhere; he wandered around for a while and eventually he heard some guy say that she was watching screens.

"Operations," he said to no one in particular, and stumbled in that direction.

The door was open. He was torn between the desire to march right in and woo the woman and the desire to piss—which had gotten pretty overwhelming. He compromised and peed on the entry frame before his imminent conquest.

She was reading some kind of porn hard copy, he could see that much. Damn, but she was fine! He imagined that small mouth all over him, on his dick; and she wanted it, too, he could tell.

They did the small talk thing for a minute or two, and she told him she was into being dominant—'call me ma'am'—and the little vixen played chase, backing up, her cheeks flushed with desire.

And he reached out to touch her, to put her hand on his ready-and-willing equipment—and then he wasn't sure what happened.

He must have tripped—

Noguchi grabbed his arm above the elbow with her free hand and hooked one foot behind his. She twisted, pushing up and over at the same time, and the pilot went down. She jumped back and struck a ready pose, left foot forward, fists made. It had happened so fast, she was barely aware that she had done it.

The drunk groaned loudly; he didn't get up. Noguchi relaxed slightly, but kept her distance.

Another man stepped into the room, dark-haired, wearing glasses.

"Scott?" He looked down and moved immediately to the fallen man. "Jesus, what happened?" He stared up at Noguchi, at her fighting stance; realization dawned on his face.

"You next?" Adrenaline still pumped through her system.

The drunk's friend stood, hands in the air. "No, no, I was just coming to tell you that the ship is loaded and that we'll be making our first shuttle run as soon as the inspectors give the rhynth a clean bill of health—" He spoke all at once, in a rush, but seemed to catch himself.

Noguchi nodded. "You'd better have them check out this pilot, too." She looked down at Conover and frowned. "Especially his judgment."

"I'm Tom Strandberg, ma'am. I'm sorry about this, he's the designated drinker on this run." As the man spoke, he bent down and tried to help Conover to his feet. He grinned sheepishly. "Tomorrow it'll be my turn."

With a grunt of effort, Strandberg stood up, Conover half over one shoulder.

"Your turn to drink or your turn to get some of what I gave him?" Noguchi spoke sharply; she knew that none of this was Strandberg's fault, but damn him for excusing his friend so lightly; attempted rape wasn't particularly funny.

Strandberg edged toward the door with his heavy load. "Look, I'll make sure he doesn't bother you again, okay?"

It seemed to be the perfect cue. Conover raised his head slightly. "Damn bitch," he mumbled, and nodded back out.

Strandberg carried the other pilot out without another word.

Noguchi sat back in her chair and felt her heart slow down little by little. If she didn't receive a formal apology the next morning, she would file a complaint with the company.

Maybe I'll do that anyway. Conover certainly didn't deserve anything less, ol' I-got-your-ramrod-right-here.

She surprised herself by laughing out loud. How classically dumb *male*. Did they teach lines like that in Neanderthal 101?

Noguchi picked up the papers she had been reading, a smile still on her face. Well, it had broken the tension she'd been feeling.

After she'd read the same paragraph three times, she sighed and put the report down. This was important stuff, but she couldn't seem to regain her concentration after the rush of adrenaline that idiot's advances had created. Besides, it was late. Revna must have gone to the party or just gone home.

She stood, stretched, and yawned. Maybe she wasn't so very out of martial arts' practice after all. She had tossed him without thinking about it. It came back quick enough when she'd needed it.

She made sure that the recorders were all on and pulled her jacket off the back of the chair. She would talk to Revna tomorrow about these "specimens"; from the sound of it, there might be some crucial things going on out at Iwa Gorge—and it was her job to know about it.

It was dark and hot. The smell of burned materials worked its way into that darkness, and with the scent came pain.

Dachande opened his mouth to scream at the young males to fall in line, but nothing happened. He sensed no movement, no sound of the students came to him. He tried to lift one arm to clear his vision, but nothing happened. Only heat and blackness and far-away pain.

And then only dark.

Scott hurt. He rolled his head and opened his eyes, but closed them again immediately. The whole fuckin' *planet* was spinning. And there was an earthquake or something.

What planet?

"Wha' the fuck?" he mumbled. He opened his eyes again.

"Back to the land of the living?" Tom's face swam into view next to him. They were riding a small cart outside, back to the ship—the earthquake was the rumbling motor. On Ryushi. *The Lector.* Cowboys.

Japanese babe—

Scott focused on Tom's face. "Nogooshi," he said. It was coming back.

Tom grinned. "Scott, you're plowed. Apparently you tried to have sex with the head of the company here, a very capable woman who knocked the shit out of you before you got around to figuring out she wasn't interested." He paused for a second and then added, "And if you ask me, you're lucky she didn't rip your dick off and feed it to you."

"Great," said Scott. He closed his eyes, exhausted. "Nice to have you on my side, ol' buddy ol' pal."

Scott was almost asleep when the cart stopped. He growled and pulled himself upright. They were back at *The Lector.*

"Need help?"

"*No.* Fucking Judas." He got out of the cart okay, but discovered that his legs weren't particularly interested in staying straight. Tom grabbed one of his arms and pulled it over his own shoulder. Scott leaned on him heavily.

"Yeah, okay." He shuffled along next to Tom as they walked onto the second loading ramp. "She can't treat me like that, you know."

"Maybe you want to go back and tell her that," Tom said. "What's with the lights? Prindle's team is getting sloppy, maintenance is going to hell—"

Scott sighed. "Fuck the lights. But you know what I mean, right? I mean, I'm a goddamned *star*-pilot, you know?" On top of the humiliation of it all, he was getting a *huge* headache.

Tom leaned him up against a wall. "Hang on a sec, let me get a light."

Scott went on. "Who the fuck does she think she is, you know?" He stared at the floor. Goddamn rhynth all over the place, looked like one of them had thrown up on the floor. He toed the puddle of wet, mucusy goo with one foot and then looked away quickly; that was enough to make his stomach pretty damn unhappy.

"She's corporate," said Tom. "She pulled rank on you." He reappeared holding a flashlight and reached out to steady Scott with his free arm.

"That's not all she pulled," said Scott glumly. "I think my back is broken or something."

"Who in the hell left this hatch open?" Tom stepped forward and shined the light into the dark rhynth pen.

"You're not listening to me." Scott leaned back on the wall. Fuck the hatch.

"Hey, Ackland warned you, right?" Tom's voice had

taken on an echolike quality. He had walked into the pen.

With the last of his coordination, Scott followed him, narrowly missing a renegade doorway. Rhynth puke *everywhere*.

Tom continued. "But you wouldn't listen, *no*. You just had to go mess with the queen—"

Tom stopped short. The flashlight hit the floor and a low hiss filled the room, coming from all around.

Scott shook his head and followed Tom's gaze. There were four. Or seven. Or twenty. A flurry of horrible images: long, dark skulls and dripping razor teeth. Gigantic, black, all arms and legs and spiny tails, hissing. Moving forward.

Reaching toward them—

11

*T*here was darkness. Not
with the cold that she had once associated with the
black hours, not with a sense of night or time. It was
a stifling darkness that echoed with soft, wet sounds
of rhythmic movement—the insistent pulse of body
against body, but far from any act of love. It was the
black of a huge machine, steadily devouring light,
continually working, thrumming. Eating. Building
toward the inevitable scream. The darkness was the
dragon, calling her name, calling its prey, and there
was no escape . . .

"Machiko?"

Light blared, loud and unwanted. Noguchi started,
sat up. She rubbed her eyes. "What—?"

Hiroki stood in her doorway, his hand on the control panel.

The darkness machine, insatiable—

She shook her head. "I had a dream . . . Hiroki. What time is it?"

"Almost noon." Hiroki smiled apologetically. "I know you were up late last night, sorry to disturb you—"

"What is it?" Noguchi felt the last of the dream slip away as her eyes adjusted to the brightness. She was suddenly aware that she wore only an undershirt, and a tight one at that.

"Doc Revna still hasn't returned, and Mrs. Doc is starting to worry. I've sent out a crew in the copter to search for him, but I thought it would be best if the staff saw that you were in on this, too."

Noguchi nodded. "Thank you, Hiroki. You're right. Give me two minutes to get dressed."

Hiroki averted his eyes politely as she walked to the 'fresher to splash water on her face. Revna wasn't back? He'd been gone—fifteen or sixteen hours, at least. Too long.

She dressed quickly and rinsed her mouth with water. In spite of the cool liquid, she felt hot, her eyes sticky and full of sand. Not enough sleep. Noguchi combed through her hair with her fingers and stepped out to meet Hiroki. She glanced longingly at her bed; a nap later, perhaps.

Doc had probably just had some engine trouble; he would know to stay put and wait for help. Hell, the copter was most likely on its way back with Revna already; nothing to worry about.

Except for the darkness.

She shuddered as they reached the door to the building; her dream—

"You okay?"

Noguchi smiled and gave up on the half-remembered image. "Fine. I just—I dreamed it was hot."

Hiroki laughed. "Pure fantasy."

Noguchi smiled again, but felt the shudder deep inside. She hoped the dark feelings were just that, fantasy. She donned her sunglasses and followed Hiroki into the blazing day.

David Spanner had one fuck of a nasty headache. The pressers on the goddamn copter were incredibly noisy—no, more than that, they were *deadly*, that was it. He had been sent out because of all of his sins to die by slow torture. *Loud* torture.

"How about after this we go to the cafe and get some sushi, Spanner? Nice and fresh, maybe the abalone, all squishy and raw, or the octopus—"

"Fuck you very much, Ikeda." Great. Only big party of the year, everyone in town is sleeping it off, and *he* gets sent to pick up the doc. With the only person in town who wasn't suffering a severe hangover.

His copilot grinned, her smile relaxed and easy. "Or we could have a few cold ones. What do you say? Couple of big frosty quarts of beer, to wash down the snake-roll?"

Spanner scowled. "I could just throw up on you now, save you the trouble of making me."

"No time," she said. "We're almost there."

Ikeda pulled up on the stick as they rounded a cliff and flew into the gorge. Spanner's stomach protested at the sudden dip. He wrapped his arms around his chest and closed his eyes, taking deep breaths.

"You did that on purpose, Ikeda."

"Maybe. Help me look, lush."

Spanner shook his head, eyes still closed. "Uh-uh. You look. I'm just here for the fresh air."

They flew without talking for a few minutes, but it was far from silent. The pressers. It was the goddamn age of science, and no one had invented a decent muffler; what were the techs thinking? Spanner considered jumping. At least it would be quiet . . .

"What the *fuck*?"

Spanner sat up quickly. They had just come over a low cliff, and on the floor of the gorge—

There had been an explosion, a big one.

Huge metallic arches like the rib cage of a giant stretched up from still-smoldering wreckage. The charred ground around the arches were strewn with large chunks of blackened debris—of what, Spanner couldn't tell.

His hangover was forgotten.

As Ikeda started to set down at the edge of the site, he wished he had thought to bring a weapon more powerful than a rhynth-stick.

"It's a ship, isn't it?" Spanner scanned the gorge side to side. Lots of places to hide . . .

"Yeah, I think so." Ikeda's eye were wide. "*Was* a ship. But not any human design I recognize."

She shut off the pressers. The sudden silence wasn't so welcome anymore. Spanner gripped his rhynth-stick tightly.

They got out of the copter carefully and walked toward the burnt-out shell. It was very quiet. Spanner's fear dissolved into awe as they neared the towering arcs. It was—

"Incredible," Ikeda said softly.

Spanner nodded. And from the smell of it, the fire had been recent. Like yesterday, maybe.

"This thing—you ever heard of *anything* like this?"

Spanner looked at her. Ikeda kicked at a chunk of the odd substance.

"Never." She turned and started to poke through the rubble.

"Think of what this *means*, Ikeda! We're talking intelligent life here, not just some new strain of amoeba! This could be the first real proof, you know?" His brain kicked in to overdrive. Fucking *wow*!

"Think of the new information! If we could figure out who made this ship, could figure out some way to test this material—" He trailed off, mind alive with the possibilities.

"Why don't you just ask him?"

Spanner twisted around to see Ikeda crouched down by a fallen figure. He stepped closer. "Doc—?" And stopped short.

It wasn't human. Some sort of armored animal, but humanoid form—except this thing was *big*. Spanner himself stood a little under two meters, and he was probably the tallest man in Prosperity Wells. This guy had half a meter on him, easy. Jesus fucking Buddha.

"Careful, Ikeda."

"I think it's dead," she said, and then watched the figure for a second.

Spanner joined her.

"No, it's breathing," said Spanner. "What the fuck?"

Ikeda shaded her eyes and looked up at him. "You tell me," she said quietly. Her words sounded flat in the hot, dry air.

The initial anxiety he had felt surged back. They were an open target down here. And maybe this guy's friends were nearby . . .

He looked at the steep walls of rock on either side

of them and suddenly felt claustrophobic. "Let's get outta here, what say?"

Ikeda nodded and dropped her gaze back to the creature. "Yeah. But help me get him into the copter, first. We'll have to come back to look for Revna later."

They loaded the thing into the copter as quickly as possible considering he weighed about a ton. They did their best to strap him to the stretcher with the human-sized bonds. It was a tight fit. When they finally lifted, Spanner felt relieved. No way was he coming back later unless everybody in town came with him.

On the trip home he kept his eyes open and aimed at their passenger; his headache had crept back, and it pulsed sharply at his temples as the suns beat down hard in piercing shafts of brightness.

Dr. Miriam Revna was an attractive woman even when she was worried. Which she was—in spite of her calm composure, the lines on her brow and the concern in her smile gave her away. Noguchi felt an instant sympathy for the woman; her attempt to maintain cool and continue functioning in spite of her emotions was a state Noguchi was quite familiar with.

"Is there anything you can think of that might help us locate your spouse?" Hiroki said.

Revna walked over to an examination table and motioned for them to join her. "He went to Iwa Gorge to find more of these," she said, and lifted a plastic sheet to expose some kind of spider. Hiroki frowned and stepped closer.

"They're unclassifiable," the doctor continued.

"Their structure bears characteristics of both carbon-based and silicon-based life forms."

Noguchi nodded. "Yes, I read the report. But what made him decide to look all the way up in Iwa Gorge?"

Revna smiled weakly. "That's where she said she'd found them."

" 'She'?" Noguchi and Hiroki almost spoke in unison.

The doctor nodded. "Jame Roth. The young woman who works for Ackland."

"Thank you for your time," Noguchi said. "We will contact you as soon as we know anything, Dr. Revna." She smiled warmly and touched the older woman's hand. "I'm sure everything will be fine."

They walked into the searing heat together and started toward the garage.

"What would Roth be doing at Iwa Gorge?" Hiroki said. "Ackland doesn't have any herds within twenty klicks of there."

"Those things weren't found in Iwa Gorge, Hiroki." Of course! It was obvious once she thought about it.

"What?" Hiroki stopped to look at her.

"Think about it. If you were Ackland and you found some new life form the night before the roundup, would you risk having three years' profit tied up in quarantine? No. You'd say the creature was discovered far from where your herd was pastured."

"But why would he report it at all? The things we saw might not be any threat to rhynth. I mean, if they were like ticks or something, they'd be easy to spot."

Noguchi felt a spark of anger deep in her gut. "To cover his ass. Say his rhynth *do* come down with some disease. Maybe the crab things are carriers, they bite an animal and infect it. He's done his duty, right? He reported it, even though they were found a long way from his animals."

Hiroki nodded thoughtfully. "So do we talk to Ackland first, or Roth?"

"Roth. She'd be more likely to admit to something like this than Ackland. Besides, if we go to Ackland first, he might bribe her to stay quiet before we can get to her."

Hiroki smiled appreciatively. "Good thinking, Machiko."

Noguchi barely heard him. "If anything has happened to Kesar Revna, Ackland will be sorry," she said softly. "He sent the doc to chase dust up there. He could have had an accident, hurt himself, and that's a long way from help."

After the ooman craft left, Tichinde and the others moved back to the smashed and burned wreckage to see what they had done.

M'icli-de had wanted to kill them, but Tichinde had held them back; he had a better idea.

Dachande was gone. He'd been dead already, of course, but the oomans were *h'ulij-bpe*, crazy. In a way, it was fitting. The oomans had taken the old Leader, had left him to be the new one. He was a warrior now, 'Aseigan had been his first kill. And so he would Lead them to their first Hunt. Later, he would Blood himself, design his own mark, and etch it in place with Hard Meat *thwei;* and he would also mark the other students as his own.

The ooman craft had surely gone in the direction of

their dwellings; and if not, it did not matter. They
would go and find the ugly small ones wherever they
might be. It was only a matter of how long it would
take, and that was not a concern.

They had nothing if not plenty of time.

12

Math sucked, and it sucked *hard*; if Bobby Sheldon had children someday, he would see to it that they never had to do fractions if they didn't feel like it. Because fractions sucked worse than anything. In fact, they sucked *shit*.

"Bobby?"

He jerked around in his chair and flushed slightly at the sound of his mother's voice. The s-word was totally unallowed, even if he'd only thought about it.

"Yeah?"

"Finish what you're on and go wash up for lunch. You can do the rest later, okay?"

Bobby nodded at his mom. " 'Kay."

He looked back at the screen and sighed. One-tenth of ten was one. So three-sevenths of twenty was—

Stupid. Why the hell did he have to know this anyway? He tapped the save control and went to wash his hands. He was going to be a rancher, and what rancher needed to know fractions? His dad said that they came in handy for counting heads, but his dad was a rancher and so far as Bobby could tell, Dad had *never* used that shit.

Bobby walked back into the living room of their small house and looked out the window for Dad. Tomorrow was school day, which he looked forward to as usual; not that class was so great, but it was the only time of the week he got to hang out with the guys. They lived too far out of town for him to go every day, like some of the other kids. Although he'd gone to see the ship come in last night, that'd been cool. He had played spy-tag with Dal and Alan and Hung and eaten about a ton of banana popsicles.

Bobby heard his dad before he saw him. Actually, he heard Dax first; the terrier always sounded like a bike out of fuel after a morning's work. Dax padded into view a few seconds before his father and headed straight for the water dish at the side of the house.

"Hey, how's the best eleven-year-old in the world?" Bob Senior opened the door in a blast of hot air and smiled at Bobby. The joke was old, but Bobby grinned; he *was* the only eleven-year-old on the whole planet, at least for another month. And then Hung's sister, Ri, would have a birthday. Stupid *girl*.

"What's for lunch, hon?" Dad stood in the doorway and patted his thigh. "C'mon, Daxter, we don't have all day." Dax hurried inside and Dad shut the door against the simmering heat.

Mom walked into the room and smoothed her short blond hair down. She was pretty for a mom, although she was old, at least thirty-six or so. She smiled at Dad and kissed him on his cheek.

"Tuna casserole."

"Tuna! Where'd you get tuna?"

"I traded some of our jerky for three cans of it from one of *The Lector*'s crew." She sounded pleased with herself.

"Good deal. Maybe tomorrow when you take Bobby in, you can see what else you can get."

Bobby followed them into the dining room and listened to them talk about their days. Dad's boss, Mr. Cho, was going to give him a raise; Mom still wanted to build another room onto their small house, a reading room. And there was a rumor that some of the rhynth had contracted a virus of some kind, although none of Cho's got sick.

"It's probably just talk," his father said. "Like that thing about the flies last year. That had everyone going crazy, until the doc declared the whole thing a farce."

"I heard the doc was missing," Mom called from the kitchen. "One of Chigusa's people called this morning to tell us to keep our eyes open. He may have been near the gorge . . ."

She carried a steaming dish into the room and set it on the table. Bobby felt his mouth water; they mostly ate meat and canned vegetables.

"This looks great. Yeah, I heard the same thing, but they've already sent out a copter, probably found him by now. I'll check later, but I doubt they'll need any more help."

Mom spooned the casserole onto their plates. Dax ran into the room and started to whine.

"Hey, no chance, Daxter! You'll get yours later." Dad reached for the water pitcher.

Dax whined louder and went to the front door. Dad

sighed and pushed back from the table. "Good timing, Dax; why couldn't—"

He stopped short as Dax growled at the door, teeth bared.

Bobby stood. "What is it, boy? What's the matter?"

Dax continued to growl, and then barked, the sound deep and fierce.

"Bob?" Bobby's mother wore a look of concern. Bobby started around the table, but his dad motioned him back. Dax barked again.

"One of those damned briar-wolves again," his father said, and went to the door. "I thought we'd gotten 'em all." He picked up the carbine that they kept by the coat rack and checked it. And then opened the door.

"Sic 'em, Dax!"

Dax ran outside full speed, his barking a continuous war cry.

Dad stepped onto the porch, Bobby and his mother behind him.

Dax stopped in the middle of the yard and circled, growling. He acted like there was something there—but there wasn't. The dog backed away and edged forward, all the time barking and growling at nothing.

Bobby's eyes widened. There *was* something! A ripple of—dust and light. Dax flickered like he had gone into some kind of magnifier as he circled again.

Bobby felt his mom's hands grip his shoulders.

"Dad? What—?"

"Both of you, in the house, now!"

His mother pulled him backward, but he still watched. And saw as Dax was lifted off of the ground in a gout of blood. A huge beast—a monster!— appeared from out of nowhere, he held the spear stuck into Daxter!

Bobby heard a dull sound like an ax hitting meat. Dax made one short howl of pain and then went quiet.

"Good God—!" his father whispered.

The monster was tall, masked, inhuman. It shook the dead dog on its spear, sent a rain of red to the ground.

"Be careful, Bob!" His mother almost screamed it.

Bobby was petrified, unable to look away.

"Dax?" He watched as the monster tossed the dog over its shoulder and turned to face his father.

Dad brought the carbine up and aimed. There was a sudden shift and creak from the roof, like when Dad had patched the tiling, like somebody was *up* there—

—and a ripple of light and dust plunged into his father's skull. Bobby screamed. Dad reached up to clutch at the now-visible metal claws that had worked into his face—

Mom spun him to face the kitchen. Her breath came in short gasps.

"Run, Bobby!"

"Mommy? Is—"

"Run! We have to get to the truck! Out the back!"

He tripped and sprawled on the floor. His mother pulled him up and shoved him toward the rear door.

There was a giant, splintering crunch from the front porch. Bobby and his mother both turned.

The monster crouched in the doorway.

Impossibly fast, it reached for Mom, grabbed her—

And ripped her throat open.

Once again, the sound of meat being cut.

Warmth dotted Bobby's face, turned his vision to red.

He screamed, "Mom!"

He ran. There was no time to think, only move. The

flier outside his parents' room, Daddy had shown him how—

Bobby ducked across the hall and into their bedroom. Without a pause, he ran and jumped through the thin plastic window. There was another scream—his—as the window shattered, and there was the bike, within reach—

He hit the ignition button as if he had ridden a thousand times. The machine roared to life, raised up from the ground—

—and behind him was the sound of some evil bird, screeching, hoarse and piercing. Something touched his shoe, still inside the house—

—and the bike lurched forward, pulled him away. There was another, and another of the murdering creatures, all claws and hate. They came out of nowhere, appearing like magic.

They reached for him—

—and he took off, tilted wildly. He aimed the bike east, toward town.

He kept his sweaty hand jammed to the accelerator. Behind him the things howled and screamed, horrible, horrible, Mom, Dad—

There was a noise like gunfire, but hollow—and the wall of rock in front of him to the left exploded, sharp pieces hammered the bike, stuck into his skin, but it didn't matter, it didn't hurt. And beyond that, Bobby knew nothing.

Tichinde was pleased. True, they had lost one—but they had faced the deadly oomans and come away unscathed, with two kills. The escaped one would die soon enough, with the rest. It had surely gone to alert the others; they would have to be prepared . . .

Tichinde watched as the other yautja danced and cried over the victory. He himself had killed the second ooman; it had been without weapon, but as dangerous as he had heard oomans to be, that was allowable. Hunt or be Hunted . . .

Dachande would have disapproved. Tichinde flared his tusks in amusement at the thought. Dachande was *thei-de*; his opinion no longer held meaning. Besides, with no one to hold judgment over their actions, they would take what they wanted; from what he had seen so far, the oomans were not so dangerous as the yautja had been led to believe.

13

Roth cleaned the dirt from under her nails with her teeth. It was a nervous and dirty habit; Cathie was always getting on her case about it. But considering the circumstances at the moment, she didn't really give a flying fuck about biting her nails.

The two heads of Chigusa onworld stood over her small table in the rec center and glowered at her. Creep snuffled blissfully by her feet, probably thrilled to get out of the sun; she wished she felt the same.

"Do you know what charges you could face if Ackland's rhynth turn up infected with dangerous bacteria or a virus?" Hiroki had always been an amiable sort, but his eyes flashed with anger. At her. "And you were responsible for sending them to Earth?"

Roth opened her mouth to speak, but was cut off by the Noguchi woman.

"Ms. Roth—if anything has happened to Kesar Revna, you will be held accountable." She leaned toward Roth, expression cold. "How do you feel about that? He's been missing for almost a day now. He might be injured. Or dead."

Roth nodded slowly. She had lied for Ackland, had put her reputation at stake for him—after all, he was the boss. But she wasn't about to get caught holding *this* bag; it was just a little bit too heavy.

"Ackland told me to," she said quietly. "I realize that doesn't excuse my actions, but I just work for the man, you know?"

Hiroki and Noguchi exchanged glances.

"So Ackland told you to tell Revna that the spider creatures were in Iwa Gorge?" Noguchi leaned forward again, but her eyes weren't as angry as before.

"Right."

"What the hell is going on here?"

Roth looked up, surprised.

Ackland marched across the room, his face sweaty and red.

"Roth? What have you done?" Ackland stopped at their table and glared down at her accusingly. "What's this I hear about you lying to Doc Revna?"

Roth felt raw anger hit her system. He was going to let her take the fall, after she'd worked her ass off for him for three years!

What a surprise.

She stood abruptly. "Mr. Ackland, I've already explained the situation. And I quit. I'll expect to be paid within the month." Roth nodded at Noguchi and Hiroki.

"Please let me know if I can help in any way, and

contact me about charges as soon as you've decided."
She whistled softly; Creep jumped up to follow her to
the exit. Already she could hear Ackland's voice
raised in a huff.

"... I thought a man had a right to be present when
his accusers were testifying against him!"

She was glad to get out. Ackland talked big, there
would be quite a scene—but he had enough sense to
know when he was caught. Hiroki was a fair man ...
but Noguchi? Something about her was pure steel.

Roth would hate to cross that one; nitrogen queen
was right.

"So you were planning to try me in absentia? Don't
you need a judge to hold trial? Or is that some old-
fashioned notion—"

"Shut up, Ackland."

Stunned, he did.

"You've violated company policy and jeopardized
the security of this complex and its personnel,
Ackland. I figure that's all the legal authority I need."
Noguchi was royally pissed, but she kept her voice
low. This overblown rancher had the *gall* to try to
screw things for everyone and then cover it up?

"You really think you've got the backing to make
charges stick? In case you haven't noticed, you aren't
exactly the most popular person in this settlement."
Ackland was shaken, she could tell, but he smirked at
her.

"You're right, I'm just the new boss." She had to
make a conscious effort not to shout. "But Doc Revna
has been here since the beginning, treating the ranchers' stock, treating their families—delivering their ba-
bies. So far, he's just missing. But if he turns up dead,

who do you think folks are going to side with, you? Or his grieving widow?"

Ackland seemed to shrink a little in front of her. He dropped his gaze to the unlit cigar he held and spoke uneasily.

"Look, I didn't expect the doc to go out looking for more of those things—"

Hiroki stepped in. "But if he did, you wanted to make sure he looked in the wrong place."

Ackland flared again, but his anger seemed weak. "We had no way of knowing whether those rhynth were infected or not! I didn't want to delay the whole operation—"

Hiroki frowned angrily and pointed his finger at the rancher's chest. "Didn't it occur to you that trouble with your herd could be the reason *The Lector* is still parked out front?"

Noguchi raised her eyebrows. *"What?"*

"I meant to tell you—" Hiroki started, but she was already headed to one of the wall screens. She punched up a southern compound view and looked in disbelief.

"Those rhynth are going to be hell to manage after standing in the sun all day!" She turned to glare accusingly at Ackland. He looked away.

Noguchi tapped into operations. Collins appeared in front of her.

"Collins—why hasn't *The Lector* taken its first load back to its orbiter?"

"I couldn't say—ah, Machiko. We've been trying to contact them all day, but they haven't responded . . ."

"Send someone in person."

Collins nodded. "I'll go myself."

"Good. And don't waste your time with Conover,

talk to Strandberg. Remind him we're on a tight schedule. Report back immediately, okay?"

"Gotcha."

The screen went blank. At least *that* was taken care of. She walked back to the table where Ackland had sat down, his face blank.

"If this has anything to do with your little lie, Ackland," she said smoothly, calmly, "I'll see to it that you are put away for it. Until hell freezes solid."

The look in his eyes, defeated and guilty, was exactly what she wanted.

Scott ached all over. It was the hangover, and that Japanese woman, she was responsible—

Except he couldn't move his arms. And he was standing up—?

He opened his heavy eyelids and blinked several times. It was dark, but he was inside; there was weak light coming from somewhere ...

"Tom?" His voice was a raspy croak. God, he was thirsty! He cleared his throat and tried again.

"Tom. Can you hear me?"

No answer. Was he in a med center, maybe? There might have been some kind of accident ...

He took a deep breath and spoke as loud as he could. "Hello! Where am I? Tom!" His throat protested; it felt like he'd swallowed a bucket of sand.

A slow hissing filled the room. The shadows in the room moved, unfurled themselves from the walls and the dark corners. He could make out—

Teeth.

Jesus!

He tried to move, but his arms were pinned.

"Oh, God, no—" His voice was barely a whisper.

The room swam with darkness, and then once again, there was nothing.

". . . the company has billions invested in this project," she continued. "Where the hell do you get off fucking with us? Not to mention possibly endangering the lives of millions, maybe billions of people? You think the quarantine laws are there just for the fun of it?" She was still on a roll and unwilling to doppler down.

Ackland hadn't spoken for several minutes. Neither had Hiroki.

"Well?"

Ackland looked up at her and said nothing.

The tension was broken by an incoming message over Noguchi's com. "Ms. Noguchi, report to the med center immediately. Ms. Noguchi to the med center." Miriam Revna. She sounded agitated.

Noguchi tapped the received button and looked at the rancher. "You'd better pray they've found Revna, Ackland."

"I didn't make him go out there! And if he hurt himself, it's his own fault!"

She hurried out of the rec center and was blasted by the afternoon heat.

Ackland and Hiroki followed; she deliberately walked ahead of them to avoid further conversation for the moment; by the sound of it, Ackland was trying to reason with Hiroki, his deep voice apologetic and contrite.

Asshole.

Noguchi waited at the entry to the lab for them to catch up; if Revna was dead, she wouldn't want to walk into it alone.

The three of them stepped into the lab together. Noguchi saw what was strapped to an examination table, and took in a deep breath, to scream or faint she didn't know.

Dragon!

14

So much for your precious quarantine," said Ackland softly.

Noguchi closed her mouth. Miriam Revna and two local pilots were looking at a readout on a small screen across the lab.

One of the pilots, Spanner, turned and grinned. "Hey, look what we found!" He pointed at the creature unnecessarily.

Hiroki took a step toward it and then paused. "Is it—alive?"

Miriam Revna stood and walked over. "Yes. It's injured, but not in any danger. At least, I don't *think* so. Four cracked ribs and extensive contusions in the dorsal region. And it's male, I'm fairly certain."

Noguchi saw what she meant about the maleness. She couldn't miss it.

The thing was a giant, maybe two and a half meters tall. Humanoid, but its head like some sort of mutated crab. It wore armor, and was bound to the exam table by several thick straps of rhynth hide—its long, taloned arms were speckled, reptilian, but not scaled. Noguchi saw the slight rise and fall of its chest. There was a mask over its face. What was it breathing? she wondered.

After the initial shock, she tried to remember what the company's off-planet manual contained on the subject of possible XT encounters; something like "Avoid direct contact until trained personnel arrive!"

Looks like we're going to write a whole new chapter . . .

"We found a ship, too," Spanner said. "It's mostly blown to shit, but we should get a salvage team up there!"

Noguchi found her tongue. "Any idea what it is, Doctor?"

Revna looked at her blankly. "Hmm? I'm sorry, I'm not thinking clearly today."

Noguchi nodded. "Of course. We are still looking for Kesar. I just wondered if there was any connection between this and those unclassifieds that Roth brought in."

The doctor shook her head. "This creature has a completely different cell structure. No relationship at all. He"—she nodded at the monster—"is more like us than the little crablike things."

Hiroki walked over to a table covered with pieces of the alien's armor. He held up a broken staff tipped with a vicious-looking blade. "Quite an arsenal."

Noguchi joined him and picked up a large chunk of dark metal with a strap. She could barely lift it. At closer inspection, it was apparently some kind of weapon, a rifle or a flamethrower. It was damaged.

She set it down and picked up a mask.

"This is stuff you'd pack for a hunting trip. Or an invasion," she said. "This guy's no peaceful explorer."

Hiroki fingered the strap on the odd weapon. "I don't think this is his first trip to Ryushi, either. I can't place the rest of it, but this strap is definitely rhynth-hide."

"Any sign of the Doc?" Ackland nodded at the pilots.

The slender young woman, Ikeda, sighed. "Negatory. But Iwa Gorge connects with a maze of canyons and arroyos; it'd be easy to get lost. We'll go back out pretty soon."

There was a small shield of some kind with the other weaponry, a plate-sized disk with a strange-looking creature etched on it. Noguchi ran a finger over the blackened metallic substance. The drawing was the head of an unknown animal or bug, an elongated skull with sharp teeth and no eyes; she traced the outline thoughtfully. There was something familiar about it.

Was it a dream? It was dark and hot . . .

She looked again at the unconscious alien and shuddered. Maybe Doc Revna hadn't gotten lost—

There was a scream from outside, followed by a crash. Noguchi started; what now? She and Hiroki ran to the door together with Ackland behind them.

A flier had slammed into the transmitter building directly across from the med center. There was no fire but a lot of oily smoke; a small body lay on the hot pavement next to the accident. Several others had come out of the op center and were also running toward the scene. Hiroki got there first.

"What happened?" Noguchi called out.

Hiroki knelt by the victim and carefully touched its face. "It's the Sheldon boy," he said.

Noguchi looked down at the child's still, tear-streaked face and felt her heart tighten. So young . . .

The boy opened his eyes and started to scream.

Bobby woke up with a scream. It was hot, the air smelled burnt, and his parents—

He sat up quickly and looked around. He was in Prosperity Wells, there were a bunch of people gathered around him and the flier lay nearby, broken.

"Bobby," said a calm voice. Mr. Shimura was next to him. "Are you hurt—?"

"Monsters," he whispered. And he started to cry.

Ms. Noguchi was there, too. She leaned down next to Mr. Shimura and smiled at him. "It's okay, Bobby. You're safe now. What happened?"

He closed his eyes, unable to stop the tears. "Mu—monsters killed my dad and then my mommy and then before that they kuh—kuh—killed Dax and we couldn't *see* them, but then I got away—"

He couldn't say anything else; he wanted to tell them how scared he had been, how there were so many of them, and how Dax had seen them first—but all that came out were loud sobs of terror and sadness.

"Let's get him to the med center," someone said. Gentle hands lifted him off of the burning ground and carried him away. One of his legs hurt really bad and he cried harder.

Cool air washed over him as they went inside, the world dimmed.

"We've got an emergency here, Doc!" the person holding him shouted. Mr. Shimura.

Bobby opened his eyes and looked past Dr. Revna at the medical room. And he started to scream again; just like the tears, he was unable to stop. Fear and hatred and sadness and anger for the thing that they had lying on a table.

"Monsters! Monsters! Monsters!"

Dachande remembered movement after the loneliness of pain, the new pain. Once, he had opened his eyes and seen that he was indoors, in a moving ship. There had been heat and then cool, and strange, animal sounds—

He realized he could see a little, but could not focus. Dark and light shapes folded and formed in front of him. But now his gaze sharpened, just for a second, at the horrible cries of some creature in front of him. It screamed and howled its nonsense language, the thing. It was pale and little, like—

Like an ooman?

Dachande sank back into the quiet darkness. Fear fought to rise in him.

He was caught by monsters.

15

Noguchi and Hiroki walked into a room filled with low, nervous chatter and grim faces. The gathered ranchers and Chigusa staff fell silent and looked at them, their expressions fearful and expectant. The rec center was packed, but suddenly a hundred-plus people didn't seem like so many.

Noguchi cleared her throat. "Before we start, is everyone here?"

Mason stood from his seat near the door and read from a piece of paper. "Everyone except Ikeda, both Revnas, three ops people, two of Marianetti's people who are on their way—and the Sheldons. Oh, and the Barkers haven't answered yet."

Noguchi nodded. "Ikeda will be here shortly, and Miriam Revna is tending to Bobby Sheldon—"

A slender blond woman called out from a back corner of the room, her voice tinged with worry. "Is it true? About the Sheldons?" Noguchi recognized her as one of the garage maintenance workers, a mechanic.

Noguchi took a deep breath; she and Hiroki had discussed how to handle the situation after Ikeda had called in, but it wasn't going to be easy—the Sheldons had apparently been well liked on Ryushi.

"I'm not sure what you've heard, but I'll tell you what we know," she said. She consciously kept her voice low and firm; panic in the crowd would help no one.

"Approximately two hours ago Bobby Sheldon came into town on a flier, alone. He said that his parents had been killed by a group of XT life forms. Just before he arrived, Spanner and Ikeda found an injured ... being in Iwa Gorge that is currently unconscious in the med center. Bobby Sheldon identified this being as similar to the life forms that killed his parents." Noguchi took another deep breath. "When we were unable to reach Mr. and Mrs. Sheldon by radio, we sent Ashley Ikeda on a flyby. I am sad to report that she just called in with the news that the Sheldon house is in flames, and their breeding stock has been slaughtered.

"We must assume that an attack is imminent."

There was a slight murmur through the crowd. A few people coughed, a few children started to cry softly.

Loren Gaunt, one of the ops screen-watchers, stood and raised his voice to be heard above the uneasy group. "So what are we going to do with the thing in the med center? And what is it, exactly?"

Several others nodded.

Hiroki stepped forward. "At this time, we know

very little about the creature currently in Miriam Revna's care. It is a large, humanoid being, unlike anything previously registered in the EXT guide. It is under restraint, and has shown no signs of recovering so far—although Revna doesn't seem to think it's in critical condition—"

"You mean you haven't *killed* it?" Gaunt sounded incredulous. "After it murdered Bob and Sylvan?" A couple of others called out agreement.

Noguchi raised a hand for silence. "The creature in the med center was not involved in their deaths; the time frame—"

"*Fuck* the time frame," said Gaunt. "For all we know, that thing was responsible for sending its buddies out to murder them!"

The calls of agreement were shouts now.

Noguchi felt that spark of anger she'd had for Ackland. She clapped her hands sharply above her head and yelled.

"*Be quiet!*"

The room quieted. An infant howled loudly in the back and was soothed by its mother.

"Perhaps if we all panic and turn ourselves into mindless animals, we'll get out of this situation! Who else wants to add to the problem?"

Her voice carried well. She could feel her cheeks flushed with anger, and was gratified to see that Gaunt's were also red—he dropped his gaze to the floor and didn't speak again.

Noguchi nodded. She had everyone's attention.

A young boy raised his hand.

"Yes?"

"Is Bobby okay?" The boy was no more than twelve; his voice was high and shaky, obviously upset by the situation. His father placed a hand on the child's shoulder.

She nodded and attempted to smile. "He has a sprained ankle and is in shock, but he'll be all right. Squires has agreed to watch him for a while."

Noguchi motioned at the young teacher who chewed nervously at her lip.

She scanned the room, watched the fearful crowd with a calm eye.

This is bad, but we will handle it. She felt in control; for once, the people of Ryushi looked to her to tell them what to do. She wouldn't let them down.

"If we could hold other questions for a few moments, I'll tell you what we propose. Mr. Shimura is in charge of security. All ablebodied personnel will be expected to take a shift on watch, and anyone not on duty will remain within the main complex. First, we'll do what we can to barricade the town with the cargo crates from the move here—" She nodded at Mason. "Mason here will head up that maneuver. Anyone trained on lift equipment will report to him after the meeting. There is a thirty-three-hour curfew in effect as of now; no one will go anywhere alone unless they've cleared it with me or Hiroki, and it will have to be a good reason. Those of you with weapons, please list them with Spanner ASAP. Ben Davidson and Jess Jonson have volunteered to show our younger members holovid graphics at the school this afternoon, so meet with them afterward for specific times."

People nodded; she could almost feel the fear in the room become less tangible. It was a good thing to remember that most crises just needed some organization and clear thinking to be handled efficiently.

Hiroki read from a list the first watch team and

then suggested another meeting later, at dusk or when the work was finished, whichever came first. As the gathering drew to its close, Noguchi was pleased to see that order and confidence had been restored quickly after Gaunt's outburst.

Except—

Except only a few people had heard what Bobby Sheldon had said. Or seen what the thing in the lab looked like . . .

Noguchi shook her head. It didn't matter. Wishing for other circumstances was pointless.

She took a deep breath and went outside to do what she could.

Twilight was almost there when it occurred to Noguchi that she hadn't heard back from Collins.

Under Hiroki's capable direction, they had set up an admirable line of defense; the house-sized moving crates had been lined up around the perimeter of the compound quickly; with the willing aid of both the ranchers and the staff, the work had been neatly done.

A copter crew had made runs to fetch all of the weapons listed by the ranchers; Noguchi had felt her heart sink at the inventory. Twenty-seven scatter guns, ten pistols earmarked for a police force that had never been needed, and six old-fashioned flare guns. There were also a few hunting rifles and handguns. Not much.

She sat in the ops center hunched over a cup of black coffee that was barely tepid. Her body ached from all of the work; Hiroki had insisted that she take five, and she was only too glad to comply. Hiroki was going to take a team to walk the compound and secure any place they had missed. Around her, four staffers watched screens. Noguchi was exhausted, and there was still too much to do, too many variables to consider—

Like *The Lector*.

Noguchi straightened. The crew outside was just finishing up, and another meeting was coming up within the hour—but had she seen anyone from the ship? That obnoxious Conover—?

"Weaver, have you seen Collins anywhere?"

The tall, dark-haired staff woman looked up from her console. "No. *I* haven't at least—Downey, have you seen Collins?"

Sid Downey shrugged. "No one's seen him since he went to talk to *The Lector*'s people."

Noguchi sighed and stood up reluctantly. "Any progress?"

Downey shook his head. "The Barkers still don't answer. And Dr. Revna refuses to be moved to the main building—other than that, everyone is accounted for."

Noguchi patted him on the shoulder as she walked toward the door. "Keep up the good work. I'm going to go talk to *The Lector* folks, see if they've kidnapped Collins."

She almost collided with Hiroki in the doorway.

"Where are you going?" Hiroki looked like she felt. Dark smears of dust painted his face, and his eyes looked weary and old.

"Collins still hasn't come back from the ship; I'm going to find out what's going on with them. But first, I'm going to see if I can talk some sense into Dr. Revna."

Hiroki frowned. "It's not safe, Machiko." His tone was gentle.

She felt oddly touched by his concern, but she was also tired of not knowing what the hell that ship was up to. "Someone has to go; may as well be me."

Hiroki looked at her seriously for a beat and then unhooked his holster strap. He handed the revolver to her, butt first.

"I see you've made up your mind—but take this. It's a 12.5 mm Smith. It belonged to my grandfather. It is loaded with jacketed bullets, for hunting big game."

She stared at the weapon.

He pushed it into her hands. "If you have to shoot something, make sure it has a thick wall behind it— these bullets will go right through a rhynth. I'll call the sentries and let them know you're on your way."

Noguchi accepted the weapon gingerly and nodded. She knew how to shoot, of course, it was SOP for offworld execs to take a course. Never knew what you'd run into out on the frontier. For once, the company was right.

"Fine. Have Weaver set up the sat-link as soon as the suns set, and ask them to cut a deal for Marine support." She smiled tiredly. "And thanks, Hiroki. Be careful."

He smiled in return. "You're doing a good job, Machiko."

She walked into the late-afternoon heat and headed for the med center, her thoughts jumbled with exhaustion. There was still a crew of a dozen or so outside, setting the final walls into place. Amazing, that in the space of one day, they'd gone from peaceful town to armed camp. The gun was heavy in her hands. She paused long enough to strap the holster on and settle it on her hip. Still heavy but comforting. She wanted desperately to believe that their measures were needless, but her gut told her otherwise; tired though she was, there was a chilling certainty in her bones that tonight would be a long one, and come morning, things might be very different . . .

Miriam watched the stats on the screen with something like awe; she was glad to have something to do besides worry over Kesar, and the alien was distracting, to say the least, now that Bobby was gone.

Her stomach tightened at the thought of her husband; she had always thought that she would know if he was gone—that deep knowing that two people shared if enough years had passed. But there was nothing; she just missed him; she kept thinking of what he would say about the incredible reads that flashed across the console . . .

"Doctor . . ."

Revna turned in her chair, heart pounding. "Ms. Noguchi?"

The attractive Japanese woman smiled gently. "I'm sorry, we haven't heard anything—"

The doctor took a deep breath. "Then you've come to check on our patient." She tilted her head toward the prone form on the exam table nearby. "He's still not awake, but he's making remarkable progress; his respiration has deepened, and I believe that two of his ribs have begun to heal."

The gentle smile never left Noguchi's face. The obvious sympathy there made Revna want to cry, so she turned back to the screen.

"I'll let you know if he regains consciousness," she said.

"Doctor, I'd like to move you and our 'visitor' to the main complex; the security is better there, and—"

"Thank you, no," said Revna. "I prefer to remain

here. I have everything I need to look after my patient . . ." She hoped she sounded collected and normal, but she heard her voice crack slightly on the truth. "Besides, this is where Kesar will come when he returns."

She didn't turn around, but she sensed the Noguchi woman's hesitation. Before, they could have hoped for an accident, with her husband lying injured, waiting for help. But now? Revna could almost hear her thoughts—that she was fooling herself. Kesar Revna had undoubtedly met the same fate as Bobby's parents. He had gone right to where the wrecked ship lay.

Miriam spoke again, her voice firmer this time. "I'm fine, Ms. Noguchi. Really."

"Very well, Doctor," she said. "I'll check back on you later."

"Thank you, Ms. Noguchi. Machiko."

When she heard the door close, Revna finally relaxed a bit. A lone tear trickled down her cheek; she wiped at it absently and concentrated on the task at hand. He would be back soon; and if he wasn't, she would find him somehow . . .

Mason rolled his head and yawned; he and Riley had run out of things to say about twenty minutes ago. The initial adrenaline of the situation was long gone, and their nervous small talk had disintegrated into a watchful silence. At least it wouldn't get any hotter today; the suns were headed down. And in another hour or so, he and Riley would be inside drinking beer and shooting the shit; he pitied the next watch; being out here after dark would be a bitch.

"Hi, Riley. Hi, Mason." The boss lady walked toward them smoothly, a smile of greeting on her lips. *Speak of the devil.*

Riley nodded back and Mason stepped forward. He dropped his cigarette on the dusty ground and squashed it with one boot.

"Ms. Noguchi," he said politely. "Mr. Shimura said you were coming. I'm to escort you to *The Lector.*"

"Let me guess, Mason—Hiroki ordered you to follow me even if I declined your escort?"

"Yes, ma'am."

She nodded and sighed. "Well, come on then." She stepped ahead of him and headed toward the ship.

Mason glanced over his shoulder to see Riley grinning at him and shot him the finger; smarmy bastard. He jogged to catch up to Noguchi and walked in front of her. This would be a prime opportunity to tell the management what he had been thinking.

"You know, I think we're worrying too much. I mean, look at the size of the complex. You'd need an army to attack, right?" He looked back at Noguchi and stopped at the base of the ramp for her to catch up. She didn't answer, didn't even look at him, really. He might as well be talking to a block of plastecrete.

"I think those XTs are gonna take one look at Prosperity Wells and go back home," he continued. Fuck her, anyway. He stepped into the open door at the top of the ramp and pointed his scatter gun at nothing in particular; it was dark in there. He took another step inside and then turned his head to call back to the ice queen.

"Just give me a second to get the lights." He edged to the left and groped blindly with one hand. Something wet dripped on his hand.

"Hey," he said under his breath. Another drop of warm liquid splashed the top of his head. Fucking disgusting! Where was the goddamn light switch anyway?

He got the impression of sudden movement overhead—and then there was only pain.

Noguchi stood at the top of the ramp and listened to Mason babble mindlessly. Mason was something of a jerk, that was certain. He stepped into the dark and fumbled for the lights, still chattering away. She turned to look at him—

—just in time to see him lifted straight up into the darkness. There was a strangled, wet cry—

—and the darkness rushed forward to greet her, a dozen arms and a thousand teeth, all screaming, all hungry.

16

Noguchi grabbed for the revolver in slow motion. The single patch of darkness separated into many forms; she fell backward as the dozen or so nightmares came at her.

What—?

She fired four times and stumbled down the ramp without looking. The deafening shots echoed from the walls and in her head and two of the things dropped.

She backed up against the shield wall, revolver extended toward the huge bugs, Jesus, they were half again her size! They came, but slower, their short, twisted limbs reached for her. They hissed and cried out like demented banshees. Double rows of teeth snapped and dripped a clear, slimy mucus.

Noguchi didn't take her gaze off them, even as she heard more of the things come down the ramp.

She was going to die—

She panted shallowly and backed farther up the incline, revolver heavy in her trembling hands.

Another of the bugs rushed forward with a scream. She jerked the trigger again and again. The thing howled in fury and pain and fell—

She fired again, only—the shots were quiet, dull clicks. The gun was empty.

Was there more ammunition on the belt? Did she have time to reload?

Yes. No.

The nightmares advanced; she backed up, her last moment of life. Nothing flashed before her eyes save the horror coming for her; no memories, fond or otherwise, came to haunt or comfort her. She was in the moment and in this moment, the leading bug cried out and jumped—

—and a hollow thump sounded behind her, as if something had imploded. A rush of heat stirred her hair, and the creature closest flew backward in a rain of hissing liquid, its head gone.

The horde screamed in unison but stayed at the bottom of the wall, their dark limbs clattering on the ground in—anger?

Noguchi risked a glance behind her.

The dragon—?

It was the monster, masked and armored. It held the spear with the broken shaft—except it was whole now, the long pole mended; the heavy dark weapon it held was slightly different—

It wasn't the creature from the med lab. It was one of the others, the killers.

It aimed the weapon at her and fired.

Noguchi felt a cry escape her throat—

—and another of the bugs exploded behind her.

She looked back down at the advancing army and felt a rush of air again behind her.

The monster warrior leapt *over* her and landed on the pack of seething black bugs.

Noguchi could do nothing but stare.

The dragon fell into battle, its movements so swift she could barely follow them. The savage spear sliced and cut another bug in pieces. Another shot from the strange weapon and dismembered limbs clattered to the ground.

The blood of the dark spidery bugs hissed and melted into the plastecrete; some kind of acid—?

She couldn't tell from the screams which was which. As the warrior spun and hacked two of the bugs at once, a flash of Noguchi's childhood came to her—

—*Samurai*—!

More of the bugs came down the ramp, scrabbled wildly to get at the warrior.

Noguchi, still unable to move, looked on at the storm of death and battle.

Gkyaun had been sent in to scout, but the Hunting he had found was too good to walk away from. Here was a sickly, pale ooman—with *no defense*! He had watched as the cowering ooman's small burner died, then as the *kainde amedha* swarm approached the ooman. It did not seem able to defend itself. Where was its spear? Its wrist knives? This terrified creature was the monster of which he had been frightened as a suckling? It was a joke.

The ooman was *thei-de* without him; he would save the ugly creature for later.

First, the Hard Meat—

Gkyaun's heart hammered with glory as he caught the ooman's attention by burning the first drone. The drone exploded.

The others cringed, drew back, looked upon him with the respect befitting a Blooded warrior. On some deep cellular level, they knew his kind. Knew the danger he presented.

This *dtai'kai'-dte* was nothing! He could have won in infancy! Yautja would cry his name this night, victor of drone and ooman alike. He would bring the ooman's blackened skull to drink from—

He fired again, and was again rewarded with a shower of acidic *thwei*. The Hard Meat screamed in loss.

Gkyaun howled the war cry and jumped. He landed amid the hissing drones and moved among them like the *setg'-in*, deadly and quick. So easy! He spun and slashed, burned and cut at the same time.

Two bugs fell with one slice of his spear.

A drone from behind lost its head; he gutted yet another.

He was *Paya*, the conquering warrior! *Thwei* ran at his feet, the Hard Meat shrank in terror—!

More came at him, a relentless flow of fury and sound. He pivoted, Hunted, his every movement was an arc of doom and pain.

Noguchi gulped air and pushed herself backward, toward the top of the shield wall. The warrior was a dervish of wild energy and prowess—the nightmare creatures fell all around him.

But more monsters flooded toward him. And despite the fighter's speed and strength, he fought poorly; he hadn't allowed for any outcome other than victory. It was as if he were a *karateka* who had mastered *kata*, but had never faced an opponent in actual combat . . .

The clamoring dark animals surrounded him, pulled him down. The warrior struggled, but to no avail; one of the giant bugs ripped off his mask with one spidery clawed arm and plunged its razor teeth forward—

Noguchi scrambled backward and to her feet, atop the wall. She ran back toward the complex and didn't look back. The cries of hunger and triumph followed her, told her the warrior was no more.

What *were* these things? What new disaster had come to visit them?

17

The noise came from a million klicks to his right. It was a familiar sound, one he had known for a very long time—back on Earth, from before he knew what it meant.

He felt his consciousness as it rose upward, swam to the surface of a depthless abyss—the knowing part of him, the tomes of understanding. He fought to keep it from happening, but was helpless to stop it. There was something that he didn't want to know, was terrified of knowing . . .

The sound again. *Scott? Scott, are you?*
Scott?

Scott was him. The blissful nothing dwindled away as the aches in his body stepped in to greet him, coupled with a horrible, consuming hunger.

"Scott?"

Scott opened his swollen eyes to blackness and took a deep breath. He almost choked on the cloying, wet air.

"Scott, are you awake? Can you hear me?"

He coughed, the minor movement sparking a thousand pains. "Yeah." He swallowed gummy spittle and turned his head toward the voice. "Tom?"

"I think I can get my arm free," the other pilot said.

Scott couldn't see him, but his friend was only a few meters away from the sounds of hurried struggle.

The rest of the nightmare clicked in to place. "Where did they go?" Scott strained to see in the dark room, memories of hissing motion and giant teeth adding sharp panic to his dull and clouded mind. "Tom, did you see them? Where did they all go?"

"Shh! I'm almost out—" A grunt of exertion and Tom's welcome face appeared in front of him, grimy, fearful, pale.

"Hurry! Jesus, where did they go? Get me out of this, hurry, please!"

"Be *quiet*!" Tom spoke in a harsh whisper and reached for Scott's immobilized hands. The ropes of resinous dark material holding him in place snapped and crumbled to the floor.

Tom glanced over his shoulder every other second, eyes wide.

As soon as one of his arms was free, Scott tore at the weird matter at his midriff and leg—and tumbled to the floor.

He had been suspended a half meter in the air.

Tom slipped an arm around his waist and helped him up, speaking quickly and quietly.

"They were all around us, and something happened outside, I guess; they swarmed out of here like mad bees, and I didn't know if you were here—" Tom seemed to realize he was babbling and cut himself off.

"It's okay, man. Let's just get the hell out of here, okay?"

Leaning on each other heavily, they stumbled toward the emergency hatch. It was hard to see anything, but Scott could make out areas of the dock where the shadows were denser, more solid.

A raspy breath came from one of the darker corners of the room. Scott stopped and turned toward the noise. At first he couldn't see what was the cause—and then he was unable to believe what he saw.

It was one of the creatures.

It was bigger than the others. Its huge, flattened skull was curved downward, its limbs drawn up in front of its dripping jaws. The thing was curled up, a horrible caricature of the human fetal position.

"I think it's asleep," Tom said softly. "It hasn't moved since before all the other ones left."

Scott couldn't pull his gaze away from the dormant monster, the slow rise and fall of the thing's furled body with each slow breath. It was the most frightening thing he had ever seen, like a giant spider-lizard with knives for teeth, deadly, insectile. Strings of sticky goo fell from its jaws, the dim light from the partly opened dock door reflected in the glistening slime.

"Let's go before she wakes up," Tom whispered urgently.

"She—?" Scott shook his head and looked at the pilot, but Tom was already pulling him toward the hatch.

"Yeah," Scott whispered back. He wanted nothing more than to get the fuck out of there. Get help, get weapons; just see another human *face*. But as they hurried to their escape, Scott glanced over his shoulder to look at the thing once again. Where had they come from? What were they capable of? There was something strangely familiar about them . . .

He did a double take. His heart pounded. The angle of the creature's head seemed to have changed slightly . . .

"Come *on!*" Tom pulled at his arm.

Scott nodded mutely and followed. There would be time to think about *why* later, not now, not fucking now . . .

Scott shuddered as they reached the emergency hatch. The thing was frighteningly similar to the picture in his head of the jabberwock, from that old poem.

He had the sudden, certain feeling that this was far from being over with.

Noguchi ran through the deserted streets of Prosperity Wells. There was distant thunder, harsh and unreal—

Thunder? She grabbed for the comset around her neck, feeling like an idiot for not having thought of it before; everything had happened so *fast.*

"Hiroki, this is Machiko! Do you read?"

A hiss of static, and then thunder assaulted her ears. She twisted the volume switch in a panic. Not thunder. Gunfire.

"Hiroki! Come in, please!"

". . . achiko?" The reception was bad, but it was him. The sound of his voice was music.

"Listen, I'm approaching the south lock. We're in real trouble, you're not going to believe this!"

"At this point, I'd believe anything," Hiroki said. His usual calm was gone, replaced by tension and worry. The sounds of weaponfire clattered loudly through the com, blocking out whatever he said next.

"Hiroki? Where are you?" Her thoughts buzzed and clamored loudly as she stopped in the street and listened. Nothing. "Hiroki? Are you there?" Her voice cracked in tension.

". . . welding the inner doors of the west lock. We'll hold them off as long as . . ." Static. ". . . wish we could see what the hell we're . . ."

Noguchi slapped the receiver, hard. "I can't *hear* you!"

His next words came through clearly. "Get everyone to *The Lector*," he said. And the com fuzzed out.

"*No!*" she breathed. "Hiroki?"

He was gone. There had to be another way! *The Lector* wasn't an option anymore, there was nowhere to go—

Noguchi ran toward the main well, where Riley and Mason had been only a few moments before. Riley would still have his weapon, they could—

Riley lay facedown in the dust, the late sun shining on the pool of red that had formed around him. The dry soil drank deeply; even as she watched, the blood drained into the earth, leaving a wet stain of crimson mud. A large hole had been punched through Riley's back, the ragged edges raw and meaty. His rifle lay nearby.

She ran to the fallen form and crouched next to it. She pressed numb fingers to Riley's throat and gagged on the thick, metallic scent of fresh blood. No pulse.

"Shit," she whispered. She looked around, eyes wide. The warriors, like the one that had saved her life—

She reached for Riley's rifle quickly, stood. And heard a sound right behind her, nothing so much like a sharp intake of breath. It wasn't Riley, that was certain. She turned in slow motion—

—and saw nothing. She let out a sigh of relief. There was a lot to be worried about, but no immediate threat, at least.

That was when the earth rose up, the dust wavering in the dimming light, to knock her to the ground.

18

Tichinde led the willing yautja into battle as the light grew shallow on the arid world. The *kwei* oomans had barricaded themselves behind a heavy door, their stingers on the outside but controlled from within. Their weapons were hot and deadly, their fire had already taken two of the warriors before Tichinde had decided to pull back and organize a stronger attack. Tricky devils, to hide behind the door and kill from a distance.

There were now only six other students left. They crouched behind one of the ooman structures and looked to him for command. Any doubt Tichinde had felt after watching two of his yautja fall evaporated as he saw the eager Hunters before him; Mahnde and Da-ec'te had been slow and foolish, but these warriors would go on to the victory Hunt.

"Skl'da'-si, you will be *hult'ah* and stand behind." Skl'da'-si had the best eyes; they would need sharp vision to watch for any ooman who might be waiting to ambush.

The yautja tilted his head and stepped away from the rest.

"It is time for the Hunt of *nain-de*," the new Leader growled. He raised his voice steadily as he spoke the truth aloud to the others. "Time to kill until the *pyode amedha* trophies sit on our spears, until their *thwei* flows in our honor and the fight is done. A thousand stories will be sung in our names, for we will conquer!"

Tichinde flared his mandibles in pleasure at the low hisses that came from his warriors. They were ready.

It was Etah'-dte who began the chant of the Midnight Kiss. One by one, the yautja raised their spears and voices to the sky, the screams true and harsh in the dry dead air of the ooman world. Tichinde howled loud and long with his warrior brood; the Soft Meat would die in scores this night, and he would Lead the slaughter.

The Hunt was all.

Noguchi scrabbled backward on her elbows from her bizarre attacker.

There's nothing there—!

Even as the thought popped into her head, the magnified dust rippled and changed. One of the warriors suddenly towered over her, its thick arms high over its head. The spear it held was pointed at her.

Earlier, in the ship, she had forgotten in her panic

that she'd had a rifle strapped on her back. She remembered now.

She swung the heavy rifle up.

Too slow. Time expanded, flowed like thick oil. It took a millennium to thrust the weapon against her shoulder and aim—

Darkness sprang and covered the dragon.

From the main well structure behind the creature, the metallic black bugs shrieked and swarmed and fell on him, their talons fast and sharp.

Noguchi had not seen them there, hadn't heard them come. It didn't matter. She jumped to her feet and stumbled backward, watched as the warrior hit the ground and screamed horribly. The nightmare insects cried and tore at their prey. A pale green fluid, the dragon's blood, sprayed the dark animals. They threw back their obscenely long heads and screamed.

Fuck this!

Noguchi turned and ran.

Roth stood behind Cathie at the ops panel near the south lock when Ackland shouted from his position near the heavily fortified entry.

"Get ready! Something's coming!"

Roth gave Cathie's shoulders a light, reassuring squeeze before she picked up her carbine and joined the other armed men and women at the door, Creep at her heels.

Her heart thudded dully in her chest as she ran the dozen meters or so. Hiroki's broadcasts had been coming in from the ops console for the last twenty minutes or so. His team was doing their best to ward off the attackers, but they had wasted a lot of their ammo on thin air; the going belief was that the alien creatures had some kind of invisibility cloak. The camera angle was such that only a few of the team could be seen—not what they were fighting.

Roth took a position toward the front of the group and trained her weapon on the reinforced plexi door, arms steady. The tension around her was heavy; they didn't know enough about the aliens, what they were after or what they could do. Maybe they wouldn't be so easy to kill . . .

Reuben Hein, one of the geotechs, was on watch. His face was pressed closely to the loophole in the wall. He held up one of his dark hands for silence as the seconds ticked by.

Roth felt a trickle of sweat run down the nape of her neck; she closed one eye, finger rested lightly on the trigger.

"It's okay, don't shoot!" Hein called. "It's Noguchi!"

Roth hadn't realized how nervous she had been until his words flooded her with cool relief. She and the others lowered their weapons and stepped back from the door.

Noguchi had obviously been in a fight; her clothes were rumpled and dusty, her normally sleek hair was plastered to her head in strings, her face flushed. She walked in quickly and surveyed the situation.

"Did you see them? What the hell are they? How many were there?" Ackland half blocked her entrance, his red face betraying the fear he was hiding.

"Too many," said Noguchi. She turned to the assembled group of ranchers and company people and spoke clearly, her voice one of authority. "Fall back to the inner doors and get someone with a welding torch over here. Seal all of the doors—upper level, too—except the east lock. And no one goes in or out without my authorization."

She looked at Hein. "Are we organized enough to get this done without tripping over each other?"

He nodded. "I'll make sure of it."

"Are the children here?"

Loren Gaunt spoke up. "Yeah, they're eating back in the conference room with Davidson and Jonson."

Noguchi exhaled slightly, and some of the tension left her shoulders. She picked out Spanner in the crowd and walked over to him, her revolver extended butt first. "Please load this for me. And get me some extra rounds for it. More of the armor-piercing hunting rounds like it had before."

He took the weapon carefully. "How much extra ammo you think you'll need?"

"Ten speedloaders. And seal those doors ASAP."

She walked back toward the ops panel, not noticing the effect her words had on the group. *Ten speedloaders?* A low murmur rippled through the room.

Roth followed Noguchi to the back to tell Cathie what was going on.

The Japanese woman stopped near the board and spoke calmly to one of the staffers.

"Downey, do you have that sat-link hooked up yet?"

"Little Cygni's still interfering—but it'll be below the horizon in the next hour."

Noguchi nodded at that and turned to Weaver. "What do you have on the cameras? Can you get me a fix on Hiroki and his team?"

Cathie stepped up behind Roth and grabbed her hand, both of them watching the conversation. Weaver looked up at Noguchi slowly and said nothing; her brimming eyes said enough.

Noguchi threw her comset on the panel and took

the one that Weaver held out. She stood behind Weaver's chair and looked at the scant visual.

"Hiroki! This is Machiko, do you read?" Her voice held an edge of panic.

From their position, both Cathie and Roth could see what little there was to see on the small screen. A med kit lay open on the floor, its contents scattered. There was a white cable in one corner of the visual—which Roth realized, with dawning horror, was a human arm. The body of the fallen person was offscreen. Cathie's grip tightened in hers. Muted sounds of gunfire rattled through the com.

"Hiroki, this is Machiko! Do you—"

"Ma . . . iko?" The reception was terrible, but Roth felt her spirits lift slightly; he wasn't dead . . . bzzt. "—you in the tower? Friedman, get down!"

More static.

Noguchi grasped the com tightly, as if doing so would help somehow. She spoke in a rush; it was maybe the first time Roth had seen her with her cool exterior completely blown. The nitrogen queen was terrified.

"Listen, Horiki! Tell your team to stand by, we're going to open the doors and pull you in, do you read me? Tell your team to *stand by!*"

Hiroki had backed up so that part of his profile was visible in the screen. He held a rifle aimed offscreen and pulled the trigger uselessly.

"No time," he spoke in a half shout. Onscreen, Hiroki held the rifle up by its barrel, like a club. Static. ". . . team left, anyway! Just . . . and Friedman." Static. "I don't think we've hit any . . . them! Ammo's gone, us, too, I . . ."

He said something else, but his words were

drowned out by the sound of breaking plexi. Hiroki held his empty rifle higher.

Someone, Friedman, shouted offscreen. "... they come!"

"Stay safe, Machi ..." Static.

Roth watched as huge, dark shapes, the alien warriors, swarmed onto the screen. Hiroki brought the rifle down, hard—to no effect. The attacker he had tried to fend off knocked him to the floor easily, as if he were a child. Mercifully, he fell out of the camera's range. But the pool of red that flowed sluggishly into view must have come from Hiroki.

Noguchi made a strangled sound deep in her throat and looked away. And then Cathie was crying, and Roth turned to comfort her as best she could.

The mighty yautja burst through the shoddy ooman defenses with no further losses. There were only two of the Soft Meat still upright, and they fell in the span of a breath. Tichinde himself took out the smaller of the two. The ooman tried to stop him with a dead burner, like a staff—there was no contest.

The new Leader relished the decapitation of the small creature; it had put up a fight, however meager. Its skull would look fine on Tichinde's trophy wall, once it was polished clean of the sickly pale flesh.

Tichinde howled, the head of the ooman dripping *thwei* from his spear. Perhaps the Soft Meat were not as deadly as the yautja had been told. If this was the best they could do, he and his warriors would have many trophies to take home.

19

Scott figured that the ranchers and staff were probably holed up in the main operations building; there was no one in sight as they stumbled through the empty streets toward the structure. Twilight had fallen over the town with no respite from the heat.

Scott felt a sense of déjà vu as they walked. Deserted town, lights low, unknown dangers—he looked over his shoulder several times to see if *The Lector* was still there. He was aware that there was no reason it wouldn't be, but he couldn't shake the feeling that he was in deadly danger and that there was no escape from it.

They were near the first set of holding pens when they heard the shriek.

From behind them somewhere, a long, shrill squeal

that seemed to echo in the still air rose in pitch and then dwindled into nothing.

Not human, whatever it was. Those things in the ship?

Scott glanced at Tom. He had gone a deathly white, his eyes huge in his face.

"What the fuck—?"

Before Tom could finish, the horrible cry came again. Closer.

Gaining.

Scott grabbed Tom's arm and they ran for the nearest holding pen. His gut had twisted at the alien scream; this whole thing was some kind of bad dream, one he didn't want to be in anymore.

I'd like to wake up now, please.

The entry to the pen stood open. They scrambled in just as another long howl came—louder, closer still—and slammed the heavy door shut.

Inside, the dark, stuffy room stank of perspiration and rhynth shit. At least they seemed to be alone.

"What are we gonna do?" Tom managed, his voice nearly a gasp.

Scott shook his head, tried to catch his own breath.

The only light in the large room came through a row of small, dirty windows set high on one wall. Other than the door they both leaned against, the only other way in was through the loading hatch—which was closed and locked.

"We're going to stay here," Scott said finally.

"But the other people must be—"

"Fuck the other people. The other people have guns, you heard the shooting. We don't. Do you want to go back out without a weapon?"

Another scream from outside. Tom's silence was answer enough. They would wait. If somebody wanted in, they could knock and ask politely and if the voice wasn't human, they sure as shit weren't gonna get an open door.

Noguchi sat on her bed and stared at the floor, one shaky hand on her forehead. She didn't feel much of anything; at first there had been a huge sadness, but it had been replaced with a kind of dull acceptance.

Hiroki was dead. He and the others had sacrificed themselves for the rest of the colony, and she had failed to use the time he had bought for them; she had failed at everything.

Part of her mind kept shouting at her: *Organize! Get this under control! Get yourself together!*

It was the same voice that had pushed her through most of her life, the driver of the strong Machiko who allowed her to hold her head up. It clamored in her thoughts now, directed her to get up, get up now! and get going—but she let it run itself in circles.

Where was there to go?

Noguchi felt as if she had been sitting there for hours, but she knew it had been only a few minutes. Funny; all she really wanted to do was lie down and sleep until she woke up at home. On Earth, back in the tiny apartment she'd left a million years before . . .

Would that be so bad? Just to give up and wait there until help came, until the damn company sent someone to pick them up? They could probably hold out, just do some heavy reinforcing of the locks and then sit tight. Maybe she could even stay here, in her room. The people downstairs could make do without her. They would figure out something. Hide away, do nothing, wait. Yes, that felt right—

"Ms. Noguchi?" A soft voice crackled over her com.

Noguchi felt her stomach tighten at the sound. Why did they need *her*, it wasn't fair! She couldn't run a battle, she was an *overseer* for Christ's sake!

"Ms. Noguchi, this is Weaver." The hesitant voice called again.

Noguchi sighed. "Yes, what is it?" It didn't matter, none of it did.

"I'm sorry to interrupt or anything. I thought—I mean, I know you and Mr. Shimura were friends, and I'm sorry to bother—"

"What?" She wanted to feel angry, but there was still nothing.

"There's something you should see. I could transfer it to your screen, it's the feed from the security cam on the southwest side of the tower. It's dark, though I've boosted the gain—I guess there are a lot of lights out over there—"

Noguchi turned wearily and looked at the console on her wall, already sorry she'd admitted to being there. Fuck these people. They didn't even *like* her. What did they expect? Why did she have to take care of them? Why her?

The screen snapped on.

It was a bonfire. At first, Noguchi didn't recognize that it was a picture from anywhere on Ryushi; she was reminded of old holos she had seen on Earth, of tribal dancing, ritual stuff.

But the dancers were the warriors. The dragons. Well, no, not really dragons, aliens.

There were five or six of them, the creatures who had killed Hiroki and the others. They ran and stumbled and jumped high in the air all around the fire, which was probably built with debris from the west lock. Sparks flew, flame cracked and rose into the early evening sky as the aliens danced and circled. And they carried spears . . .

There was no audio, but Noguchi could imagine the howls of victory. For the spears they held high in the air were decorated with their conquests. As she watched, one of the warriors danced past the cam with one of the black nightmare-bug skulls jammed onto the point of his spear.

And the next warrior—

She quickly looked away, then returned her gaze to the screen. She didn't want to believe what she had seen, but it was true. Fuzzy and distorted by the heat and bad lighting, but there.

Hiroki's decapitated head on the tip of the creature's spear, the sharp, bladed end running through his neck and out of his mouth.

For just a moment, she thought she might vomit.

The alien danced from view, but Noguchi had seen what she had needed to see. The nausea passed. Something new, some new feeling was filling her up. It wasn't sorrow or sickness, although she felt both of those things. No, it was dark and solid and throbbing, like a huge, black machine had started running deep inside, at the core of her being. It was a physical sensation, this feeling, a rumble of newness.

It was many things, but the easiest to understand was the anger. She watched the celebrating warriors and felt the apathy get eaten by the new machine, chewed and burned away, fuel for the thing at her center. It cleared her mind for what she would need to do.

She was going to kill them. All of them. Not just for Hiroki's death or the lives of the ranchers or her career—she felt almost selfish about her reasons, but in the end, it wouldn't matter. They would die because they dared to try her. She was a woman of honor and they stood against her.

Roth and Cathie stood near the table where Spanner sat, Noguchi's gun in front of him. A lot of the others watched also, although there really wasn't much to see. Spanner had already filled eight speedloaders, and was working on his ninth. He fed the rounds in slowly and the metallic clicks were loud in the quiet room when he closed the latch knob. It had been pretty silent here since Hiroki's last transmission.

Noguchi had been gone for twenty minutes or so, which was just as well. Roth hadn't liked seeing the new overseer choke up. Tears would have been okay, but Noguchi had just—swallowed it and gone inside of herself. It was too bad; Roth had seen an iron thread in Noguchi during the setup of the barricades, and had hoped they would all see more of it. Bitch or no, she was competent under stress. Or so they had thought. They were gonna need that, given what they were up against.

Ackland had made a short speech after Noguchi had walked out, about how they were all going to have to pull together and decide what their next move would be. But he was dry-mouthed and scared, he didn't have any suggestions after that, and finally he sat back down. He didn't know what to do, either.

Cathie kept a firm grip on her arm as the silent tension grew. Roth knew her spouse didn't want her to step forward, although she was as qualified as anyone else, maybe more so. She didn't want to lead the colony, but someone would have to. Much as she wished it would have been Noguchi, Roth didn't think she was going to come back.

Spanner continued to load the bullet holders methodically. High velocity hunting rounds, jacketed slugs that would punch through a wall. Someone would need them.

Noguchi stepped into the room quietly.

"Ms. Noguchi—" Ackland looked and sounded confused.

She had pulled her hair back and knotted it tightly at the base of her neck. She wore a fully padded coverall, the kind that the rhynth workers wore during gelding time; the suit was designed to dull impact from stray kicks, and had saved Roth herself from a lot of injuries. She had strapped a carbine to her back and wore knee and elbow leathers, as well as gloves. A comset hung loosely around her neck, and her eyes were cold and hard.

Roth grinned nervously, and felt Cathie's arm slip around her waist. Noguchi was back—and looked like a woman to reckon with.

"Who owns the fastest hover bike?" she said, her voice cool. Cool, strong, authoritative.

Roth said, "I guess that would be me."

Noguchi nodded at her. "Where is it?"

"East lock. Keycard's in it."

Noguchi smiled briefly at her, the expression calm and yet somehow chilling. The nitrogen queen was back, only this time, there was something else under the icy facade.

Ackland laid a hand on Noguchi's shoulder and turned her roughly to face him. "That's it? You're taking off? What about the rest of us?" His voice was heavy with anger, his composure blustery. "I thought you were supposed to be in charge! Where's your sense of responsibility?"

Noguchi took a deep breath. And then she punched Ackland low in the gut, hard.

20

The anger rested in her like a dormant but wild animal, waiting to be awakened and used. Noguchi knew she had bigger things to deal with than this overblown rancher who stood fuming, his fat finger pointed at her chest. But she had had more than enough from him. She took a breath and jabbed. It was a reaction more than a decision.

Ackland folded, gasped, and fell to the floor.

She heard the people all around step back; two or three applauded.

"Responsibility?" Her voice sounded strange to her ears, cold and furious. "Hiroki is dead, Ackland! And a big part of this shit sandwich is on your plate! *If* we live through this, you're going to find out what happens to people who are *responsible*!"

Ackland was still on the floor, face red, trying to catch his breath. The anger suddenly coiled back to a resting state, left her exhilarated and exhausted all at once. Ackland was an annoyance, but nothing to slow down for.

Like a headache.

She raised her gaze and looked around at the watching crowd. The faces she saw weren't angry, just somber. Maybe Ackland wasn't quite as popular as he thought. The only important thing now was getting the job done, the job she *was* responsible for— hunting down the things that had disturbed Prosperity Wells. But not simply for vengeance.

For honor.

Noguchi raised her voice so that everyone could hear. "Weaver, you're in charge until I get back! The rest of you will follow her orders to the letter, is that clear?"

A few of the ranchers nodded. It would have to do.

Spanner had holstered Hiroki's revolver to a rhynth-hide belt with pouches for the extra ammunition carriers. Noguchi smiled briefly at him and strapped it on without another word. No one spoke.

Several of the ranchers and employees followed her down the long hall to the east lock, but she didn't have anything else to tell them. She had an idea, but the details weren't quite worked out yet; she had told Weaver the basics over the com, so help on this end was covered. But judging from how fast Hiroki and his team had been taken out, time couldn't be wasted on planning; she'd have to play it mostly by ear.

Noguchi reached the lock and peered out of the loophole window; the bike was only a few meters from the entry. The deepening dusk was deceptively peaceful-looking, quiet.

Roth stepped up behind her, expression set. "I could come with you," she said softly.

Noguchi considered it, then shook her head. "No. If I don't come back, someone will have to come up with other plans. You'll help most by staying here. Talk to Weaver, she'll fill you in."

Roth nodded. "Let me cover you, then."

"Okay. I'll signal here in approximately twenty minutes; if I haven't called, weld this lock and keep a CDS going to the corporation's sub-HQ. If you keep backing up and sealing the doors as you go, you might be able to hold out until they give up, or until my idea pans out."

Or they get in . . .

It didn't need to be said. Roth nodded again and shouldered her rifle.

Noguchi opened the door and broke into a run in the hot night air.

The pain had been flowing away for a long time, how long he didn't know. Or where he was, or what exactly had happened. More than once, he had risen from the dark to feel that he was still alive, still *nan'ku*. There were straps on his body, which conjured images of a snarling dark creature in bands of dlex.

Queen. *Kainde amedha.*

He surfaced briefly with the familiar image and then decided to sleep a little more. He must still be unwell, although he felt that his strength had somewhat returned. The sickness was sensory; the smells in consciousness were alien, strange. The air was wrong. And he sensed no yautja nearby . . .

Dachande slept, but left his inner eye open and

watchful. He would investigate the situation later. Soon.

Noguchi jumped on the bike and stabbed at the key at the same time. Her adrenaline was in overload, her breath shallow. Everything around her had slowed down, but she was at light-speed.

She jammed the accelerator down and flew toward *The Lector*, free from fear. Death wasn't so scary once decided on; Noguchi didn't want to die, but the odds weren't in her favor. After seeing Hiroki's head on a spear, she had accepted the futility of the situation. She would probably die—but not without company.

There was an overpass ahead, the second-story walkway between the sewage treatment plant and the main well. Noguchi floored the pedal; the shadows there were thick and secretive.

She was halfway through when the dark exploded to life.

The attack came from her left. A high shriek, then something big and heavy hit. The bike tipped, veered toward a wall in the dark, claws ripped, the bike righted—

—and she was back in the open. The creature had fallen off of the unbalanced bike. There was another shriek behind her. She got the impression of great speed from behind, as the thing ran—

Noguchi grabbed for the rifle on her back and circled wide. It was one of the bugs. Because everything had slowed, she saw it in perfect detail as it ran. Long black skull with razor teeth, an impossible body, segmented, black, metallic. There was only the one.

She flew straight at it, a part of her mind screaming at her to get away, fast.

She aimed the rifle . . .

The creature's head blew apart in a spray of blood.

Another jumped out from the heavy shadows, ran at her—

—she hit it, heard the cry of pain and rage. It clutched at the cycle, scrabbled up, loomed above her.

There was a meter-thick beam under the walkway, barely visible in the dark. Noguchi ducked low and flew straight at it.

The bug's howl was cut short and the bike lifted again.

Noguchi circled back and headed again for the ship, heart pounding. In spite of the physical reaction, she felt calm. Very awake, but not panicked; she felt in complete control, she knew exactly what she was doing . . .

She slammed on the brakes suddenly and cried out, enraged by her own stupidity.

"Shit, shit, *shit!*"

Miriam Revna. She had forgotten.

The coms had been out for several hours before Miriam heard the shots echo through the compound. There had been gunfire before, but it hadn't been so close. Several times, she had heard weird screams, alien sounds.

Miriam held the bonecutter tightly and tried to breathe deeply. She had stood by the door for what seemed like days, and she was exhausted. The patient had not regained consciousness, although his readings had jumped several times, indicating a raise of bodily functions—increased heart rate, blood pressure, temperature. The readings could be wrong, though, probably were; she had never seen a creature quite like it. Neither had Kesar . . .

Kesar.

Miriam closed her eyes and breathed deeper. She didn't want to think about him, not yet. She wasn't ready to admit that he . . . she wasn't ready to grieve.

The two coms in the lab were notorious for fuzzing out, sometimes for days at a time. They had never bothered getting them fixed—the lab was only a few dozen meters from the main transmitting antenna, not a hassle to walk. No one had tried to contact her— although she wouldn't know, of course. She was scared, and she missed Kesar more with every second.

A hover bike pulled up outside, and Miriam heard running footsteps. Perhaps it was Kesar—

She knew it wasn't somewhere inside even before she heard Machiko Noguchi's voice.

"Dr. Revna! It's me, Machiko!"

Miriam gripped the bonesaw closer and went to the door. She punched the entry button and looked outside, cautiously.

It *was* the overseer. She wore a padded coverall and held a rifle. Her gaze scanned from left to right as she edged into the lab, facing out.

As soon as she was inside, Miriam hit the control and the door slid shut.

"Machiko, I heard shooting! What happened?"

The younger woman turned to face her. Miriam was struck by the changes she saw in Noguchi's cool expression. Something huge had occurred, something that had made everything different. It was in her eyes, in the set of her mouth—

"Things are bad, and they're about to get worse." In

spite of the circumstances, Machiko Noguchi sounded calm. "Can you handle a hover bike?"

Miriam shook her head and set the cutter on a table. "No. I never learned. Kesar was going to teach me, but we never—"

"Do you know how to use one of these?" Machiko cut her off, held up the rifle she carried. "I don't have time to get you back to ops."

Miriam shook her head again.

Machiko handed it to her anyway and spoke quickly. "It's a semiautomatic, so it does all the work for you. Just point it at what you want to shoot and squeeze this trigger." She motioned at the crook of the rifle. "You only have six rounds, so don't waste any on warning shots."

Miriam took the rifle hesitantly and frowned. "Ms. Noguchi, I'm a doctor, not a soldier . . ."

"This isn't war," Noguchi said softly. "This is survival."

Miriam felt tears in her eyes, but wasn't sure why. "Who might I be—shooting at?" The words were strange in her mouth.

"Your patient's brothers. Or something that looks like a two-meter-tall black insect with a banana-shaped head full of teeth." Machiko said. She walked over to the patient and the table of artifacts and picked up the odd shield she and Hiroki had studied before. She held it up toward Miriam.

"The unclassifieds that Roth brought in—Kesar's report said he thought they might transport eggs, or spores, to host bodies. Is it possible that when those spores grew up, they'd look like this?" She pointed at the strange animal etched into the surface.

"It's impossible to say," Miriam said slowly. She felt horribly confused. "Why?"

"Because I've seen some of these things tonight. There were dozens, maybe hundreds of them in *The Lector*. And I think Ackland's rhynth were infected"— she paused—"or *impregnated* by these things. And they've spread it to all of the herds on the ship. I think our two unclassifieds are connected somehow."

Miriam looked at the etching and then over to the specimen strapped to the table. "Not biologically. They're quite different in chemical makeup."

Machiko nodded. "There's no time to worry about it now, anyway." She looked at the injured alien. "We ought to shoot that thing," she said. "But maybe we'll need it as a hostage later." She walked toward the door.

"What are you going to do?"

Noguchi turned. "I have an idea or two. Listen, I want you to *stay here*, okay? Outside is not safe. Keep the door locked. I'll come back for you as soon as I can, but if you haven't seen me within the next hour, start thinking about how you can get to ops. Wait until daylight, and take the rifle when you go. I'll tell the ranchers to watch for you."

And she was gone, just like that.

Miriam set the heavy weapon on the table and stood with her eyes closed for a moment. It was all like a dream, surreal and frightening. None of this could be happening. She looked at the alien creature on the exam table and tried to get her thoughts in order.

Kesar was dead. Thinking anything else was folly. Perhaps the broken-tusked alien had something to do with it, but there was no anger in her heart, only a soft, wishful ache.

"It's so wasteful," she said quietly. "We could learn so much from one another . . ."

There was a sudden scratching sound at the door, a sliding knock.

"Dr. Revna! It's me, Machiko!"

Why had she come back?

Miriam hurried to the door. "Machiko? What happened?"

She hit the entry control and stepped back. "Did—"

Words escaped. The patient—no, it was a creature like the one on the table—

Miriam turned and ran, even as the armored monster clutched for her.

The weapon, table, trigger—!

She ran, but the thing screamed behind her, too close.

She was going to die.

21

After the initial conquest, Tichinde left the yautja to circle the ooman dwellings and get a feel for where the others might be. There were many in the same structure as the first group, but he wanted to be certain that there weren't more, perhaps waiting to ambush them.

He walked. And heard the sound of machinery behind him, coming closer. Tichinde blended with the shadows as they had all been taught and waited to see what would come. He patted the mesh sack on his belt; there were already three ooman trophies in it; there would be more.

A single ooman drove a small aircraft into view, landed it, then ran to one of the dwellings, a short burner in its hand.

Tichinde pressed the loop control on his shiftsuit,

one that he had salvaged from the wreck, to record the language spoken. The tiny ooman shouted and then entered the building at the beck of another ooman inside.

A short span passed and the flyer ooman came out and went away. He thought it was the same one—they looked much alike to him.

Tichinde waited a few breaths and then walked to the same door from which the creature had come. He pushed the loop control on the arm of his suit and listened to the odd language spill from the copier.

There was movement inside. And the door opened to reveal a lone ooman, defenseless. The creature's face distorted in reaction and it howled.

Tichinde ran forward and screamed for blood.

The ooman stumbled back, turned, and ran for a table. A table with a strange burner on it.

Tichinde raised his bladed staff high, ready for the final cut—

—and there was something familiar here, a scent he knew, but it didn't matter because the ooman must die—

—the ooman raised the burner slowly and fired at nothing, the shot far and wide, then another—

—and Tichinde brought the blade down, prowess and certainty in the fatal cut—

Noguchi heard a shot, then another. It came from the lab, or somewhere near it.

She had stopped at the main control hatch for the front six buildings of the compound and studied the numbers, not certain of the proper codes for what she needed to do. She'd punched buttons, pretty sure that she had gotten it right, and checked her chronograph.

The shots made her jump; they were accompanied by a shrill and primal scream.

Noguchi jumped on the bike, turned it back toward the lab, and hoped she would get there in time.

Dachande opened his eyes at the sound of the yautja death cry and growled softly.

Tichinde. And he pursued the creature, the ooman whose smell had become familiar.

The desperate ooman ran to the table in front of Dachande's resting place and snatched at a burner clumsily. Tichinde towered over it in classic pose, ready to deliver the death blow to the panicked ooman. The ooman who had nurtured him through the dark, what could have been his final moments until *dhi'ki-de.*

Dachande lifted one of his arms. The strap holding it snapped. He thrust his talon forward and caught the staff right below the blade.

Tichinde's head jerked up in surprise. The ooman fell to the ground.

With a quick shove, Dachande rammed the staff upward and knocked Tichinde backward.

Tichinde jumped up and popped his wrist forward, extended the double bladed *ki'cti-pa* toward Dachande.

The Leader growled in fury. Tichinde would raise a weapon against *him?* Had he lost his memory?

Dachande freed his other arm easily and struggled, tried to leap. His lower body was still bound—

Tichinde jumped to meet him, *ki'cti-pa* raised to slash.

And the world exploded into a million flying pieces.

The sounds of battle were unmistakable. So was Miriam Revna's scream.

Noguchi stamped the pedal and ducked.

Miriam cried out and fell to the floor as the wall cracked open in a roar of thunder and shattered around her. A chunk of something sharp and heavy gouged her right calf. The pain was horrible. The terror was worse.

The thunder ceased. Miriam pulled herself around a table leg and turned to see what had happened.

Noguchi had come through the wall. The bike was turned on its side and Machiko was propped on her elbows, pistol aimed behind Miriam.

The doctor snapped her head around and saw that the attacking creature was sprawled facedown on the floor. It didn't move, but she could hear its labored breathing.

The patient was still on the exam table, pinned there by one remaining bond across its abdomen. He fumbled with the strap frantically.

"Lay down flat, Miriam!"

Noguchi had her gun pointed at the struggling patient. Her finger tightened on the trigger.

The doctor stood up, right in the line of fire.

"Jesus, get *down!*" Noguchi's heart pounded.

Miriam didn't even look back at her. She held both

of her hands up and walked slowly toward the tethered warrior.

Dachande redoubled his futile attempts at freedom as the ooman came at him. The creature held its odd, clawless hands open and moved slowly. The other, dressed as a warrior, had a weapon on him—but the approaching ooman blocked the small warrior's efforts.

It could be a trick, a ploy to calm him before the Soft Meat ripped him open . . .

But the slow-moving creature was the one that had tended to him; the *ki'cti-pa* was unmistakable. If it had wanted him dead, wouldn't it have struck when he was injured and unaware? There was a thick bandage of some kind around his chest—not the work of a Hunter. A healer, then.

Dachande stopped his labors and held still, but kept his body tensed and ready. He hissed a warning to the ooman.

And it leaned toward him, very slowly, and unlatched the restraint.

Miriam unhooked the bond and stepped back, careful not to move suddenly. The creature had growled at her, a foreboding gurgling sound, but didn't attack when she was in reach.

"What are you *doing*?!"

Miriam kept her eyes on the patient. "I think it's okay," she said softly.

The creature studied her for several long seconds. Miriam held still, not wanting to frighten it.

"Are you insane?" Noguchi was furious. "They killed Hiroki and six others!"

She didn't move. "*They* did. He didn't."

Miriam was scared, in spite of her intuitive feeling that the creature wouldn't harm her. Intuition wasn't a lot in the face of death.

The patient moved fast. It slammed one clawed hand down on her shoulder.

Dachande inspected the ooman thoughtfully. *This* was what he had wanted to Hunt all of his life? It was ugly, but certainly not dangerous-looking. It was stupid, too. Approaching a warrior with no weapon didn't indicate a particularly high intelligence. Or it was incredibly brave and ready to do battle. Small as it was, if it wanted to fight, perhaps it was also mad?

The armed one babbled at the ooman next to him. Dachande got the impression that the defenseless creature had kept him from being killed. The ooman with the hand-held burner lowered the weapon slowly.

Overcoming a lifetime of yautja lore was not a thing he wanted to do—but good warriors stayed open to new information. Perhaps the Soft Meat on this world were different.

Dachande decided. He placed one of his claws on the ooman's shoulder and shook, the symbol of greeting.

The ooman shrank slightly, and the other raised its weapon again. Dachande took his claw away and waited.

After a pause, the tiny ooman stretched itself high and returned the gesture.

Dachande tilted his head at her. Fascinating!

Then it was that Tichinde clattered his mandibles and slowly got to his feet.

Dachande's anger flared. The *s'yuit-de*! He would die!

Dachande jumped past the ooman and whacked Tichinde's skull. The blow knocked the student to the ground.

Tichinde said nothing, but scrabbled at the pouch on his belt.

Dachande snatched the sack from the idiot yautja and held it up. Trophies.

Ooman trophies.

His rage was blinding. Tichinde had Hunted with no supervision—and had Hunted ooman!

Dachande lifted the yautja by his tresses, the fury boosting his strength. He could smell his own musk, hot and heavy with the desire to kill. He raised one fist and smashed Tichinde in the mouth.

Tichinde tried to pull away, responded with a weak blow to Dachande's gut.

Dachande howled in his face, a shriek of pure disgust and outrage. He struck again.

Tichinde was his student, once. He had broken the rules of the Hunt. There was only so much slack Dachande could give him, even as a Leader. Now the rope must be pulled taut. Now, Tichinde must be destroyed.

It was the law.

It was a matter of honor.

22

Noguchi watched in amazement as the two huge warriors fought. The broken-tusked "patient" was the more skillful—and was winning easily.

Myriad half thoughts ran through her mind. The patient was grateful, the other was with the killers, the broken tusk was better, older, brighter perhaps, the doctor was insane, they had to *get out*—

Miriam stood a few meters from the battle, just stood there and watched.

Noguchi ran forward, pistol ready, and grabbed the doctor by the arm.

"Come on!"

The monsters could slug it out to the death for all she cared; they had work to do.

She and Miriam ducked through the shattered wall

and ran across the compound. Noguchi steered them toward the main garage, to the east. The med center was closer to the holding pens, but they would need a flyer for what she had in mind and the hover bike was totaled; there would be other bikes at the garage—

Except Miriam can't fly one and they won't carry two people.

Noguchi wanted to scream. Fuck, fuck, *fuck!*

And on the heels of the panic, she remembered the copter.

The copter!

She ran faster.

Miriam had trouble keeping up; blood ran down one of her legs. The compound was completely dark now. Many of the building lights had been broken at some point, and the few remaining only seemed to add to the shadows. A faint breeze had sprung up, hot and fetid. A death wind, full of carrion stench.

Behind them and ahead, shapes moved and shrieked. It was hard to see what was happening. Noguchi guessed that the two alien races were fighting.

Maybe they won't even notice us—

A giant black bug leapt in front of them from a shadow and raised its strange arms to attack.

Miriam screamed.

Noguchi pointed and fired twice. The first shot was too high. The second tore out the bug's throat. Blood sprayed.

A drop of the fluid spattered against one of Noguchi's padded suit arms and hissed, ate through the fabric and burned her skin.

Acid, some kind of acid—

The noxious substance ate deep into her flesh. As

they ran forward the garage, Noguchi felt her own blood soak into the coverall. She ignored it as best she could; they were almost there.

They reached the garage, Miriam now stumbling badly. Noguchi half dragged her toward the back of the building. The copter was usually kept at the med center, on the roof's helipad; the doctors used it to get to emergencies. But Noguchi remembered that it needed some minor adjustment after the weapons-collecting run.

I just hope it wasn't engine trouble—

Noguchi laughed sharply as the rounded the corner, a short bark of relief. It was there! She looked around for trouble, but the yard seemed clean.

Miriam stumbled behind her and fell.

"Oh, *shit*, I can't get up, I'm sorry, Kesar, I'm sorry, I can't—" The doctor tried to hold it together, but she looked close to a breakdown. Her face was the color of dust, her eyes rolled upward.

Noguchi pulled Miriam to her feet and dragged her to the copter.

"It's okay, Miriam, you're going to be fine, okay?" She hoped she sounded soothing. "Everything will be fine, really, okay?"

They reached the vehicle. She opened the door and hustled Miriam in, still talking. "Don't worry, we're going to get out of here, okay? I'll help you fly this thing, just tell me what to do and we'll be fine."

That seemed to cut through the doctor's hysteria. Revna raised her tear-streaked face to Noguchi, eyes wide.

"Kesar always flew. I don't know *how*."

* * *

Dachande didn't want to spend too much time on Tichinde, much as he felt the idiot deserved to die slowly. He had to find the other yautja, if there were any. Find out what was going on, how he had come to this state. It did not feel good, what had happened.

Tichinde fell again. His tresses were matted with *thwei*, two of his mandibles broken and crushed against his worthless, dying skin.

Any fight the student had in him had fled. He tried to crawl away.

The sight of the yautja slowly inching from his Leader was infuriating. The *kwei* would die as an animal, a coward, rather than go out like a warrior.

Dachande waited no longer. He snatched Tichinde's bladed staff from the floor and raised it over his head, aimed it at the base of his student's upper spine.

Brought the sharp blade down—

Shiiink!

Dachande jerked the blade from the body in a patter of blood and then spit on the corpse. The Leader donned the *kwei*'s armor and took his weapons; he left the bandage on his chest. There was some pain there, perhaps the dressing would help. After a second's hesitation, he pulled the recording loop from Tichinde's chest; there might be a use for it later.

Armed and ready, with a fire in his gut that screamed for justice, Dachande stepped into the dark night to find his other students. Perhaps Tichinde had been alone, but he doubted it. Hunting alone was not common behavior to the young.

And if they were here, in the ooman camp, on a Hunt—nothing would stop him from the lessons he would teach them.

*   *   *

"What?"

Revna nodded. "He was going to teach me—"

Noguchi tuned her out for a second.

Okay, she can't do it, we're fucked—

She searched the myriad of buttons and switches on the console and found one that said MAIN. She flipped it.

The copter's engine hummed to life.

She tapped her comset. "This is Noguchi in copter"—she looked over the board quickly—"copter one. Do you read me, tower?"

A hiss of static.

And then Weaver's welcome voice.

"We copy. What's happening?"

"Miriam Revna and I are at the garage and neither of us are checked out in a copter. We could use some help here."

Weaver sounded calm. "Okay, we got you. Hit the switch that says MAIN."

"Did it."

"Do you see the button that says COMP? Punch that."

Noguchi spotted it and did what she was told. A small screen flickered on with program questions. She and Revna both sighed at once.

"Okay, we're on a roll," Noguchi said quietly.

"David, get over here." Weaver's voice was distant, then came back through the com. "I'm going to let Spanner talk you up, okay?"

"Fine. What's the situation there?" Noguchi touched her arm lightly and grimaced at the pain. At least the bleeding seemed to have stopped.

"We're all set for your signal. Everything's locked up, for a while at least. But you should see what's happening in the southwest quad; looks like an all-out war."

"Consider the signal given. Wait until we get off the ground, and then go as soon as you hear it. Good luck."

"Copy that, boss."

There was a pause; Noguchi waited for Spanner to come on and tapped the comset, anxious to get out of there. She turned to look at Miriam—

—a dark shape popped up in front of the copter, a nightmare bug. Its teeth dripped and gnashed as it plunged one claw through the windshield.

Scott and Tom had stayed quiet for a long time. The sounds outside of weapons fire and death cries were incentive not to move around much. The monsters were out there and maybe if they stayed under their rock here long enough, they'd eat each other and go away.

Scott figured out that they were in the southwest quadrant of the compound, in one of the two empty holding pens. There were six others, full of bellowing rhynth; their cries mingled with the alien screams.

Harmony à la hell.

"I'm starting to think we were better off in the ship," Tom whispered.

"Yeah, right. Stuck in the spider's web waiting around for dinner. Their dinner."

Scott cracked the door slightly to see if anyone was coming to help. So far, they had seen nothing. Well, no *people.*

Strange humanoid creatures were at war with the bizarre animals that had taken over the ship. It was too dark to make anything out clearly, but the situation was obvious; between the screams and the weapons, there was one *fuck* of a battle going on out there. They couldn't tell who was doing what to whom and for what reasons, but it was bad.

Scott was exhausted and he felt like shit. They had been stuck there for what felt like days. He wanted a shower, a steak, a few beers, and a soft bed. No way he was going out there to get it, but it helped to take his mind off of the situation at hand. Which looked like Armageddon. It was all so . . . unreal.

Tom groaned softly and shifted to sit on the dirty floor. He was sick, had been coughing and having cramps for over an hour, but he was trying to keep it to himself; the look on his face expressed enough. Scott looked at his friend, worried, then back out at the bloody combat.

Something screamed piercingly and then was silenced.

"Hang on, Tommy," Scott whispered. "We're going to be okay."

Yeah. Maybe we'll sprout wings and just fly back to Earth.

Noguchi jabbed her leg forward and up and pushed as hard as she could. The bug barely moved, but it was enough. Maybe.

She pulled the trigger four times, fast. The animal's head exploded, sent a spray of deadly blood across the windshield and onto the console. The noise of the gun hit her ears like hard slaps. The plexi material began to smoke immediately and the small compartment filled with a foul and acrid stink.

Noguchi whipped her head around. Nothing else coming at the moment.

"You okay?"

Revna held up one shaky hand and nodded.

Noguchi took a deep breath and strapped herself into the chair. "Buckle up, Miriam."

She ejected the spent shells and slammed another speedloader in before she looked down at the controls and took a deep breath.

"Let's do it, Spanner. What's first?"

The copter rose in a series of sharp jerks before Noguchi turned it toward the south end of the complex. Miriam still wasn't sure what the plan was, but she was glad to get off of the ground.

She felt her injured leg carefully and winced. It was a bad wound. Each second that passed left her weaker, dizzier; she had lost a lot of blood, maybe too much—

Miriam applied pressure to the wound with part of her jacket and prayed silently that she and Kesar would be together soon.

Dachande ran through the oddly structured system of ooman buildings toward the sounds of battle. He ached all over and at least two of his ribs were broken, but he put the pain aside for now.

Shattered buildings and other rubble littered the grounds. Dachande hopped over the torso of a fallen drone; its life fluid still hissed on the soil.

He heard burners and screams in the distance, to the left. He cursed mentally and ran in that direction.

The *s'yuit-de*! They Hunted oomans, worse, they did so without proper surveillance. It was bad enough to have broken the law; to use poor strategy and tactics only compounded the error.

The other two Blooded must certainly be dead; they would not have allowed this. As sketchily trained as these yautja were, the bugs would be more than just a minor challenge. Armed oomans would be worse.

A small torrent of the Hard Meat appeared suddenly, leapt from the dark shadows to scream at him. Dachande pulled his burner. He was in too much of a hurry for prowess feats.

There were four. They circled him.

The first darted forward, teeth chittering. The outer jaws spread wide, the smaller teeth on the inner rod gaped.

Dachande burned it, the hollow thump of the weapon exploding the drone's gut into bloody bits. Without turning, Dachande took out the second and the third. He shot one, and used the spear in *hiju* position to disembowel the other.

The final drone screeched, turned, and ran. Unusual behavior, but they sometimes did that when there was a queen nearby. It was not fear, for they had none, but instinct to warn the nest.

Dachande sped on. Perhaps a few of the students would be salvageable. If not, he would have to kill them. Whatever they had stepped into on this world, they had sunk up to their necks in it and the stink was bad. Real bad.

Roth loaded food and water packs into the AVs with the others. With any luck they'd be back the next day, but they had taken almost everything. Most of the ranchers were seated and ready; just a final check and they could move.

Weaver had outlined Noguchi's plan briefly; it was shaky, but there was a chance it could work. Only a few people had protested—Ackland's voice above the rest, of course—but Weaver had shut them up with a few well-chosen words. Roth had liked "or we'll kick your fucking ass" in particular.

Roth stood cover outside the east lock as Weaver directed the last few people to either an AV or a ship loader. The largest piece of machinery, one of the carts that had carried most of the building supplies for the shield wall, now held thirty-seven people. Most of the transmitting equipment was also loaded—they would continue the CDS from the desert.

If they got that far.

Creep whined softly at the sound of one of the children crying. He kept saying that it was too hot outside. Roth silently agreed; she was reminded of the thunderstorms in southern Texas, where she had grown up. The stifling summer air would get even hotter as the clouds pressed down; as a child, she had waited eagerly for the first drops to fall, filled with the joy of expectation. There was a wild feeling in the air that had always made her think of carnivals in the dark, although she didn't know why. And then the rain, heavy and warm—

Weaver interrupted her thoughts. "We're ready."

Roth nodded and whistled for Creep to get on the bike. Cathie was watching some of the children in one of Harrison's AV; they would hook up later.

A low rumble shook the ground with no warning and then grew louder. Roth hopped on a bike and started it up, the sound quickly lost in the rising tremors that beat through the soil. Goddamn if that didn't sound like thunder; Roth hit the accelerator and headed east, the AVs and loaders behind.

Miriam opened her eyes and looked down when the noise rolled over them. There was an ocean of life directly below them; the entire compound was moving, undulating in a quake of heaving bodies and animal cries.

Noguchi had stampeded the rhynth.

23

Dachande heard the rumble and immediately ran for the nearest structure he could climb.

Directly after he had attained Leader, he had taken a group on a Hunt and he had heard the same rumble; it was the sound of many animals running in mindless *gry'sui-bpe*. The yautja had clambered onto a low rise and watched as a herd of four-legged hosts had stampeded past in front of them. Had they stayed on the low ground, they would have been trampled.

He spotted a ladder bolted to a tall structure and ran for it.

He had not found the students yet, but before he could do so, he needed to avoid being crushed by the stampede. He hoped the students would understand

what the sound meant and seek high ground or pro-
tection.

He growled in irritation as he climbed the rungs of
the ladder. If they paid attention to his lessons, maybe
they wouldn't die. If they had not listened, then they
deserved to die. That was the way of it. His hope was
not all that good.

Considering how well they've learned so far . . .

Dachande climbed as the rumble thickened into an
all-encompassing roar.

Noguchi buzzed the pens as low as she dared and
hoped the locks had opened according to the codes
she'd set.

The rhynth had been in the hot sunlight all day
without food and a minimum of water. The sound of
the copter must have echoed loudly in the pens. It
only took one spooked animal to get it going. And as
soon as one rhynth jumped forward, the rest followed.

The animals tore through the doors she had un-
locked.

Within a few seconds, all of the rhynth joined the
stampede, headed straight through Prosperity Wells.
Anything small enough to get in their way was trampled, crushed, kicked aside.

The searchlight on the copter illuminated the scene
dimly. Noguchi only glanced at the panicked herds;
she had her hands full piloting. Miriam Revna cried
out in delight.

"They just ran over about two dozen of the unclassifieds!" It was hard to hear over the clatter of hooves
and the bellows of the frightened rhynth.

Noguchi smiled tightly and pulled up on the control

stick. She wanted to check and see if the ranchers had gotten out—

She veered east. All she needed to see were the lights of the AVs—

Noguchi allowed herself a short rush of relief. The low red and white lights were visible. The ranchers and staff were headed away from town into open desert.

It was working! Her plan was working!

She circled the copter back toward *The Lector* to make another run on the animals. The colonists were headed to relative safety, and the rhynth were stomping everything in sight. Maybe she wouldn't have to sacrifice anything else.

Of course, there were still the creatures on the ship to deal with—and it was probable that a few of the other kind had survived. But to take out the majority . . .

As they neared the transmitting tower, Miriam sat up straighter and pointed. Noguchi shot a sideways glance at what the doctor motioned at—it was one of the warriors. It had climbed the ladder and was almost to the top—and there were three or four of the huge black bugs clambering up after him.

Miriam saw the broken-tusked warrior nearing the top of the transmitter and pointed. He still wore the cast she had strapped him in for his damaged ribs.

"Machiko, look!"

"What?!" The stampede was deafening.

Miriam shouted louder. "It's my patient! We have to save him!"

Noguchi whipped her head around. "No fucking

way! Those things are the reason we're in this mess!"
She looked back at the controls.

Miriam chewed at her lip in frustration. How could
she make Noguchi understand? It was important, the
most important thing in the world right now. She
could not have said why.

"He saved my life, Machiko!"

Noguchi opened her mouth and then closed it.
"Look, I don't—"

"*Please!* Machiko, he risked his life to save mine!"

The doctor looked at her patient, getting closer to
the top now. The dark, segmented creatures were also
getting closer.

"*Please!*"

Noguchi didn't say anything. She veered toward the
tower.

*I must be out of my mind, that's it, I finally went
insane—*

Noguchi steered the copter toward the tower in
disbelief. What the hell was she thinking? Dr. Revna
was a nice lady, ordinarily she wouldn't mind doing
her a favor, but this—?

She watched as Broken Tusk kicked at one of his
pursuers and then stabbed the closest one; the bug
screamed and fell. He refused to give up fighting,
she'd credit him that much.

But she could barely fly! Even a trained pilot would
have doubts about trying to hover next to a *tower*.
And to save an alien that they knew almost nothing
about.

Except it had saved Miriam's life.

Right.

It would break every rule in her book, to risk their lives on this. And she had about a second to decide.

Below them, the rhynth ran on.

Dachande kicked at one of the drones and then used the spear to take out the gut of another. It fell, still kicking—but there were two others.

He heard a ship over the sound of the running hosts but he ignored it. He had enough to worry about. On the ground, the bugs were no match. But fighting while hanging one-handed and almost upside down—

The metal he gripped let out a high groan; he could feel the structure shift under the combined weight of himself and the drones.

Again the weak substance creaked—and started to separate from the building.

If he didn't think of something, he would be on the ground in a few breaths.

Fighting the Hard Meat and in the path of the stampeding hosts.

The Black Warrior must wish for Dachande's immediate company.

And the Black Warrior eventually won all battles.

Noguchi lowered the copter toward the tower. Which had started to quake dangerously. It was collapsing under all the weight.

"Shit—"

Miriam fumbled around the console for a second and then hit a button. Her next words blared incredibly loud.

"Grab the strut! We'll take you to safety!"

Noguchi winced. The doctor had found the PA.

She lowered the ship a little more. It was hard, but not as hard as she had expected. On the other hand, a series of red lights had lit up on the control panel. She was too intent on the task at hand to figure out what they meant, but she also didn't want to find out the hard way.

"Grab on!"

Noguchi screamed to be heard. "I can't do this forever, Miriam! He doesn't *understand*—"

The copter dipped, and then pulled up again. He had grabbed on to the strut.

Noguchi let out a cry of disbelief. It had worked! Broken Tusk had jumped to the copter!

Now what the fuck are we going to do with him?

And then everything happened at once. A dark shape lunged at them. Noguchi just had time to register that it was one of the bugs before it landed on top of one of the compressors, on the same side as Broken Tusk. It scrabbled to hold on, screamed.

The copter tilted alarmingly and Noguchi jerked the controls instinctively upward—

—there was a rending screech of metal as the tower collapsed—

—and everything turned the wrong way as—

—the copter went down.

24

They were both sleeping when the stampede hit.

Scott hadn't thought it was possible for him to nod out, but he was exhausted, hung over, and probably coming down with whatever Tom had. There was still fighting outside, but the pen they had holed up in seemed safe. The sounds of battle had almost become a background drone, and had moved away after a while.

Scott had been dreaming that he and Tom were explaining what had happened to them to a doubtful audience of company people back on Earth. They were all sitting around a huge wooden table in a dim conference room. At first, the suits had seemed interested as Tom spoke. Except Tom kept saying all of the wrong things, and every time Scott opened his mouth, nothing would come out.

And all at once, the people started slamming their fists down on the table. One of them, a very tall man in a black shirt, kept yelling, "Liar! Liar!" And the sounds of their knuckles hitting wood get louder, more insistent, deafening.

Scott snapped awake as the table broke.

"Oh, shit—" Tom jumped up and lurched to the door. Even in the dark pen, Scott could see that Tom didn't look too good, pale and strained.

Scott pulled his aching body off the floor and joined him. By now, the noise had drowned out all else. He looked out the crack in the door and felt his mouth gape.

The rhynth weren't running past the pen, at least not the front. But they could see the dust kicked up by the animals to their right, maybe six or seven meters away. The whole building shook as the thick stream of animals tore past, headed north. Tom said something that Scott couldn't catch.

"What?!" Scott couldn't hear his own scream.

Tom shook his head and pointed.

At first, Scott wasn't sure what he was looking for. Tom was motioning at a transmitting tower, two structures away.

Tom finally pointed straight up, and then back at the tower.

Scott looked at the top and felt his heart jump. A copter hovered there shakily. It was involved in some kind of rescue mission; there was a person trapped on the tower, being pursued by—

Scott peered closer. The alien creatures from *The Lector.*

They watched as the person on the tower—who seemed to be some kind of giant—reached for the strut of the copter and made it. Scott grinned widely as the stranded person made it to the copter in a breathtaking leap and looked at Tom. Tom laughed without sound and clapped Scott on the back.

The excitement on Tom's face melted suddenly into horror.

Scott looked back at the copter just in time to see it spin down toward the ground, toward them. Something had gone very wrong; one of the creatures had jumped on the roof of the copter and the pilot had panicked. They watched as the flyer spun out of control to crash, a few dozen meters past them to the left.

The explosion was loud enough to be audible above the stampede; it was getting quieter, the majority of the animals already gone.

By silent assent, he and Tom opened the door and ran toward the crash, the stench of burning fuel and cooked dirt heavy in the air.

The hot night had just gotten hotter.

Noguchi opened her eyes as the thunder fell to the sound and heat of a bonfire. Above her, the Ryushi night sparkled with stars. She had a sunburn and there was something wrong, she couldn't move—

"Miriam?" Her voice was barely audible.

A face appeared over hers, familiar, bearded.

"Conover."

"I should've guessed it'd be you!" The pilot had to shout to be heard over the final remnants of the stampede. "You're lucky to be alive, lady!"

Noguchi remembered all of it at once as Conover unbelted her and half lifted her out of the wreckage.

Broken Tusk, the rhynth are stampeding and the people went to the desert and Miriam—

"Who the hell taught you to fly?" Behind Conover stood the other one, Strandberg. He looked sick.

"Nobody, yet," Noguchi said. She sounded weak, hated that she did. All around them were bits of burning wreckage; the main part of the copter was behind them, still on fire. The flames crackled and danced.

She leaned heavily on the pilot as they stumbled away from the smashed cockpit.

"Where's Miriam?" she said. The doctor hadn't been next to her when she had come to. It was an effort to look around; her neck didn't seem to want to hold her head up.

Strandberg stepped forward and grabbed her other arm.

"Listen, we gotta get out of here! The bugs will be back soon!"

On closer inspection, she could see that Strandberg *was* sick. He looked like she felt; shaky, pale, nauseous.

The last of the rhynth had gone. Besides a fading rumble, the only noise was the hiss of fire—and somewhere close by, the piercing trill of a nightmare creature.

"Miriam," she said again. "Broken Tusk, Miriam had to save him—"

The pilots ignored her and started pulling her toward one of the holding pens.

Noguchi pushed them away and turned back to the remains of the copter.

"Dr. Revna, the woman who was in the copter with me! I'm not leaving without her!"

Conover's voice was both apologetic and irritated at once. "I didn't see anyone else," he began. And then stopped.

"Oh, Jesus—"

Noguchi glanced at both of the pilots, who stood with looks of awe and terror on their faces.

She spun back around and felt her heart sink.

It was Broken Tusk, surrounded by flames.

He carried Miriam Revna in his arms.

Dachande hit the ground, hard, but shouldered the impact well. It helped that he had the time to jump before the ooman flyer had crashed.

He stood and winced at the tight feeling in his chest; he had probably rebroken what had started mending.

But the host stampede had passed, and the drones were nowhere around, at least for the moment.

Dachande looked around at the burning pieces of material and walked around them slowly. The oomans had been trying to save him; there was no question. And they had probably died for their efforts.

He saw a fallen form on the ground, thrown clear of the wreck. Dachande approached it carefully. It did not move.

The small figure was turned on its stomach, but he knew what it was before he turned it over. It was the ooman who had tended him, then released him. It was the ooman who had tried to save him from the drones and had lost its life trying. There was no question that it was *thei-de*; thick *thwei* dripped sluggishly from deep gashes in its face and neck, and its position suggested a snapped spine.

Dachande scooped the tiny body up and paused for a moment, uncertain of what to do with it. Now that the animals were gone, he heard sounds of ooman language from somewhere near; past the largest part of the burning flyer, just a few paces away.

The other oomans would want it. For such a brave being, they would want to properly care for it before it's *u'sl-kwe*, final rest. It was no warrior, but it had a sensitivity that Dachande had never seen before, except in the smallest of children.

He carried the ooman to the others. There were three. One he recognized as the armed ooman from before. The other two were bigger, but unarmed. They held very still as he approached.

The small warrior held no weapon against him now; it ran toward him, the hold of its body frantic.

Dachande could see that it was not an attack. The warrior reached him and then gently stroked the face of the dead one that he carried, its composure one of sorrow.

It repeated something over and over as it touched the dead face. Dachande suddenly remembered the animal loop on his forearm, and tapped it quickly.

The ooman's language babbled back at it. The warrior looked up at him and then motioned for him to set the corpse down.

Dachande did it gently; the ooman had shown him respect. He would do no less for it in its death.

Noguchi stared in shock as she heard her own voice spill out from behind the creature's mask.

"I'm sorry, Miriam."

She pointed to the ground and then back to Miriam's body. Broken Tusk carefully set the doctor's body down and then stepped back.

Noguchi knelt over Miriam, could already see that it was too late.

That's okay, Machiko. Someone else you cared

about, someone who depended on you, dead. No big deal.

Just because it's your fault.

She allowed herself one second of pure grief. Her head dropped into her hands, and she let out a soft moan of despair and sorrow. The pain was sharp and cruel, the guilt tremendous and stabbing. And she didn't have time for it.

Noguchi stood slowly and took a deep breath. The pilots kept their silence, in respect or embarrassment she didn't know. She turned to look at the warrior, who also gazed at Revna's broken body; his odd mask flickered with strange shadows.

"It's time to put an end to this," she said quietly.

Broken Tusk stepped toward her and put one clawed hand on her shoulder. Noguchi did her best to return the gesture, although she couldn't quite reach.

It looked like she had an ally, at least for a while.

25

Scott and Tom followed the Noguchi woman through a deserted alley in the dark town. Scott wasn't sure where they were headed, but Noguchi moved with certainty.

He glanced over his shoulder from time to time, wary of the huge alien that brought up the rear. They had left the dead woman behind, soaked her corpse with fuel, and set it ablaze.

After listening to Noguchi's summary of what had happened in the last twenty-eight hours, Scott hurried to talk to her.

"Are you saying that *they*"—he tilted his head back at the giant—"let those bugs loose on a populated planet so they could *hunt* them?" He kept his voice low.

Noguchi nodded. "Just a theory, but it fits. Except

I don't think his kind knew there were humans on Ryushi. And from his actions, they weren't supposed to be shooting at us. We haven't been here that long, and it looks pretty certain that they were here before."

Her voice was edged with dry sarcasm when next she spoke: "I imagine we would have remembered if they'd visited recently."

Tom stumbled behind them. Scott stopped and started to turn back, but the giant stepped forward and set the pilot back on his feet as if he weighed nothing.

Tom nodded at the creature, waved a hand, and moved to join Scott and Nogushi.

She continued talking. ". . . and I imagine our presence probably screwed up their plans."

Scott raised his eyebrows. "Screwed up their plans. Oh, that's great. I feel so much better knowing that this whole fucking mess was an accident."

Noguchi shrugged. "Hey, at least he's on our side."

"Until he gets hungry," Scott mumbled under his breath.

Noguchi stopped at the end of the alley and waited for the giant to catch up to them. She kept her revolver barrel pointed up.

"Okay. The stampede started just around the corner here; we're going to walk through its path and see if there's anything left alive that shouldn't be."

Swell.

Scott looked around for some kind of weapon. Besides a few small rocks, they were out of luck. They'd have to stick close to the woman.

The giant hefted a large spear and seemed to wait for Noguchi's signal.

"Go."

The alien and Noguchi crouched out into the open compound, weapons ready.

Scott's heart raced; he looked over at Tom, who shrugged. They stepped out together to join the other two. It wasn't as if they had a whole lot of choice here, now was it?

"Holy *shit*," Tom said.

Scott forgot his fear for a second or two.

The stretch of open ground was littered with dozens of bodies, rhynth, bug, and giant alien. Large patches of soil were eaten away to reveal charred black splatterlike stains, as if the blood from the corpses was toxic. The rhynth were cut or blown open, chests shattered, throats slit. The black bugs were mostly crushed, so also the giants.

The only light was from a sole street lamp that hadn't been broken or shot out. The resulting mix of dark and death and shadows was forbidding, ominous. Ugly.

"When you kill something, you don't fool around," said Scott.

Noguchi wasn't listening. Her gaze darted from side to side, her revolver still up.

The giant's head was cocked to one side, his stance ready. The two of them moved forward slowly.

The pilots stayed close.

The four of them made their way cautiously down the ravaged street, stepped over torn bodies and corpses smashed down deep into the cracked earth. Apparently this was where the fight had ended.

After a moment of tense silence, Tom whispered loudly to Scott as they followed their armed escorts.

"Do you think the stampede got them all?"

Scott started to reply, but stopped short. He had

heard something behind them—the cry of a bird, perhaps, a chittering sound—

Behind one of the storage buildings, sudden movement. Scott felt his mouth go dry. He had heard it before—

"Run," he said, hardly able to get the word out. *"Run."*

Dachande heard the Hard Meat and spun around. He sprinted past the two ooman strangers toward the threat, staff forward. He was dimly aware that the small warrior was right behind. It shouted something at the other two.

They came in a single-file stream, flowed from around a structure, ten, maybe twelve. Dachande leapt to greet them.

Two arrived first, angled in from the sides. Dachande spun, swung completely around, cut them both through their midsections in one strike. He didn't watch them hit the ground; there was no need—they were dead and all he need do was avoid the throes.

He extended his *ki'cti-pa* and slashed through the throat of the next drone nearest, to his right.

The drone's death cry was garbled through its own *thwei.*

A split second later, he jabbed the staff point through the jaws of another, twisted the sharp blade and dug a hole through the top of the skull. The weapon's metal was proof against the Hard Meat's *thwei,* but there was no time to hesitate and enjoy the kill—when you fought the ten thousand, you did so one at a time, but you also had to do so *quickly*—

He thrust the spear's butt back, hard, and knocked

one behind him down, then turned and slashed its gut. Digest *this*, foolish creature!

The *ki'cti-pa* blurred again, jammed backhand into yet another Hard Meat chest. The drone howled, fell, did not die but did not rise again. Acid pumped into the dark air, pooled, smoking.

Dachande jumped forward, stabbed the throat of yet another, and then spun to meet the next. Death fell all around his feet as he and the Hard Meat danced.

Noguchi heard what sounded like a bird and turned; Broken Tusk was faster—he ran past the two pilots toward the main storage shed. He was eager and if he had any fear of the dark monsters, it was not apparent.

"Follow the tower around to the east lock!"

She would just have to hope that the pilots listened. She hurled herself after the warrior.

Several of the bugs streamed from behind the shed and toward Broken Tusk. He stepped in to battle without hesitation. Too many of them, ten, twelve. She aimed at one of the bugs—

—and it was dead before she fired. She took aim again—and again, her target had fallen already.

She took a step back, transfixed by the swift movements of the giant warrior.

Here was no inexperienced novice; every step was measured, every strike timed and sure. Within the space of a few seconds, most of the bugs were down, dead or dying. She had enough training to recognize a Master when she saw one. This one's skill had been gained in battle, against deadly enemies.

Broken Tusk whirled and jabbed, crouched and

slashed with precision and confidence. Never a misstep, never a hesitation. He was no dojo tiger, covered in padding and fighting for points.

Wherever he had come from, they had a martial arts more complex and dangerous than any she'd ever seen. It was like a choreographed dance—

Except we don't have all day.

She aimed and fired several shots, then aimed and fired again. The last two shrieked and stumbled. Broken Tusk hesitated, confused perhaps, then finished them both with slashes to the gut.

"Sorry." Noguchi ejected the spent rounds and slapped in a loader. "But we've got to go."

Broken Tusk stared at her for a second, then raised one claw—in understanding or camaraderie, she couldn't know. She returned the move, then started toward the east lock.

The warrior caught up to her easily, then slowed and strode at her side as they rounded the front of the ops building toward the lock. He made thick growling noises, strange,, but somehow not threatening.

Ahead, the lock was open. Conover stood by the control panel inside, face pale.

Noguchi heard now familiar chirping noises behind them, not far.

"Hurry!" Conover shouted.

Noguchi and Broken Tusk ran through the entry together. The door slammed down.

A second later there were several thundering crashes. The metal door shook as the nightmare creatures threw themselves at it, but it wouldn't give.

Noguchi collapsed against the frame and closed her eyes. They were safe, at least for the moment.

Safe—and fucked. They hadn't gotten them all.

The plan hadn't worked.

26

So what's the plan?"

Noguchi didn't answer. She continued to take deep breaths, her eyes closed. The giant alien stood at her side, still enough to be a statue. Its face was turned to watch the woman, but the odd mask it wore covered most of any expression it may have had. Given the faces of some of the dead ones who'd lost their masks in the stampede, Scott was just as happy about that. Ugly bastards.

He stepped away from the door and started to pace. He was feeling pretty goddamn tired of not knowing what was going on.

"Look, lady, I realize that you're under a lot of stress, but you do *have* some idea of what we're going to do, don't you? The stampede didn't work out quite the way it was supposed to, obviously. Now if I were you, I'd start worrying about what—"

"What?" Noguchi had opened her eyes to reveal an icy anger. "If you were me, you'd worry about what?"

He shut up. Then, "Well, shit. What next?"

"Lay off, Scott." Tom sounded bone-tired.

Scott looked at his friend and felt his anger spark higher. Tom looked worse than he had before. Whatever he'd picked up was making him really sick. The younger pilot had fallen into a chair and rested his head on a console; his body shook.

Scott stopped in front of Noguchi and lowered his voice. "My friend is sick, okay? We have to do *some-thing.*"

Noguchi smiled softly, humorlessly. "No shit. But unless you or your friend come up with some brilliant revelation, I suggest you *shut up*; I'll listen to you when you've got something to say."

She closed her eyes again.

The spark fizzled. She was a cold bitch, but he didn't have any ideas to contribute. And he sure as fuck didn't want to lead this little party.

"Right. Sorry, okay? I don't feel so good. It's been a bad day."

Noguchi nodded, then walked toward an ops panel. "The colonists made it out safely, that's something. We've got power here, and supplies; we can hold out for a while here and come up with something."

"There's a screen still on over here," Tom said.

Scott and Noguchi both walked over to where the ailing pilot sat. The giant remained at the door, motionless.

Across the top of the small console was a series of numbers.

"That's my code," said Noguchi. "It's a hyperstat

from the corporation substation! The æther driver got through."

She leaned in front of Tom and punched a few keys excitedly.

Scott blinked. Æther driver? What the hell was that? Some new equipment the company was too cheap to put on their ship? Shit.

He read over her shoulder.

Attn: Machiko Noguchi, Prosperity Wells/from BAE:683 Takashi Chigusa, New Osaka. re: possible XT specimens. Take steps to preserve all specimens of species described in Revna's report; nearest Marine ship will enter area at approx. 5/14. Keep BAE:683 apprised. Await further instructions.

YFNT677074/TC.

Noguchi slammed her fist against the screen and stalked over to a chair. She plopped down and put one hand to her forehead.

"Five weeks," she said softly. "All we have to do is survive for five weeks."

As if on cue, there was another slam to the lock. A creature screamed, the sound muffled through the thick metal.

"And preserve for them 'all specimens,'" she said. She laughed. It wasn't a funny noise.

Christ. Don't lose it, lady. We need you.

It was looking hopeless. Noguchi had never felt so frustrated in her life, or so angry. There was nothing she could do—

"Well, fuck this!" Conover had started pacing again. "I say we scram out of here and join the colonists!"

She looked up at the red-faced pilot and shook her

head. "Yeah? And how long before the bugs run out of
food and head into the desert looking for more?"

Conover dropped his gaze and said nothing.

"I don't know about you two, but I'm tired of
fucking with all of this. I want to finish this, and I
want to finish it *now*." She wasn't sure how, but there
had to be a way—

Conover snorted. "Sure, great. You gonna burn
down the whole complex?"

Strandberg coughed loudly. "That wouldn't work,
too many of them would"—he coughed again—
"would get away. It'd have to be something fast."

Noguchi started running off possibilities in her
head. Maybe they could formulate some kind of
bomb, or gas—

Conover jerked his gaze at Broken Tusk. "Why
don't we ask the hulk over there? Maybe he's got a
death ray or something."

Strandberg shook his head. "I'm serious. I think
Ms. Noguchi had the right idea with the stampede,
crush them like bugs—" He broke into a fit of coughing.

Noguchi looked at Strandberg with sympathy; he
really didn't look well, and he had at least tried to be
helpful—

The pilot had regained his wind and raised one
hand weakly. "Something big enough to take out the
complex and the ship at once—"

Conover interrupted angrily, "Forget it! I can't even
believe you'd bring it up!"

Noguchi stood and faced the asshole pilot. "Don't
hold out on me, Conover! If you know something that
might stop those things—"

Strandberg started coughing again.

Conover glared at her and jabbed a finger in her

general direction. "Look, I have some shares in this little investment along with everyone else! There is nothing we can do, okay?"

Strandberg tried to stand up, and fell to the floor. His coughing suddenly turned to hoarse choking sounds, and he spasmed and convulsed, clutched at his chest.

Heart attack or epileptic seizure—

Noguchi took one step toward him and felt a hand on her shoulder. Broken Tusk. He hissed and hefted his spear.

Conover rushed to his friend's side and then stepped back at the sight of blood on Strandberg's abdomen.

"Tommy—?!"

Noguchi gasped. The convulsing pilot screamed again and again. And at the same time, there was the sound of ripping, shredding, the sound of flesh parting—

A creature the size of Noguchi's forearm burst through Strandberg's chest in a spray of red. Dripping with blood and slime, the animal looked surreal, its head dominated by rows of teeth. It coiled its long, flesh-colored body in the frame of Strandberg's bloody rib cage and screeched at them.

And jumped—

27

Dachande watched from the door as the oomans battled verbally. Although they did not give off a musk, the anger was clear. He imagined they were worried about their deaths and the proper manner of them, not an unreasonable concern in the situation. There might not be any witnesses to carry the tale to their friends and relatives, no one would know if they had died bravely or not, a concern to any warrior, of course. But in the end, *they* would know, just as he would know. All beings died, later, sooner, no one escaped the Black Warrior. But—if it happened in battle, did you meet the gods with blood on your blade, your laughter at Death still echoing around you? That was the thing; that way lay honor.

He had counted five of his students crushed into

the soil on their way here, their weapons destroyed or missing. There was no way to know if there were more still alive, but he guessed not. He was vaguely disappointed in their performance, but they had been served with what they earned. Especially if they had followed Tichinde. The nature of would-be warriors was to obey the strongest among them and Tichinde had been that. Unfortunately, when a Hunt needed strategy and tactics, strength did not make up for stupidity. Even a good teacher could fail and that rankled, but one worked with what one was given.

Dachande watched the ooman debate with interest; the small warrior was in charge, and the other disagreed with whatever the small one wanted. He waited to see if there would be physical combat, but for some reason, the larger ooman did not strike. Dachande guessed the small one must be a Leader to merit such respect. He decided to support the warrior; from its actions so far, it was surely braver than the others. Certainly it stood in better balance, it flowed better.

When the third ooman fell and went into *z'skvy-de*, Dachande moved. The oomans had no experience with such things and did not recognize the eruptive phase. The small warrior stepped forward, but he stopped it, quickly explained the situation, and stepped past.

The larger ooman stood in his way. He pushed it aside and reached the ooman host just as the *kainde amedha* lunged forth.

The newborn creature snaked across the floor and almost made it under a table before Dachande lifted his spear and brought it down, hard.

He could feel the young drone's back snap beneath the weapon. Hot intestine squirted, blood hissed.

Dachande stepped away and looked at the oomans. He waited.

Scott couldn't seem to catch his breath. He was sprawled on the floor next to Tommy, where the giant had shoved him and Tommy was—

"Oh, Jesus, no," he whispered. His voice sounded faint, far away.

Tommy still quivered all over. His fingers clenched and unclenched, and then nothing.

The giant had squashed the alien parasite quickly and neatly. It was over, that fast. And Tommy lay next to him, the slick innards of his body exposed, his eyes open.

Scott turned away and dry-heaved a few times, the retching bringing only sour spit. And then he understood.

He sat up stiffly and put a hand on his stomach. And coughed. And started to cry.

Noguchi grabbed someone's coat off the back of one of the chairs and draped it over the dead pilot. She shuddered and stepped back.

Conover's shoulders shook with grief.

Noguchi looked up at Broken Tusk, who watched mutely, and then back at Conover.

Broken Tusk had known. Her theory had panned out. For what that was worth at this point.

She crouched down next to the crying pilot and put a hand across his back. She kept her voice low, but didn't hesitate.

"I'm sorry about your friend, Conover. But I need your help right now, okay? Before Strandberg—"

She cleared her throat and started again. "He was about to tell me something—something that could wipe out the bugs; I need—"

Conover turned his tear-streaked face up to look at her. "You don't get it, do you? What happened to Tommy—that thing that was inside of him. We were together on *The Lector.* That means I've got one of those things inside of—"

The pilot's face crumpled in despair. He buried his face in his hands and started to sob loudly.

Noguchi let him cry for a moment, then patted him gently on the back. She felt like a real bitch for what she was about to say, but there was no way around it.

"You're not dead yet, Conover. We still need your help."

He continued to rock back and forth. "Leave me alone. I'm doomed, I'm a dead man."

Noguchi stood up. "Maybe if you help us, I can help you."

Conover looked up at her and wiped his eyes with the back of one hand. "Are you a doctor? You gonna perform surgery and make me all better?"

Noguchi shook her head. "No, I can't do that. But you can have a shot at revenge—" She took a deep breath. "And I can make it quicker, easier for you."

The mixed look of pain and self-pity and gratitude on the pilot's face made her stomach clench. Conover was an asshole, but he didn't deserve to die for it. If she had one of those things inside of her ...

"Okay," he said quietly. "Fuck it. Yeah, okay."

Scott sat at the terminal, his eyes gritty and his hands trembling. He was going to die. He was going to die. The thought was a repeating loop in his mind, a horrible and constant statement of looming black truth. He was pregnant with a monster, he was going to die—

Scott shook his head and finished the sentence he had typed onto the screen; almost done. His stomach hurt, and with each second, it got worse. He coughed into his hand and tapped a few more keys. Real, or in his mind?

"Everything you need is on the disk," he said. His voice sounded dead, too.

Noguchi nodded. She sat next to him and watched carefully as he worked.

"Thanks, Conover."

"Scott," he said softly. It suddenly seemed very important that she knew his name. Because he was going to die.

"Thanks, Scott."

He felt a few more tears trickle down his face and into his beard. It had been like that for the last twenty minutes. Knowing you were about to die was bad, very bad.

"It's going to be tough getting in," he said.

"We'll find a way."

Scott nodded and glanced at the giant. It was back by the door, spear at its side.

"I don't doubt it," he said. He coughed, the painful spasm filling him with dread. He took a deep breath and coughed again. It was getting worse.

He smiled weakly at Noguchi. "You know, if this works, the company's gonna be really pissed."

She straightened slightly and then laughed. She seemed surprised by the sound. So was Scott.

You can still make a pretty woman laugh, Scott.

"Fuck the company," she said.

"Yeah."

On a sudden impulse, Scott grabbed at a piece of paper on the console and a pen. He made a quick sketch, studied the drawing for a moment, and then added a few more details.

He folded the paper in half and handed it to Noguchi.

"It's a going away present," he said. He coughed and pressed one hand to his stomach. He tried not to think about it—

You're going to die—

"It's a map of the ship," he continued. "I should have thought of it before."

She slipped the paper into a chest pocket and nodded. Behind them, at the door, the shrieks of the alien bugs had gotten louder.

"Sounds like every bug in the place is trying to get in," he said. "Well. All but one of them. It's already in."

"We're ready to go." She stood.

Scott nodded and coughed again. He was going to die.

A kind of calm slipped over him, a sense of unreality that made him feel far away from all this. It didn't matter, not really. He should be scared, had been scared, but now, in this moment, he was somehow floating above it, watching himself as if he were someone else. It was a done deal, end of the line, and while he had never dreamed it would happen this way, here it was and what choice did he have?

At least he had helped. Maybe it would even make some kind of difference—he wouldn't be around to see, but at least he wouldn't be in pain, and the damn repeating line would end.

The giant alien walked over to meet them when Noguchi stood. It gestured with its spear at Scott.

Noguchi's voice came from the creature: "I can make it quicker, easier for you."

Noguchi held up one hand. "No. I made the promise, I'll do it."

The giant seemed to understand. It stepped back.

"Weird," said Scott. He coughed—and with it came an odd nauseous feeling. Like he had swallowed something alive.

"Just do it, okay?"

Noguchi held her pistol up. "Close your eyes, Scott. Count to three."

Scott closed his eyes. He sensed the barrel of the weapon behind his skull and he clenched his eyes tighter. He was afraid. But he was ready.

"I'll remember you," said Noguchi gently.

"One. Two—"

The warrior looked away from the fallen ooman and stood still for a moment. Dachande said nothing, but after a short span, he growled a time reminder at the standing ooman and motioned at the door. The Leader had done what a Leader had to do; there was no cure for an infected host and the larger ooman's death was quick and honorable. It had not fought or tried to run.

He moved to the dead ooman, judged where the unborn Hard Meat embryo was, and raised his spear. Looked at the remaining ooman.

The ooman nodded and turned away as Dachande drove the spear downward. Felt the blade hit the harder substance of the embryo. Felt it struggle to escape the point, then give up.

He pulled the blade free, hammered the shaft of the weapon with his free fist to shake the blood from it. Done.

The other ooman walked to join him. Glanced down at its dead comrade, then away. It looked tired. It motioned at a side entrance with its weapon and nodded at Dachande.

He nodded back and followed the small warrior to crouch by the entry. The drones still scrabbled madly outside the main door, but there were no sounds outside this one.

The warrior raised its burner. Dachande readied his staff.

The door opened.

28

Roth yawned and glanced at her chrono for the third time in fifteen minutes. They were out in the middle of nowhere in a quick and dirty makeshift camp and she was watching the darkness for monsters. Monsters.

Life sure wasn't what you expected, at least never for more than a few minutes at a time.

The suns would be coming up soon, which meant her shift was about done. In the dim predawn light, she leaned against Ackland's AV and whistled softly for Creep. The mutt had wandered over to stand watch with Leo, an older Chinese man who always seemed to have candy in his pocket.

After a few seconds, Creep padded quietly through the maze of vehicles to join her. She scratched his head.

"How's Leo, dog? Still awake?"

Creep whuffled softly and sat down, tongue hanging out.

"I heard that, Roth," a voice crackled in her ear.

"You been feeding my dog crap again, Leo?" Roth spoke quietly. Most of the camp was still asleep, except for her and five others. On any normal night, they would've swapped jokes and insults, maybe taken turns napping. But the day before had been too long and too frightening. The shift had been tense and silent, and except for one false alarm when a few stray rhynth had wandered into camp, uneventful.

Leo chuckled. "Yep. You don't give him anything good; if I were him, I'd be hungry for something besides soypro in a can, too."

"You'd make a good dog, Leo."

There was a short pause and then Kaylor came online. "Sorry to interrupt, folks, but shouldn't Noguchi be here by now?"

Roth sighed. "Yeah, we know." Kaylor had a bad habit of stating the obvious.

Leo cut in. "Maybe someone should go back . . ."

He trailed off. No one replied. Roth concentrated on the twins suns as they sneaked up on the far edge of the desert and began to lighten the clear sky.

Twenty minutes later, the door to Ackland's AV banged open.

Roth jumped. She had been lulled into a trance by the silence and purity of the early morning. Asshole.

Within a few minutes, the camp was up. Bleary-eyed ranchers and their children stumbled out into the almost-cool air and trotted off to relieve themselves behind various rocks and low shrub.

Roth shouldered her rifle and rubbed at her eyes.

Sleep would be bliss, but she wanted to stay awake for a while and watch for Noguchi.

"Jame?" Cathie walked over with two cups of coffee.

"Thanks, hon. Get any sleep?"

Cathie smiled. "An hour or two, at least."

She handed Roth a mug and kissed her lightly. "I figured you wouldn't be ready for bed quite yet."

Roth motioned with her head at a small group of people who had gathered by Luccini's AV, Ackland and Weaver among them.

"What's the deal?"

Cathie shrugged. "Ackland's being a dickhead, what else?"

Jenkins arrived and took over from Roth. They nodded at each other.

As soon as the shift was covered, Roth and Cathie walked over to join the circle; several other ranchers had also stopped.

". . . and I think it's suicide!" Ackland looked blustery and irritated, as usual; Cathie was right, he was a dickhead.

"What's suicide?" Roth asked.

Weaver's cheeks were flushed. "Oh, nothing. Ackland is being a coward, that's all."

"Bullshit," said Ackland. "There's nothing we can do until the Marines show up, that's all! If one of you wants to go back and get killed, that's fine by me!"

Paul Luccini spoke up. He didn't talk much, but people tended to listen when he did. "The Marines might take a while, Ackland."

Cathie stepped in. "In the meantime, she could be hurt, or in need of help."

"Those are the chances she took when she accepted the job," said Ackland. His voice was now patronizing and slow, as if he were addressing children. "The Chigusa Corporation is responsible for the safety of the colonists, not the other way around."

A red haze seemed to settle over everything for Roth. She took a deep breath, tried to control it, but something snapped while Ackland spoke.

"You *bastard*!" She stepped forward and poked him in the chest with one trembling finger. "You can't shove this off on the company! *You* had me lie to Doc Revna about where we found those creatures! And it was your idea to sneak those rhynth past quarantine!" She took another step toward him. "I'm ashamed to admit to my part in it, but I take responsibility for *my* stupidity! What's *your* excuse?"

Ackland held up his hands, as if to defend himself. "Hey, look—you know what a hardass Noguchi is, right?" He searched the assembled ranchers for support. "I was just trying to protect my investments. *Our* investments."

Luccini spoke again. "Fuck the investments. I've got a family."

Several others chorused agreement.

Weaver glared at Ackland. "You can say what you want about Noguchi, but when it came down to it, she risked her life to save all of us—including your ass!"

Ackland opened his mouth, his fat face angry—and then closed it again. He turned and walked away.

"He'd better pray she's still alive when this is all over," Cathie whispered to Roth.

Roth nodded. The rush of adrenaline was gone, had left her exhausted. She caught Weaver's gaze. "Are you looking for volunteers?"

Weaver considered it for a moment and then shook her head. "No. Not yet, anyway. Machiko told us to wait, so we'll wait. If she'd not here by late afternoon, though ..."

"Right. Let me know, okay?"

Roth and Cathie walked over to a makeshift table that had been assembled and stacked with trays of rolls and a couple of pots of coffee.

"Do you think she's still alive?" said Cathie.

Roth started to say no, but then thought better of it.

"If anyone could survive that place right now," she said carefully, "it'd be her."

Dawn had come.

Broken Tusk stepped past her, out into the open compound, and then motioned for her to follow.

Noguchi crouched outside of the door and pointed left, then right with her handgun. It was clear.

She could still hear the screaming bugs around the corner to her right; they continued to slam into the main door, apparently unaware their prey had escaped.

Noguchi and Broken Tusk circled to the back. From behind them, Noguchi heard several loud cracks as the door finally gave up the fight.

Looks like they got tired of waiting for us to let them in—

Broken Tusk glanced back at her.

She pointed forward and he moved on.

Noguchi covered the rear as they headed to the other side of the ops building. They hurried, but didn't run. She took her cues from the warrior; he had dealt with these things before, and he stepped cautiously.

In spite of the situation, part of Noguchi could appreciate the dawn. The compound was illuminated softly by the early light, so unlike the Prosperity Wells she had known, harsh and glaring. It seemed tranquil and cool, like a dream—

—or a memory—

Pay attention here, Noguchi. Daydream when you don't have to worry about being eaten.

Good thought, but a little late.

She didn't see the thing until it was almost on top of her.

Dachande heard the splintering of the weak door behind them as they circled. He wasn't sure of what the ooman warrior had planned, but he knew what he needed to know and it was simple: kill everything that got in their way.

The ooman pointed past him and then turned its back again; it watched for threats from the rear.

Dachande glanced upward and then went on. They should step a little faster. The drones would run through the ooman structure quickly, and then come back out. They were stupid, but good at finding live meat.

Dachande heard a cry from above and looked up again, too late.

A single drone howled and jumped, its long body twisted in the air. It landed behind him. In front of the ooman.

Noguchi spun. The hellish creature reached for her—

She whipped her arm around, tried to aim, no time, fired—

Missed.

The nightmare bug towered over her, shrieking.

Slime dripped from its metallic jaws. Its huge mouth opened, exposed a set of inner teeth, razor sharp.

Noguchi stumbled backward as the inner jaws snapped forward and smacked into her chest.

Something ripped. Hot pain seared her skin, blood flowed—

—she shoved the gun like a punch as the creature prepared to leap—

Before she could pull the trigger, the bug convulsed and shuddered wildly. A thick silver blade had suddenly appeared in the middle of its segmented torso. The thing's acid blood sprayed across the dusty floor, flowing toward her.

Noguchi passed out.

Dachande speared the drone in the back and then tossed the body across the ground. It wasn't dead yet, but it would be.

He spun, searched for others. He could hear the attacker's cry answered from structures all around. They would be here in seconds.

He scooped up the ooman and ran.

He had not had time to study the ooman dwellings properly, save the tower he had fallen from the night before—but the two larger oomans had been in one of the buildings nearby, he was sure of it. With luck, it was still safe. And the warrior had seemed to want them to head in that direction.

The warrior weighed almost nothing, hardly more than his staff. It made a low sound of pain as he pounded the dust. Speed was of the essence; he could not fight with it in his arms. The drone had clawed open the ooman's soft armor, armor now soaked in *thwei.* Red blood unlike his own. How different they were.

He heard screams from where he'd left the dying bug; it had been found.

Dachande ran faster.

She was flying.

Noguchi opened her eyes and blinked hard. Her abdomen felt shredded and her head ached.

Broken Tusk carried her. They ran through the compound, incredibly fast. Something had happened, she had been attacked—

She lifted her head slightly and panicked for a split second before she realized that the gun was still clenched in her fist. She winced at the pain in her chest and belly and closed her eyes again. Broken Tusk had saved her, but there was nothing she could do until he put her down.

From somewhere not so far away, the nightmare creatures howled.

Dachande saw the open entry to some long, low structure directly ahead.

The drones hadn't spotted him yet. He ran to the building, scanned the interior quickly, and ducked through the ooman-sized door.

It was empty. He set the warrior down carefully and then closed the door. He fumbled for a minute with the latch mechanism, and finally smashed the door hard enough to drive it into the frame. It was a flimsy barrier, the drones would get through it in seconds—but they didn't know where he was, not yet.

He turned to look at the ooman, and was surprised

to see it sitting up. It still held its small burner—not aimed at him, but not down, either.

He approached it carefully and crouched down next to it to study the wound. The ooman seemed to protest at first, but relented quickly; it lay down.

He pulled the soaked padding away from the warrior's body and touched it gently. The ooman moaned.

"It's not going to kill you," he said. The ooman didn't reply.

He tried again. "No *thei-de*, understand?"

It didn't understand. It babbled for a minute and then fell quiet again. Frustrating.

Dachande lifted the rest of the weak armor away from the warrior's chest and then hissed, surprised. If ooman anatomy was anywhere similar to yautja, this warrior was a female; he hadn't thought of it before. It had a pair of what were obviously milk glands.

Stupid! Of course it's female!

Yautja females were bigger than males; it was apparently the reverse for oomans. It had never occurred to him. That was stupid; simple mistakes like that could lead to bigger ones, fatal ones.

It also explained why this warrior was smarter than most of the yautja he taught. Females of any species were usually smarter than the males.

Dachande assessed the wounds; minor. There was a fair amount of blood, but it had already stopped flowing, and most of the acid burns had been slowed by the armor.

He used some of the torn armor to stanch the wound and then sat back on his heels and studied the ooman. It watched him, curious perhaps.

They didn't have much time, but Dachande thought they could spare a few seconds.

He pointed at his chest and gave her his honorary name. "Dachande."

The ooman shook her head.

"Dah-shann-day." He stretched it out.

The ooman tried, but couldn't make the right sounds. Dachande shook his head.

She reached out hesitantly and touched his shortened mandible. The new style masks covered only the nostrils, leaving the fighting tusks bare. She said something in her own language, then repeated it.

Dachande tilted his head. It wasn't his name, but she seemed to understand the meaning. "Brr-k'in dusg?"

The ooman exposed her teeth and then pointed at herself and spoke.

Dachande tried. "Nihkuo'te?"

The ooman shook its—no, *her* head.

He looked at the creature for a moment and then named her.

"Da'dtou-di." It was the feminine of "small knife." A brave name, and it suited her.

Da'dtou-di pointed at herself and did her best. "Dahdtoou-dee?"

Dachande hissed with pleasure. It was a start, and it was enough; it was all the time they could waste on pleasantries. Should they survive, they would talk later.

He stood. "Da'dtou-di," he said, "we must go."

The ooman got up, staggered slightly, and then nodded. She was all right.

Dachande turned and walked to the door. He listened.

The drones had run past their structure and were assembling elsewhere. Which likely meant their nest was close by.

The Leader waited for Da'dtou-di to join him, feeling older than he'd ever felt before. His bones ached. He had been on many Hunts, dangerous Hunts, but for the first time, the outcome was not obvious. There were more drones here than he'd ever fought, and where there was a nest, there would be a queen—the drones could do that, change to female when no others were around. And a queen was not an easy kill.

He sighed deeply. If his Final Hunt were not today, it would be soon.

Noguchi got to her feet carefully and fought off dizziness. Broken Tusk started to reach toward her, but she nodded and held up a hand. The wounds weren't as bad as she'd feared; the light-headedness was more exhaustion than anything else.

She joined Broken Tusk at the door and held her handgun ready. Her new name rang through her thoughts, Dahdtoudi. If someone had told her a year ago that she'd be fighting XTs with an alien warrior, the fate of a hundred people on their shoulders, she would have laughed for a week.

As it stood, she allowed herself a tight grin. It was actually pretty funny; she'd laugh later, if there was time. If she woke up.

Noguchi motioned at the door, then pointed toward the south, where *The Lector* sat. Broken Tusk tilted his head to one side in agreement.

Next thing you know, we'll be talking philosophy.

Broken Tusk growled something at her and then pushed her back from the door slightly. He had jammed it.

Noguchi stepped back and watched as the warrior took a deep breath—

—and the door flew open to expose one of the warriors, a twin to Broken Tusk, holding a spear, its arms raised to strike.

29

Noguchi reacted without thinking.

She dropped her weapon to chest level and fired into the warrior's belly until her gun ran dry.

The warrior fell backward. Its strange gun discharged harmlessly into the air with a hollow thump and an eye-smiting flare. The spear it held in the other hand fell and clattered on the door stoop.

He had not had time to scream.

Broken Tusk jumped in a split second later, but it was done.

A low, guttural gurgle came from the dying warrior's throat, punctuated with a spew of thick, greenish, milky, almost glowing fluid.

Blood.

Broken Tusk hefted his staff and brought the

weighted end down on the warrior's skull. The head split with a dull, wet crack.

Broken Tusk's posture indicated anger and sorrow, his huge shoulders tensed, head bowed. She had killed one of his people. Would he be angry with her?

Noguchi scanned the immediate area for other dangers and then looked at Broken Tusk again.

He was much more adept than the one she'd shot had been.

It dawned on her.

It would explain the difference in prowess, the difference in behavior—

Broken Tusk must be the commander.

Dachande was disgusted with himself. He had been so intrigued with the ooman female, so intent on opening the door, he had not scented the yautja.

It was Oc'djy, one of his less adept students. The dead yautja's attack had been, as it seemed with all of their moves since they arrived, stupid. "Look before you shoot" was one of the cardinal rules. If you aren't *sure* of your target, the burner stays cold, the spear does not fly. Shooting a brother warrior accidentally was the height of bad manners.

And quarter-wit Oc'djy breathing his last on the ground would surely have killed them both if Da'dtou-di hadn't fired first. No doubt of it. He was embarrassed that his students were so inept.

Dachande clattered a respectful appreciation to Da'dtou-di and then cracked Oc'djy's head open. That his thick skull could no longer be any Hunter's trophy was a disgrace, and one he had earned. Too bad he had not broken Tichinde's. Ah, well. It was not likely anybody on this world would ever find the dead student, save for scavengers.

Dachande took a deep breath and frowned slightly. The yautja's musk, the *h'dui'se*, was weak, covered with the stench of dried feces and blood. At least that explained his inability to detect the student before . . .

He snatched the burner from the ground in irritation. A Leader should not make excuses; in Hunting, they did not matter—you died or you did not.

At least he had a decent weapon. Dachande checked it over and growled. Four more fires; not much, but better than his spear alone. Tichinde's burner had been empty.

He glanced at Da'dtou-di, who studied him carefully. He did not know contempt on an ooman face, but she probably felt it.

Da'dtou-di motioned again toward the nest as she finished reloading her weapon. Dachande tilted his head and stepped forward, slinging the burner over one shoulder. She was right; now was not the time for recriminations. He could dwell on his incompetencies later.

Maybe.

Noguchi pointed at the ship, only a few structures away, fifty or sixty meters.

Broken Tusk moved again to the fore position.

They edged forward, Noguchi careful to check the roof.

They made it past the south end of the pen they'd been in before the first attack.

Broken Tusk walked into the open space between two of the pens.

Noguchi backed toward him cautiously.

He hissed a warning.

Noguchi spun, handgun extended.

Broken Tusk crouched, hissed again, his arms spread wide, spear pointed at the sky.

Two of the bugs sprinted toward them from the shadows of the alley, joined by a third. Then a fourth. And a fifth.

Dachande counted them quickly, then stood. Only five.

As the first two rushed to attack him, he side-stepped and thrust the bladed staff out.

The closest one caught it in the throat; it screamed, collapsed, hit the ground.

The second rammed its head directly into the durable blade; the top of its head sliced neatly from its body. Acidic blood fountained.

Da'dtou-di fired her burner from behind him, the sounds loud and sharp.

Two of the running drones fell. Four of five.

Dachande stepped in again to take out the last.

It seemed not to see its fallen siblings. The creature ran straight at him, shrieking.

Dachande hopped to one side as the creature neared, spear held to the other side—

—except the drone hopped and matched his move. And hit him, running full speed.

Noguchi aimed past Broken Tusk and fired. The first two shots missed, but the third took out one of the black bugs, still a dozen meters away.

She trained and fired again, this time right on the

target. A second fell, its corrosive blood sprayed and began to sizzle and eat into the nearest wall.

She tried for the last, but Broken Tusk was in the line of fire. Noguchi turned quickly, alert to other threats.

From *The Lector* or close to it, she heard what sounded like a hundred of the nightmares. They shrieked and howled and pounded the earth, but none came into view.

Noguchi spun, just in time to see the fifth bug barrel into Broken Tusk and knock him down.

Dachande felt ribs snap as the drone tackled him. He'd lost his spear—

The snarling bug drove its head downward, opened its mouth, exposed its inner jaws—

—he plunged his fist into its mouth.

The alien gagged and bit down. Dachande felt the dagger teeth pierce his arm but he drove his claws in deeper, dug deep into softer flesh—

The drone jerked its talons away from Dachande's throat and clutched at its own. The Leader brought up his other fist and slammed the bug's neck, hard.

The drone spilled to the side.

Dachande let the weight of the creature pull him over to land on top of it. He grabbed for the burner—that sent a shooting pain through his side—and brought the blunt end down on the bug's slender throat.

The drone let go of his arm and died.

Broken Tusk staggered to his feet and retrieved his spear. He turned and jogged toward her. His arm was dotted with green spots where the thing had bitten him.

If he felt any pain, Noguchi couldn't see it. She covered him until he reached her, and then turned toward the ship without her pointing to it.

He knew that much, and she had figured it out on the way.

They were going to where most of the creatures called home.

Dachande ignored the jabbing pain as they edged closer to the nest. The drones would surround their queen now, protect her. They made it past the second and third structure with no more attacks.

Da'dtou-di paused for a second to reload her burner. Dachande glanced at her thoughtfully.

She was the prey he had waited most of his life to Hunt. They were small but powerful, obviously more intelligent than the yautja had thought, and as brave as any warrior he had Hunted with.

Of course, Da'dtou-di could be an exception; she was obviously trained better than the other few oomans he had been in contact with. The kind one that had died, for instance—it was not trained to Hunt, and had been blind to the danger he could have represented.

He would have enjoyed Hunting oomans. But he was proud to Hunt at Da'dtou-di's side. This would be a tale to tell for generations to come . . .

The ooman saw that he watched her and raised her fist into the air. She exposed her teeth again at the same time, probably a sign of aggression.

Dachande still wore his mask, but he raised his

arm also and then clattered, as loud as he dared, the Kiss of Midnight.

Kill or die. He was ready.

They crept into the open space in front of the shield wall as quietly as possible. Ryushi's suns beat down on the nearly lifeless compound. It seemed like hours ago that Noguchi had been thinking of how beautiful the town was. Not now. Especially since the heat of midmorning had taken on the cloying stench of rot and decay. A lot of bodies—humans, aliens, warriors—must be cooking in the hot sunshine.

The Lector seemed deserted from the outside. A lone dead rhynth lay on the ground in front of the ship, its intestines ripped out. It must have staggered from the stampede to die there . . .

Noguchi figured the bugs had nested in the ship, and that they waited there now, grouped to attack. Their actions reminded her of a bee colony, the way the drones of a hive lived only to feed and protect their queen.

She shuddered slightly at the thought; she wouldn't want to meet with whatever those monstrosities called "mother."

The distance to the ship slowly dwindled as they crossed the compound. Noguchi's heart thumped louder with each step. She stifled an urge to go back to the empty holding pen and study Conover's map for a while longer.

Like five or ten years.

Broken Tusk walked cautiously, but not too much so; Noguchi figured he knew something she didn't. That wouldn't take much.

As they neared the main loading entrance, her worries about what they would do if the door was closed vanished. The middle steel entry was halfway open as it had been when she and Mason had gone in—

Another pleasant thought. They reached the bottom of the ramp and Noguchi looked up into the black interior of the dock; the metal door was raised horizontally, exactly the right height to let the bugs come and go.

The bugs didn't seem too smart, but she wondered. Conover had spoken of one that was much larger than the others, that had slept near them when they were captives.

Queen?

She might have stood there for a lot longer, but Broken Tusk growled at her. Noguchi took it as impatience. She took a tentative step onto the ramp.

From somewhere inside the blackness, a low hiss.

Noguchi took another step, gun ready for the first thing that moved. Broken Tusk was by her side, his weapon also out. He had slung the spear over his back.

The dark lock stirred, shadows shifted. She heard the clatter of alien movement, and then silence.

Broken Tusk moved in front of her. She let him.

They were halfway up the ramp when a sudden flurry of motion in the dark ahead of them surprised her. She fired into the dock, twice.

The gunshots clapped loudly in the still air. Whatever had moved wasn't moving now.

Broken Tusk made a few guttural sounds and then walked without hesitation to the top of the ramp. He turned and motioned at her to follow.

Noguchi joined him and peered inside. Nothing, at least nothing she could hear or see. It felt empty, too. But there was alien spoor all around. An odd, wet-metal smell. What looked like meaty chunks of slaughtered rhynth—or human.

She edged inside, adrenaline pumping. On the dark floor there were several of the unclassifieds that the Revnas had dissected, their spiderlike bodies curled and motionless. Dark shapes lined the walls. She looked closer and then shuddered. *The Lector*'s crew, at least some of them, with chests ruptured, webbed like flies in the nest of a demonic spider. Some of them had not died easily, from the expressions locked on to their dead faces.

Where—?

A jagged hole at the rear of the dock answered her. The edges of the torn metal looked melted, scorched. All around it were bizarre formations of shiny black material. It stretched and hung in thick ropes, appeared both organic and deliberate.

It seemed twice as hot as outside in the burning sunlight with the humidity added. Noguchi took a shaky breath and then moved into the darkness. Broken Tusk walked ahead of her to the hole and waited.

She heard a chittering movement come from deep inside the ship somewhere, and steeled her nerves as she approached.

They were going to have to find the control room. Which meant going in, navigating a labyrinth of corridors, climbing two flights of steps, and unlocking a locked door.

Broken Tusk watched her for a second and then stepped into the hole.

Noguchi prayed silently to anyone listening, and followed him.

30

Dachande went first.

He crouched down immediately and searched for life, sweeping back and forth with his burner. Nothing moved.

Da'dtou-di slipped in after him. He ignored her for the moment; she could take care of herself. What she lacked in skill, she made up for with intelligence; it would have to be enough.

He scanned the long dark corridor through the eyes of the mask. More of the alien spittle secretion, *te'dqi*, lined the steep walls. It was a brittle substance, but could provide camouflage for hiding drones.

The lenses showed nothing. He glanced at Da'dtou-di. Her sickly pale skin seemed whiter than before.

"Nothing," he said.

She babbled a short reply. The words were nonsense but the tone was watchful and ready.

They crept forward.

Da'dtou-di stumbled behind him. Apparently oomans didn't see well in the dark. She followed closer.

At the end of the corridor, another door, open. Dachande heard the *kainde amedha* as they skittered somewhere beyond. He ducked his head to get through the portal and discovered that he would have to move in a crouch through the next hall; the ooman ceiling was lower here.

Dachande had gone into three nests before this one. But always with fully stocked burners and at least a handful of armed yautja with him. Not to mention that he felt like a month old *rjet* turd—his side ached from the drone attack and each deep breath burned somewhere inside. From his experience and the way he felt, the wounds were fairly serious. Well. Nothing to be done about it.

He wasn't afraid, Blooded warriors seldom were in battle. But he accepted that dying could come easily here. He hoped it would come with honor. The real pity would be that there would be no one to tell the tale. No one except a small ooman—assuming she survived as well.

They moved forward in the thick dark.

Noguchi tripped on something and caught herself before she fell. There was virtually no light. Every dozen paces or so, a small dim emergency torch set high into the wall illuminated just enough to make it seem darker. She could make out her own weapon and Broken Tusk's back; beyond that, nothing.

The warrior seemed to be able to see better. He

must have done this a dozen times, and he obviously knew something about the aliens' behavior—

Noguchi felt her gut clench at the sound of movement ahead somewhere. She gripped her weapon tighter, her eyes wide and semiblind.

They stepped into a second corridor, the air grew muggier as they progressed. Their footsteps were oddly muffled by the strange alien material that lay thick on the floor.

She should be in front, she knew that; Dachande had looked at the map Conover had given her, but his understanding of it couldn't be clear. Then again, he could *see* better, and was stronger—

As they neared the end of the second hallway, Noguchi heard another alien chitter, close.

From *behind* them.

Dachande whipped around at the drone's cry and pointed his burner.

Da'dtou-di had also heard it. She fired at the bug as it ran for them.

The shot from her burner hit the drone in the shoulder and spun it around. It didn't fall.

Dachande aimed his burner at the screaming creature. Light and heat spewed in a tight beam.

The drone's back exploded outward in a spray of corrosive blood and cooked entrails.

Footfalls. He spun. Two drones attacked from the front.

Dachande turned, got the first with his bladed wrist, a sharp slashing jab to the bug's throat.

The second clambered over its falling brother and reached for him. Dachande knocked it down, used the burner as a club to crush its jaws. Blood hissed over the durable metal and dripped to the floor, ate holes in the hard material.

Da'dtou-di inhaled sharply and fired past him, at a third drone.

And missed. The Hard Meat turned and sprinted away from them, down the third winding corridor, shrieking an alarm to the others. It was too stupid to be afraid so it must be a sentry.

Dachande cursed. Behind him, he was pretty certain Da'dtou-di did the same in her own language. He didn't need a translator to understand that.

Well, it just meant they'd have to hurry. He had hoped to make it farther . . .

The Leader picked up his pace and hit the hallway at a jog, Da'dtou-di right behind. Ahead, the Hard Meat waited.

She was terrified but ready. This had to be done or else the colonists would die—

And you, too, Machiko.

No shit.

At the end of the third hall, the corridor came to a T-junction. Noguchi pointed for Broken Tusk to turn left; she hoped she'd remember the rest as they came to it.

She moved blindly behind Broken Tusk. There would be a rung ladder on the right pretty soon—

—a bug hissed behind her. Noguchi turned and fired. The shots were deafening in the closed area. The alien's dying screams were quieter.

This was getting old real goddamn fast.

She turned again, just in time to see a bolt of hard light come from the warrior's weapon, accompanied by an echoey thud. It acted as a strobe, showed them a nightmare of dark limbs and shiny teeth.

More screaming.

Noguchi breathed the stifling air shallowly. Her body twitched and jumped as she searched the darkness for the ladder. Her chest had started to bleed again.

Maybe she was already dead and didn't realize it.

Maybe they were in hell.

Dachande felt the ooman slap him on the back and turned.

Da'dtou-di pointed up, her face distorted. She seemed disturbed, as far as he was able to read her expression.

He eyed the flimsy ladder and then started to climb; the narrow rungs allowed him to take three at a time.

Dachande reached the top and looked down at the small warrior. She swung her weapon in an arc; dull light glinted off the small metallic burner.

He looked up again, reached for the floor of the next level—

—a clawed hand dropped down to cover his own. The black talons etched into his wrist, raising small fountains of his blood.

The drone bent down and hissed into his face.

Noguchi looked up just in time.

The bug leaned toward Broken Tusk and opened its jaws.

She aimed and squeezed. The AP bullet went into the alien's mouth and out the back of its head. It fell forward, almost toppled Broken Tusk from the ladder, and then clattered to the floor. If the maker of this ammunition ever asked, she would give them a testimonial they wouldn't believe. This here stuff is a monster killer, never leave your cube without a few dozen rounds . . .

A shriek from her left.

She fired and fired again as they seemed to come at her from all sides. The noise was incredible—

Click.

That was louder.

Dachande stood up and hit the first drone to come at him with the weighted staff. It dropped, still alive but out of the fight. There was nothing behind it, at least for a few seconds.

He turned to cover Da'dtou-di on her climb, at the same time her weapon fire stopped.

A drone leapt at her, knocked her back against the ladder.

Dachande felt pure rage. He jumped from the second level, staff in front of him—

—and landed on the drone.

Like that, tarei hsan?

The drone did not. So he killed it.

Noguchi was dizzy. Broken Tusk stamped the life out of the bug that had grabbed her. He tucked her under his arm and ascended the rung ladder easily.

He set her down first and then pulled himself up after her. Noguchi reloaded her gun and then covered him, but the last few hissing shapes that were below backed away, then turned and scampered off. That didn't really seem like a victory, somehow.

She looked down the second level corridor. The next ladder would be at the end, but their escape was only a few meters away.

Much as she wanted Broken Tusk to come with her, someone needed to guard the escape pod. And Broken Tusk probably couldn't run a human computer—

At least the passage was clear for the moment.

They started down the second level.

The ooman paused midway down the hallway and then pointed at a doorway with odd figures scrawled on it. Ooman language.

She spoke something. Dachande hit the animal loop on his suit to record, in case it might later be helpful. Da'dtou-di motioned at him and then again at the door.

She wanted him to stay *here*?

Dachande growled, but Da'dtou-di was adamant. It was important to her.

It had been a long time since he had trusted another in battle. And now he was being asked to trust an *ooman*, not even an *un-Blooded* yautja!

She held up her clawless hand again and then backed away a few steps.

Dachande tilted his head at her.

Da'dtou-di spoke again and bared her teeth at him. And then she turned and ran ahead. He could take her head off with a swipe of his wrist blade and yet she showed him her teeth. Brave Little Knife. If she risked his wrath it must be important to her indeed. Well.

This was her kind's ship. She surely knew things about it he did not. She must have a plan.

Dachande stayed.

He tilted his head, which she thought meant affirmative.

Noguchi felt a rush of relief. She didn't want to part with him in this hot, deadly maze, but she'd need a clear path to get back. She only had maybe a dozen rounds left. It did not matter how good the ammo was if you were out of it; she hoped Broken Tusk had more for his weapon.

"Hold the fort," she said, and grinned tightly. She was scared and she hurt, but it felt powerful to be doing something. Something that might kill the infestation in her town ...

You hope.

"I'll be back when I'm done."

With that, she turned and ran. And prayed that he would be there when she got back.

If she got back.

The second ladder looked empty, but she couldn't see the top. The strange alien formations were thicker here, looped around the rungs and covered the wall.

She checked behind her again and started to climb, revolver in hand.

A drop of odd, warm goo smacked onto her arm. Then another.

She looked up.

Da'dtou-di hadn't indicated if she wanted the door he guarded open, but Dachande opened it anyway. The ooman wanted him to watch it for *some* reason.

It was locked, so he pounded at the frame with the end of his staff until it cracked.

It was a *tyioe-ti*, an escape pod, small but large enough for the two of them. He stepped in and surveyed it quickly. Not a nesting area. Three ooman-sized chairs and a panel of controls. He'd never be able to squeeze into one of those tiny seats to fly this craft.

He turned and stood at the entry to wait for Da'dtou-di. And he heard a resounding crash from the direction they had come from, followed by a low, scratchy hiss.

Dachande tensed. It was a sound he had heard before.

A queen. Heading in this direction.

Was it the one they had brought on their ship, egg-layer of their prey? Or had one of the drones shifted hormones and metamorphosed into a female?

Not that it really mattered, just at the moment.

He waited.

Noguchi looked up and stopped breathing.

One of the bugs had leaned down from the third level, its long, misshapen skull right above her. Another drop of slime fell from its jaws—

She brought her pistol up and rammed the barrel into its mouth. She jerked the trigger again and again.

The creature didn't even cry out. It fell past her with a clattering thud. It was a small miracle that none of its acidic blood splashed onto her.

Her hands shook as she topped the ladder. Surely there would be another at the top, waiting to tear at her, to rip out her throat—

Noguchi pulled herself up and on to her knees. The

platform was coated heavily with the dark alien material, but otherwise empty.

She jumped to her feet and ran down the hall. At the end was another tee. Without hesitation, she took a right and continued on. The hot, sticky air made it a struggle to breathe. It smelled like rotten mushrooms in here.

It wasn't until two more turns in the twisted corridor that she realized she had gone the wrong way.

Dachande took a deep breath and waited. There was no doubt that it was the queen, or that she was headed toward him.

Drones were target practice, but a queen egg-layer—

No lone yautja had ever survived combat with one, unless he had a burner. Once, a dozen Blooded warriors had taken one down with only blades and spears, but the queen had killed nine of them before she died.

Metal creaked and groaned from below. At least he still had a fire in his burner. Two of them.

A crest of shiny black appeared at the top of the ladder . . .

Dachande pointed and fired.

Missed.

The Hard Meat ducked and screamed, but was uninjured. He took aim and waited for her to come up.

Nothing happened for several beats. Dachande remained ready.

Suddenly she howled and a dark shape sprang into view at the top of the ladder.

Dachande fired, his last shot.

The head of the creature exploded.

He roared in triumph and threw the empty burner at the bubbling mess. The useless weapon skipped over the platform and disappeared. He had killed her, had Hunted a queen and killed her! The stories of their intelligence and skill had been wrong, she had been an easy target—

The queen hissed again and the crest of her unmistakable skull rose into view.

Dachande's eyes widened. But he had blown her to pieces—!

Decoy. She had sent a drone to take the shots; he had been tricked.

But how could she know that—?

It didn't matter. The deadly queen was alive, and she was coming.

S'yuit-de!

He watched as two huge talons screeched across the metal platform and pulled the grinning monster into view.

Noguchi didn't bother with the map. She knew where she'd fucked up.

There was a second of initial panic. She'd actually *left* him there to wait for her, stupid, stupid—!

Noguchi brought it under control and turned back.

She was almost back to where she had taken the wrong turn when one of the nightmare creatures leapt out of nowhere to land in front of her.

She pointed and fired several times. The snarling animal shrieked and fell.

Behind it was another. She pulled the trigger again, and it toppled on top of the other. There were no others.

Idiot! Your ammo!

A cold hand clutched at her heart. The gun was empty.

She ejected the spent shells and loaded the final rounds, hands shaking harder now.

Six rounds.

Noguchi came to the tee and ran straight. For one terrifying moment she felt totally lost, but then she saw the door. Yellow and black lines, just as Conover had said.

She aimed as carefully as she could and blew the lock off of the door. Bits of plastic and metal spewed and stung her face and hands. The door opened to reveal a room full of panels and screens. This was the central computer room, according to what Conover told her. The ship's brains.

Noguchi slammed the door behind her and ran to the second chair.

Second chair, straight on, disk slot next to red and black strip—

She hit the transmitter's power switch and waited for the panel to light up. She took Scott's disk from her pocket and held it tightly. The seconds stretched like minutes. Hours. Eons . . .

There was an empty coffee cup on the console in front of her with "Conover" stenciled on the side. She felt a stab of pity for the pilot; he had died bravely.

The screen glowed to life with a stream of numbers and letters at the top. She carefully inserted the disk into the slot and pushed the lock button.

The computer hummed and blinked. Noguchi felt her breath catch.

If this doesn't work, you're dead—

A light flashed: *Dir. received/pil. S. Conover, 93630/navigational complete.*

She slapped the board. "Yes, yes, *yes!*"

It had worked.

She turned just as the door burst inward.

Dachande straightened his back and took a deep breath. If this was to be his Final Hunt, he would die fighting. Combat against a queen with only a staff—it was an honor. He would fight and he would lose but that was the only choice.

From the way Da'dtou-di had gone he heard her weapon crash several times. He tuned it out. She would have to complete her mission alone.

The queen was huge, twice as large as a drone. Her arms were longer—she had a second, smaller set protruding from her chest—her crown sleek and branched almost like antlers. Her double jaws held more than two rows of shiny teeth. And being female, she would know how to fight.

She moved toward him slowly. Her long, pointed tail dragged across the metal floor.

Dachande raised his staff and held it out slightly, legs spread wide. If she came at him like he thought she would, he would get in at least one clean cut.

The queen towered in the corridor, bent almost in half to move.

Dachande held steady. He said, "Come, Hard Meat. I killed your children. Come and join them." An unlikely boast and neither could she understand it, but smiling into the face of Death was said to sometimes unnerve even the Black Warrior.

A sudden noise behind him called for his attention, but he didn't take his eyes from her.

She swung her head to look past him and hissed.

Dachande's eyes flickered. Was there someone—?

The queen leapt—

* * *

Noguchi blew the bug's brains across the hall with two shots.

The dark jellied mass splatted against the corridor wall and ran down in clumps.

She jumped over the corpse and into the passageway. She sprinted for the tee.

It was over, or it would be soon. The barge was going to fall like a meteor, like an atomic-powered meteor and when it hit, it would take out what was left of Prosperity Wells. And the rest of the alien brood. There wouldn't be anything remaining here but a smoldering crater.

The escape pod should get them far enough out of town—

At the turn to get back to the ladder, the corridor beyond exploded into motion.

Noguchi let out a cry and then aimed at one of the bugs that sprang for her. The bullet knocked it down, still shrieking.

Two shots now, only two left—

Noguchi reached the top of the rung ladder down to the second level. The ladder was twisted, torn loose from the wall. Shit—!

"Broken T—!"

She stopped. Below her, the warrior stood. And faced one of the nightmare creatures, a giant, huge, it filled the entire corridor!

At the sound of her voice, the monster looked up and hissed, a horrible, raspy sound that chilled her to the pit of her soul.

—Queen—

It spun and lashed out at Broken Tusk as Noguchi aimed her handgun at it.

The impossibly long and heavy tail crashed against the warrior's chest. His spear flew and he was knocked flying.

She heard the sound of the impact from where she was. Broken Tusk smacked against the door he guarded and bounced off it. His blood seemed to glow against his dark armor. He didn't move.

Noguchi fired, her chest tight. The queen screamed and turned toward her.

The bullet missed.

Without thinking, Noguchi jumped to the second level, revolver in front of her. One shot left. One chance.

Her knees buckled as she hit the platform, but she didn't fall.

The queen shrieked and started for her.

Noguchi prayed that one bullet would stop her—
—fired—
—and the monster fell backward, screamed, and thrashed on the floor. Chest shot.

Not dead, but down.

Noguchi ran to Broken Tusk. She dropped the empty weapon. The nightmare queen's tail lashed out and would have knocked her down if she hadn't jumped.

Broken Tusk took the lash again in the chest. Blood spattered.

Noguchi kicked at the door to the escape pod and stumbled. The inner hatch was open.

The queen screamed, a piercing howl. Her death chant, Noguchi hoped.

She bent over the injured warrior and got one arm under him. With strength she didn't know she had, she lifted with a grunt—

—and he slid with her into the pod.

Sweat ran down her face. She pulled again, and his feet cleared the door.

No time, no time—

She half fell into a chair in front of the panel and searched frantically for the control.

Behind her, the alien screamed again in pain and fury.

Broken Tusk groaned and rolled toward Noguchi.

Noguchi found the button, right in front of her. In her panic she had missed it.

Movement behind her. A scream that sent hot, charnel, rotting air across her back.

She half turned, hand on the button—

—and the queen was *there*, her head in the pod, her huge claw came down—

—and embedded in the warrior's shoulder.

Broken Tusk screamed.

Noguchi slammed the door's override button.

The thick metal door closed. The grinning head seemed to rush at her—

—and then toppled to the floor as the pressure door, designed to seal the ship against hard vacuum, crunched the exoskeleton of the monster's relatively thin neck and beheaded the queen.

Her disembodied hand was still buried in the motionless warrior's back.

Noguchi hit the next button.

And they were free of the larger ship, flying.

The pain was bad, but Dachande let it happen.

He didn't understand it for a moment. It. Something. Da'dtou-di, was she here? Had they killed her?

He felt oddly weightless for a short time—

—flying—

And then the floor rose up and slammed against him.

There was a burst of new pain. Gravity returned, with more aches than he'd ever had. He was hurt, badly hurt.

Then a rush of hot, clean air. Light assaulted his eyes. His breathing mask was gone. Too much of the planet's combustive oxygen flooded into his lungs. He couldn't last more than a few hours breathing such potent air.

He coughed. Warm liquid ran down his throat, but it still felt raw, wounded.

A shadow moved over him. He was lifted slightly and pulled.

He growled in pain but couldn't seem to form a protest. The air blinded him. He was outside.

He opened his eyes slowly and focused on the face that hovered over his.

Da'dtou-di!

He felt a burst of pride. She had survived, had helped him.

Dachande started to speak and coughed again. More pain.

He reached for the loop on the arm of his suit, but his fingers had grown clumsy.

Da'dtou-di placed her fragile hand under his and moved it for him.

Noguchi's throat felt tight. There was a stone in her chest, heavy and painful. Pale blood covered the warrior, his breathing slow and labored. He was dying.

They had made it. The pod had landed with a jarring impact somewhere in the east desert, far from

Prosperity Wells; the chute had opened at least. But . . .

Broken Tusk raised a shaky hand toward his other wrist, but couldn't seem to maneuver it well. Noguchi guided it for him.

It was the recording device. She felt her eyes brim as her own voice spilled out.

"Hold the fort. I'll be back when I'm done."

Broken Tusk grabbed at the alien claw, still embedded in his shoulder. "Hang on," she said. "Help will be here soon, the colonists will come—" She faltered and choked. Then gave him what she felt he needed. "We did it. We killed the bugs. The queen. You and I." She waved her hand, feeling helpless.

He pulled the queen's claw loose and looked at it.

She pointed at it, nodded, made a throat-cutting gesture.

He understood. She was sure of it, because he nodded in return. Then he grasped one of the long, spidery digits and snapped it off, groaned with the exertion. Hissing blood dripped from the finger.

Broken Tusk then motioned at the mark on his face, a jagged bolt between his eyes. He motioned at her and then at the scar again.

Noguchi nodded and leaned closer.

Da'dtou-di had to be Blooded. It was his responsibility, as Leader.

Dachande tore off one of the queen's fingers. It hurt to move, to breathe, to live, but this was important; it was all he had left.

Da'dtou-di came closer, closed her eyes. Something wet splashed on Dachande' face; he ignored it. It was time.

The warrior dipped one claw into the alien blood and then spat on the claw. His own blood mixed with the alien's acidic ichor. That was part of it. His blood would partly neutralize the potent chemicals from the Hard Meat. Moving with great care, he reached out and etched his mark into her pale skin, on the forehead, between her eyes. He managed to keep his hand from shaking long enough to draw his symbol.

She hissed in pain, but didn't move. She was brave, Little Knife. She had helped him and they had killed the queen. That was something to take and lay at the feet of the Black Warrior.

Dachande dropped his hand, exhausted. The animal loop played again, some ooman speak from long before. It didn't matter; he had been ready for a long time and now was the moment. He had no complaints.

He wished he could talk in her language, teach her what he could—be brave, Hunt well, respect your Leader. But she already knew most of that. The rest, she would surely learn. She was Blooded now, and somehow she would learn. Even though they had only been together a short time, he knew all about her.

The best student he ever had.

Tears fell before Broken Tusk even touched her. She started to wipe at her eyes, but then closed them instead. The dying warrior was going to give her his mark, she understood what he wished. She leaned down.

The pain was short and burning. A trickle of green blood ran down her nose.

Broken Tusk dropped his hand, and her voice spoke again from the loop, softly this time.

"I'll remember you."

Noguchi lowered her head and started to sob, the first real tears she had cried in a long time.

Behind them, a light appeared in the sky. A ball of flame plummeted through the Ryushi sunlight, headed for Prosperity Wells.

Noguchi glanced behind her as the explosion thundered through the desert. The air around her compressed suddenly. Fiery air washed over them with the sound, the roar and rumble of it.

When the sound died, the town was gone. As quickly as that.

She turned back to the warrior. Buried her face in her hands and rocked slowly, back and forth.

Dachande had stopped breathing. Like the town, he was gone.

Epilogue

Dahdtoudi woke up early on the morning they came.

It was first light on the open plain that unfolded in front of her small home. She yawned and stretched as she climbed out of bed and glanced out the window. The air felt different somehow, electric—

Only two years before, she would have disregarded the sense of change as nonsense, superstition. But "quiet" didn't start to describe the experience of living on a world where she was the only human; she had developed a feel for Ryushi, the way an athlete could feel her body and its fluctuations. The air was different, no question. Something was going to happen.

Something.

She pulled on a coverall and slipped on her boots. She pulled her shaggy hair into a knot at the back of her neck as she walked into the tiny kitchen for a glass of water. The new well between her home and the near cliff was clean, the water sweet. No more riding twenty klicks for a shower at the old well, either.

Dahdtoudi drank the cool water slowly and thought about the day ahead. Yesterday, she had run through forms, so today was weight day. Also water day for the sheltered garden in the glassed shed behind the house. Tomorrow she would ride the east sector and check for visitors ...

She finished and set the glass in the sink. It was feeding time first.

Dahdtoudi walked outside and almost tripped on Creep. The dog jumped and wagged his tail, excited to see her.

She scruffed the dog behind his ears. "I'm excited, too, Creep. It's been what, six hours since last we met?"

Creep barked happily and followed her to the rhynth pen. He ran between her legs and almost knocked her over.

"Dumb dog," she said fondly. He barked again.

She couldn't look at the mutt without thanking Jame and Cathie silently. Creep had been good company, had kept loneliness from getting too big. They had acted as though it would be best for the dog, to be able to run free—but the gift had been for her, too.

"Good morning, kids."

The three rhynth that she kept turned their heads slowly to watch her approach. Spot, Milo, and Mim. They weren't as good at conversation as Creep, but they were tame. They also acted as transport; she had a flyer, but eventually her fuel would run out, so she saved it for emergencies. Keeping them as pets made it harder to eat meat, but it was a matter of survival. Besides, she only had to hunt once every two months or so . . .

Dahdtoudi dumped some grain in their trough and scratched Mim behind her leathery ears. The beast snorted and started to eat as if she'd been starving.

"Should have called you 'pig,' " said Dahdtoudi. The rhynth ignored her.

She walked back to the house and sat down on the front porch to watch the suns rise. There was enough light for her to see the queen's skull, bleached by the hot suns where it perched on her roof. Her trophy, hers and Broken Tusk's.

Creep lay down next to her and nuzzled her legs.

"What's different today, dog? Something is different."

Creep glanced at her and then rested his head on his paws. She patted his side and smiled.

They had been here alone for almost two years. After Broken Tusk had died, she had joined the colonists for the long wait. It had taken nearly two months before help had arrived, and by then her decision was made, was firm. Was irrevocable.

At first a couple of the ranchers had argued with her, but they soon gave up.

The company hadn't tried to change her mind at all. She could have been charged with something, however trumped up the charges would have been, but the final word was that "her actions had been dictated by necessity." Her executive contract had been quietly bought out, which was fine by her. Chigusa was worried about liability and declared the whole thing a write-off. The old man wasn't stupid. He gave her a permanent, official position as a "caretaker," and pulled his interests out of the Cygni system. He never threw good money after bad, so it was said, and he was superstitious about staying on a world so cursed as this one. The galaxy was full of worlds and the old man owned hundreds of them. He would never miss this one.

Only Roth and her spouse and Weaver had seemed to understand why she wanted to stay.

So the colonists had gone to start over again in the Rigel system, and she was left alone to start over on Ryushi. And she had been happy. For the first time in her life, there had been no dragons. There was only peace.

"Everything I care about is right here," she said softly.

Creep sighed, most likely bored. She'd had a lot of time to replay conversations and events in her mind, and the dog had suffered the same stories for two years.

A flash of movement in the morning sky caught her attention. For several seconds she thought she was seeing things; it had been so long . . .

The flash grew brighter and brighter. She watched its progress as it ripped through the air, the sound far away. Creep sensed her excitement and sat up, whining softly.

The object fell gracefully in an arc to land to the west, maybe half a day's ride by rhynth, maybe less. Dahdtoudi Noguchi stood quickly and tried not to get her hopes up.

Probably a meteor, that's all . . .

But she didn't really think so. She went to get ready.

* * *

Seven hours later, she dismounted Milo and moved through the harsh sunlight toward a small stand of rocks. She carried her binoculars and carbine; the company had left her with plenty of supplies.

A thin stream of smoke still rose from where the object had landed, in a small valley set among a stand of steep rock walls.

Dahdtoudi slipped between the rocks silently and propped herself up on a baked stone. She scanned left to right until she picked up the smoke—

A small vehicle on treads buzzed across the cracked dirt, maybe a hundred meters away. She zoomed in, her heart hammering.

Behind it was a trail that extended beyond her range of vision. A trail of spheres, oval-shaped—

Dahdtoudi lowered the viewer and stood for a moment. She rubbed absently at the jagged scar between her eyes, faded white now.

"It won't be long," she said. She would make them understand, tell them of Broken Tusk's bravery and skill. And how everything had gone wrong . . .

Milo gazed at her. She stretched her sore muscles and then mounted him for the ride home.

The Leader sighed inwardly at the yautja assembled before him. They were as ready as he could make them, pumped and hungry to kill. They stood in line next to the ship, their burners loaded and blades sharpened.

But he also had orders to seek after Dachande's group on this Hunt, an extra pain he could have done without. That ship had never returned.

He had known Dachande. Old broken tooth had been a good Leader and a strong warrior, but something had gone wrong, and those in charge wanted to know what. As they always did when it was not they who had to determine it.

Vk'leita shook his head as he reviewed the young yautja. He had Hunted with Dachande, he respected him, as had many—but he was surely dead, and dead was dead, all that mattered was the way of it. More than a long cycle had passed, probably too much time to ascertain much of anything. The dead from that trip would be sun-grayed bones scattered by the local scavengers by now.

He nodded at the other Blooded, Ci'tde. Ci'tde would take the group on the initial scouting trip. The Hunt would start in earnest after the light fell away.

The Leader stayed at the ship and ran through some practice drills while he was alone. Young males took a lot of energy to train, and he relished the time away from them. Besides, he would have to check the *ui'stbi*, the geography, for remnants of recent Hunting. He could do some through the ships' *gkinmara*, but much would have to be done on foot. He was looking forward to stretching himself, covering ground, loosening up the ship-stale muscles.

He finished practice and then sat on the ground to clean his armor. The yautja would not be back until the suns had passed through their high point, so he had plenty of time . . .

Behind him, a sound of movement.

Vk'leita was on his feet instantly. The sound had come from the other side of the ship. He snatched up his burner and started toward the sound.

He reached the front of the ship and let out a warning hiss.

Nothing.

Suddenly a small figure stepped into view. Vk'leita pointed at the creature and almost fired—

—he lowered the burner uncertainly. The creature was no yautja, it was the size of a child—but it wore armor and a wrist blade. The creature moved slowly toward him, hands out.

Ooman!

The Leader raised his weapon again. The sickly, pale, *ugly* face of it—

It stepped closer and tilted its head to one side.

He could have fired. Had the other yautja been there, he might have, that was the proper response to a threat. But this small creature did not seem particularly threatening, even though he knew the stories. And neither did it seem to be afraid. If anything, it carried itself proudly, almost as if it were a warrior. Oomans were supposed to be cowards, sneaky, deadly when cornered, but seldom stand-up face-on fighters. And it made him curious.

"Who are you?" said Vk'leita.

The ooman pointed at itself. "Da'dtou-di."

Vk'leita flared his mandibles. The creature's accent was awful, strange, but he understood. Female? An ooman female? The name was "small knife," feminine form—

Going against a lifetime of training, the Leader reslung his burner and moved closer. This bore investigation. The ooman stood still.

When he was a few paces away, he stopped and eyed the ooman carefully. It wore tresses like yautja, and carried the weapon; its pieced-together armor was part warrior—he recognized the Hard Meat shell—and part unknown.

The ooman motioned at itself again. "Da'dtou-di," it said again. It reached up and touched its face.

The Leader peered closer. It had a mark on its head. It looked like—no, it couldn't be. He took another two steps and bent to stare at the ooman. It did not flinch as he practically stuck his mask in the thing's face.

The mark—

It was *Blooded*! A Blooded ooman! That couldn't be! It was not possible. But there was the mark, right *there*! and, and—the mark was—

Dachande's.

What the unholy *pauk*?

Vk'leita growled. "You know Dachande? Where is he?"

Da'dtou-di shook her head and then pointed at him. She touched her own face again, now where mandibles would be if she were yautja. With one of her fingers, she mimed a break.

As if a mandible were broken. Dachande.

"Go on."

The ooman used her hands as teeth and made tearing movements with them. Then motioned "Dachande" again. *Thei-de*. Dachande was dead.

Da'dtou-di moved closer to him and then cautiously reached up to rest her tiny hand on his shoulder. She *greeted* him.

Vk'leita tilted his head, fascinated, and returned the gesture. This was unheard of. He was standing here as if he had a brain listening to a *pauking* ooman talk to him in sign language, telling him about the death of a Blooded warrior. She was *ooman*, but she called herself Da'dtou-di in the warrior's tongue. She bore Dachande's mark, no way around that, no warrior would tell an alien what that mark meant, much less how to apply it, not under any circumstances. And she had come to him to speak of Dachande's death. But something else, too . . .

"Hunt?" Vk'leita asked. "You've come to Hunt with us?" He unsheathed his blade and made jabbing movements in the air.

Da'dtou-di tilted her head and exposed her small teeth. She raised one arm into the air and threw back her head. A long, strange cry came from her, of aggression and eagerness, he guessed.

The Leader listened to the eerie sound and then circled the ooman. She was little, but moved well; she carried the marks of a warrior, and she had known Dachande. He studied her thoughtfully.

This was unprecedented, but there was really only one option. She was Blooded. However it had come to be, there it was. The rules of the Hunt had never been stretched so much, he was sure of that. But what could he do? He was a warrior, he had his code and he had lived his life with it too long to deny it now. He would let her Hunt with them. Perhaps they could exchange languages, and he would learn Dachande's fate. Perhaps she would choose to leave with them, to return to their home and teach them ooman ways—surely that would be a great victory, to have found an ooman warrior?

Well. Perhaps covered much of the galaxy, didn't it? Who could say?

The Leader raised his own arm and howled. After a moment, Da'dtou-di joined him.

There was much that they could teach one another.

ALIENS
VS.
PREDATOR
HUNTER'S PLANET

For Donald Maass

Special thanks for the able editorial input from Kij Johnson and Janna Silverstein

PROLOGUE

Dtai'k-dte sa-de nav'g-
kon dtain'aun bpide.

"The fight begun would not end until the end."
Tarei'hasan shit.

Nat'ka'pu illustrated how silly the old yautja saying
was by feinting to the left, then slipping around the
sparring spear thrust out by his opponent. With aston-
ishing speed the Leader followed through with a lightning lunge, grasping the edge of the student's mask
and ripping it off his face, shearing off a couple of
tightly bound ringlets of hair in the process. Yellow
eyes blazed with surprise. Mandibles clicked with
shame. The student yawked with displeasure, at-
tempting to slap Nat'ka'pu back with the blunt side of
the spear. But with a creaking heave of his armor the
Master took advantage of the cocky student's bad po-

sitioning, hacking down on the elbow with the blunt edge of his leather gauntlet, forcing the weapon to slap down onto the floor. Then, before the snot-nosed fool could even begin another sorry howl, the expert reached in and boxed the warrior's right tusk so hard that it looked to the others as though the young one's head would be ripped from his muscle-grieved neck. The student could only give to the force so adroitly positioned. With a gasp he toppled to his knees.

"Nain-desintje-da."

The pure win, of course. Nat'ka'pu expected nothing less of himself. However, he spat upon his victim with open contempt. The fool should have lasted longer in battle. For all his young pride and strength, he was one of the more thoughtless sparring partners that the Leader had ever faced.

"You have much work before you if you wish to feel the sting of the Hard Meat's *thwei* upon your brow—if you survive that long."

The student—a snarly, oily fellow named Ki'vik'-non—just glared back silently and woodenly.

"Get away from my sight," snapped the Leader. "Go and wash disgrace and defeat from your eyes. And cleanse your ears as well. You smell of childbearer's musk. Hurry, Ki'vik'non—or your betters will wish to mate with you."

The cruel joke set the others on the deck of the ship into a braying, clicking laughter—derision. With as much dignity as he could muster under the circumstances, the fallen would-be warrior rose to his feet with a clatter and creak of his *awu'asa*. Sunken deep in their orbs, his yellow eyes shone hatred and disrespect before he clanked back into the ranks. Something was wrong with this one, Nat'ka'pu thought. This Ki'vik'non lacked the sense of honor that drove a good warrior. He bore watching. Nor would it be a good idea to turn his back on Ki'vik'non when they were alone.

Suddenly the enunciator in the wall of the *kehrite* blared.

"*Kainde amedha!*"

The Leader's mandibles rippled with satisfaction, even anticipation.

He turned to the younglings, his eyes blazing with challenge.

"Prepare your souls for some *true* action!"

The ship of the yautja descended from the clouds and skated across the tops of trees. This was a fertile planet, which suited yautja purposes just fine. Besides its variety of terrain, it had plenty of species of life, many quite vicious and dangerous, making it prime Hunting material.

The yautja were Hunters who traveled from world to world, proving themselves with the skill of their kills. Nor was Hunting just sport for them; it was a way of life. It was the Path. The philosophy that bound their bones more surely than did their sinews. They were Predators, and they often ate what they could, but more often they collected and preserved only trophies to testify to their prowess. They were Predators of meat physical, meat spiritual, and below their ship now was one of their favorite tastes in predatory effort.

Kainde amedha. Hard Meat.

And Hard in more ways than one.

Upon this Hard Meat, sown in chosen areas, the youth of this race cut their tusks. Upon this Hard Meat, the inexperienced learned the Truth of the Path, turned experience into value, came of age, became a true yautja and could father younglings with pride and pass on the courage and honor that separated Beings of Will from the dross of mere instinctual life.

The Hard Meat was valuable prey for the Hunter, because it could turn the tables with a flick of a claw.

There was no more valuable target for Predators than
other predators, for in difficulty is there courage and
honor. And honor and courage were of paramount
value in these creatures' lives.

Their ship looked like a combination between a
fish and a huge engine tube. With a strange flash of
greenish hue, it landed in a clearing. A broad ramp extended from it, and down the ramp the Hunting party
strutted. Seven of them there were: four students, the
Leader, and two adjutants. The students and Nat'ka'pu
carried only spears; the adjutants carried burners.

They were giants, these warriors. Their average
height was two and a half meters, and even the short-
est, at a mere two meters, had broad shoulders and
biceps that strained against their leather jerkins. They
wore armor and masks, and their tough, wirelike hair
hung in dreadlocks from the back of their necks. The
first step toward becoming a warrior was the agony of
the pleating of these locks, a process that took
months of ritual and scalp pain, performed in public
sessions. If there was any sign of tears or even the ti-
niest voicing of pain, then the intricate weavings
would be undone, and the candidate had to start from
the beginning.

Nat'ka'pu was in the forefront of the party, as befitted his rank. The two adjutants held sight-amplification
equipment. They quickly scanned the terrain. The short
one grunted, then pointed.

The prey was spotted.

Nat'ka'pu called for the binoculars. He trained
them on the bushes, saw the squatting, partly hidden
form of the Hard Meat.

How odd. It was not a Queen, and yet it was dis-
cernibly larger than the average drone. The Leader
tapped his mandibles thoughtfully against his mask,
then turned to face his charges.

"Who demands the honor of facing this fresh Meat
first, alone?"

They all brandished their weapons as one, fiercely and yet quietly. This was all part of the ceremony.

Nat'ka'pu laughed mockingly. "You are fools, all of you, and yet at the first part of the Path lies the door of the fool."

"Perhaps you should show us the door, Leader," suggested Ki'vik'non.

"Perhaps I should show your intestines the point of my spear!" barked the commander.

"It is true," said the short adjutant, whose name was Lar'nix'va. "These are rank beginners and have never sucked Hard Meat before. It is not fitting that a few feints be made by the Blooded—especially when the Blooded is said to have fought the Hard Meat bare-fisted."

"And torn off its head!" spat Nat'ka'pu proudly. "Very well. But mark my methods, for I will leave the final killing to you, my students."

That said, the Leader turned and walked jauntily. He'd weaken the thing so that his charges could dispatch it easily. It had been a long day, and he was looking forward to going back and selecting a bulb of *c'ntlip* to drink with his bloody meal, to the relaxation it would bring and the pleasant dreams of his wives, waiting for his valiant seed back home.

The yautja called this world Var. It was used only off and on for Hunting, despite its merits. The Brave People were vagabonds of a sort and had a wide field in which to range, touching on a variety of worlds. Too long in one place created stale *kv'var*—exercises. It blunted the warrior's soul, and made the Path rocky and illusory.

When a flotilla of ships had returned to Var, however, there was a distinct change. There were *oomans* here now, that new growth of intelligent Soft Meat who were colonizing worlds. Nat'ka'pu knew that yautja lore spoke of many expeditions to the homeworld of the *oomans* with delicious results. Adventures to make a warrior smack his lips. The notion of performing *kv'var* on a world where humans had settled—albeit only in one small area, and with odd purposes and circumstances—stirred his blood. At the very least, hiding their activities from the Soft Meat would give him a sense of superiority. And if Nat'ka'pu actually encountered them and was forced to hunt *oomans*? Well, then, all the better. Nat'ka'pu could use some *ooman* skulls to dangle from his trophy cages. Perhaps that would even gain him some new conquest with females.

The thought stirred his seed within his loins and churned up his blood. He could feel the aggression knotting in his muscles, and his great heart beat a song of battle.

He advanced, his spear held out in front of him, part of the ritual of Readiness.

The Hard Meat did not stir behind the covering of the bush, which was not unusual. It was daylight, and though the Hard Meat was not nocturnal, it preferred to slink through areas of darkness. That it was out in the open at all was a wonder, but then, Nat'ka'pu had seen them in such circumstances before. Nor did they usually travel alone, though the detectors showed no other Hard Meat in the area. Just as well, however. The situation suited him perfectly. It was as though it were tailor-made for such a training exercise, and Nat'ka'pu was never one to push away a challenge of fate, even when it was presented upon a tray of precious metal.

Had he merely wanted to kill the beast, he would have approached it in his shiftsuit and turned a burner on it. There was no valor in that, though, and certainly no lesson for the snot-noses.

No, he had to face the thing full on.

However, for the beast to be fought properly, it had to be aware of his presence. This one seemed to be in an odd and awkward kind of repose. If it had been dead, their sensors would not have picked up its signs.

So what was wrong with it?

Carefully, his warrior's instinctual antennae out and questing for information, Nat'ka'pu advanced, his spear firmly placed before him, ready for any sudden charges.

He came into full view of the creature.

The Hard Meat was indeed a large one.

It looked like the obscene skeleton of some larger monster, and Nat'ka'pu could feel the familiar worm of fear threatening to wriggle in his gut. His said his *kantra*, though, which kept the fear at bay, and used the spurt of adrenaline to sharpen his senses.

Yes, the monster was obscene in every sense.

Part reptilian, part insect, part arachnid, and all evil, with no glow of nobility or honor whatsoever. Just sheer vicious need to kill and procreate.

Its head was like a banana with teeth. No eyes. It had a reptilian tail, and long mantislike limbs. Pipes rose from its back like periscopes out of hell.

Something different about this one, thought Nat'ka'pu. Something odd, besides its large size.

His boot stepped on a dry twig.

Snap.

The response was immediate.

The Hard Meat rose up like a vehicle on hydraulic crane legs, and a soul-chilling hiss escaped from its mouth. Thick saliva dripped from its jaws, and it reared up for what looked like the beginning of a charge.

Nat'ka'pu went immediately into the Warrior's Stance, the position from which all martial-arts moves in such Hunt battles derived. His mind spun ahead, calculating the maneuvers that would be necessary when this creature attacked.

The Hard Meat always attacked. These were not shy creatures. They were vicious fighters, albeit with limited intelligence. They were tenacious and cunning, with a terrible focus, and deadly weapons at their disposal. Even in Death they could be deadly; their blood was acid that could eat through some yautja armor, all yautja flesh.

The review flashed in his mind.

When facing Hard Meat with only a spear, the best course of action was a penetration into the thing's inner defenses and then a quick upthrust through the bottom of the head, into a portion of the brain that would paralyze it. At that point, one could carve the thing up at leisure. The challenge in this situation was to duel with it only awhile, perhaps slightly incapacitating it, so that the students would have an easier road to the final victory. A wound to the thorax perhaps, or a lopped-off limb.

Hiss.

The thing rose up and down, almost challenging.

Nat'ka'pu's mandibles bristled. He could taste the blood of victory in his mouth, even against the harsh, fearful smell the thing was exuding.

He raised his spear and chanted that most Holy of Holies, the Warrior's Song, that blast of wind and rain that terrified greater prey than this.

Then, pride and joy brimming in his veins, he advanced upon the next leg of the Path.

The *kainde amedha* suddenly stooped.

When it came back up, it was holding something in its limbs.

That was one of the things that was different about the thing, Nat'ka'pu realized. The limbs were different. At their ends were structures very like hands.

And in those hands now was a weapon.

No! Was this a dream? Hard Meat couldn't hold weapons.

But before he could think anymore, the weapon gave off a blast of fire that cut through Nat'ka'pu like a giant saber, and the Great Path suddenly dropped away like a trapdoor into pitiless darkness.

Lar'nix'va watched as the explosive bullets rammed through his commander's armor, watched as they blew his head and chest apart like ripe *naxa* fruit.

He did not watch for long, however, for action in the life of the warrior was the stuff of survival. This was no longer an exercise, this was the real thing, and something incredibly unexpected had just happened.

Raising his burner, he ran forward, calling out a terse command for the other adjutant to do likewise. The moment he was within striking distance, he pressed the trigger. A stream of power and flame streaked out, attaching itself to the Hard Meat before the creature had the chance to swing its weapon around.

The thing screamed and fought against the power, but it was blown back, blazing, pieces of its chitinous body tearing off.

The blast of his fellow adjutant pushed it over, finishing the destruction. The Hard Meat was soon a pyre of death.

When the flames died down, the group walked through the gory ground, littered with the blood of their commander.

"I am Leader now," stated Lar'nix'va matter-of-factly. "Is there any challenge?"

There was none. Astonishment hung heavy amid the stink of Death.

When the dead creature had cooled, one of the students stirred the remains with the end of his spear.

Lar'nix'va looked down, deeper astonishment filling him at the remains of the creature.

A guttural snarl tore from his lips.

"What is happening upon this planet?" he said.

None of the others had an answer.

Lar'nix'va swung back and walked to his ship through the splattered body of Nat'ka'pu.

The flotilla would need to be contacted.

This business bore evil portent, and from his life experience, the short yautja suspected who lay at the root of it all.

For whenever there were *oomans* on a planet, there was always trouble.

Peace can kill."

Machiko stared at the blocky letters she'd just written on her blotter for a moment, then with a red pen commenced to illuminate the *P*, like a dusty old monk at work on some Gothic Bible.

The cursor of her desk-bulb computer blinked blindly at her. A stack of input crystals lay inert atop her IN compartment. A mug of coffee with a dead multilegged, multieyed insect afloat on its turgid surface sat to one side, beside a half-finished piece of dunktoast. The gray, flat plains of Alistair Three stretched out from her window like nothing, squared.

The warrior was bored.

The memories of battle lived inside her like bloody monuments to a time when she'd been truly alive.

A time of danger, nobility—

And yes, honor.

She'd been a different person then.

Buddha, how she'd changed.

Ryushi had changed her. Her time with the yautja pack had changed her. Both to the better, she thought. At the core of her soul, before, there had been shame. Her father had brought shame upon her Japanese family in Kyoto, embezzling from his company and then taking a coward's way out by killing himself before he could be jailed. "You are my flesh, Machiko," he had said. "You must restore the family's honor."

And then his blood had spilled.

Machiko Noguchi had tasted honor when the bugs had been loosed upon her town of Prosperity Wells, fighting alongside Dachande and his warriors. When she had joined the Hunter Pack, she had literally *become* honor. But then, later, her humanity had called to her upon that miner's world, and although honor demanded that she fight against the pack to save her *ooman* genetic kin, it had meant betraying her place in the pack. And now, stuck back in the muddle of humanity again, she had lost that sense of honor, become merely quotidian.

And oh, yes—a little snarly, a little bitter.

She stared morosely at her vague reflection in the computer screen. A few lines had formed beneath her dark Japanese eyes, and her short black hair was a little gray, but otherwise she was an attractive woman. Small-breasted, muscular, a compact beauty. It was lost on her, though. She longed for more.

She sighed.

You'd think the Company would at least let her bring Attila on shift. At least then she'd have someone to talk to. She wouldn't have to resort to doodling. However, the last thing the Company was interested in was her mental health. As far as they were concerned, she could *drool* and doodle here, just as long as she got her job done. Just as long as she stayed out of trouble.

If only they didn't have that contract hanging over her like the sword of Damocles. If only she had money, a ftl-ship—a business plan ...!

If only ...

A high-pitched voice from a grille molded into the framework of the desk beside the computer facet interrupted her reverie.

"Ms. Noguchi!"

She started, then immediately realized who it was. How many times had she wished that she could yank this infernal radio-comm from its mooring and toss it into the garbage blaster? Freedom would break out. Peace from the incessant whine of the planet's Company president ... a man who made certified anal retentives seem relaxed and carefree.

"Yes, Mr. Darkins."

"How's that oversheet coming?"

"It's going well."

"Good. Glad to hear it. I need not remind you that it's due in my office at the end of the week. Company heads are expecting a subspace transmission then, and a comprehensive one. I trust that it will be a better job than last time."

"I think it will satisfy them."

"Good. Glad to hear it. You've got an important job, Ms. Noguchi. An important job, on an important planet."

The transmission ended, with a faint buzzing sound like the annoying song of a rat-fly.

Sure.

Important, her *butt*.

Alistair Three—also known as Doc's World—was a planet with a perfect rotation, a perfect distance from the sun, a perfect atmosphere ... perfect, that was, for a blandly uniform surface, with bland cattlelike grazers on its vast plains, few mountain ranges. Its weather was boring, its oceans were dull and luster-less; all its specifics were the epitome of monotony. One of these days humans from other planets would get around to fully populating this planet, but for right now there were far more appealing planets to go to, with much less distance between them and the rest of the human part of the galaxy.

What interested the corporation enough to dip its tentacles down into Doc's World (named after one of the men who'd discovered it, Doc Warden, an alco-holic ne'er-do-well whose ship had gotten lost, and whose comment on Alistair Three was "Makes me want another drink") was simple.

The mining.

Not that Doc's World had anything like rubies or di-amonds or unusual precious gems.

No, what it had was *narkon* ore, a curious grade of ore created by Alistair Three's unique mineral vulcan-ization process, which the corporation liked to use in its starship engines. Thus it had set up this Blakean "dark satanic mill" to mine and process said ore, then to transport it to satellites and moons where the ship-building was accomplished. Almost ten thousand peo-ple lived here in Solitaire City. Many were miners who took a daily troop train twenty miles south to a moun-tain range where they worked. Many were the miners' companions who often as not went with them. A few were supervisors and managers. A few more were bu-reaucrats. Machiko was one of those few—albeit on a top echelon—and she loathed it.

And to think of what her past had been.

To think that she had once run with a Predator pack.

Oh, how the Mighty had fallen.

She sighed and tapped up the spreadsheet. She be-gan to examine the data that had been entered by oth-ers, and to send the computer through its analytic paces so that the corporation would have the precious vital statistics it needed. She stared awhile at the screen, and then she put in another crystal, adding a new matrix of information.

Juggle, juggle.

Toil, trouble.

After a while, she saved her work. She sipped her coffee. And then she stared off into the plain plains of this nothing world, remembering what it had been like to fly with lightning in her wings.

2

Machiko, warrior, looked around and found herself surrounded by Death.

The bugs.

For a brief moment fear exploded inside her. Then she realized that fear was her friend. It helped limn the borders between life and death, light and dark. It plumbed the depths of her soul and biochemistry, bringing up the thunder of valor and the controlled explosion of adrenaline.

Up ahead Top Knot, running point, aimed a strafe of plasma. The fiery stuff raked across a line of the aliens, cracking their chitin into cinders. Lethal acid splashed back, boiling into acrid steam.

Others of the pack added to the fire, tearing a wide hole in the jumble of the bugs, the swelling ranks pouring forth through tunnels to protect their hive.

The pack had just landed on this planet in the majestic and silvery craft that was their starship. Their mission was simple: secure this hive's Queen for their own purposes. Simple though their goal might be, the road there was not.

She was working with a pack of yautja on perhaps one of their most dangerous objectives—indeed, so dangerous that the Predator Hunter's normal codes of conduct in the pursuit went right out the window.

For this expedition, anyway, the ritual laws of matching the quarry weapon for weapon were suspended.

The naginatas and scatterguns prescribed for hunting the *kainde amedha*, the Hard Meat, were replaced by plasma-casters and lasers.

This was no Hunting trip.

This was war.

Just as it had generally been in the history of her own *ooman* peoples, there are no rules in war.

Only objectives.

Machiko, warrior, was no longer Machiko Noguchi. No longer a streamlined ramrod for the corporation on a planet of alien cattle. She was Dahdtoudi, proud and brave warrior, who had proved herself on the planet called Ryushi and was Blooded by no less than the great Dachande, a great Predator Leader. Dahdtoudi. "Little Knife." The lightning scar that he had etched on her forehead just before his death with the acid of a broken bug finger, partly neutralized by his bloody spittle, marked her glory for life. When the pack searching for Dachande and his ill-fated mission, headed by the valiant Vk'leita, had discovered Machiko, she was Dahdtoudi, and she bore Dachande's mark and had a Queen's skull hanging above the door of her home. She'd been one of the surviving *oomans*—humans—on Ryushi. She had no particular reason to stay, seeing as she no longer felt committed to the Company, and every reason to go with the yautja. With the alien Hunters she found the core of honor, a state that eradicated the shame that had descended upon her family when her father, having been caught embezzling funds from his family, had committed a bloody seppuku. But a suicide without honor. Though she had excelled scholastically and then corporately, this was a pain and shame that had always hung over her, crippling her relations with other people. She had found it difficult to get close to people, but there was always the desire. Now there was no reason to get close to the yautja. Here, thus released, she could test herself, test her courage and skills, test all the things that would lead her into the state of grace shown her by Dachande.

As a Blooded One, she'd been entitled to come for Hunts.

She felt a real and profound need for that now, a vital desire to pursue honor and valor and the ways of the yautja.

A desire she needed to explore.

And so now, here she was—

They moved through the birthing chambers. Remains of ill-fated denizens of this foggy world—apelike creatures with four arms, big jaws, and elephantine ears—hung from the walls, their chests burst, their innards in various states of decomposition. The smell was beyond description, beyond bad—cloying and gagging. If not for the filters in the mask they'd given her, Machiko would not have been able to make it through that funk. Well, perhaps ... After all, she was no longer Machiko, she was Dahdtoudi, and she had not yet fully tested what Dahdtoudi could take.

Whatever it was, she knew it was going to have to be a lot. She'd braced herself for this raid. She'd braced herself when she'd gone off with the pack. Her whole life now was one big Brace—

Payoff time now.

The big guns having paused momentarily for their metaphorical breaths, the Leaders stepped aside, staggered English-line style, for their backers to let loose their volleys.

Machiko and the youngers to the rear discharged their weapons, cutting into the throng of aliens, slicing, dicing, and generally churning up the Hard Meat into chunky-style puree, acid flavor.

Machiko wore the yautja armor, sleek and economical and oddly comfortable. The material worked well in the movements of her lithe muscles, and the air circulation was superb. The armor was blessed, and it felt almost like augmenting prosthetics, as though the lines converged into power that boosted her own. Her hair was worn now in the ceremonial ringlets, rather like neat dreadlocks bouncing energetically at the back of her head as she moved forward, her discharges blasting through the dying, spindly creatures.

They broke through.

As though this knowledge was as instinctual as it was empirical, the pack moved as one through the opening presented to it. The wedge of the older, valor-hogging frontmost went first, and the others, including Machiko, allowed this. All were equal in honor, all were esteemed. However, Machiko had quickly glommed on to the fact that these Predators were pretty much like an Earthly predator pack. The members jostled for dominance, and the older, smarter, and more experienced members were generally either given deference or simply plowed past the more awkward younger members.

"Ha ha ha!" whooped one of the younger warriors, a snot-nosed kid about a head shorter than the others; a difference in height was almost made up for by the chip on his shoulder. This dude had bridled at Machiko's presence in the pack from the word go and had been on her back ever since. He took guff from the others for his lack of stature, then handed it to her coated with a little shit for good measure.

"Ha ha ha!"

It was garbled laughter. He'd heard Machiko laugh once, and he would imitate her from time to time, out of spite. She jostled right back generally; jostled just short of a set-to: no reason to make unnecessary waves, when all she wanted was to sing in the band.

No, especially right now, smack in the middle of a den of the most vicious killers in the galaxy.

"Ha ha ha!"

The tide had let up under the slash and burn of their weapons. The elders were hurrying along, intent on their goal, the other youngers tagged along, just behind them.

She called her tormentor Shorty, though before she'd assumed he didn't know English.

Now, though, she wondered.

He turned around and shoved her.

"Ha ha ha!"

She went back a few feet, surprised at the push. She'd already figured out that the very last man had the least honorable position in battle, albeit a necessary one. That must have been what Shorty intended: to make sure that she came up in the rear.

"All right," she said, "let's just go," hoping her tone was understandable, if not her words.

"Ha ha ha!"

Shorty fairly skipped ahead, waggling his locks at her in a defiant, teasing manner.

Oops.

She saw the thing way before he did. It was coming out of a tubing in the ceiling: a mean-looking bastard, its diseased banana head already dripping saliva, its claws outstretched and ready to jump.

"Watch out!" she cried, pulling up her plasma gun.

Shorty may have been young and stupid, but he

was quick. He spun around, looking up immediately at the trouble.

She waited.

Not because she wanted to see Shorty killed.

Worse. She wanted to let him sweat a moment, until she did something much, much worse. . . .

Fast as he was, the bug was faster.

It jumped down, leaping for the certain kill.

Machiko fired.

The blast caught the bug in midsection exactly at the point she had calculated, not only smashing the thing to fiery bits but blowing back those pieces and their acid blood against the wall, preventing them from falling on Shorty.

Shorty stepped back away from the devastation. He had stopped laughing. Through his mask Machiko could see the ice of his glare.

"Ha ha ha!"

One of the other youngers, up ahead, had stopped. A brawny arm pointing an accusing finger.

"Ha ha ha!"

They'd learned the laugh, all right, and now the derision was being heaped on Shorty.

A bark of communication. Shorty turned and stormed off. Machiko followed into the harsh acridity of the smoking advance.

Time to get back to work.

Sometimes, at lulls like these, when Machiko felt a little sick to her stomach, more than ill at ease with her companions, she wondered about how the bugs had spread across the galaxy. Simultaneous evolution? From what she could gather, Hunter folklore seemed to indicate that. But could that folklore have been created to mask a troublesome possibility? Could the bugs have spread because of the Predators' blooding rites? Could "accidents" have occurred on many others worlds—"accidents" of containment, like that which had occurred on Ryushi?

Of course, the cultural pride of these Predators could never stomach that notion, and so the possibility was washed over with insistent folklore. Besides, who could really say? The bugs had a way of spreading, like disease. And interstellar-vector theory really had no bearing on what they were doing now, on this planet.

The bugs had this planet. That was all that mattered. The Hunter mission now was not to dispute the bug domain, but to appropriate their Queen, for their own purposes.

And their destination was not far away. Machiko could sense that much.

Breakthrough was imminent.

The elders, honor and glory and ego etched in flesh and bone and armor, blasted their way through one last tissue of defense. By the blaze of their weapons, Machiko could see a much larger chamber, lit in a feral spectral glow.

Closer, she could see that it was like a chamber of the devil's heart.

And squatting inside that chamber was its own particular demon.

The Queen was about normal size. Which was to say, *big*. It hunkered in its hold like a cornered jabberwocky, its fingernails-on-blackboard hiss already aroused by the surrounding Hunters.

As rear guard, it was the youngers' duty now to keep the Queen's drones away while the more experienced Hunters did their jobs.

Machiko performed that duty, but made sure she didn't turn her back on Shorty. These creatures were supposedly made of honor, but she'd never really trusted young males of any race, and now was *not* the time to begin.

The Predators knew their prey well.

One of the bugs' collective strengths lay in their complete subjection to their Queen. Another was their total dedication to the proliferation of their species.

But within these strengths was the key to their one major weakness: the warrior-drones would do nothing to endanger the life of their Queen.

In turn she would do nothing to endanger the lives of her unborn brood.

Armed with that knowledge, the success of the Hunters was assured.

Still, it wouldn't be easy. Trouble along the way was virtually guaranteed, despite the strutting self-confidence this pack had displayed toward the effort from the very beginning.

As the youngers picked off any of the drones who dared to poke their misshapen, horrific heads into the chamber, the elders expertly shot off their grappling devices around the numerous limbs of the Queen, around her neck, effectively hog-tying her.

The mighty weave of the cords pulled tight. The Queen raged and heaved, but her powerful huge body was held in vague check. Even though she wobbled and surged from time to time, it would have to do.

The Queen thus reasonably subdued, the drones seemed to check themselves, keyed intuitively to her vulnerability.

Now came the most dangerous part. . . .

The capture team had to maintain control of the Queen as Top Knot, their brawny leader, prepared her for travel.

This was a ticklish business, as it consisted of separating her from her egg sack.

Top Knot advanced, his long, sharp blade held high and glistening in the halogen portable lamps carried by the others. He raised it high, tensed himself, aimed—

And brought it down like a surgically trained executioner upon the fleshy interstitial connective tissue.

The blade cut down and through the stuff hard. There was a shriek from the Queen.

Unfortunately, the Hunter whom Machiko called Three-Spot was caught napping. His stance had been improper, and so when the Queen unexpectedly threw all her ample strength into that limb and pulled it away, he was lifted bodily into the air by the rope curled around his arm.

The Queen hurled him around like a yo-yo and dashed him down onto the hard ground.

Stunned, the Hunter could not move.

But the Queen could.

With a vicious vengeance she brought down her own scythelike claws directly onto Three Spot's chest. So sharp were the claws, so much momentum did the Queen have in her blow, that they drove down directly through that armor, burying deep into the warrior's chest with a sickening splash and thunk of released blood.

Three-Spot wriggled and spasmed for a moment. Then he was dead.

That's what tended to happen in these situations.

On their way out of the unfortunate Hunter's body, the razor claws slashed through the rope.

Part of the Queen was free.

This wasn't good.

The situation was pretty obvious to Machiko. The capture party's continued safety rested on their ability to control the Queen. Her freedom would be the signal for her brood to attack.

Back when she was corporate ramrod on the planet Ryushi, Machiko would have examined the situation ... weighed her options.

People would have died.

Now, instead, she simply acted.

Dropping her gun, she leapt for the loose rein. She had a split-second grab for it before the thing whipped back out of reach. Her leap was automatic, but there seemed to be magic in it, talent in it, a skill and precision that she hadn't owned before her experience on Ryushi.

She'd leaped out of her position, darted past the others, still seemingly frozen in the confusion of the moment—

Her fingers folded around the rope, grabbed it, held it just long enough for the other mesh-glove to grab it, wind it around her hand. When the thing went tight, it felt almost as though her arms were being pulled out of their sockets. . . .

Fortunately, she'd dug in and was pushing down with all her power.

Just hold it, Dahdtoudi, she told herself. "Little Knife," the name that Dachande had given her. Her handle on strength and pride and honor.

Just keep that thing in control. The others will do the rest.

Mere moments seemed to stretch as long as her arms wanted to. Sinews creaked and her bones felt close to cracking. The feral alien smell of the place threatened to overwhelm her. However, she concentrated on stillness. She would not be moved. She pretended she was sitting *zazen,* totally centered, totally within herself, and lashed her mind to this planet's gravity.

She sensed more than felt the others gaining control. And then two Hunters took her place.

She stepped back, breathing hard.

The Queen was still straining at the ropes, but she was in control again.

By stepping in like that she'd prevented a possible disaster.

Top Knot approached her.

She expected . . . what? A pat on the back? A bend of the mandibles by way of smile? Some kind of medal of honor?

No. She didn't expect that at all, not from this race of beings, and she braced herself.

Top Knot slammed his arm against her chest with such power that she was knocked down. Despite her preparation her breath was knocked from her lungs. She did not offer resistance, she did not take offense, she did not complain.

What she'd done, besides saving these Hunters, was to go against her station in stepping out to grab that rope.

By abandoning her post she had disobeyed Top Knot's orders. Though she helped avert disaster, she had revealed herself as untrustworthy.

Her insubordination might be forgiven, but it would never be forgotten. These crab-faces might not have been around to forget without that insubordination, but she'd still flown in the face of tradition, honor, and authority.

Oh, well.

They started to haul the Queen back to the ship.

She picked herself off the ground and simply stood for a moment, waiting for the chamber to stop spinning around her. Eventually, on their way out, Top Knot turned his attention to her.

He gestured forward, and she understood.

She was to take position at the advance guard.

She picked up her gun and hobbled ahead.

It was a token position at best. The Queen's pheromones would do the work of scattering her brood before her. It was rather like pulling out a hostage with a great, big, sharp machete held to her throat.

The older, more experienced members of the troop—the ones with the necessary muscle and alien-wrangling experience—hauled the reluctant Queen forward toward the ship.

As much as Broken Tusk/Dachande's mark allowed

her entrance to this society, her behavior that day had branded her as an Outsider.

She still had much to learn about the ways of the Hunters, but nonetheless, she knew that had she had choice over again, she would have done the same thing.

The haul back seemed to take forever, what with the bitch digging in from time to time and needing a quick stun to take some of the fight out of her.

And what a job they had ahead of them, to boot:

According to Top Knot's briefing, bringing a captive alien Queen onto a ship was the most dangerous part of any capture mission.

When they got to their destination, Machiko soon found out why.

The ramp was lowered by remote control. It was narrow and posed quite a problem. She could see that the tight confines of the ship would allow no margin for error, no room for slack.

According to Top Knot, many times the captive Queen made a suicidal last-ditch attempt at the door of the nesting chamber.

With great effort the Hunters hauled the Queen up the corrugated ramp. They pulled her through into the area that would be her prison—a chamber separated from the rest of the ship.

Machiko took up her position by the end of the ramp. She could not help but cast concerned glances back at the progress the others were making, getting that monster into her own private suite.

She expected it to make a last break for freedom at any moment.

What she did not expect, what came as a surprise, was that the bid for that freedom came not from her, but from her children. Somehow she got off an unseen signal or a silent call that spurred her offspring into action. They came roaring out of the cavern,

more fiendish than ever. Their cries spurred Machiko
into action.

She swiveled around, took stock, reacted instantly,
swinging her weapon around and spraying streams of
bright death into the burgeoning hordes. In conjunc-
tion with her fellow youngers, they must have killed
thirty of the bugs in the next fifteen seconds.

The aliens just kept on coming.

Top Knot bawled out a retreat order. . . .

A bawl that turned into a howl of consternation.

Machiko had already started up the corrugated
ramp. The bugs seemed to pay no attention to the fact
they were being slain by the score. A few broke
through the fiery onslaught and started up the ramp
as well.

Machiko turned around to see what the commotion
was and was horrified to see that the ranks of the
brave, valiant senior Hunters were splintering. The
Queen had turned into a raving fury, trailing lines.
She leaped to one side.

Another cry.

In the confusion Machiko realized that Top Knot
had called out for the ramp to be lifted, and not a second too soon. Even as the lip of the thing yanked
from the ground, two bugs clambered onboard.

Fire from the retreating Hunters tore them off, but
two more took their place.

Meanwhile the ranks of the Hunters frantically
fought for control.

Machiko stood aside to allow the last of the youngers to climb onboard. She fired one last salvo, tearing
the final bug off the edge and hurling it back into the
frenzied roil of its companions.

And then with a chuffing sound, and the shriek of
hydraulics, the ramp/door shut.

The bastards were outside.

The bitch was inside, though, and free.

Machiko turned. The Hunters were scuttling about

to the exits and their posts while the Queen howled out her frustration and anguish.

The Queen had only one path open to her—directly into the waiting nesting chamber. Behind her was a grillwork-covered vent from which a cable dangled, but it was too small for her to fit through.

The others knew this ship much better than Machiko, and they had hurried off to be out of danger. In her confusion and consternation, Machiko had simply stood her ground watching the Queen rampage.

The Queen turned and headed straight for Machiko.

Automatic response drew her gun up as the Queen approached at full bore. In fact the gun seemed to move of its own accord, expertly swinging into place, aiming directly at the Queen's head. At this close range one blast would tear even that huge head off.

Just a pull of the trigger would do it.

Her finger tightened.

But then she stopped herself.

No.

Too many of her companions had paid with their lives that day trying to reach the Queen. To kill it now would negate their sacrifices.

In this situation even honor offered only one course of action.

Retreat.

She dropped the gun and ran.

Her breath came in ragged gasps, echoing inside her helmet, her heart drumming a machine-gun beat in her chest. Her feet pounded a counterrhythm on the steel floor of the nesting chamber.

She barely heard any of it.

All she was aware of was the sound of the Queen's pursuit. . . .

And the implicit sound of her own mortality.

Leaving Ryushi and joining the Hunters had seemed like the logical thing to do at the time, the *right* thing to do. The yautja code, as she perceived it, seemed enviable, clean. As she had waited alone on Ryushi, she had waited for just such an opportunity, feeling herself changed in the crucible of her experiences at Prosperity Wells.

Now the decision just seemed stupid and vain. A romantic fantasy. Hard to think of anything but fear and survival when there were tons of drooling Death bearing down upon her. Whatever had made her think that she could match the ways of these half savages? What had she hoped to prove to herself?

She ran for her life.

It seemed as though she could feel the heat of the creature's breath on her neck. She certainly heard the clank and clack of its chitin, the stretch of its tendons.

Up ahead was the door . . . the passageway to safety. It was round and small and could close quickly.

Standing on the other side, hand up and off to the side, was an unexpected figure at the controls.

Shorty.

She could not see his expression because of his mask.

Hell, she didn't know if these things had expressions—she just couldn't read mandible positioning.

Shorty's arm twisted.

A *chak* of controls.

The door slammed down hard, cutting off her exit.

In its very middle was a triangular window. Two of the Hunters—neither of them Shorty—moved up to that window and gazed into the chamber.

Neither of them moved a muscle to get the door up. Neither of them made an effort to save her.

They just stared at her, spectators of some deadly morality play.

Whatever had made her think that she could live by these creatures' bizarre laws?

Much less gain their respect?

She spun around.

The monster Queen was not as close as she feared, but neither was she far.

And she was gaining all the time.

Well, she'd worry about saving face after she saved her own skin.

She feinted in one direction, and the Queen quickly responded, shifting its weight in a twinkling and investing its momentum in its bid to make quick work of this available tormentor.

Then Machiko shifted, dodged, and sprinted for her true objective.

There was more than one way out of any trap.

She headed for the vent and the restraining cable she had noted before.

Machiko leaped with all her strength and began to scramble up this rough ladder.

She made the climb in record time, but even as she made the grill, she heard the beast below her. It apparently wasn't going to just sit around and watch her get out.

She didn't waste a moment.

Perched upon her shoulder was a laser.

She fired it, and its brilliant beam cut through the wires speedily. She turned it off and pried off the grillwork, making a hole wide enough for her slender body to slip through.

Just about it. A moment or two and she'd be out of—

Even as she was tasting her safety, she felt an awful tug on her hair.

The Queen had reached up and grabbed her dreadlocks.

Fortunately, the Queen wasn't the only one with sharp and nasty claws.

Machiko let go of one of her grips and twisted her wrist forward in a manner that triggered her retractable blades. With almost the same movement she slashed backward.

She cut off her dreadlocks.

She also severed most of the Queen's hand.

It shrieked.

She could feel it thump back onto the floor noisily and messily, the wound spilling acid, none of it, fortunately, over Machiko.

Machiko pulled herself up through the hole she'd made in the grating, her muscles performing the function smoothly and efficiently. She once more was grateful for her training, her workouts, her endurance . . .

. . . and her luck.

She wiggled through quickly, not giving that bitch down there any time to renew her attack. It was wailing pretty fiercely, and she could smell the acridity of its pumping blood wafting up through the opening.

She did not pause to make sure it was okay but scuttled through the pipes as quickly as she could. There was still the possibility, after all, that it would thrust its good claw through the opening and grab her foot.

Her dreadlocks were expendable. She wasn't exactly trying to attract male action among the Hunters. Hell, maybe they even had some glue-ons she could use.

Her foot, though . . . her foot was a different matter.

She needed her foot.

Too bad about the Queen's fingers. But the Hunters would be able to get control of the thing, and it would certainly still be quite able to do what they needed it to do: namely, lay the eggs they needed for their blooding exercises.

Negotiating her way through the air venting was a matter of relying on her intuition and sense of direction.

Over. Up. Down.

Eventually, she came to another grate.

She put her back against the wall, brought her legs up. Kicked. Kicked again.

The grate banged out of its fixture, fell back onto the floor.

She slipped out lithely and fell the few feet onto the metal deck, landing on the floor on all fours, sleek and ready as a cat.

The Hunters were standing there, watching her.

Just standing there in expectant repose.

She tore off her helmet and took in a deep breath.

She gave the ritual greeting of a warrior's victory.

She wasn't sure what she expected. A thank-you? As far as she knew, there was no such phrase in the Hunter vocabulary.

She'd saved their bacon, and they had nothing to say.

They just looked at her, as though trying to perceive what this strange Outsider that Dachande had Blooded was composed of. This honored companion they could never understand . . .

Then they did something remarkable.

They bowed.

She'd bowed for them before . . . something from her Japanese ancestry she'd shown them. They'd just stared at that, seemingly uncomprehending. . . .

And now they were bowing.

All but one.

The others turned and left to be about the business of taking off from this planet. Of dealing with this captive Queen . . .

All but one.

The one lingered. He took his helmet off and his eyes were like lit coals in the darkness.

Shorty.

His mandibles danced menacingly.

He took a step forward, quick and menacing.

Machiko stood her ground.

Just inches short of her, the young Hunter stopped.

Machiko did not move. She did not blink. She just stared directly back at her challenger.

The mandibles bristled.

But then the Hunter spun, stalked away.

His steps echoed in the hallway.

She'd stared him down. Shorty dared not challenge her now, dared not hurt her after her incredible display of valor, after she'd risked her life to ensure the success of this operation.

No. She wasn't one of them.

But they owed her more than ever now.

She felt the bliss of an endorphin rush. . . .

. . . *wings of lightning* . . .

3

. . . heart of thunder . . .

Machiko crouched, holding her blade steady, waiting for the first move of her opponent.

For a moment the samurai warrior, in full medieval regalia, was just as motionless. His own long blade gleamed in the late-afternoon sun like a slender medallion of death, pendant from an azure sky.

The samurai warrior stepped forward, pleated armor ajangle off an obviously immaculate build. She fancied she smelled the musky competence wafting off him.

She tasted a backbeat of fear.

He moved again, and he stepped forward with a familiar and startling arrogance.

He seemed in a hurry, as though he wanted to finish up this particular butcher's order of slice 'n' dice and move on to the next bit of delicatessen fun.

"Hey," she called in Japanese. "Are you hiding a salami in that codpiece, you miserable, impotent coward!"

The eyes shot open with fury.

The samurai raised his sword and, screaming, ran forward.

Machiko Noguchi feinted to meet him headlong, then at the last possible moment stepped aside. She flicked her sword down, then up and under the skillful but infuriated blow, and its blade slammed up the vulnerable break in the armor, cutting into the man's body.

The man's face grimaced a suitable expression of pain and surprise, and his mouth opened to let out a howl of extreme anguish.

Machiko's sword whipped through shimmering light, coming out on the other side at full speed.

The man disappeared in a snap.

Machiko had to control the sword. She deflected its passage so that it whacked down into the sod.

She took a breath and steadied her nerves.

"Excellent," piped a voice beside her. "Absolutely excellent, Machiko."

She turned and looked at the speaker. There he was, beside that rock, crouching down so as to be out of the scenario that he had so ably created.

The holo-tube was already retracting into its compartment in his forehead.

"Thanks," she said.

She suppressed a smile. It would not be advisable to give old A the H *too* much encouragement.

He stood up, dusting off his khaki knees, straightening his immaculate bush jacket just so.

"You've utilized the Sun Tzu's principles very well," pronounced the android in a clipped, punctilious tone that had an old-time mid-Atlantic quality to it.

"Pardon me?"

"Sun Tzu. The *Art of War*, of course."

"Oh, yes. I thought you were talking about some kind of disease-carrying fly."

"That, I believe, is the tsetse."

"Yes, yes, along with many other fine principles, Attila. You reiterate them to me constantly. I don't necessarily have to be able to cough up whole sentences at the drop of a nunchuck! At some point, however, it all gets assimilated into my subconscious. It looked like a pretty obvious opening, though. You made the samurai display the flaw of pride and anger. I'm well acquainted with those flaws, and I know how to use that weakness in others. It's a common trait, I believe, in men—and I traveled awhile with super— well, if not supermen, then at least *exaggerated* men."

Attila looked a little troubled. "I wouldn't know. I don't have a subconscious. Perhaps I should save my money and buy one some day."

They were about three kilometers out in the plains of Machiko Noguchi's workworld. It was the corporation's bureaucratic equivalent of Saturday, and Machiko used the day in her usual fashion.

Exercises.

Fighting exercises with Attila the Hun, her robot, to be precise.

Keep the body trim. Keep the soul sleek. Keep the old noodle *alive*. That was the ticket. Even when she'd been assigned out here in Zerosville, she'd realized that she was going to have to have some kind of trainer, some kind of companion, and since she wasn't quite certain of the human availability in these departments out here in the hinterworlds, she'd bought herself a robot.

Well, "android" was the proper term, really, but as far as she was concerned, Attila was a robot. He'd been a number when she'd bought him, and she'd renamed him. It wasn't often that a private citizen was able to afford the expense, and she'd had to get the Company's approval. However, she'd explained in no uncertain terms what she'd needed the thing for, and since the Company was quite aware of her past and wanted to placate her as much as to get this loose cannon off their main deck, they'd complied. She had the money, and if she wanted to use it on a fabricated companion, well, what difference did it make if she used it to fight with or to fornicate with?

Attila the Hun was not the normal android used by the corporation. He was not an Artificial Person in the usual semiorganic sense, but rather a more mechanical sort. His strata of models was created to be affordable to the average populace, and used for commercial or private reasons rather than military or space exploration.

She programmed Attila to her specifications.

Unfortunately, she didn't know quite what to do with the personality that came along with the whole package.

"A beautiful day, Miss Noguchi, is it not?" said Attila, casting a smile across the plains.

Machiko grunted.

"Not feeling particularly articulate today?"

"I just get really annoyed when you call me 'Miss,' dammit."

"You're not married."

"Look, we've gone over this a hundred times before. I wasn't aware that I hadn't had your previous programs erased, okay? I didn't realize that you had such a complex background. I realize that I can't erase them now without erasing you in toto. Can't you try to selectively erase habits—like calling me 'Miss'?"

"Certainly."

"Well, *do* it."

"You're not in a very good mood today, are you, Ms. Noguchi?"

"Machiko. Please, just call me Machiko."

"Oh, excellent. I enjoy our informal exchanges. It's nice to relate to you when you unleash me from the closet to do your will with me."

"Right. Like you haven't got a life."

"My life is to serve."

"And to watch your tapes and catalog your music."

"One has to fill the spare moments."

"I should have had you programmed to clean and cook. That's what I should have done."

"I do my share."

"You can boil water and that's about it."

"You forget that although I have senses, they have to be calibrated to the proper specifications to cook to your taste. Also, I would clean more, if your odd meditation exercises did not call for such Spartan quarters and your regimen did not call for your cleaning it yourself, as part of your *kata*."

"Okay, okay. I'm sorry. I guess I'm just in a bitchy mood. Maybe defeating holographic opponents isn't quite as satisfying as the thunk of real flesh, the splash of real blood."

"I'm sorry. I'm not equipped with those sorts of simulations. Again, you attempt to make me feel inferior."

"Nothing of the sort."

Attila suddenly smiled, and it was a revelation. Usually when in repose that face was dark and dour. With a dark complexion, dark eyes, a natural frown, and a sharp, perfect nose set in a thin face topped with a perfect short gentleman's haircut, Attila looked more like a mopey Neapolitan young man than a Germanic Hun. However, when he smiled, showing perfectly shaped white teeth, the entire face seemed to light up into a different dimension. Moments like this made Machiko forget entirely that he wasn't a human being.

Moments like this also made her remember that *she* was a human being.

She'd always prided herself on her cool, her control. Her glacial characteristics had caused associates to dub her "Ice Princess" or "Snow Queen." She had had very few friends. Her pride in life was remaining tough, cool, and efficient.

She had changed somewhat after her experience with the yautja. True, she had been more comfortable in some ways with creatures who had rules of behavior among them and who generally obeyed those rules. However, they were alien, and she was human. Her experience on Gordian made her realize that she had a deep instinctual love for, and loyalty to, humanity. She respected the yautja. In many ways she had become one of them. But she had discovered that she would have to do so in *human* terms and so was now trying to explore different dimensions of her humanity. This did not mean that she could deal with other people that well. However, she was trying. One of the best parts of being with Attila was that she felt comfortable with him and could be playful or bitchy, cold or charming, and experiment with emerging aspects of her personality.

"Oh, good," said Attila. "Then you'll snap out of your funk and agree with me that it's a beautiful day. I mean, all the evidence is here before you."

Machiko looked around.

The scent of her own exercise had dissipated somewhat, so she was able to notice the smells around her. Prominent, of course, was the grass. Not Earth-type grass, but on the same principle, short and green and cast over everything like a luxuriant rug. It was this area's version of summer here, pleasantly warm, just as the area's version of winter was pleasantly cold. In between were the long, long autumn and spring, king and queen of this world of the bland and the mild.

Flowers.

That was what Attila was talking about, of course.

The floral addition was truly pleasant and combined with the odd shadings of color combed into the surroundings, poking out of unexpected spots in ochers and magentas and bright slashes of camellia. That, along with the uncommon blue-green of the sky, the way the cumulus clouds navigated the vasty, silent reaches of it, and out beyond the reaches and humps of hills and flats, the faint suggestion of mountain peaks.

A slight, fragrant breeze ruffled Machiko's still-short black hair, cooled the still-hot blooding mark on her forehead, that afterimage of lightning. . . .

"Nice."

"Nice?" The robot's eyebrows rose with surprise. "Merely 'nice'? Where are your aesthetics?"

She shrugged. "It has a kind of unruly, boring attractiveness, I suppose. You forget my background, though."

A curious cock of the head. A finger lifted in understanding. "Ah, yes. As Japanese, you must prefer the more regulated and disciplined beauty of a garden."

"I'm not saying I don't enjoy wild beauty. I learned to thrill at the wastes of Ryushi, the violent dawns, the harsh sunsets. . . ."

"Perhaps your opinion is presently reflected by your state of mind."

"Oh?"

"You are not a content individual?"

"Oh, right . . . and you *are*?"

The robot shrugged. "As an android, I am merely content to be an individual."

"Freedom in bondage, eh?"

"I do not consider my service with you as bondage, though I suppose legally and technically it might be considered so."

"Oh, for emancipation! Let my people go."

Attila's face assumed a rather hurt expression.

"Perhaps we should continue our exercises."

Machiko took out a scarf and wiped away a residue of sweat from her exertions. "I think I want to break for lunch. Maybe we can do some war maneuvers later this afternoon."

Attila shot an arm forward and made a show of scrutinizing his wristwatch. "I believe I can fit you into my schedule."

"Well, how thoughtful of you. There's a nice little bistro in town I thought we could go to."

"Well, since there's only one bistro in town, I believe I know the one of which you speak. It's a shame you didn't bring a picnic lunch. We could have lingered and enjoyed the day. . . ." He slapped his chin with exaggerated revelation. "But oh, my. How could I have forgotten?"

Attila fairly skipped over to the omniterrain vehicle, opened the trunk, and pulled out a basket covered with a red-and-white-checked towel. He whipped this off to reveal sandwiches, apples, and a bottle of red wine.

Machiko gave a grudging smile. "I didn't realize that you were programmed to be thoughtful."

"All androids have areas of latitude within which to move."

"It's the areas of longitude that trouble me."

Attila sniffed with fake huffiness. "Perhaps you should just partake, enjoy, and then criticize if the fare does not meet your high standards."

She laughed. "Come on, Attila. You're just trying to cheer me up." She followed him over to the boulder, where he motioned to a place where they could sit.

"Yes. I confess. And with good reason. Life is so much more pleasant when you're in a reasonable mood." He began to unpack the basket and place the meal on the tablelike rock. He lifted a small vase, complete with diamond-petaled flower, and made it the centerpiece for this sumptuous display. "There. To your liking?"

She nodded. "A pleasant surprise."

"There is more to existence than the *Art of War.*"

"That's nice to know. What kind of sandwich is this?" She began to unwrap the cellophane.

"Taste it. Guess."

"I hope this isn't some kind of new martial-arts exercise."

"What? Sandwich karate?"

"Complete with the Movement of the Lettuce and Mustard?"

"And the Pickle on the Side Kick? Hardly. May I suggest that you taste it?"

She did. From one look at the contents between the rye slices she was able to guess that it was some kind of meat pâté, and the color was liverish—but surely not . . .

She bit into it, and her eyes lit up.

"Foie gras!"

"The genuine article."

"But where—"

"Oh, a little barter with the gentlepeople in Shipping and Handling. I thought it would go well with a picnic, and you seemed so down in the dumps lately."

She took a bite of the delicious fatty pâté and just let it linger meltingly in her mouth. She closed her eyes and savored it.

"Can you blame me?" she said finally.

"I had thought that you were happy when you were dating that mining foreman."

"Who? Edward? That was a laugh. Just a diversion. It's all pretty bland now, Til. It's all anticlimax."

"Hardly a very positive attitude. Surely those Predator sorts didn't have foie gras sandwiches?"

"No. They ate their liver raw."

"Surely they didn't have clever and valuable android assistants?"

"No, and they didn't have robot slaves, either. They were quite resourceful, those fellows."

"Hmm. Sounds like they ate honor and valor for breakfast, lunch, and dinner."

"Oh, no. There's a biological reason for their interest in Hunting. They're quite carnivorous. You can pretty much tell by their breath."

"What a lovely bunch. And you say you actually miss them?"

"Miss them? I wouldn't go so far as that, Til. They're not exactly the lovable sort. No, they hardly inspire much sentiment." She sighed and thought of a different way of putting her feelings. It pretty much came out exactly the way it came out before. "I felt *alive* then."

"You're alive now. You want me to engage my diagnostic functions?" He grabbed her wrist. "Ah, a pulse. A very good sign."

"Sorry. I felt fully alive. Fully in the *now* of existence."

Attila shrugged. "Dangerous sportsters report the same kind of rush. It's all the human body's internal drug system. I'm told that they have some nice rushes on the black market as well."

"No, no, you just don't understand."

He nodded. "No. Perhaps I do. Perhaps, with all this proving of your mettle, your own honor and valor in this society of hypermacho creatures, you were able to somehow momentarily blot out the shame and guilt that rest so heavily upon your family's name because of what your father did, and what that means in the culture that you cling so stubbornly to."

"I hate it when you get like this."

"Get like what?"

"What—did I buy a psych-bot for God's sake? What kind of bullshit are you handing me?"

She got up, red-faced, and threw the half-eaten sandwich at him.

Attila flinched.

"Simply pointing out things we've already discussed."

She was immediately sorry.

She realized the reason why they didn't call these things robots anymore. Robots didn't have feelings. Androids did. And though perhaps those feelings weren't as screwy and cantankerous as human feelings tended to be, they deserved respect and consideration.

"I apologize, Attila." She went over and picked up the sandwich, biting into it as though she were eating the words she'd previously spoken. "A delicate area." She brushed some dirt and grass from the sandwich and took a large bite, masticating with emphasis. "Hmmmm. Lovely."

Attila the Hun folded his arms. "Perhaps I refuse to be tricked in such an obvious way."

"Oh. You won't forgive me?"

"I was never upset. What's to forgive?"

"Oh, *now* who's dissembling?"

"I find our course of conversation extremely unproductive and will now resume my role as your trustworthy, faithful, and *silent* robot servant."

"In other words, you're going to sulk."

"Precisely."

"Well, before you do that, maybe I can have your input on what I'm presently looking at over there."

She directed her finger skyward.

Attila swiveled his head, responding immediately to the seriousness of her tone.

The spaceport lay to the west of the makeshift town. They had driven immediately south. Coming down on incandescent impellers was a starship, flashing in its own exhaust and in the exultant sun at its zenith.

"A moment."

There was a click and hum as Attila's oculars focused on the object and made the appropriate telescopic adjustment. Attila had shown her some of the mechanical aspects of his composition. All truly impressive. Hidden compartments. Perhaps even hidden weapons? He even claimed that portions of his body could operate independently of one another—by remote control. At his more exasperating moments, Machiko sometimes felt like testing this out with her sword.

"Well?"

"Impatience is not a virtue of a warrior."

"My humanity is leaking. So . . . spill."

"Your metaphors are mixed."

"Come *on*."

"It's a most curious spaceship, Machiko Noguchi. Some kind of KX model."

"KX models . . ." She whistled. "Those are exclusive *yachts*."

"Indeed."

"Why would anyone who owns a KX want to come to this godforsaken planet?" wondered Machiko Noguchi.

4

It didn't take long for her to find out.

"Well," said Livermore Evanston, hoisting his own glass of fine wine to his guest, "here's to health, happiness, and a mutually beneficial business arrangement."

Machiko looked at him suspiciously. She sniffed the brimming crystal glass of startling red he'd just poured. Superb. This, coupled with the foie gras, would just about make her gourmet quotient for the year. Nonetheless, she managed a noncommittal expression.

"I only know your name and that you zoom around in a big private starship. As for business arrangements, that remains to be seen."

He smiled, his red cheeks glowing like cheery

Christmas bulbs. His merry eyes were wide and open and seemingly wanted to hide absolutely no secrets.

"Oh, I think what I've got for you, my dear, will be of emphatic interest."

She sipped the wine. Truth in advertising on this. It was the best burgundy that had ever crossed her lips, a glow of grapey warmth with a dry yet clever finish.

She took another sip, though, just for the alcoholic content.

"May I sit?"

"Certainly."

He gestured to the streamlined though well-appointed seat before her. Everything on this ship was sleek and streamlined, but with touches of quality and class that could come only from wealth.

She sat, and the cushioned chair was very comfortable indeed, ergonomically accommodating her body.

"More wine?"

"Why not?"

She put her glass out and had it topped off.

"Excellent stuff, no?"

"I see nothing on this ship that's not excellent."

"I'm so happy you could take the time to come here and visit me."

She shrugged. "I miss out on a frozen dinner, my vid, and my robot. You owe me a lot."

"An attractive woman like you, not being wined and dined on the evening of a weekend. Somehow the very notion appalls me. I am happy that coincidence brought me here today."

She took another sip and leaned over, all politeness wiped from her face now, replaced by a pure business expression.

"So. Let's cut to the chase."

"Gladly." He sipped at his glass. "I have an offer for you, a business proposition, that I think you will find most interesting."

She leaned back to listen.

When she and Attila had returned to her apartment, there was a message waiting on her communications module. It was a man's voice, requesting her to return the call to a certain number.

She did not return the call.

She had a bath. Time was a luxury, and always after a strenuous workout she took the chance to have a languid bath, filled with scented oils and topped with delicious bubbles. She'd never taken time for them as a corporate ramrod in those frenetic pre-Ryushi days. Just quick showers. Her baths on Ryushi had been generally cold water. And with the Hunters ... well, they seldom took baths, and so she'd just learned to live with her own true grit.

Now, though, her baths were opportunities to shut out the universe. Machiko-time she called it. She had all kinds of interesting gadgets in her bath.

Dried off and in her synthsilk robe, she'd been in a reverie that she liked to think of as meditation but was actually a regretful daydreaming that she'd started at this dead-end job here, when the phone had rung.

She ignored it.

Attila, however, had not. Attila had answered and then had insisted she take it. This made her think seriously about selling Attila. However, she did take the portable phone and placed it to her half-listening ear.

That was the first time she had heard the name Livermore Evanston.

It was only after she'd rung off and discussed the phone call with Attila that she realized, with the android's help, that the address she'd been invited to that evening was a docking bay at the spaceport. In all likelihood she would be heading that evening to the spaceyacht she and Attila had witnessed landing. Attila had been all atwitter about the possibilities, but Machiko remained stoic and suspicious.

There was too much to lose if any kind of hope
crept into the mix.

"Let me put my cards on the table from the beginning," said Livermore Evanston. "I know quite a bit
about what happened on Ryushi than most people.
And I know more about *you* than the corporation
does."

She raised an eyebrow. "Oh? You want to spell out
exactly what you mean by that?"

He knew about the Hunters? That seemed unlikely.
They kept a low profile, and their maneuvers through
human as well as universal history had been veiled
with secrecy. That, after all, had been part of their
Game.

Her time with the yautja was officially "unac-
counted for" in Company records; the Company didn't
know what had happened in the time she was missing, but they knew enough to bury her someplace
safe. They'd thought they had done that when they
left her on Ryushi after the colony was moved.

"I know about your experience with the alien
arichnida."

"The bugs, you mean."

"Yes. They are, frankly, the reason I'm here."

Something sparked in Machiko. She could not help
but move forward. Doubtless, interest flamed in her
eyes. It wasn't a good poker face anymore. Fuck it.
Bugs were Bad. Anything that had to do with squish-
ing them was worth paying attention to, and every little bit of help she could extend to eradicating them
from the galaxy she did not begrudge.

"I'm listening."

"You seem to have a reaction to the creatures."

"I do. They need to be destroyed."

"So your dossier would indicate. And if your survival on Ryushi proves anything, you're quite talented
in that area. Although your settlement was all but
wiped out, your experience, your skill, and your valor

were noted—however, you disappeared for years . . ."
He let the sentence hang, waiting for her to fill in the
blanks.

She sipped her wine and left them empty.

". . . and then suddenly you reemerged on that mining planet, in better shape than ever."

"Yes. Gordian."

"A planet with a bug problem."

"Yes."

"Along with some sort of other mysterious problem. . . ."

Again she sipped wine. He did not probe.

She remembered how it had been on Gordian—
another human colony world seeded with bugs by the
Predators she hunted with. She had to make a decision there. She had to choose between the yautja she
Hunted with for two years and tried so desperately to
win honor from, or the colonists, creatures of the
painful race that was her own, that had caused her
and her family so much shame. Her sense of humanity
had won out. She had thrown in her lot with the colonists and beside them had fought off the Hunters.
The margin of victory had been slim.

Evanston had assumed a serious, closed aspect,
sealed with a frown during these last sentences. Now,
though, he smiled and assumed a jolly openness once
more.

Livermore Evanston was a round and pudgy man,
but there was no sign of a lack of strength, either
physical or mental, in his face or body. He exuded a
vitality of power and enthusiasm beneath his mask of
indolence. He wore beautifully tailored and color-
coordinated clothing in a business-suit ensemble that
looked as comfortable as it was neat. Expensive, like
everything else around here, no doubt. His hair was a
lovely mass of artfully coiffed curls—dappled brown
and gray—and he wore a tastefully cut goatee. He
smelled of lemony sandalwood cologne and pipe to-

bacco. He was the epitome of the excesses and might of civilization, and Machiko Noguchi had to admit to herself that she was very, very intrigued.

"Ah. I'm getting ahead of myself. I am a creature of curiosity. I forgot my promise to you. I have the advantage here. I know far more about you than you know about me."

He paused then and slipped his hand into his pocket as though he were digging around for a pipe. Then, as though deciding against it, he pulled his hand out again and reached for his glass of wine.

He did not drink it, just stared into its clear, deep red as he spoke.

"A little rectification, then, is called for."

A scratch of the nose, as though an aid to considering the best phrasing.

"I have this planet, you see . . ."

That was a little too much for Machiko to take, right from the start. "Wait a minute. You're clearly a wealthy man—but you're telling me you own a *world*."

"Hmm. Yes. A bit off the beaten track, but then so is this wonderful little place."

"Never has sarcasm been so truly used. You mentioned before you're not a member of the corporation."

"No. I *trade* with the corporation. I got my start in the Rigel system, you see. A huge inheritance and I've been nothing but a pure entrepreneur since I can remember. All sorts of businesses and technologies and conglomerates. Much of what constitutes the modern starship engine was designed in *my* engineering think tanks." He shook his hand expressively and dismissively. "Enough of that. I'm loaded, okay? So loaded that I personally sent out an expedition in an unsettled and unexplored region of the galaxy, personally colonized it, and set up an enterprise unlike anything in human history." He took a deep breath and exhaled through a tentative, chagrined smile. "However, we've got a problem."

"I suspected as much."

"Yes. There's been a sudden and unexpected bug infestation . . . and the hell of it is that we don't know where they came from or how they got there." He looked at her with an arched, bushy eyebrow. "A situation very similar to that on Gordian, right down to the mysterious and unexplained deaths. Also similar to Ryushi. It's been said, you know, that planet is haunted."

"Yes, I've heard that theory too."

He tapped his fingers on the table, looking at her expectantly, as though she were going to solve his problem with a pronouncement of some sort.

She, however, said nothing, even though the interest still burned in her eyes, undisguised.

"I suppose you'd like to know what sort of planet it is I own."

"Something that would make money, I presume."

"Oh, yes. But it's something that's important to me as well." Tap tap tap. "I have your dossier. I'm aware of your abilities with weapons, and your excellence in martial arts. However, your write-up is not complete. Have you ever *hunted*, Machiko Noguchi?"

She smiled. "Yes."

"What?"

"Bugs."

"That wasn't sport, that was necessity."

She let that go. He said it, she didn't. The further away the subject stayed from the Predators, the better. She smelled possibilities here, and there was no reason to louse them up with a little jaunt into Alienland. Let that business be her little secret. It was bad enough, betraying her pack to save her humanity. She didn't want to broadcast that little personal bit of mixed courage and shame.

She shrugged. "I went duck hunting once."

"Then you know something of the thrill of the sport."

She nodded.

That was the understatement of the year.

Hunting with her pack had come to make multiple orgasms feel mild and mundane.

"Good. I had that feeling about you."

"Is this suspense thing to keep me interested? I mean, I came to your ship, didn't I?"

"I'm sorry. A bit of sales technique. I've never quite gotten out of the habit." He leaned back and rubbed his pudgy hands together gleefully. "You see, it's a hunter's planet, Machiko."

"I kind of guessed."

"Good. I suppose you're aware of the restrictions that have been placed on blood sports on many worlds."

"You have governments and they tend to make laws. You have corporations and they make laws too."

Evanston nodded soberly. "Yes. And as civilization proceeds its dizzy climb up the ladder of Progress, the elevated few who think that they can legislate morality have lost track of some of the needs of humankind."

"Like hunting."

"Precisely. It's in the fiber, the very marrow, of humanity. The *hunt* . . . Instincts die hard." He winked at her and patted his chest. "I know. They're right in here."

"Hmm. I'm catching the drift. You find and colonize your own world. You go and shoot its creatures without any threat of reprisal."

"That's not the whole story. I import creatures as well . . . fine, ferocious creatures. Worthy of glory. I then sell tickets to people who can afford them."

"Ship them out, let them chase beasties about."

"Yes."

"Sounds ideal."

"That's what I thought, Machiko. I didn't bargain, though, on the arrival of the bugs."

"A bit more than your hunters can deal with."

A grave nod. "At the moment I'm pretending it was all planned. There have been deaths, but that just adds spice to the sporting. However, deaths are one thing . . . catastrophe's another. I'd like to hire you to avert catastrophe."

"One little problem, Mr. Evanston. As the song says, I owe my soul to the Company store."

"Ah, yes, the beloved corporation. They didn't know quite what to make of you when you came back, did they? They considered you a loose cannon, and so they put you out to Pasture World. Yes, yes, I'm well aware of the confines of your life, Machiko. However, I'm a man of means—and a man of contacts. If you'll sign on to help deal with this alien manifestation on my planet—with the understanding, of course, that you'll be well remunerated for your effort—I will not merely get you leave from this backwater nothing of a planet"—he smiled—"I'll get your contract torn up."

She blinked. "You can do that?"

Evanston nodded.

"Hmmm." She stood up and paced.

It was too good to be true. There had to be a catch.

She looked the gift horse in the mouth.

"How do I know that I won't be stepping from the frying pan into the fire?"

"Oh, it's a fire, all right. But you hate the frying pan, I know, and it's my take on you, Machiko, that you *love* fires. Your element, so to speak."

"I don't know. You're telling me the whole story here, right?"

"No. Of course there are details . . ."

"Details that would make me regret my decision to jump on your horse?"

Again the shrug. "You'll have to wait and see. Look, I'll tell you what. Come with me, and I'll make you an advance. Work for a week or two. If things aren't to your liking, the advance will be enough to start a new life somewhere."

"You'd pay that much up front?"

"Indeed. And you won't even have to spend any of it for ship fare. I'll put you on one of my ships."

"I can get this in writing."

"Yes, and I'll be legally bound to let you free."

"You must know I hate it here. How do you know I wouldn't just use the opportunity to get out of this bureaucratic hell and then skip?"

"Like I said, I have a dossier full of information on you. Including your family history. That would be a shameful thing to do, Machiko, and you know how shamed your family's name is already."

Machiko nodded. "Yes."

"And may I also suggest that a successful completion of this task will not merely make you an independently wealthy individual . . . it will add just about all the honor and self-esteem to your individuality you crave so much."

She sat back down. "I wonder if there's enough in the entire universe." She looked up at her prospective employer. "You've certainly done your homework."

"Money buys a great deal."

"You certainly want it to buy me."

"As I said, I think I understand something of your psyche. I'm not buying you. Money isn't your thing, Machiko Noguchi. I'm offering you freedom . . . and self-respect within human society. You'd be able to go home again, Machiko. Go home, with your head high."

She thought about the offer for a moment more.

And then she gave him her answer.

5

The yautja danced.

Lar'nix'va danced the dance of Death. Not just a Path dance, but The Path dance.

His opponent hissed and clacked before his spear, seeming aware of the importance of this battle. Beyond life, above Death. It smelled of its acid, though it had not bled yet. It had just been detected with a sensor and then beaten from the bush where it had been hiding.

The pack had challenged Lar'nix'va's assumption of the role of Leader. The *kainde amedha chiva*, the Hard Meat Trial, would prove his worthiness.

To Lar'nix'va, though, it was just one more step on his personal path, a path that had engraved itself upon his soul at a very early age.

The Hard Meat lunged.

Lar'nix'va dodged backward and performed a graceful flip. A showy maneuver, certainly, but then this kill wasn't just for sport or for blooding—it was to illustrate for certain that he was worthy of not just a questionable Leadership, but a brilliant and honorable Leadership with more than a touch of pride and swagger. Thus would he take the next step up the ladder, for the other packs that Hunted on this planet would surely have to take note. The situation merited extreme scrutiny, and by his careful and panache-filled Leadership, Lar'nix'va knew that he would attract the attention of the elders. Thus he hoped to command many yautja, not just a pack. Thus he hoped to attract many females, breed many children, and make such a name in the genetic pool as had not been heard in many Passings. To think that the elders had once considered him unsuitable for breeding, had even considered severing his gonads. It was not just ambition that drove this warrior, but outrage. Soon there would be many yautja a few *noks* shorter than the norm. But they would be superior warriors and good solid breeders, without question. His name would not just be in history books, but written in the annals of the genome.

With this fire of intention that burned in him, he took a couple of fancy steps, confusing the Hard Meat and impressing his fellows with his nimbleness. Then, before the *kainde amedha* had the opportunity even to consider the possibility of fleeing, he raced forward and with stunning speed lopped off one of its forward limbs. Even as the sword-sharp length of special steel sliced through the last bit of chitin, Lar'nix'va yanked it back and stepped away from the spray of acid blood, not merely in the prescribed training fashion, but with a glorious flourish and a deep bellow of victory.

The Hard Meat shrieked, but it bore forward, its long head darting out, drooling and snapping.

The good thing about the *kainde amedha* was that, while they could be wily and hard to deal with in the closed space of tunnels and darkness, out in the open they were highly predictable. They sought to attack and kill, and that was it. A warrior merely had to time his attack and defense in cadence to the instinctual performance of his prey.

Now Lar'nix'va played with that. This was his Dance.

The Hard Meat struck, its limb dangling horribly. Fortunately, the limb had ceased spurting acid, merely dribbling now, so that Lar'nix'va dared to dart in and attack once more. He saw a perfect opportunity to slash open the creature's thorax. However, the fight would have been over too soon then, cheapening his glory. He signaled with a whistle his decision to attenuate the battle, and then instead of making it a quick kill, he whacked down with the blade upon the thing's leg.

The limb was tough. The blade bit into it but did not sever it. The spear was stuck. Acid streamed out. Rather than pull on the spear and risk a slash from the jaws or remaining limbs, Lar'nix'va abandoned it, leaping back with fancy footwork.

Then, rather than receive another spear from his fellows, he did the glorious thing.

Lar'nix'va pulled out his short blade.

He heard the mandibles of the pack behind him chatter with disbelieving approval. This was an insane thing to do, but a little insanity in the Leader was always respected.

Lar'nix'va capered around the Hard Meat speedily, and then, before it could do anything in defense, he jumped. His leg muscles drove him up onto its back, and with a powerful blow the new Leader brought the blade down upon the back of the cranium. The sharp steel pierced the armor, driving perfectly into a node that controlled the creature's reflexes. Before he could be grabbed, Lar'nix'va bounded away.

The Hard Meat screamed.

It rolled and convulsed.

Maddened and in terrible pain, it tried to leap toward the warrior responsible, but its limbs would not respond. With a clatter and clunking it fell into a hellish heap.

Lar'nix'va darted in, grabbed his spear, which had fallen away, and with a fluid motion rammed the weapon down and through the thorax with such force that the Hard Meat was pinned to the ground.

Then Lar'nix'va leaped away.

With the life of the thing leaking into the dirt, he turned to his fellows.

"Can you doubt now that I am a Leader?" he said.

"No," said a tall warrior named Bakuub, sullenly. "We cannot. However, there is more to a Leader than an individual feat. You well deserve your skull here, and the honor that this kill heaps upon you, a milestone on your Path. However, we must see how the pack works under you. Times are serious, and we cannot hazard a bad choice."

Lar'nix'va could feel the blood rush to his head. However, he controlled his temper. By rights all he had to do was call this a challenge from the troublesome fool and defeat him in a duel. However, Bakuub was correct. They were in a troublesome position. Most likely Bakuub would be killed in such a duel, and the pack—Lar'nix'va's pack—would thus lose efficacy.

This, after all, was the pack that would lead Lar'nix'va to greatness. It was a good pack, and the yautja knew it well. No reason to dismantle it when such was not necessary. What was the saying? *Thin-de le'hasuan 'aloun'myin-del bpi-de gka-de hasou-de paya.* "Learn the gifts of all sights, or finish in the dance of the fallen gods."

Lar'nix'va had no intention of moving his feet and shaking his spear in that particular festivity.

"Very well. We should have an exercise. A portrayal of teamwork."

"Yes," said Bakuub.

"A Hunt!" said another.

"A challenging *Hunt*," chimed in a third bellow.

"But what is worthy of such a Hunt? What will truly test our merits as a working unit?"

Lar'nix'va's mandibles clattered together in a sly yautja smile. "The most truly worthy prey. The other creatures who hunt on this planet, who have no doubt caused the death of our Leader. A prefatory foray into their realm."

"Yes."

"Pyode amedha," cried another.

"Wait," said Bakuub. "Is it wise to do this before we know what truly transpires upon this planet?"

"You are not revealing cowardice, are you, Bakuub?" said Lar'nix'va.

"Soft Meat!" cried a warrior.

"Yes. A true challenge," echoed another.

Lar'nix'va nodded. "The others agree. We must hunt the *oomans*. We must hunt the clever hunters. And we shall hunt our loosed Hard Meat at the same time." He grabbed a spare spear and waved it in the air. "Hunt and thus our glory as a pack will be restored!"

The cheers of his companions buoyed his spirits, and his soul began to yearn for killing.

6

I don't know about this," said Attila the Hun. "I don't know about this at *all*."

"Don't know about what, Til?"

"This entire enterprise. It smacks of duplicity. It smells of trouble. It reeks of—"

"I think the phrase you're groping for so literarily is 'It's very suspicious.'"

The android looked taken aback. "Well, don't you agree? I mean, from out of the blue comes a Greek bearing a gift. I believe the dictum states clearly that one should be chary of such."

"I don't think 'Livermore Evanston' sounds very Greek, do you?"

"The fact that he didn't come with a bloody Trojan horse doesn't change the fact that ... that ... well, that this whole thing sounds not only *fishy* but *dangerous!*"

The look on Attila's face was so sincerely chagrined that Machiko Noguchi slowed down to a walk. She halted her assistant and trainer, who was of course not at all winded. She herself spoke breathily, and a light patina of sweat covered her forehead.

"Aren't we wading a little deep into the ancient kingdom of mixed metaphors?"

Evanston had agreed that Machiko should keep in shape, and as there were no exercise machines or rooms devoted to same, she was allowed to avail herself of the circular corridor on the second deck, which was pleasantly similar to a short track.

Round and round and round . . .

Puff and puff and puff . . .

The thing was, if Machiko didn't do some strenuous exercise as well as her *kata* and her little softshoes with holographs thrown up by good ol' AH, she'd be so antsy she'd be in a thoroughly nasty mood and probably insult or hit someone. And if not him, then one of his several toadies who ran this boat.

What had happened was this:

She'd signed on.

That simple. She'd accepted Livermore Evanston's offer, laid down her Joanna Hancock right by his own squirrelly scrawl.

As promised, it took only the weekend for all the red tape to get bleached and snipped. Evanston had advised her to take the day afforded her to pack and make arrangements for what she wished to bring with her.

All she'd wanted to take with her were a few paintings she'd grown fond of, some phones and some music cubes, a painting set she found helped her meditate . . .

And, of course, Attila.

Attila was a little trickier, since her license for him

extended only to Company territory; and Evanston seemed a little nonplussed about taking a training android to Hunter's Planet (that simple term seemed to be the favored appellation, spoken with a wide range of irony and emphases and melodrama by both the impresario himself and the crew). However, once assured that Attila would not only help keep her in tip-top fighting and physical trim, but, with his multi-faceted abilities, actually be of help in the effort, the Boss agreed.

Besides, he *adored* the name.

People at the office were appropriately stunned and impressed by her company and her swift departure. She gave them a quick toodle-loo and showed them her backside, though not quite in the way that perhaps she would have preferred.

She and Attila were ensconced in luxurious quarters aboard the spaceyacht. Evanston asked if perhaps "the Hun" wanted his own room, or perhaps just a broom closet somewhere, and when Machiko had answered that Attila always slept in the same room, like a "big teddy bear," the fat man had just leered.

All to the good, if it kept the guy's mind away from the possibility of any midnight peregrinations. Machiko honestly doubted that Evanston had any designs in that direction. Doubtless, money, power, and sheer personality kept him deep in whatever sexual activities he pleased to partake of. No, he surely hadn't taken ages to trip out to Buttlick, Milky Way, to try to jump a scarred, overmuscled, stringy-haired gal's bones, no matter how sexy she might be. He had come because she was, in his words, "unique."

That didn't mean, though, that he wouldn't try, the lech.

Actually, Evanston was fortunate.

Starships could go lots faster now than in days of yore. And though Blior, in the Norn system, was a far way out of the normal sphere of interstellar activity, it happened to be in the same Einsteinian neighborhood as Dullworld, relatively speaking.

"I'm as much a warrior in the land of mixed metaphors as I am in any other land," said Attila. "But truth to tell, I rather liked it back where I was."

"Even though I was miserable?"

"Ah, but you would have been so much more miserable without me. I had a purpose, a positive value reinforced every single day. What being, biological or manufactured, can truly look for comfort in his duties?" Attila sighed. "For a while I could." He looked off sadly at a stolid bulkhead, as though staring through some imaginary porthole into the depths of space. "Now I'm just a bag carrier."

"Come on. You're my trainer, my associate, my secretary, my alter ego, my—"

"Your robot slave."

"No . . . that's absurd. Again . . . you're my . . . my . . ."

She wanted to say "friend and boon companion" or something sweet and supportive, but somehow the words stuck in her throat, like peanut butter.

Maybe that was why she'd run off with the yautja. They had hard and steely emotions, just like her. Honor and valor were all, and emotions soft and tender or simply good-natured were nonexistent.

A reality where shame and weakness could be fought with and defeated, and a noble Death was as much a victory as a noble conquest.

"My better half."

"Oh, dear. Don't strain yourself." But Attila the Hun was smiling, happy with whatever crumbs of genuine approval she threw his way. "Still and all, I *am* on record: This is a bad idea. You will regret it, and I already regret it. But, then, I have very little choice in the matter."

"That's right, guy. And don't you forget it." She smiled. "Would you rather have assumed my lovely job back there? How well would you have done on a mining world without me?"

Attila was silent for a moment. "Very well. Point taken."

"We do this job, make some money . . . and we can start up something on our own . . . our dream, Til. . . ."

"*Your* dream, you mean." Truculently.

"Hey. You came up with it, not me."

Still walking, round and round and round.

"A suggestion, merely." The accompanying sniff was affected, Machiko knew. Attila didn't have sinuses.

"Our own school of martial arts and 'Spiritual Training through the Physical.' That's the exact phrasing you used. I liked it then and I like it now."

"What, back on Earth?"

"Still a world of opportunity. . . . That, or some other older civilization. With culture. Plays, musical events . . . *art*, Til. Real art, not just books in some dank library. Panoramas, cities, things to do . . ."

Although he was fighting it, the android clearly was brightening. "Yes . . . yes, I do admit . . . it all sounds very tasty indeed." Darkness again, lowering of the prominent brow ridge. "But we've got to survive this next leg first. And we don't know exactly how long it will be."

Machiko shrugged. "I told you about my experiences with the Predators, Til. I told you about what I had to do to reconnect with human beings again. I told you about the hell on Ryushi. My anguish on Gordian. I survived. I'll survive again."

A look of profound thoughtfulness had taken hold of the android's face. "Yes, but it all proves that you're a magnet for trouble."

"C'mon, Til. If that's true, you'll actually be able to prove out all these great fighting theories of yours . . . and actually see me in action."

A sheepish look appeared on Attila's face. He said nothing, and Machiko did not needle him.

It had always been one of Attila's private embarrassments that he'd never actually had a fistfight or a street scuffle, let alone been involved in anything like a battle or a fight for his semilife. That was, as far as he knew. All the war stuff, after all, had been fed into the neural complex center of a practically tabula rasa android. His body had been around for a while, and his personality and odd subaware stuff were still clinging to his artificial neurodes and dendrites and synaptic colloids, but he had no substantial memory of his past. Machiko used this fact to reassure him. Perhaps, she claimed, he'd in fact been a valiant warrior in some antilitter campaign and had been taken captive by the slobbish enemy, his brain hastily and poorly scrubbed of memory. Identity he'd never felt in short supply of; memory was an entirely different affair.

Not that Attila was ever in short supply of things to do. While Machiko was doing her forty-hours-plus of bureaucratic nonsense per week for the corp, he would read, paint, master musical instruments, and compose music, becoming a well-rounded—indeed, a renaissance—robot. However, when Machiko was around, his focus of attention was entirely upon her, as if he were some sort of faithful Labrador retriever. At first ever-single and self-sufficient Machiko found this annoying. However, she rapidly got used to it and now actually enjoyed it.

Attila was along on this trip as much for company as anything else. She enjoyed the surprising aspects of her personality that she displayed around him. It was like discovering a new Machiko inside her, a funny and clever Machiko, though more vulnerable, more hurt than she'd ever admit to anyone else.

"Maybe that's what I'm afraid of," said Attila.

"Okay, okay. This kind of mopey attitude is not the

sort of thing I'm in the mood for. Maybe I should just take the dry sleep that Evanston offered."

Attila shook his head adamantly. "Not and stay in any kind of trim or tone."

"Ha *ha*! There's the drill instructor I know—*that*'s why I need you. Had I gone alone, chum, you can bet I'd be snoozing in one of those chambers right now, with a nice little sleep aid for company."

Attila seemed to take that well.

They continued walking along the hallway, chatting lightly as was their wont. The corridors of the ship had nothing of the metal-and-glass sterility usually associated with Long Drag boats. In fact, they were more like an odd penthouse, what with the colorful and tasteful wall patterns and artwork, along with the occasional piece of antique furniture. Livermore Evanston tended to prefer rococo, baroque, and Victorian decorations, and the principal rooms had a strangely cluttered look for a starship. But, then, it was all very homey, especially the fireplace in the dining hall, and it *was* the private spaceyacht of a rich man. Machiko thought it fascinating.

Attila's mouth made a slight tic, a sure sign he was consulting his internal chronometer. "All right, that's fine for the exercise."

"Anything special you'd like next?" said Machiko.

"Yes, as a matter of fact ..."

"Be my guest. Your choice."

"Actually, if you don't care to accompany me, you need not," said Attila.

"You're too kind. No, actually, I'm enjoying seeing what you get up to when I'm not around. Go ahead—shoot. What did you have in mind?" said Machiko.

"Hmm. Well, maybe we *should* go over some exercises ... can't be too careful about preparation."

"Nonsense. I'm up to here with exercises, anyway. Let's have fun. *Your* kind of fun."

Attila brightened considerably. "Yesterday I did

have a peek into the library and thought it most interesting."

"Oh."

Attila nodded his head emphatically. "Not boring
old microfiche or computer screens. Real volumes.
Some with leather binding and marvelous illustra-
tions. Exquisite."

"So you'd like to pore over some antiquities."

"I'm sure you'd be bored."

"Not at all. Let's go."

Attila looked positively ecstatic. "I'm sure there are
rewards. I thought I saw a volume of haiku that would
interest you. You are aware of the poetry of your ancestors."

"Oh, yes. I think I wrote one or two in my romantic
youth. Certainly, Til. That all sounds quite grand."

The library was on the second level. They took the
antigrav pneumatic tube box to get there, one of the
few items on board the craft with streamlined modern
design. The first thing that Evanston had done was to
give them a tour of the boat, including a brief glance
at the library and art room. He'd given them access to
these throughout the trip; at their destination
Machiko placed her palm on a light strip. It read her
DNA pattern. A door whisked open, revealing a room
full of shelved books. The place had a wonderful,
comfortable old booky smell.

Attila immediately gravitated to the poetry section,
poring over a vellum volume with great awe and rev-
erence.

Machiko discovered a whole section devoted to
classic comic books. Now, that interested her. She
was looking over a collection of ancient Superman
stories when Attila looked up suddenly from his reading and said, "Machiko." Softly.

"Yes."

"Shhhh. We're alone, right?"

"I didn't see anyone in the corridor, and unless

they've got visibility dampers on, there's no one in here."

"Good. I believe that this library has an annex."

"No, it doesn't. Evanston showed us just one room."

"I'll bet he has more books. I bet the truly interesting ones are in the annex."

Machiko got a little annoyed. "*What* anex?"

"Shhh. I detect no observation equipment in this room, but I've noticed that voices do tend to carry through the corridors in this environment." He got up and walked over to a shelf of books. "My sensors picked up a control box here, behind these books." He carefully took the books down and placed them on a table. Sure enough, there was some kind of electronic switch on the wall—nothing like on the outside, either.

"Hmm. Curious. Purely mechanical. No identification required."

"I really don't think you should fool with that." Normally, Machiko would be just as curious as Attila. However, she didn't want to go ruining a good thing by getting caught snooping around where she didn't belong.

"Come on. If it was all that important, it would have an identity access seal. My spatial and analytical sensors detect a room next door, along with more paper and leather." His eyes seemed to glow with enthusiasm. "That must have some true antiquarian prizes."

He began to touch the controls.

Machiko got up. She could order him to stop, she supposed, but somehow it didn't seem worth it. Attila seemed interested and intent, and it was good to see him so fascinated with something.

Besides, she was getting a little curious herself.

Suddenly a complete panel of the library shelving opened, revealing a door.

Attila looked totally delighted. "Just like in the movies. A secret room."

He turned another switch, and a soft yellow lambency spread through the new room.

Machiko stepped forward to have a look.

Sure enough, there were books lined on more shelves.

Attila stepped forward, examining spines.

Machiko had noticed something else besides books.

"Fascinating," said Attila. "How very curious . . . our benefactor seems to be a war buff. He's got extensive biographies of generals from Julius Caesar through Napoleon, Rommel, and even Lickenshaun from just a few decades ago. He's got all the books of John Keegan from *Face of Battle* to *A History of Warfare*. He's got all of von Clausewitz's writings. Of course, the *Art of War*. Many first editions. My goodness, he's even got things by Maenchen-Helfen, the most meticulous collator of Hunnish data concerning my namesake. Perhaps he's some sort of war-gamer. He's got that sedentary look about him."

Machiko walked to the other end of the small room. There was a glass case there, like those used in museums. Set inside the case were several items.

A glove.

A broken javelin.

Half a bloody mask.

And a knife.

"An interesting collection," said Attila. "And extensive. If he just wanted the data, it would all be stored in—"

"Til," said Machiko in a sharp, hushed tone.

"My goodness. A first edition of—"

"Til!"

"Coming, coming."

The android moved to her side. She pointed down at the display. He blinked at her.

"So?"

"Til. The pack I was telling you about?"

"Yes. The yautja. The Predators."

"This glove . . . these weapons . . . theirs."

"What. The pack's?"

"Not necessarily. I mean, these are part of their general war culture."

"I thought their whole culture was war."

"War. Hunting—all to gain honor, prove themselves."

"Yes. I've heard all your stories." He looked down through the glass case again, clearly mulling over this new turn of events.

"You know what this means, don't you?"

"There are a number of possibilities. The one *I* favor is that you're being taken for a ride. I knew that Livermore Evanston was no good the moment I met him."

"These only mean that Evanston's got some relics of the yautja. Nothing more. Although it *could* mean that he knows *something* about them. . . ."

"Care to list the possible speculations?"

"One step at a time . . . right now . . ."

There was a sound of voices. Distant voices, fortunately.

Machiko and Attila looked at one another for a split second and then immediately hopped back out of the room. With remarkable speed and agility Attila punched the necessary buttons and closed the door behind them.

They reassumed their places in their chairs, perusing books. A crew member walked past, gazed in for a moment, nodded good day, and then left.

"Shall we go back in and take another look?" Attila asked after the footsteps had echoed away.

"Maybe later. We've got a few more days' passage." Machiko nodded thoughtfully. "I need to think about this."

They went back to their respective reading.

7

The hunt was on!

Abner Brookings, Esquire, lawyer to the bright and the powerful, and gun-fancier extraordinaire, strode through the *yanga* trees, a beautiful antique rifle cradled in his arms like a well-oiled baby. The sun of this world, a purplish, splotchy affair, was just topping a magnificent frieze of mountains in the distance, and the colors the rays made through the swirling mists against the leaves and vines and flowers and trees were spectacular. Brookings took a deep breath, tasting the sweet and sour life of this world, and again he felt the charge that the hunt always brought:

Total Hereness.

How often, in the docket of some musty judge's quarters, or even in rich corporate boardrooms, did his mind wander. *Thereness*, he called the state, and

73

he decided that human beings lived most of their lives in that quarter-conscious state.

Some people woke themselves up through Zen meditation. For some, music rang their chimes. Others—well, the list was endless, from grav-skiing to poga-licking.

For Abner Brookings, though, it was the hunt.

For him it was the Prospect as well as the Act of killing something.

Today, though, the sensation was particularly acute, for the something was the sort of beastie who could just as likely turn around and kill him.

"Watcha think, Ab?" said the woman walking abreast of him. "Pretty good day. Think we're going to bag that *zangoid*?" Petra Piezki grinned and shifted her hold on her large and heavy twelve-gauge shotgun. She was short and stocky with big shoulders, and she liked heavy artillery. Piezki was a lawyer in the same firm as Brookings, a little younger, and not quite the snappy dresser that the dapper A.B. was. In fact, she looked a little like Jungle Jill in her silly khakis. She was dark and gruffly friendly in her Russki sort of way, and a good gal to have a vodka martini with after nailing poor suckers in legal coffins. They'd gone hunting before, but never on this kind of extravagant planet, never for this kind of big game. Brookings could see his own excitement mirrored in the flushed cheeks and the stance of his partner.

"I think we'd *better* bag that *zangoid*, or we're going to have to buy drinks for the whole bar tonight."

Petra grinned. "We did boast last night, didn't we?"

"Like the drunk legal eagles we are."

"Well, it's not as though we haven't had any experience in this kind of sport."

"Ducks and squirrels, some deer, one mountain lion."

Petra looked taken aback. "Not! They were alien, fearsome creatures!"

"The equivalent of the above."

"Come on, Ab. Give us some credit."

"What we've actually killed, Piezki, isn't much."

"The sims, though. The sims!"

"True—but 'virtual reality' in my humble opinion is a term that should be changed to 'verisimilitude reality.' I assure you it's just not the same thing."

"We'll see."

"Right. After pointing that gun down the jaws of a charging *zangoid*, I'm pretty sure that we'll both have different views of this entire business. And goodness knows, on the plus side, it will be a bigger rush."

There was a long pause, and Abner Brookings took the opportunity to gaze over the party, taking comfort in the numbers and the fact they had a couple of guides, looking competent and hearty as they surveyed with keen eyes the murmuring alien savanna.

"You know," said Petra Piezki, "maybe we should have taken along heavier armament." She looked down at her beautiful shotgun with its elaborately carved handle and its beautiful metalwork. "Like a many-millimeter blaster or something."

"Ah," said Brookings. "Getting a slight bit of jitters, are we?"

"Of course not. It's just that—well, from what those guys were saying about the particular *zangoid* that was being let loose this morning—I don't know. Maybe the first time out here on Blior we should have been a little more cautious, a little less sporting, huh?"

Brookings hefted his own rifle. "Look, these guns are part of our collections, right?"

Petra nodded, looking a little pale.

"We paid plenty of money for them, right?"

"Oh, yes."

"So let's use them!"

Petra thought about that for a moment as the sun burned through the mist and an exotic bird with rainbow plumage thrashed up out of the foliage.

"That's the sort of game these things are suited for." He shook his head. "Man killers . . . I dunno."

Brookings grinned, showing his perfect teeth. Some of them were implants, and they were all personally attended to by an expert dentist at extraordinary price. However, Abner Brookings had learned that nothing befitted a good sharky lawyer like a flashy set of choppers. "Petra, Petra! This isn't paddle tennis. This isn't null-grav ball! We're here for the challenge. We're both gun collectors, right?"

"Absolutely."

"And a sport gun isn't truly a sport gun until it's been christened by the blood of a challenging kill."

Petra cocked a civilized eyebrow. "So you say."

"I speak from a long tradition of gentlemen hunters. Believe me, there will be absolutely nothing like the feeling of composure, contentment, and satisfaction you'll feel in your old age when you sit down in your study with your snifter of cognac and view the trophies on your wall, right beside your tasteful gun collection." He coughed and shivered exquisitely at the very notion. He pointed over to the guides, two brawny extrafabs slightly bent under weaponry and powerpacks. "Besides, should we run into trouble, we've got friends here with blasters." He pulled out a bit of Tartonian snuff and snorted it up his nostrils. "People don't pay the money they do for this expedition to get *killed*. They pay for the illusion of danger."

Petra shook her head. "I don't know. I'm feeling somebody squatting on my grave, doing something obscene."

"How amusing. It's called *fear*, my good friend. It's fresh and original and primal, and when you're through it, you'll go back to your normal humdrum— and then, before you know it, be back for more."

"I just want to get through this now, and maybe later I can buy you a drink, pat you on your back, and tell you how right you were."

They were an odd couple, Abner and Petra. When they did criminal law work for the corporation, their nicknames were Bad Cop, Bad Cop. When they did any other kind of work, they were called Shark and Sharkette. There were a whole raft of names they were called behind their backs, but in Brookings's opinion when you were called nasty names as a lawyer, that just meant you were doing your job well.

Abner Brookings was a full head taller than his compatriot in torts, and blond to boot, a handsome devil. He was forty-five years old, although with his rejuv treatments and his regular exercise and vitamin injections, he still looked a rigorous though experienced twenty-seven. There were those who whispered that Brookings sucked blood to stay young, and he would always air these statements to his office and colleagues with the addendum that if he indeed sucked blood, it was only metaphorical—and could you undo that collar a bit . . . I can't quite get at your jugular.

He had a straight nose and a square chin; he almost looked prefab. Money had bought him his good looks, and he made little secret of that either—although he added that this way he didn't have to buy women. This was the one area of modesty in a generally arrogant and immodest individual, and he cherished it. He'd had a few wives here and there through his life, and a few children, whom he saw irregularly. Mostly now what he had was an exciting and fulfilling life and lots of money, beautiful women, adventure: a life, in his opinion, far beyond the dreams of lesser human beings.

In truth, his allusion to "paying" for this expedition had been mere rhetoric, since there were actually professional matters to which the corporation had sent him here to attend.

Business mixed with pleasure, so to speak.

However, as true as that may have been, he was

quite impressed with what had been done with this
planet. As a hunter himself, when he'd heard about it,
he'd been intrigued, but he'd had no idea of the true
wonderland old man Evanston had concocted on this
world so far from the system that laws didn't matter.
This made the lawyer in Brookings nervous; but the
man, the hunter, it excited.

Anything was possible.

They walked through the warming day a little farther in silence. The other hunters in the party chat-
tered; Brookings could smell their jitters. And no
wonder. These weren't true hunters; not even true amateurs. They were just rich wanna-bes who thought by
plunking down cool credits they could put on some
macho, some stink of *cajones.*

Ha!

There were ten of them, ranging from scrawny to
obese. Some Company people; mostly remoras, entre-
preneurial hangers-on to corporations or to the Independent Man himself, Livermore Evanston. The Man's
dream, of course, was to make this world a business-
man's rite of passage—all corporation flunkies, all
"free market" sorts; anyone with a couple million to
rub together and make some money to burn, money
to spare should they want to get away and blow apart
some unlikely game.

Chances were, when those Disneyland days came,
it would be a cream-puff planet, with no edge. Brookings would have to look for his thrills elsewhere.
However, right now he'd get his kicks while he could.

"So, Nickelson," he finally said, calling out to one
of the prefabs. "Any sign of our guest of honor?"

Hank Nickelson turned and looked through heavy
lids at the lawyer. "Yo, Mr. Brookings." He lifted one
of his brawny arms and indicated. "I got a reading
from about five hundred kays ahead." The man's accent was gilded in Bronx. Brookings wasn't sure it
was real. It was a pure tough-guy accent, and maybe

The Man had trained his guide especially to talk in Tough Guy.

Take the other hunt leader, Hans Beinz.

"*Ja*. Ve haf der pheromone tracker on high. She is in our sights." Big teeth shone through a scowl on the Wiener-schnitzel face.

A fake German accent, no doubt learned from old World War II films.

Give me a break, thought Brookings.

Then again, maybe it made the excitement and uncertainty more entertaining for the others. For Brookings, though, it was like being in a bad VirtReal Adventure.

Oh, well, when the actual shooting started, *real* reality would take over.

"Good," asserted one of the newbies, a twitchy little geek in glitter-blue sunglasses and mousy mustache. Name of Sherman something, and he'd drunk milk the night before at dinner. "I . . . I can't wait for the action to start."

"You sound as though you're trying to convince yourself, friend," said Brookings, unable to resist the opening.

"Going to be nasty, I can just feel it," said Petra. "I just hope we all coughed up the insurance premiums that were strongly suggested. Particularly the mauling-and-lost-limbs charge."

That got some eyes bugging.

"Hey, goofball," said Hank. "We don't need none of that, now. Everybody's gonna be safe, long as they follow the rules. And rule number nine is, Keep your big mouths shut if your group head tells you to." Glare. "And I'm tellin' you."

Petra shook her head and laughed. She looked over to Brookings for backup, but the lawyer just gave her a "This is *your* shit you just stepped in, colleague" look that he'd perfected with partners in court.

Petra shut her mouth.

After a while Hans looked up from his machine-encumbered arm, a puzzled expression knit over his meaty face. "Funny. I'm not getting anything on the motion sensors."

"Maybe the *zangoid* is asleep."

"What? With the sun up? The thing had a good rest last night. Morning is its most active period."

"Maybe it's caught something, and it's chowin' down."

Hans tongue-probed his cheek thoughtfully. "*Ja. Ja.* Must be!" His eyes, though, did not look sanguine.

"What you think, Petra?" said Brookings, drolly. "Perhaps the fearsome critter has found a perch on a tree somewhere and is presently patiently waiting to feast on your liver."

Petra smiled. "No, on your brain, good buddy. It likes soft food."

Brookings let off a hearty chuckle and slapped his colleague on the back. "That's the spirit. Stupid jokes. Bonhomie. Bonding. That's what makes this a hunting safari of some quality and note."

With renewed vigor they advanced to the forefront of the party, following immediately behind the two leaders. The others in the group, though, did not look so reassured. In fact, the general consensus, if expressions were to be read, was that perhaps they should all just go back and play something lighter and less troublesome, like a few holes of golf.

The *zangoid* had been beacon marked. Hans and Hank followed their sensors and tracers into a large copse of tall trees, a denser part of junglelike terrain. The smells were more pungent here, the rising damp steam more oppressive.

They filled out into a small clearing.

There was something in the middle of a clearing, and Brookings could see the digitals and dials grow excited.

Hans pointed. "*Ja*. There."

"What's it doing?"

"Just lying there," said Hans.

"Odd," said the other leader. "*Zangoids* prefer to remain in the brush. You generally have to flush them out. What's it doing in the open?"

"Maybe it's a retarded specimen," said Brookings.

Both leaders flashed dirty looks at the lawyer. They were big and dominating enough that Brookings cringed a bit at their obvious displeasure. He'd have to be a little more discreet with his quips out here. He couldn't hide behind the robes of a judge, and these boys could kick his tail, easy.

Still, it gave him a little thrill to be so saucy with them; a part of the dare of this whole expedition.

They approached the *zangoid*.

The beast was lying prone on the ground, on its back, quivering.

Zangoids are generally feline in principle, with a lizardy head and hide and six limbs—four legs and two arms. Some called them "snake centaurs" because of their resemblance to creatures of Greek mythology. They were fearsome beasts with talons on mobile limbs, claws on their "hands," and sharp teeth in their head. They were most definitely carnivores, preferring their meat from the fresh, quivering, and bloody counter. Although they hunted in packs, a *zangoid* on its own was a far more fearsome and dangerous beastie, which made it an ideal hunting animal. Thus it had been imported to Blior, and thus it was being used for preliminary safaris. The leaders had hunted lots of *zangoids* before and knew their habits, making this a reasonably safe expedition, despite the obvious snarling viciousness of the things.

However, Abner Brookings could tell from the expressions on Hank's and Hans's faces that lying down on its back in the middle of a clearing was not generally one of the *zangoid*'s known habits.

"What's it doing?" piped one of the subamateurs.

"Is it having some kind of attack?" asked another. "Maybe it's sick."

There were other suggestions, including calling it a day and going home. However, Hank put up his hand for silence.

With his gun poked forward, he took a few steps closer to the creature.

Brookings watched, his own safety off, as the *zangoid* went through what appeared to be a series of seizures. Its wide eyes were rolled back in its head, and its splayed legs trembled spastically.

"Look. There's something growing in its chest," whispered Petra.

"Looks likes a pulsing growth or something," added another hunter.

"Shhhh!" said Hans with full Germanic sibilance.

Brookings watched with interest and disappointment. There was plainly something wrong with the *zangoid*, which, while interesting enough, meant that in all likelihood they weren't going to be able to hunt the thing.

A bulge had indeed formed in the creature's lower chest, and it seemed to pulse, as though the *zangoid*'s heart was beating far too hard. The animal's mouth had opened and snapped closed, and it had bit off part of its tongue. Rich red blood streamed down its side.

Every movement of the beast screamed its clear state of delirious agony. Its lizard eyes seemed expanded to the point of popping out of their sockets. It stank of blood and urine and feral fear.

The whole atmosphere around it was charged with an electric precognition of terror and violence; Brookings could feel it thrumming through the very ground. It raised his hackles.

He thrilled.

He could tell that Petra felt it as well. The young, stocky woman looked on the verge of bolting and running. Brookings placed a comforting grip on her arm, staying her. Then he turned his attention back to the event at hand.

"Stay back," cautioned Hans. "We don't haf any idea what's happened."

"Shit, man. The Boss pays a lot of money for dese things," said Hank. "He's gonna wanna know just what went wrong with dis one and—"

"Jesus Christ!" cried one of the new women.

With good reason.

The chest was expanding again, this time not retracting, just growing like some fleshy, bony balloon. A bulbous, puslike, veiny head formed at its peak, as though it were some kind of gigantic carbuncle in bad need of lancing.

It burst.

Blood spattered in all directions, a particularly large splatter falling and drenching Hank. But this was all peripheral to the main show, which Brookings watched with horrified fascination, rifle down and ready.

Emerging from the hole came a crimson-drenched wormlike creature the size of a heftily muscled arm.

"What the hell is that?" cried Petra.

"Some kind of parasite, it would seem," said Brookings. "Some kind of creature on this world they don't know about? If so, it has an amazing gestation period if the beast was just let loose this morning."

"*Nein*," said Hans. "This *zangoid* was let loose several days ago to adjust to the environment. Experiment."

Both the hunter-guides looked as though they were undecided about whether to try to capture the creature or just blast it.

The creature didn't wait for their decision. It squiggled out of its host—clearly dead now, damaged tongue lolling, ribs spoked up like tombstones—and scurried for cover.

"Quick," cried Hans. "Hank—shoot it!" He raised his own blaster.

Hank wiped off a layer of blood and raised his own weapon.

Before either could twitch a trigger, however, something tore through the shrubbery. It was going almost too fast to see, but Brookings, who had excellent eyesight, made out the dim outline of some kind of boomeranglike device.

It whooshed through the air.

It sliced into the thick worm creature, cleanly lopping off its head.

The wormthing writhed in death throes.

The device that had killed it whisked back into the bushes, disappearing from sight.

"What the hell—" said Hans.

Brookings crouched, looking around. "It looks as though we're not the only ones hunting today."

"What do we do?"

"For right now, we just stay put and see what happens."

The others, however, paid no heed to this advice.

Two men broke and ran back in the direction in which they'd come.

"No, you idiots. Wait!" cried Hans. "There could be danger! Stay *together*!"

Neither listened. They cut through the quickest way back to the savanna, to civilization.

"Let 'em go, man," said Hank. "We've got our own problems."

"What's happening—"

"I dunno. Those weird signals we been getting. The tech boys have been saying that something weird's been going on for a while now, but the head honchos have been just forging on, you know. Turn on the cameras. We better get this down for posterity."

"And posterior holes, from the sounds of it," said Brookings.

"Camera's been on ever since I saw that thing," said Hans, backing away slightly, as though just in case something else was going to blow out of that chest cavity, or even the head maybe. "Bad stuff." His blaster was up, and his eyes were easing back and forth, catching a wide arc of vision. Feet apart, ready. A professional's stance.

"What do we do?" asked Petra.

"I suggest we see how our guinea pigs do in their path, eh?" said Brookings.

"Stalking horses of their own making?"

"Precisely."

The stalking horses were galloping along, indeed, at a rapid clip.

However, they did not make it.

Before they were halfway through the glade, immediately under a large palmlike tree, something shuddered in the foliage, and something black, something netlike folded around them from beneath, hoisting them into an elastic-gripped ride. They bounced in their tree-prison only once, before other things rippled through the foliage.

Spears.

Simultaneously these javelins transfixed the attempted escapees. One through the head. The other from shoulder through groin.

Both men had just enough time to let off a yelping screech and wiggle a little bit before the streams of blood started streaming out like beet juice through a colander.

"Oh God, oh God, oh God," cried one of the newbies.

"Shit and damnation. That fuckin' tears it!" said Hank. "This ain't supposed to be happenin'."

"Hank! Stay in formation!"

Ignoring his fellow hunter, the well-muscled man ran forward, spraying a huge plume of energy up into the treetops from where the javelins had emerged.

Defoliation on a massive scale. The leaves did not even have time to burst into flame. They were simply blown into carbon along with many of the surrounding trees, leaving only blackened skeletons behind.

Hank turned around, a satisfied smile broadening his lug's mug. "There. That should hold the bastards down awhile, so we can see what the hell's going on. Hans, what are you showing on your sensors?"

"Nothing."

"Can't see anything up in the trees, either," added Petra.

"Maybe we got whoever it was," said Hank.

"I thought I saw something hopping from tree to tree up there," said a slender, bespectacled woman, who in Brookings's estimation wasn't quite as geeky as the others.

"What—now?"

"No, before."

Hank shrugged. "I guess we're just going to have to sift through the ashes. What do you think, Hans? Some kind of assassination attempt on one of dese worthies here with us?"

"I don't know. Any of you have reason to think somebody's after you?"

"Maybe they were after Blake and Alvarez," suggested Petra.

"Those guys. Unlikely," added a jowly man named Gustavson, profusely sweating.

"May I, as a lawyer, remind you gentlemen that we are presently all on audio and video, and doubtless this may be used in some sort of hearing," said Brookings.

"You can turn *that* off, buddy," said Hank. "There's no law out here but The Man's."

Brookings shrugged. "Sorry. Guess I'm just on automatic."

"What are we going to do? Take the bodies back with us?" said Hans.

"I'm afraid that I kind of blew them apart as well."

"Pick up the pieces, then."

"May I suggest that we pick up our own pieces and get out while the getting's good?" said Gustavson.

"We could send back an armored vehicle to paw through the wreckage," said Hans.

"I think that would be wise."

"I just can't figure out what went on there," said Hans.

"I really think we should leave that to the experts," said Hank. "We'll just get the data on this situation now, then get the hell *out* of here."

"*Ja.* I'm working on it, I'm working on it."

"Christ, you rube. You're going to have to get a little closer than that to get anything."

All this time Abner Brookings had been growing increasingly nervous. Before, the prey had certainly been capable of turning back and biting, but that was all part of the fun. Before, this place had been alien and strange, but that had been the frosting on the cake, fun stuff as well.

Now, though . . .

Now, with an armed and *civilized* menace mysteriously skulking about among the trees, things were profoundly altered into the truly unknown. Abner Brookings generally faced intelligent opponents in court, and those were not armed. Now he was in quite uncomfortable territory, and the threat to his mortality was not thrilling; it was unsettling on a deeper level than he knew he had.

"Perhaps you should be thinking about a higher calling, gentlemen," said Brookings.

"Yeah?" said Hank absently and brusquely as he made his way closer to the unharmed trees, holding out his sensors to get the best possible reading. "Like what?"

"I'm talking about your charges. You're responsible

for twelve lives here, two of which have been extinguished."

Hank shrugged. "Look, buster—you signed the agreement. Did you read the thing?"

Brookings was a lawyer. Brookings read everything he signed. Only as a consultant of the corporation, he hadn't signed anything—this trip was free for him and was all included under his umbrella agreement with the corporation.

"Well—er . . ."

"What it says, Shylock, is you fucking pay your money, you fucking take your chances."

Voices raised among the group. Voices that seemed to be in general disagreement with that sentiment.

"Shit. Fuckin' Sunday hunters."

Hank shook his head sorrowfully and waded out into the unknown. He directed the sensors in a wide arc.

He stopped in his tracks.

"Shit, Hans."

"Vat?"

"There ain't just something out there . . . there's *several* somethings out there, *moving*, and I can't see a goddamned one of them."

"Look—over there . . . ," cried one of the Sunday hunters.

Brookings followed the pointed finger.

Yes. There looked like something fuzzy and displaced among the trees. Leaves shook and a branch visibly bowed.

"Get your asses down here," shouted Hank. He pointed his blaster up at the trees. "Or I'm going to mow those trees down, just like I did—"

There was only a brief flicker.

A thunk, and a tearing.

A sharp intake of breath.

The next thing Brookings knew, Hank staggered, equipped with a new appendage.

A javelin just like the one that had killed the others had almost magically appeared, transfixed in his chest, bloody barb sticking out of his side.

Hank looked down at the spear.

For a moment he tried to pull it out of his body, and then he keeled over dead.

"Damn!" Hans said no other words of benediction for poor Hank's departing soul. He just ran forward, screaming, pouring out a blast of energy from his gun.

For his trouble he was rewarded with one of the boomerang devices. It sailed through the air, again seemingly out of nowhere, and cleanly sliced through most of his neck.

The head whipped back on the remaining strands of skin and muscle. A fountain of blood whooshed up into the air. The blaster scorched the earth harmlessly under Hans's clenched fingers. Upside down, horrified and stunned eyes stared at the party for a moment, aware . . .

And then the light died in them.

The body toppled over, still twitching. A gout of fire churned up some more dirt.

And then it was over.

For Hans . . .

A rush of adrenaline and panic suffused every cubic centimeter of Brookings's body. He looked down at his antique, expert rifle—and it seemed as useless as some stick.

The stink of death was in the air, and Abner Brookings had no desire to add his own to the mix.

He reached over with his rifle and tapped Petra on the shoulder.

"I don't like the turn of events. Let's go."

"Maybe we should grab the blaster."

"Uh-uh. That's going to invite another attack. Let's see how fast you can run. Follow."

So saying, he turned and started running back the way they'd come.

The remaining hunters were mostly frozen, transfixed with terror. Their protectors, after all, had been
killed, and now they were effectively alone in the wild
in a confrontation with an unknown enemy.

Two of them began firing randomly into the brush.
Mistake.

Deep in the pit of his instinct for survival, Brookings knew this was a mistake. Exactly *how*, he had no
idea ... but there was *something* ...

He didn't dwell on the subject. He just ran on it, offering absolutely no resistance.

Petra's footsteps and huffing sounded behind him.
The woman was smart. Follow the lead of your betters ... a practice that Brookings had always used
personally.

He was in good shape, a good runner, and he felt
the chemicals of his fear charging through his muscles like well-oiled, high-octaned pistons.

The path back was beaten, and the other end was
clear and free. If he could make it back there, Brookings had the feeling that he could make it.

Behind him he heard the shrill sounds of shots and
screams.

The massacre he'd foreseen was in the offing.

He put on a burst of speed.

Behind him he heard the sound of a trip, the stutter
of attempted renewal of balance, and the *chuff* of
bushes swept aside by a fall.

"Brookings. Give me a—"

A muffled yell.

Brookings's natural inclination was just to keep on
running. However, he sensed he was in an area of
safety, for now. He could spare a few seconds. . . .

And boy, would Petra *owe* him.

It was better than money. It was a power that
Brookings actively cultivated. He stopped, went back
to where his fallen colleague was lying on her stomach, struggling to get up.

"Come on, chum." Brookings reached down and pulled Petra up by her arm. "No time for lying about. We've got to save our—"

He realized that the squelched screaming wasn't coming from the distance.

It was coming from Petra.

Affixed to her face was some sort of crablike creature. Brookings could see the ridges of blood where it clung, like some hellish mask.

Brookings let go and backed away.

There was nothing he could do. *Nothing.*

Abner Brookings was a man of quick, decisive powers, and he made a fast decision now. He was going to have to leave Petra to fend for herself.

The sound of the dying filling his ears, he turned and ran for all he was worth.

8

he planet Blior was an Earth-type world, fourth of seven planets around a GO sun. It had five moons, none of which were large.

When Machiko had read the specs on the computer in her prepping work, she had understood why Livermore Evanston had taken the time, the trouble, and the huge expense to settle and colonize this world for his own business purposes. It was an ideal world, with a nice atmosphere, a perfect axial spin, which gave it mild seasons, and a terrific balance between sea and land. There were twenty-nine Australia-sized continents distributed around the planet. Evanston had actually started his colony on only one, leaving lots of room for growth.

This island continent was called, arrogantly enough, Livermoreland, with its capital city dubbed

Evanstonville. When the rich man's yacht landed at the compound's spaceport, and Machiko stepped out onto the fresh tarmac and got a lungful of the air, any doubt of the planet's beauty and worth was immediately erased.

However, she was distracted by what was waiting for them: a group of twenty-one people, dressed in exaggerated military garb, reminiscent of the plumage sported by officers in the Napoleonic wars. They raised rifles and fired into the air in salute to the return of their obvious leader.

Evanston saluted them, smiling broadly.

"A little flourish of mine I enjoy. I employ a great many people, and we often have old-fashioned reenactments of famous battles from various parts of history. Gives my security forces a chance to exercise. We have an adequately trained force of two hundred people, with a hundred reserve. Of course, they also have other jobs and functions."

"Security force? You're in the middle of nowhere. What do you need a security force for?"

The smile became a frown. "You never know. The unprepared planet is the doomed planet." He brightened. "Besides, it amuses me. Warfare, after all, is a form of hunting. And re-creation of battles is a valid sport. No one is hurt—much less dangerous than what people pay me for. I'm hoping to make these kinds of re-creations a larger part of the entertainment here one day."

"Have you had any run-ins with belligerent intelligent life?"

"No, but that doesn't mean that I won't," he said sharply, momentarily showing a harsh side. He softened, allowing the charm to flow back in. "Please. Allow a rich man his paranoia. After all, I allow you a sidearm." He nodded down to the holster, which held an old-fashioned .38 revolver, a weapon that Machiko felt comfortable with and had requested permission to use.

"True. It seems to be a scary, unexpected universe." She nodded at the uniformed people. "If you've got all these guns and warriors here, what do you need me for?"

"You and the others I've employed recently are specialists, Machiko. My security forces are merely people with guns and a lot of time on their hands. You are a past master—an artist, if you will."

She let it drop and watched for a moment as the military sorts marched off to canned martial music. She was amused by this display, but mostly she was impressed by the scenery around her.

This was an *incredible* world.

She'd seen that on the way down, through the viewers. Evanston had shown them a special travelogue detailing some of the features. The usual panoply of waterfalls, crashing surf, sunsets, throbbing music, majestic mountains, jewellike jungles, purple waves of grain, et cetera. Machiko always just sort of tuned these kinds of things right out. You could doctor the hell out of images, and even though you could get some wonderful 3-D in-your-face special effects out of the medium, there was absolutely nothing like *being* there.

Blior had that pristine, rapturous glow of nature and creation and life and rock and water and pure air that the homeworld of Earth must have owned at one time, before Man and the alien infestation sullied it with agriculture, industry, and his own fungoidlike growth.

Even when she had been in a spaceship, she could almost smell it. Blior had that quality. It was a lifeworld, and to Machiko, despite her own difficulties with that particular state of being, these were the kind of planets to her taste.

"Very habitable," she said coolly, her reserve checking her enthusiasm.

"Rather nice piquant touch to the air, don't you think?" said Evanston, who had accompanied them down the ramp. Just on the edge of the launchpad, a large limousinoid carrier was pulling up. He gestured for them to move toward it. "Like an excellent year of Beaujolais, just decanted."

Attila sniffed tentatively. "Smells of exhaust to me."

"My goodness, Machiko. Your crony has an extraordinarily sour frame of mind for one embarking on such an exciting adventure." Although Evanston clearly didn't like Attila, he bore the android's presence with a bluff kind of humor that Machiko appreciated. Odd rich duck that he was, he was the kind of impresario whose language, carriage, and demeanor were at least always entertaining.

"You have to excuse Attila. He resents anyone who enjoys life."

"To the contrary. I applaud. I'd enjoy life a great deal myself—if I had one."

"Please, just ignore him. He really does have a heart of gold."

"Is *that* how they make androids these days? Well, I suppose gold *is* a good deal cheaper now."

"Sticks and stones, Mr. Evanston." The mouthy android shrugged. "Okay, okay. Actually, I say this begrudgingly, but it *is* quite a world, and from my stay on your ship—which I enjoyed immensely, particularly your library—I'd venture to say that the eponymous city we are about to behold will be quite something as well."

"Absolutely, absolutely. But I warn you both—don't compare the ship to the world. The city is most explicitly not constructed along classic masculine lines. You will see Victoriana or whatnot here and there, where appropriate—however, for philosophic purposes I've instructed the designers to dispense with most of the curlicues."

Attila shrugged. "Perhaps you'll allow me to have access to your yacht occasionally?"

Evanston beamed. "Certainly. Glad to keep you interested. Considering your disapproving intellect, I seem to have captured some of your imagination."

"Any warlike nature is just a program I employ when necessary. The purpose of war is to bring peace."

"Ah yes. That Chinese war philosopher said that, didn't he?"

Attila seemed impressed. "Yes, as a matter of fact. Lao Tzu?"

"Precisely. But didn't he also say, 'The purpose of peace is to prepare for war'?"

"Only in terms of balance."

"Your interpretation. Allow me mine." Evanston gestured. "Besides, this is not about *war.* . . . Hunting is far more primal, elemental."

"And these days, exclusive . . . ," said Machiko. She gave Attila a "Would you please shut up" kind of look, and the android nodded grudgingly.

"Also, this world is about far more than hunting. I'm not, after all, totally bloodthirsty." The irony was rich in his voice, and Machiko's chuckle was honest. "This world is about—enterprise."

"Free enterprise?" said Attila, taking on an interested tone.

"Well, it's certainly not *free*," replied Evanston. "You've got to be *extremely* well-heeled to come here. I suppose I'll eventually make a profit. You'll have to ask my business people about that. . . . On second thought, don't. They advised against it." He shook his head. "People with no vision. Still, business, hobby, whatever—it's a *magnificent* place, and I'm sure you'll be quite impressed with it. In fact, I'll give you the Cook's Tour, forthwith."

As soon as they arrived at the limousinoid, a man hopped out of the backseat.

"Good day, Mr. Evanston," the man piped. "Welcome back. And good day, Machiko Noguchi and Attila the Hun. Welcome to our magnificent planet."

"How does he know our names?" asked Machiko.

"I took the liberty of subspacing the results of my quest back to my highest officers. This, my new friends, is my personal secretary and entertainment director, Willem Cordial."

The man gave a brisk, self-mocking bow. "At your service. I'll be in charge of your personal needs during your stay here," said the man. "Anything you want, I'll get it. If this were a giant luxury hotel, I, Willem Cordial, would be your personal concierge!"

Willem Cordial was a short, slender man with blond hair, a perfect tan, and sunglasses. He wore khaki shorts and loafers shined to a glossy finish, a short-sleeved safari jacket, and a large rimmed safari hat. He had a clean-scrubbed, young look about him, and a squeaky, obsequious voice. There was a gap between his front teeth, and a feathery caterpillar of a mustache perched precariously below his nose.

"I sincerely hope that on your agenda for this stay will be the bagging of some big game!" said the man.

Machiko could only goggle. The guy seemed more like a comic parody of a hunter than anything approaching manliness and competence. She looked over to Evanston to see if this was some kind of joke, but for all intents and purposes Evanston was very matter-of-fact with the man.

No jester here, just another unusual facet of an unusual operation.

"I'm sure we'll take time for that, if time is indeed provided, Mr. Cordial," said Machiko. "However, we are here primarily to do a job, not partake of the obvious—ah—benefits of this world."

"Nonsense," said Evanston. "You're entitled to have a good time on your leisure hours and days, and Willem here will make sure you do. Isn't that right, Willem?"

"Entertainment is indeed my job."

"Excellent," pronounced Evanston. "Now, your bags will be along presently. In the meantime we'll show you Evanstonville and then take you to your quarters."

Willem Cordial gestured to the open car door and the luxurious leather seats beyond. "Please, just slide on into this climate-controlled vehicle, and we will endeavor to be of whatever service we—"

A sudden screeching of wheels got their attention.

A small sporty car was approaching them at high speed. The low car squealed to a stop just short of the limo, its bubble top popped, and a man jumped out of the car. He wore an expensive suit and tie, but looked disheveled and out of sorts. As he approached, Machiko could see that he had flesh-colored bandages on his face. "My God, Brookings. What happened to you? Abner Brookings, this is Machiko Noguchi. I have indeed retrieved her and she's in our service."

"Great. Nice to meet you. Sorry to disturb you, Mr. Evanston. I heard you were landing. I must speak to you personally."

"Well, of course. I should be in my office later on in the day."

"I'm sorry, sir. This is a vital issue and I must talk with you immediately. Important business . . ."

There was a wild and frightened look in his eye, and Machiko could sense that this man was not used to being frightened.

"Surely—"

"If I could just have your ear for a moment."

"Excuse me."

The two men walked back toward the car, out of earshot. The well-dressed man made a few heated gestures as he spoke in a whisper.

"*Some*thing's going on," said Machiko.

"Who *is* that guy?"

"He's a prominent lawyer, working on some high-level business here," said Mr. Cordial. "Now, then, if you'll hop into the car, we'll be all ready—"

"Has it got anything to do with my assignment here?" said Machiko.

"I haven't the foggiest, really," said their host. "Now, if you will get into the car—"

"I agree totally. Machiko should know," said Attila, turning as though to walk toward the talking men.

Cordial became noticeably flustered. "Please, no ... please cooperate."

"No need to rock the boat, Til," said Machiko, placing a calming hand on her android's arm. "After all, we're just hired hands."

The little man noticeably relaxed. "I think you'll find this vehicle very comfortable. We have a variety of music, snacks, and a full beverage bar for your needs."

Attila got in first. Machiko was about to follow when she realized that Livermore Evanston was clomping back to join them.

"No, no," said the big man. "Continue. I'm afraid I have to attend to something immediately, and so I'll be riding back with Mr. Brookings. Mr. Cordial, would you be so kind as to take my place in showing these folks around?"

Cordial positively beamed. "Why, yes, sir. And I think we'll actually be able to hunt up a splendid time."

"Good. Good. I will speak to you later, Noguchi, when you are comfortably situated in your quarters."

The usually affable, in-control Evanston looked quite preoccupied, thought Machiko.

She slid in beside Attila while Cordial spoke to the driver a minute.

"Wonder what's going on," said Machiko.

Attila wore a puzzled, worried expression. "I heard a few of the words."

"Well?"

But then Cordial was back, all smiles and goofy good cheer, and they were off on their tour, their guide yak-yak-yaking away.

9

Evanstonville was clearly more a settlement than a real city; however, it was spread out over a wide area, and there were many large and architecturally interesting buildings. It was set in a beautiful valley beside a meeting of two rivers. Trees and grass and plains surrounded it, green and vibrant.

As they drove along a road that crossed one of the rivers via a lovely old-fashioned bridge, Cordial explained that rather than allow his own city to grow in a haphazard fashion, Livermore had, with the help of experts, planned the whole thing out beforehand. Vital pieces—spaceport, essential roads, bridges, quarters and residences, storage places and parks—had been set in first, and as time and tide allowed, and actual colonists came to live and work on the world, the place would grow in a preordained and contained fashion. In this way there would be an aesthetic to every part of the city when in the fullness of time it was completed.

They drove past fountains and gardens and spectacularly designed buildings, many of which were just under construction. After viewing the city hall and main hotel, Machiko had to allow that she was impressed. There wasn't just money going on here, there was taste.

Then they stopped at a duck pond in the central park, and she had to reconsider.

Not that the park wasn't beautiful. It was. As centerpiece to the entire settlement, and to the future masterpiece city, it was already galaxy class. All manner of trees and grass and flowers and other blended botanical wonders were sculpted into a paradisal vision of nature, complete with rolling fields and swooping copses, glimmering streams and waterfalls, pretty ponds, and in the very middle, a splendid lake stocked with fish and graced with a collection of the greatest variety of Earth ducks and swans and other waterfowl that Machiko had ever seen.

"*Very* nice," she said.

"Rather like an interesting Western version of a Japanese garden, don't you think?" said Attila.

Mr. Cordial beamed with the compliments. "I think that all sorts of influences can be seen in this park."

"Well, I wouldn't go that far, Til," said Machiko. "I mean, where's the Zen garden, for instance?"

"Pardon?" said Cordial, brow furrowed.

"Zen garden. You know, sand, rocks, contemplation. Meditation!"

Cordial whipped out an electronic notebook, made a quick gathering of jottings. "An excellent notion. I'll make the suggestion. And please, any other thoughts ... we'd appreciate them."

"Can we get out of the car and enjoy the fresh air by the lake?", said Machiko.

A frown from Cordial. "Well . . . actually, there are other things you should see, and we should be getting on."

"Nonsense. We need to stretch our legs, don't we?"

"Yes. After all, doesn't this vehicle make these stops? I mean, it *is* a stretch limo, isn't it?"

Cordial laughed. "Well, don't we have a sense of humor? Very well, but only for a few minutes."

"I'd like to take a look at some of these species of waterfowl," said Machiko as she got out. "You must have some sort of genetic and cloning biofactory here as well."

"Indeed, indeed. One of the features I was going to point out."

Amid the fresh floral and water smells, the sweet of grass and the sour of turned soil, they strolled down to the edge of the lake. Machiko produced a handful of crackers that she'd taken from the snack bin, gave some to Til, and together they soon had a flock of the things feeding and fluttering before them.

"Idyllic," pronounced Attila.

"Most disciplined," said Machiko. "And very interesting. I think I've already got a few questions I'd like to ask Mr. Evanston."

"Oh, I'm quite equipped with answers."

"No, I think I'll just use them for conversational fodder with our employer, if you don't mind."

"Of course not. Now perhaps we should be—"

"Say, look," said Attila, pointing to a rise just beyond the lake. "Another touring party?"

Machiko looked. She wasn't equipped with Attila's telescopic vision, but Cordial had supplied her with a pair of opera glasses to enjoy some of the scenery. She picked these up and examined the new arrivals.

They were a group of six men, all wearing stylized camouflage coveralls. Big hats and enormous goggles covered their eyes, and shoulder pads made them all look uniformly masculine and powerful.

"How peculiar. Who are these men, Cordial?" asked Machiko.

"Guests."

"Ah! So these are some of the rich men who've come to hunt."

Cordial nodded. "That is correct. Now, the limo is waiting, and there's so much more I want to show you."

Machiko put her glasses to her eyes.

"Wait a minute," she said. "These guys have guns."

"Shotguns, from the looks of them," added Attila. "How curious. Some sort of display of macho power. I also see holsters and bandoliers of ammunition."

"Yes," said Cordial with a forced cheeriness. "We of Hunter's World work to create an ambience of imagination and virility. Longtime symbols of power are utilized to create a sense of security and self-confidence in our guests. We also create exercises to prepare our guests for larger, more dangerous hunts and—"

"They're throwing bread to the ducks and swans," reported Attila. "They seem to be gathering in great numbers."

"What—feeding the birds is some sort of good-luck ritual before safari? I've never heard of that," said Machiko.

"Not exactly. This park, uhm, serves many purposes, all calculated to bring on various moods and satisfactions. In fact, if you'll just accompany me around to the other end, I'll show you something very interesting, something that—"

A gigantic, echoing blast interrupted his words.

Other blasts followed.

Machiko swiveled to see what was going on.

"Goodness," said Attila.

"Ha ha," tittered Cordial nervously. "Just a display of high spirits among our guests."

Ka-blam, ka-blam, ka-blam.

The men had lifted their guns and aimed them point-blank at the large gathering of birds trustingly partaking of the bready offerings. Now many of these ducks and such were just clouds of broken feathers and down, interspersed with a fine mist of blood and bone. Ruined duck bodies lay sprawled in the gory water. A flutter of wings took to the sky.

Whoops of joy.

Bloodthirsty success.

Ka-blam, ka-blam, ka-blam.

Flame and smoke poured from shotguns, and hard metal pellets shattered through a dozen more bodies.

The massacre was truly something to see, a Fourth of July of excess. As the shots ended and the ducks that had escaped flew away pell-mell, Machiko found herself gaping. The manly men were stomping around the flesh-and-feather detritus, laughing and clapping each other on the back.

The yautja had never done anything like this. Their prey were always hunters themselves. For food they would take down prey, yes—but never in such a disgusting display.

Machiko found herself sick to her stomach.

"My goodness," said Attila. "It seems a little excessive, doesn't it? And the waste!"

"Oh, the lab-and-factory folks can whip up more, I quite assure you."

"But the mess . . . hardly idyllic."

"A momentary thing, I assure you," said Cordial. "Look—the service robots are already coming."

A number of robots—true robots, of the servo-sort, of plastic and glass, waldo arms, and visible gears and equipment—appeared as though magically, hustling down on this barbaric scene. Quickly, the brave hunters picked up a few of the less-damaged birds for souvenirs and then let the robots deal with the rest. They set off for further park adventures, bloody and happy, tilting flasks and singing songs.

"Truly, where *else* in the galaxy can such exercises be discovered?" said Cordial. "Now perhaps another side of the park, and then on for the rest of the tour."

"Mind if my android and I take a little walk alone around the lake?" said Machiko.

Believe it or not, she thought to herself, *the brave huntress is feeling a little queasy.*

Cordial eyed his wristwatch. "I really do have to stick to my schedule ... and we do have excellent drugs in the car that will doubtless eradicate any stomach or intestinal distress."

Machiko nodded. She'd be able to get Attila alone eventually and hear those words that he'd heard pass between Livermore Evanston and the lawyer....

But apparently not now.

"That genetic factory you mentioned?"

"Yes?"

"The one that seems to be able to spew forth so many ducks and swans and all that expendable plasm and life things into this world?"

"I did mention such an establishment, didn't I?" He sounded a little uncomfortable, as though he hadn't realized the creature that had exited the bag had been a cat.

"If it's not too much trouble—could we have a look at that during our tour?"

Cordial, though obviously a bit discomforted by the request, said, "Certainly," with some of the verve and brightness returning to his speech.

Machiko followed Attila back into the car.

She wished she could talk this over with him now, without the ear of this flunky canting toward them.

She didn't feel real good about this "factory" thing.

Not good at all.

10

They drove past more houses, some built, some under construction, all dynamically engineered and brilliantly architecturally designed.

They drove past other parks, this time noticing roving packs of guests with guns, some bloody, some not.

They drove past a magnificent skeletal stadium, its promise explicit in the scaffolding that enclosed the growing shell.

All to the accompanying glowing descriptions of their guide, Mr. Cordial.

Finally, at the very end of the settlement, across a long field, crisscrossed by numerous fences, force fields, and other barriers and sentry posts, there loomed the most impressive building yet.

"Quite a building," said Machiko.

"More a compound, don't you think?" suggested Attila when Machiko made this statement.

"True, quite true."

In truth, there were more buildings than one, all of different shapes and sizes, but all were connected numerously by catwalks and gondolas and tubings and what have you, making it look like some gigantic monadic hamster colony. Machiko could see people walking back and forth, and a great deal of vehicular activity as well. It looked like a lively and productive industry, peculiarly stuck into a series of interconnected contemporary cathedrals. Glass and prismatic light; the occasional wisp of smoke stringing into the blue background of sky.

"Yes, there it is," said Mr. Cordial, gesturing absently. "Naturally we can't import the creatures we need for hunting purposes, so we grow and breed them there ourselves. A unique and still very experimental process, I might add, one that Mr. Evanston is watching over very carefully." He coughed. "Now, I'm sure that you're both tired and would like to make yourselves comfortable in your quarters before the other welcoming festivities our employer is preparing for you." He tapped on the partition between them and the driver, signaling him to drive past the intersection where a turn swung into the service road of the genetic-factory compound.

"We're here," said Machiko, "but we're not going to get to look inside?"

"I'm sure you must understand," said Cordial. "The activities inside those buildings are of a very sensitive and secret nature. Now, I'm certain that Mr. Evanston will allow you a tour. In fact, he probably wants to take you himself. However, we can't just barge in without warning. I sincerely hope you understand."

Attila said nothing.

Machiko nodded her head. "All right," she said. But

inside she still felt bothered. "Take us to our quarters, then."

Cordial relaxed. His entire attitude toward his guests seemed to change. Machiko sensed danger signals being dulled. Good. That was what she was hoping for.

"Thank you. I understand your curiosity, but I have my duties."

"Yes," said Machiko Noguchi, unmollified.

Their bags and clothes and other belongings were waiting for them at their room.

After all the luxury they'd experienced, the room itself was rather plain, one of ten lining a nondescript corridor in a brown-wrapper two-level building.

It was more like a barracks than a hotel, and while Attila seemed disappointed, Machiko was most emphatically not.

"We're hired soldiers here, in a way. I think that's what Livermore Evanston wants to remind us of." She sipped some tea Cordial had provided, looked out the window, and watched the limousinoid float away into the distance. The tea was iced, and it was exotic, rich, and cold; it sluiced away some of the stardust that had lined her throat.

"Okay, Til. Spill."

The android was sitting in a chair, looking thoughtful.

"I heard only a few words, but they were significant. I caught . . . 'hunting trip' 'all dead but me' 'bugs' "—he cocked his head—"and 'other hunters.' "

"That's all?"

"Yes."

"Well, that's what we're here for, right . . . the bugs."

"But who brought the bugs?"

"I believe you know what I'm thinking. . . ."

"I've heard your stories about Ryushi, but surely . . ."

"What do you think about that factory, Til?"

Attila shrugged. "Makes sense to me. Manufacture your own lions and tigers and bears."

"You think maybe Evanston was manufacturing bugs for hunting as well?"

"Why would he bring you to get rid of them?"

"Hell! They're bugs! Something always goes wrong with bugs!"

"I don't know. Why would he want to play with those things when he really hasn't even gotten Hunter's World off the ground?"

"Mysteries. Secrets." Machiko took a swallow of the slightly bitter tea, winked at her associate. "I like it. Puts some spin on the game, eh?"

"Makes *me* nervous!"

"Yes, well—it's a hell of a lot better than sitting behind some desk, monitoring mining operations."

"No comment here."

Machiko was about to ask him his opinion about the duck hunters in the park when there was a loud knocking on the door.

Attila got up and opened it.

Standing in the hallway were two tall, broad-shouldered men. Each gripped in his big hands a keg studded with microrefrigeration nodes.

"Hey, now!" bellowed one. "Welcome to Project Bug Spray. I'm ex-Captain Dick Daniels, late of the Colonial Marines, and this here's Ned Sanchez. Ned used to work for a security firm on Earth that dealt with the things." His eyes tracked from Attila to Machiko. "And you must be Machiko Noguchi." His eyes traveled over her firm, slim body in a taunting, hungry manner that she abhorred. She felt herself tensing: not another one of these jerks.

"Yes."

"Nice to meet you. We hear you're going to be

heading up this operation, so we thought we'd come over and introduce ourselves. Kinda been sitting around on our thumbs since we got here, and it's nice to know there's some action on the way, now that you're here." All said through an overfamiliar leer. He had a musky, hair-out-the-undershirt presence, and an overbearing, muscular aura that seemed to say, Let's get these formalities over with quick and then slip between the sheets, babe.

"Well, aren't you going to invite us in?" he boomed. He held up his keg. "We brought our own."

"I'm tired," said Machiko. "I only have a minute."

"That'll do!" A big grin split the man's swarthy, Roman-nosed face, and he lumbered in, handing the keg to Attila and offering Machiko a large, firm handshake. He smelled of hair and beery lunch, but he had a natural power to him, reflected in the firm muscles and the self-confident gait. His blond hair was tousled, but he was no spring chicken. It looked as though this guy had been in some heavy-duty scrapes and, from the scars on him, hadn't come out unbloodied. But unbowed? That was another story.

"Got some mugs or something?" he asked. Attila went to find something.

"Say, you're one solid woman. You'll have some beer with us, won't you?"

"I'm drinking tea."

"Oh, c'mon." He turned to Attila. "Get a brew for my new sweetheart, will you, guy?" he roared off at Attila. "We don't know what we're getting into here. Might as well party while we can, right, angel-eyes?"

With no warning Daniels stepped over and put his big arm around Machiko's back. She could immediately smell that he'd been drinking beer before he'd arrived. Somehow his big hand wriggled down to her backside and squeezed her right buttock as though testing the ripeness of a melon. The buffoon was large, probably weighing over twice as much as

Machiko, and probably figured he could get away with this kind of behavior by sheer intimidation.

Machiko barely thought about what she was doing; her reaction was automatic. She pulled the hand away, grabbed his arm by the wrist, stepped away, and with practiced ease flipped Daniels over. He landed heavily on the floor. Machiko stepped on his face as she twisted his arm at a startling angle, just short of damage.

"Next time I break it, chum. Understand?"

"Jeez. I was just joking!" objected Daniels.

"You didn't answer my question."

"I understand, I understand!"

She let him go, and he got up.

Sanchez's eyes twinkled, and there was a slight smile on his face.

"I told you to cut that kind of stuff out, Daniels."

"Yeah, yeah, yeah," said Daniels, getting up and dusting himself off. "Guess there's a reason you're going to be in charge." He grinned uneasily. "Can't really even say you're my type, but I'd park my butt behind your command any day. Nobody's gotten the better of Dick Daniels in a *long* time."

A rollicking partyer from the feel of him.

"I'm not here for anyone's amusement, Daniels."

"Cripes. Give me that beer. I sure need it now." He took the proffered glass and downed a large gulp. Attila handed one to Sanchez as well.

Keeping himself well away from Machiko, Daniels eyed Attila. "What—we got ourselves *another* teetotaler here?"

"Not really," said Attila. Rather than getting into android territory, potentially volatile if you weren't sure of your company, Attila took a beer. "I generally prefer to wait until dark."

"Good move," said Dick. "A smarter asshole than yours truly. Here you go, Sanchez—to the pretty powerful personality we've hitched up with. I feel sorry for the bugs."

"If Ms. Noguchi doesn't mind, I'd like to try some of the beer I noticed in the refrigerator. That's a local brew of some potency, I believe. And if I'm not entirely wrong, it's a nut-brown ale."

Machiko raised an eyebrow. "Good call, Mr. Sanchez. You know your beers, then."

"From porter to lager," said the man easily. "My favorite is bitter. At room temperature."

"An Anglophile?"

"Nope. Limey bastards are just as rotten as anybody. I just like their beer, that's all."

Ned Sanchez was slender, younger than his companion, and certainly darker, though there were suggestions of gray threading through his long black hair, tied in a ponytail at the back of his head. He was friendly and relaxed, but there was a hard and remote core of reserve to this man, and an unreadable nature to his fierce, empty black eyes. Otherwise, he had a face like a Greek demigod, and his beauty was not lost upon even so jaded a soul as Machiko's.

"Sure. I don't know about room temperature. The tea is cold. I don't generally drink beer, but once in a while I enjoy something of quality."

Sanchez shrugged. "I'll live through the experience of a cold ale. Little hot outside, anyway."

Dick slammed his big hand against his buddy's back. "Shit. Neddy and me, we done some heavy maneuvers today with the guys, just funnin', you know, but keeping in shape—and he barely pops a sweat. Quick shower, and he's ready for another evening of brews and babes." He straightened himself with feigned pain and examined a fancied bruise. "I don't know, though. Maybe just an evening of brews might be safe."

"I didn't realize this was Sodom and Gomorrah," said Attila dryly.

Machiko watched as the android sipped at his beer, amused. Attila could drink as much as he wanted without effect. He almost literally had a "hollow leg." And these guys hadn't seemed to realize yet he was an android. Of course, it was rare one could, unless the law was to have androids marked . . . and there was no such law here.

"What? You gotta be kiddin' me. You get in a bunch of rowdy and rich men to shoot it up during the day, and you're going to have to keep them entertained at night. Pretty easy, that. Some gambling, some girls—and lots of drink!"

"I can spare a little time," said Machiko. She felt herself relax slightly. Daniels's good-natured response to getting tossed on his face amused her. A yautja would have demanded immediate satisfaction of honor in a tooth-and-nail battle to the Death. *Calm down kid*, she told herself. *You've changed, remember?* She invited her guests to sit down. Sanchez sat quietly and compactly, but Daniels sprawled out over the couch, feet up on the coffee table, completely at home. "How long have you been in town?" Machiko asked.

"A whole three days," said Daniels. "We've got ourselves a company of about fifteen total now, including you." He belted a laugh, then a long swig of beer. "And let me tell you, I never did see such a mangy collection of misfits in my life."

"Oh? I'm pretty impressed so far by you two."

"Us? Oh, yeah. Mind you, we've all got the experience and pedigree and what have you, and I guess we've all seen our share of action. I'm just generally talking about the social level of the *other* guys. Mercenaries. Real pigs." He opened his mouth and let loose a long and satisfying belch without excusing himself. Then he took another drink.

"Did we come for a tiddledywinks tournament?" Machiko asked.

"Well," said Attila, "perhaps tiddledywinks and tea."

Dick Daniels looked at Attila for a moment, mouth open. Then he started laughing, and slapping his knee. "Good. Damned good. Tea! Hey, Ned, you think that Evanston can rustle up some tea for—what did you say your name was, guy?"

"I didn't."

"I'm sorry. I didn't introduce you. This is . . ." Machiko caught herself. "Attila. Oscar Attila, my assistant and personal secretary."

Obviously not feeling like getting up again, Daniels assayed a brief salute. "Howdy there, Mr. Attila." Ned nodded as well. Machiko noticed that the handsome man seemed to be retracting even further into some private space. Daniels seemed to have plenty of scars on his exterior, but Sanchez seemed to have his own as well, albeit on his interior.

It made her wonder about him. He seemed to resonate on some level that intrigued her. The fact that he was merely polite to her, taking no other particular interest in her except as the woman who was going to command him, pricked her ego slightly—and made her wonder why.

She made a mental note to have a talk with him sometime during this visit. Obviously she wouldn't get much from him now, especially with Daniels ingenuously clogging the airwaves.

Still, with the man so freely dispensing information, she figured she should probably tap what she could.

And, as always, men talked more when they had a bootful.

"You know, Dick," she said, smiling, "I once knew a guy who reminded me of you."

"Oh. How so?"

"Big. Brave. Strong and obviously a man of the universe, as it were. I admired that man a lot."

Daniels responded with a cocky grin and a pleased

twinkle of the eye. The approval he'd so desperately wanted was his, offered on a satin pillow.

"One big difference."

Double take. "Oh? What?"

"He drank a lot more beer. And a lot faster. He'd have that beer done by now."

"Sheeee—it," said Daniels. "I'm just sippin', to be polite."

The gauntlet clearly thrown down, Daniels smirked. Refilled his mug. Upended.

The remainder of the liquid, at least a pint and a half by Machiko's estimation, slid past his big, bobbing Adam's apple, very little indeed slopping over his lips and rolling down his cheeks, or snorting up his nose.

Daniels clapped down the large mug, red-faced but satisfied. "There you go."

"I am truly impressed." She was indeed. Within moments the man's face was noticeably redder. "My other friend didn't drink *that* fast."

Another burp interrupted the conversation.

Machiko sipped her own drink, pursing her lips thoughtfully . . . and then thought, What the hell, let's go for it.

"We seem to be alone," she gestured around inclusively. "We can talk now. We seem to be a bunch of pretty powerful troubleshooters. What seems to be the trouble?"

Daniels blinked a little blearily, accepting the next cup from Attila. "Crap. The bastard didn't tell you?"

"Let's just say I'm more interested in what he told you."

"Fuckin' *bugs*. That's what the trouble is. That's the biggest trouble I've heard of on *all* these planets." Daniels developed a slightly gray pallor. "Fuckin' bugs. Don't know how the hell they got here. Only with bugs, you never do, do you?"

"And that's the *only* trouble?"

"Far as I know. . . . Oh, shit—well, there's the hunters, the rich assholes who think they know which end of a gun the bullet or whatever come out of. Evanston knows he's going to have some accidents, which is why he sets 'em up with training and insurance, even though right now he's not legally bound for nothin'. Nope, there's plenty enough trouble not to buy any, I'll tell you."

"No sign of other kinds of 'iffy' activity? Any other kind of trouble?"

Daniels, for the first time, looked concerned. "Hey, lady. Aren't the bugs enough? Shee—it. I've been in all kinds of action. And bugs are the worse."

"But you're willing to face them again," said Machiko.

"For the money we're getting, and the treatment? Not really." The affable look was still gone, replaced by a startlingly sober expression for one getting into a drunk. "Look, this ain't just for the money. I guess the truth is, Evanston's offerin' me a home. A goddamned family. This pirate looked at forty a long time ago, and it's about time to commit to a goddamned bar stool. Eh, Ned?" He elbowed his companion, his good nature again suffusing his face.

Ned just shrugged. "We all have our reasons."

"That's damned right. And I'd like to know if yours are any different."

"Evanston got me out of the Company."

Daniels raised his eyebrows. "Really?"

The lug seemed honestly interested. Machiko found herself relaxing even more.

"I don't know about family, I don't know about home. . . . What I do know is that this is better than pushing papers. Would you agree?"

There wasn't a fighting person who wouldn't agree with that. No reason that Machiko had to hide anything with these guys.

'Sure," said Daniels. "But, hell, I got my fighting experience in the Marines, and Ned here's been after the bugs all his life. Where'd you get your experience?"

"Well, I'm a trained martial-arts expert, and I did time in officer's school—and I dealt with the bugs on a planet called Ryushi," said Machiko.

Daniels's mouth dropped. "Damn! Isn't that the planet where nearly everybody got wiped—"

"Not this body."

Daniels said nothing. He seemed to be trying to grope with something, like coughing up some other memory he had on the subject. He didn't seem to be successful, so he just took another chug of beer instead.

A flicker of interest grew in Ned Sanchez's eyes.

There was a knock on the door. "Hey. Guys. We hear noise. What's going on in there? A party?" The voice was thin, whiny, and annoying.

Daniels slapped his face. "Jeez, it's Lou MacCraken. He can smell fun a kilometer away and then comes to ruin it for everyone. Don't let him in, Ms. Noguchi."

"Is he one of the troubleshooters?"

"Yep. And if there's no trouble, he'll attract it."

"Then I should meet him."

She told Attila to open the door. A tall, gangly man came in with a big wide smile and a long nose. He had a shorter, curly-haired Neopolitan sort with him, who already had a bulb of beer in his hand. Introductions were made. MacCraken's friend's name was Mishka Marino.

"Glad to meet you," said Machiko. "Would you like a beer?"

"No. I don't drink," said MacCraken, eyes shining with a kind of goofy glee. "Give Marino something, though. He drinks."

"Only with one hand, Lou."

"That's so he can grab the guys. And the gals. Right, Marino? Better watch out, Ms. Noguchi. You're his type. You're all his type."

Marino rolled his eyes as MacCraken cackled a high-pitched laugh.

Machiko cringed a bit and looked over to Daniels as though to say, You're right; where did Evanston get *this* geek?

Still, this manic guy was entertaining if you didn't take him too seriously, and the conversation progressed. With the right questions Machiko drew out some little essentials about Evanstonville and Livermoreland that only a few days' stay could have obtained.

For one thing, not only had Evanston hired a great many workers and started up a colonist movement to this planet, he had somehow tapped the resources of the corporation in terms of expertise, just as he had done with Machiko. There were apparently a good many "four eyes" here—a Marine bit of slang for technicians and scientists. Many of them, Daniels said, worked in the factory and really didn't mix much with the rest of the community.

Machiko tried to milk them all for more information about that factory but came up totally dry. These guys hadn't even gotten *close* to the thing, nor were they particularly interested in doing so. They were obviously thrilled with their jobs, not so much because of the bugs, who obtained the unhealthy respect they deserved, but because of the environment here and the perks involved.

They talked about the other people who'd been selected. All seemed to have similar backgrounds: soldiers of fortune mostly, experience with bugs, a mercenary bent with an inclination to settle down in a place that had its share of thrills and excitement. Evanston must have promised them a place in his structure here, just as soon as the little problem was gone. Guides. Battle technicians. Simulators. Whatever. This was just their kind of place, no question—a paradise for men with a trade in violence, who hankered for some peace of mind.

"I look forward to meeting the others," said Machiko finally.

"Should I round them up?" asked Lou eagerly, excess energy radiating from him.

"Uh—no. No, I confess that—ah—Mr. Attila and I are a bit tired. And I, alas, have had my share of beer already. Tomorrow. Formally. It's been great meeting you guys informally, but let's just call it a day, all right?"

"Sounds good to me," said Daniels, getting up and scratching his butt.

"One last question, though," said Machiko. "It would seem that the bugs would be perfect hunting material, the ultimate experience. Do you think maybe Evanston planned to use them this way, and they got out of control?"

Daniels raised an eyebrow. "With all respect, ma'am, anyone who hunts bugs for sport has either got to be crazy, suicidal—or maybe just a little buglike themselves."

From the mouths of lumbering bruisers, thought Machiko.

They bade their adieus and filed out to find whatever other fun they could.

Ned Sanchez was the last one.

"Mr. Sanchez," said Machiko, putting a hand on his arm.

"Ned would be fine," he said easily, his dark eyes unreadable.

"You don't talk much. I get the feeling you might know more about this operation than the others."

His face remained expressionless. "I get the feeling you know more than all of us combined."

She shrugged and let him go.

But the parting seemed incomplete. She wanted to know more of what this man knew. She wanted to know more about Ned Sanchez, period.

You've been holding out on me," said Attila above the whir of the blades.

"Oh?" She adjusted her headset so she could hear him properly. "How so?"

"You never told me you could fly a copter."

She shrugged. "The way they make these things these days, it only takes a couple of engram imprints, some virt/real lessons, and then some hands-on." She smiled at him. "I bet we could just plug a new program into you and you could do it, too. Fact, I bet you could do it right now." She pushed a button. The steering wheel came off and she handed it to him.

He looked alarmed for a moment, and then he handed it back. "Ha ha ha. It's on automatic, isn't it?"

"Glad to see I haven't lost my sense of humor?" she said.

"Actually, I'm glad you haven't lost control of this craft!" Even though he didn't have the right sort of circulatory system, it was clear that Attila was white-knuckling the ride. She didn't blame him at all. She was swooping around a bit too much. Well, she'd keep the grav copter on a steady keel for a while.

It was the afternoon of the day after they had arrived on this world, and already they were out looking for trouble.

Machiko had requisitioned the vehicle that morning. Evanston had advised against looking over the terrain quite yet, but he'd been too busy catching up on other affairs to give her any real orders, so she'd talked him into at least letting her take a look at the surrounding environs, to get a feel for the lie of the land.

The other troubleshooters were out on maneuvers. She and Attila had joined them briefly. She'd met them but hadn't said much. They were pretty much as Daniels had said: worn mercenaries, looking for a home. She'd given them the usual patter: good to meet you, let's get this job done and done right, blah blah blah. Fortunately, her enthusiasm was real. All this was *so* much better than tapping input into a computer and riding herd on corporate mining nonsense.

And the possibility that she'd be dead next week, acid rotting out her brain? All the sweeter, because of the sharpened sense of life that she felt now.

They were in tree territory . . . alien trees, a kind of deciduous rain forest with large patches of plains and rivers. Wild, wild, with herds of native creatures glimpsed here and there and bright, vivid colors poking through the general green and brown.

"I wonder what kind of ecologists Evanston hired," said Attila.

"You think he's thought that far ahead?"

"Oh, yes, he would have to. There's no need to

terraform this place, but its life-forms are complex enough to take great consideration, especially if he's introducing new species."

"He's probably got a lot more on his mind now than just that."

"Probably. Nonetheless, he was talking about settling this whole planet—"

"He's most likely not too worried, since he's only settling a continent at a time. This one he figures he can mess up."

"A shame. It looks quite nice the way it is."

"I think that's the idea. A whole island continent for hunters to joyously plunder, free from restrictions and rules."

"Paradise."

"Or hell."

"Depends on your point of view."

Machiko thought for a while as the verdant land swept under the rotors and body of the copter.

"Til, something's going on here, something more than Evanston's told us about," she said finally.

Attila nodded. "I think we should talk about that. Put the pieces together . . ."

"I'm almost afraid to."

"Why?"

"I don't know."

"Sure you do. It's that gift-horse phenomenon."

"Yeah. But still—it's better than where I came from."

Attila sniffed. "We'll see about that."

"What, you want to go back?"

"I didn't say that. I'm just performing my function."

"What? Being a goddamned stick in the mud?"

"No. Being someone you can bounce ideas off of. Still, I'm entitled to my opinions, right?"

"I can think of a few other things to bounce off of you at this moment."

"You'd be so lonely without me." He smiled. Needling was such a gentle revenge. Machiko knew that deep down in his masochistic heart, Attila was rather enjoying it. Truth was, he was probably just wondering if he'd have to actually transform all that theory he was brimming with into practicality—and if the wise sage would get reduced to rubble in the process.

"Well, nothing untoward so far on sensors. You wouldn't have noticed anything, would you, with your special little nodes?"

"A great many things, but nothing that sends needles into the red."

"We'll just bank and take a look at the northwest quadrant awhile and then go back, okay?"

Attila nodded. "Fair enough."

The android didn't seem in a real hurry to get back to the fun and games of Evanstonville; he was just clearly not thrilled with being aloft, flying over unknown territory.

The wild land swept below them, a verdant carpet of mysterious life. Machiko perused it in silence. Such a *huge* area. How could they possibly hope to find any sign, any clue of what was going on there in just a quick field trip?

Nonetheless, they did.

She was about to call it a day when Attila spoke up. "I hate to admit this, but I see something."

"Where?"

He gave her the navigational reading, and she checked it on her scope.

Activity in a clearing.

Small things.

Big thing.

"Whoa!" she said, pulling up short and hovering for a moment. She thought about it and then lowered to a position still within sight of the scene, but far enough away not to attract undue attention. Then she punched up sensor screens and thumbed her telescopic step-ups.

"It's some kind of big lizard being attacked by smaller creatures."

Attila nodded. "I can't tell what kind, and I can't see what the creatures are."

"I have a suspicion. And if they're what I think they are, I don't want to go hovering around in that area." She pointed down to another adjacent plain. "I've got to have a look, though."

"I was afraid of that," said Attila. "Can't we just zip over and take some pictures?"

She shook her head. "If they're what I think they are, they'll know we know about them, and I'm not sure that's good."

"Better to be safe than sorry."

"And what is knowledge and the value of surveillance and intelligence?"

"Power," Attila said in a small voice.

"Exactly."

They landed.

"I want you to stay here," she said.

"Look, I may act truculent, but my job is to be by your side."

"I appreciate that, Attila. However, I need you here to keep the engines going in case we need a speedy takeoff."

"Perhaps I should go and reconnoiter and *you* can stay here."

"What? And let me miss all the fun? Besides, you're the reluctant one, aren't you?"

"Perhaps I am the careful one."

"Precisely. And I appreciate that. Sometimes, though, there are things that have to be done. And, Attila, this is something I have to do. This could be the key to everything."

"You could get yourself killed, too."

She shrugged. "Obviously. I also could have fallen out of my bureaucratic chair back on Dullworld and broken my neck. Now keep things revved up here. I won't be long."

She grabbed the camera, a blaster, and a weapons belt and hopped out of the copter, giving the rotors a wide berth. Quickly she loped up the grassy knoll separating the fields and then skulked through a large copse of trees. She was glad the copter was quiet; if the subjects of her quest here were as involved as she thought they were, they wouldn't have noticed the copter at its distance. She supposed they should have gotten just close enough to get a make on them and split. However, something deep inside her wanted some action, wanted to get closer. Was she being reckless? She thought not. There was something more down here than could be recorded through a telescopic lens.

And she had to see it for herself.

She made her way through the trees and underbrush, finally coming out through a glen to a perch above the clearing. Halfway through she began to hear the sounds of a most peculiar battle. Roars and snarls and cries. She could smell blood and conflict in the air.

She looked out.

Standing on its hind legs in the slight valley below, lunging and slashing at its attackers, was a thirty-foot-tall beast with a tail the size of a large tree, teeth and claws the size of butcher knives.

The attackers were ten yautja.

They could have been members of her old pack. But, then, Predators had no particularly variable fashion consciousness. They pretty much all wore the same kinds of clothing and armor. They were using spears and other manual weapons do deal with the creature, although a couple stood in the background with plasma pushers. This was a baiting game, clearly, not particularly in the realm of honorable.

She'd somehow expected to see Predators here and was glad that her hunches were paying off. It was good to have that knowledge. However, the beast provided the biggest surprise.

She'd never seen it before. She recognized it from books.

It was a tyrannosaurus rex.

So *that* was one of the things that the big DNA factory had been up to. It made a lot of sense. She'd heard that the biotechnology was available to bring back monsters of the past not just from old DNA, but from actually *building* DNA patterns according to specifics. She had just never seen it in use before.

Hard to imagine it done on a more dramatic level.

This was a ferocious beast, carnivorous savagery gleaming in its beady eyes. Blood rivuleted from cuts in its side and front, and a spear poked from its neck. However, all those pricks and nicks seemed only to have enraged it further.

The Predators appeared to be actually on the verge of retreating—or of using their stronger weapons. Clearly, they had bitten off more than they could chew.

She took out some binocs to have a closer look. Ranged it over the warriors . . .

And stopped on one.

Oh, God.

Shorty.

She tried to correct the focus, but it was sharp as a pin. A little bigger, a little more battered, but all the armor and other visuals aligned—this was the Predator who hated her.

Too bad she couldn't have killed him when she had the chance.

What was more, he seemed to be gesturing and carrying on as though he were in charge, orchestrating this odd exercise against the dinosaur. And not having a very good time, from the looks of it.

They were going to have to kill the beast, no question, and then immolate it or something; presumably the Hunters were operating secretly here, just as they always had on populated planets, and they wouldn't want their presence known. Should Evanston find one of his T-rexes dead from a spear wound (or blaster burns), he'd certainly have a better take on the mysterious things happening on his world.

Her mind was spinning with conjecture and speculation.

So much so, that she hardly heard the sound of the leaves rustling, the snapping of a twig.

Nonetheless, something deeper alerted her: a rising of her hackles, a deeper instinctual alarm.

She turned and saw the Hunter behind the tree.

Instantly, she realized how lucky she'd been. Doubtless, if they'd realized they would have had to deal with intelligent prey, they would have worn their cloaks. This bastard might have sneaked right up on her—

But then again, after living with them, after working with them, she rather doubted it.

Anyway, it gave her warning. The fact that he wasn't there to make friends was immediately apparent. He had his own blaster and was raising it to fire.

She was fast with her own, but not fast enough.

Nonetheless, at the same time, she *was* able to jump back and away. The edge of the jagged spout of energy caught the bore of her own weapon, and she let it go. It slammed against a tree and exploded. She rode the force, tumbling down a hill. Leaping to her feet, she used the momentum of her fall to give her a head start.

By the time the Predator swung around to shoot at her again, she was well away, running through a batch of tree boles.

She weaved helter-skelter.

Dodged.

Bark exploded next to her. She could feel the burn of the weapon's blast but did not take a moment to look back. She dived behind the bole of another tree, careful not to allow the vines growing at its base to impede her. Just down the glade, sunlight poured through an opening that she'd come through to get her view of the proceedings on the other side of the hill. If she could get through there, she'd have a clear run for the copter. Attila, seeing her coming, would be ready to take off immediately, and they'd have a chance. . . .

She leaped down the hill.

Ran into the clearing.

All the while behind her she heard the sounds of crashing pursuit.

She wondered if she should stop and make her stand. She had a pistol, and she could hide behind a tree. If worst came to worst, she could use the knife in her boot. The Hunter had a blaster, and even if they got off the ground, theoretically he could take a successful shot and destroy them both.

One of Machiko's talents was for quick, good decisions. Had she still been running with the pack, had she still been in that honor-is-everything frame of mind, doubtless she would have spun around and attacked her attacker.

However, her gut instinct was that her best hope for survival was to run for the copter.

Besides, life was just getting *good*.

She broke through into the clearing, began running for her life. Machiko noted to herself that next time she went on one of these little jaunts, she was going to bring along a radio unit. She just hadn't intended to leave the copter—this was supposed to be only a quick reconnaissance. Anyway, she had to live now with the realization that she couldn't contact Attila.

Which was unfortunate, in light of the fact that when she stormed down that ridge pell-mell, there was no sign of copter *or* Attila.

She hardly paused. She kept on running. Across the clearing were more woods and cover. If she could make that, there was a chance.

The thought pounded in her head, though:

What happened to Attila?

A blast ripped a fiery divot just to her right side. She zigzagged, dodging any other burst. In doing so she caught sight of the Predator, pounding into the sunlight, armed and ready for anything. Hardly a sight fiercer in the universe, and this was no ground on which to fight the bastard.

Her lungs aching, she hurled herself toward her objective.

She expected to feel the blast of a bolt in her back at any moment. *No*, she thought. *No*, came the voice of the warrior in her.

Better to meet death head-on.

Challenge.

She wouldn't make it to the other side of the clearing. This guy would be too good a shot. She had to rely on something she knew well—

The warrior's ego.

Standing in the open, seemingly unarmed, she doubted the Predator would kill her.

Not without allowing her a fight.

Unless, of course, things had changed, which didn't seem likely.

She was just in the act of turning when she heard an explosion.

Her instinct slammed her down onto the ground immediately, but her peripheral vision caught the action.

The top of the Hunter's body simply blew apart in a gale of fire and blood. Shards of armor and limbs and skull and bone went every which way, as if a ripe metal pumpkin had just exploded.

The remainder of the body teetered, fell.

Machiko hit the dirt, rolled. The taste of rich loam and blood was in her mouth, but she hardly noticed.

A familiar whooshing . . .

A dark form swooped down toward her. . . .

She raised her pistol but then lowered it.

The grav copter lowered itself, drew even with her.
The door flapped open.

She didn't need an invitation.

She jumped, catching hold of the ladder and
quickly pulling herself up and over the lip of the door.
In a flash she was into the passenger seat, the door
closed behind her.

Attila pulled the vehicle up and over the tops of the
trees, heading back for Evanstonville.

"Are you all right?" he asked, hands steady on the
controls.

"Yes . . . yes." She shook her head and shot a look
back at the biological wreckage. "How—?"

"I hadn't realized it before, Machiko, but this copter seems to be very well armed. That little exhibition,
for example, was the result of a first-rate rocket
launcher."

She took a deep breath. They'd already jumped a
goodly distance. Some of the adrenaline was seeping
out of her, replaced by surprise.

"Attila, I didn't know you could fly a copter."

"An unexplored area of my programming. When I
detected the fracas in the woods, I assumed you
would return, most likely pursued. I thought it would
be best to reach a firing point at which I would be
able to deal with a maximum of pursuers."

"Good choice. I thought you'd *left* me."

The self-satisfied look on Attila's face melted.
"Machiko. I would never do such a thing."

"No. No, of course not. I'm sorry. Thanks. Good
move. Now let's get back to home base."

"To confront Livermore Evanston on this matter?"

"No. We've got to give the situation some thought
first." She remembered then to buckle her harness.
"The Hunters are doing their bug thing—but why here?"

12

I t seems obvious to me,"
said Attila the Hun, lying on the bed in a relaxed
state.

Machiko Noguchi stopped her pacing. She looked
at her android warily. Since that little flying stunt a
couple hours before, she was seeing him in an entirely different light.

She knew he'd had a "life" before she'd bought
him. She didn't know about the programs that still existed inside him. What other residues of past talents,
past memories, existed? Attila insisted that he had no
memory of being able to do what he did—at the time
his sensors detected trouble, something had just
kicked in, and he'd had access.

This was something they would have to explore.

For now, though, there were other matters to attend to.

"I'm glad. Would you care to enlighten me?" she said, hands on hips.

"You'll have to pardon me, but I'm merely operating on what you tell me about the Hunters—your tales of your experiences with them."

"Yes, yes, go on."

"Well, it strikes me that they've got a fairly simple game plan. They like to find likely opponents, likely places to perform their rituals of honor. And, frankly, think about it—Blior is perfect. If their lives are the feral art they consider them, then for Predators this must be a masterpiece planet."

"A what?" Machiko asked.

"Masterpiece planet. It sounds as if Ryushi was being used as a training ground for young Hunters."

She nodded. "Blooding."

"That was their apprentice work, then. Whatever the word has come to mean since then, a 'masterpiece' used to be the article a craftsperson made to earn his or her master status. Blior is the place Hunters may earn 'master' status, in effect."

She nodded. "Yes, well, that's pretty obvious. But go on for a moment. Any other thoughts?"

"Yes. The reason it's a masterpiece planet is that there's nothing the Predators like to Hunt better than other hunters. . . . It's the ultimate challenge, right?"

"That's right. Unlike our race, they won't Hunt 'innocent' things—except possibly food."

"A noble breed." Sardonic twist of phrasing. "Anyway, somehow they discovered the operations on Blior, and they saw what a perfect place to Hunt it would be."

"But why bring on the bugs as well?"

"A little twist, a little spice. Who can say? Perhaps this was a world where they'd already Hunted bugs before, and they were just returning."

She shook her head. "No, I don't think so. If there were bugs on this planet before, there would have been a spillage. That's one of the problems when the Preds play with the things—they get loose and start breeding."

"Sloppy sorts."

"Let's just say that their sense of honor is a bit tunnel-visioned."

"So they're here—and they know now that we know they're here."

"I think that's what the lawyer was so excited about. And unless my guess is wrong, Evanston's got a suspicion as well."

"More than a suspicion. I mean, he has physical evidence!"

"Yes."

"He somehow seems to know you're associated with them."

"I don't think he knows as much as he strongly suspects."

"It stands to reason . . . after what happened. . . ."

She let out a breath, shook her head. "The pieces still just aren't there—"

"Seems pretty pat to me," said Attila. "He's got problems with anomalous intelligent creatures as well as the bugs—and he's just trying to get this project off the ground. Can you imagine the bad publicity if word gets back to civilization? Why, this business venture would be a total bust! Who would want to go hunting on a world where the hunters are the victims? I dare say that Evanston is a rich man, but no matter how rich he is, I'm sure that he couldn't afford a failure on this magnitude." Attila nodded. "A man like Livermore Evanston takes time to go get you to help, you know it's got to be this magnitude of importance."

"That does work . . . logically . . . but there's another level."

"Something intuitive?"

"Yes ... that T-rex ..."

"Not a curious resurrection.... Ideal, if you think of it.... What with the taste for hunting as it is, I would think that resurrected dinosaurs would be perfect for hunting."

"Yes, of course. I'm talking, though, about the level of sophistication a biolab needs to create the size and scope of a tyrannosaurus rex!"

"You're saying that it could create a lot more.... Well, isn't that the idea? To create fantastical and wonderful creatures for rich people to shoot?"

"You're not getting the point. What *else* can it create? Why is Evanston being so secretive? Why won't he let us look at the inside of that big biolab factory?"

"*He* hasn't refused—just his underlings."

"Well, then, I guess that's the next bit on our agenda, isn't it? We're going to have to ask."

"And if he won't let us see what's inside?"

She smiled. "Then we'll have to find out on our own, won't we? And we'll know that something intriguing *is* there."

"Of course. I'll take you through the factory tomorrow morning, if you like," said Livermore Evanston, absently tapping ash from his cigar. "There are more serious matters that have to be dealt with immediately, though." The large man leaned over his intercom, hit a button. "Would you send in Brookings and Zorski, please?"

Machiko had to work hard to maintain a blank expression. This wasn't exactly what she'd expected. Attila was going to give her a great big "I told you so" when she let go of this bit of news.

Evanston was sitting in a comfortable ergonomic chair, in a comfortable smoking jacket. His perch in his office building gave him a panoramic view of most of the beautiful, growing expanse of this fabulous settlement that would soon be one of the more wondrous cities in the universe.

Evanston did not look his usual happy and confident self.

The teak-paneled door opened. A man and a woman entered. One Machiko recognized: the man who had come up to them and talked to Evanston on their arrival. The woman, though, was a different matter entirely. She looked like the kind of corporate sharpshooter that Machiko was supposed to have been. A Company woman from sleek black hair to perfectly manicured fingers.

Introductions were made and remade.

Abner Brookings. Lawyer. Meet ...

Chelsea Zorski. Head of operations. Meet ...

Hello, Machiko. I hope you can help us.

Good to meet you. I did some of the background work to dig you up. You can just call me Chet.

"Sit down. Have a drink. Tea or coffee or harder stuff, I don't care. It's time not just to think-tank this situation ... it's time to take action."

They all looked like drinking people. However, they all passed over the ample supply of liquor squatting atop a corner cabinet like a model of a city of multicolored skyscrapers.

Instead they all went for coffee.

Black.

When it was steaming and aromatic before them, as Machiko took the first few acrid sips, she studied this woman Chet Zorski.

First and foremost, she was a corporate shark. Machiko could *smell* that as she walked in. It was in her perfume and shampoo, her very breath. The shine of her eyes, the flash of her perfect teeth. The tailored hang of her clothing. These people could have been made in biolab factories, for all she knew; they had the perfection of premodeling about them.

Zorski had a cleft chin, a square jaw, a nose as perfectly angular as could possibly be desired. Bright-blue eyes. Wide cheekbones. A shock of black hair. Bland stuff in general, but the congruence gave her a sharp and feral look, and the flashing of teeth made her look bright and hungry beneath the smoothness.

"We hope you're well situated," said Evanston.

"Yes."

"You've met your people," said Zorski. "Had a little dustup with one, I hear."

"Good for morale."

"Absolutely. So . . . what do you think of them?"

"Motley, but they'll do."

Zorski beamed a little at that. "Good. I thought you'd be able to look past the rough edges. I looked for a lot of special qualities in these men. Experience being paramount."

"Experience with the bugs, you mean."

Zorski looked at Evanston as though for permission.

Evanston nodded.

"Yes. The bugs."

"Look, there're some things we've got to talk about—"

"Yes. It's time to level with you, Noguchi."

She was taken aback. There was no longer confidence and control in Livermore Evanston's face. He looked, in fact, a bit at a loss, a bit desperate.

Machiko sat back in her chair, maintaining her calm, hard facade. "I'm listening."

"It's not just the bugs." Evanston turned to Abner Brookings. "Please, Abner . . . tell Ms. Noguchi what happened the other day." He swiveled to deliver a sincere stare at Machiko. "With this caveat. As my employee, you are directed *not* to discuss this with any of our other employees or guests. It's of a quite sensitive nature."

"What about my people? And my assistant?"

"Only if absolutely necessary for the men. However, your assistant is an android and clearly secure."

"I appreciate that."

"Go ahead, Abner. It's your show."

"Thank you. Ms. Noguchi, I'm one of the head lawyers for Mr. Evanston. A highly trusted employee. There are a lot of legal things that have to be worked out for this new world, of course, in its interface with the rest of galactic civilization. That's my job. However, I also fancy myself a bit of a hunter. And so I take a bit of a vacation here from time to time. I was on just such an expedition a few days ago. And that's when this awful incident happened."

Machiko listened as Brookings told his story.

A safari.

Invisible attackers.

Death.

Himself, the only survivor.

When he was finished, a silence fell upon the meeting.

"Mr. Brookings was given a thorough evaluation by psychtechs afterward. It would appear, Ms. Noguchi," said Evanston somberly, "that indeed we are *not* the only hunters on Blior. Indeed, these other Hunters—presumably alien, since there are no extant civilizations on this planet—are the source of the bug problem as well."

He looked significantly at Chet Zorski.

"Yes, Machiko. And as you might have suspected, that's one of the reasons you were selected. We believe you know who these creatures are—and how to deal with them."

She looked at them all, one by one. She said nothing. Stare for stare. They looked away.

"I should emphasize," said Zorski, "that we are not prying into your past, your background. We do not want a confession here. We are just asking for knowledge . . . and for help. . . ."

"And for you to do your job," added Evanston.

"Or bail out and take off, as our agreement states?" Machiko asked.

Evanston frowned. "That's up to you."

"No, wait . . . ," objected Brookings. "I worked up the language in that contract. There's a clause—"

"Yes," snapped Evanston. "A clause that I took out."

"It's not as if she can really go anywhere you don't want to take her," said the lawyer in a cold voice.

"Look, Brookings, I want—*need*—the best we can get from this talented woman. I told you—no goddamn legal tricks." He snorted. "Like the law has that much value out here."

"That's the idea. It's elastic. That's why I'm here," said the lawyer. "To help you form it into the shape that is best for you."

"Look, if I want to get out of this place, there are other ways than going up," said Machiko.

"Gentlepeople, *gentlepeople*," said Zorski, a conciliatory smile on her face. "Please. I don't think you need to worry about Ms. Noguchi's enthusiasm for this particular project. You see, I chose her very well. I think we have a fascinated, very enthusiastic leader on our hands now . . . don't we, Ms. Noguchi?"

"Yes. Damn you." She couldn't help but smile.

Brookings shook his head. "I don't understand. This is going to be dangerous. I assure you . . . what I went through . . . These bastards are dangerous."

"Please, let's just say I have the feeling these aliens are old allies, old enemies of our employee," said Zorski. "And besides, she's *so* much better off than she was before, under the shackles of the Company. . . ."

"Don't worry. I'm here to do a job and I intend to do it, and do it as well as I can."

Livermore Evanston visibly relaxed. "You can bet I'm glad to hear that, my dear. We *need* you."

"Okay. Now you level with me. What more do you know about these Hunting aliens?"

"Much less than you do, clearly," said Brookings.

Machiko looked from face to face.

All were unreadable.

"Well, I guess I should be grateful for what I've gotten out of you gentlemen. Now, thank you for your coffee. Maybe I should get my force whipped into shape so we can do something about scouting out this situation. Hmmm. Meantime, I'll look forward to that tour of the biofactory tomorrow."

"Why are you so interested in what's going on there?" said Brookings.

"It's just in her nature," said Zorski. "Extreme curiosity."

"No, I really think we're due an answer," insisted Brookings.

She didn't think she should tell the whole story, since she was sure they weren't spilling all their beans.

"We were doing recon. Something came up while I was checking the area."

"You just let her look around?" demanded Brookings.

"Yes. I gave her permission personally," said Zorski. "And after getting the okay from His Nibs here." She pointed playfully toward Evanston.

"Well, I appreciate that—but let me tell you, I saw something very troubling. . . ."

"Don't leave us dangling so," said Brookings sarcastically.

"I saw a dinosaur." She gave the creep the glare he deserved. "A tyrannosaurus rex, to be specific."

"Ah," said Zorski. "The T-rex."

"Not surprising. A big creature," said Evanston.

Brookings looked a bit taken aback. "But . . . those things are extinct!"

"Precisely," said Machiko. "Which means that biolab is doing some pretty heavy-duty stuff."

"Wow—that's truly *big* game!" said Brookings, looking a little disconcerted, but at the same time excited at the prospect of actually bagging a *dinosaur*.

"Yes. As I told you, we want to make things interesting for our guests," said Evanston.

"Of course. I understand. You did explain that. . . . I only thought that you might be manufacturing creatures of interest to these mysterious Hunting aliens, these Predators, as it were."

Evanston was all smiles again. "Of course. I'd never thought of that. And you'd be the person to distinguish that, wouldn't you? Excellent. As I said, I'll give you the tour myself, to be as much help as possible. . . ."

"Tomorrow morning?"

"That's right. Tomorrow, right after you get back from your maneuver, Machiko?"

"What? I haven't even gone through any training with these guys!" said Machiko. Suddenly this business with the biolab factory wasn't a primary concern.

"You'll do it on the fly," said Evanston. "Because tomorrow my hired mercenaries are going out to scout the area where Brookings and his band were attacked."

Chet Zorski pulled out a map.

13

Bakuub, Straight Spear, stared down into the holding pen of the yautja starship. There a *kainde amedha* stalked its prey. The *bisor*, a small doglike mammal from the surface of this Hunter's World, whined and barked as it scampered as far as it could go into the corner. The Hard Meat, a youngster not yet a good Hunter's challenge, crept forward infinitely slowly, drool from its secondary jaws slathering the floor, savoring its approach and kill as much as it would doubtless savor the juices of its food.

Bakuub, however, brooded upon other matters than this life-and-death drama below.

Something was happening in the *ooman* settlement. Something of great gravity and importance. The yautja named Bakuub could feel the electricity crack-

ling through the atmosphere of this planet, and he felt
entirely ill at ease.

He had sifted through the remains of the *ooman*
Hunting party they had killed, through their supplies
and weapons, but the detritus contained no clue as to
what was being concocted by their leaders.

The encounter with the female *ooman* while Hunting the big creature they had discovered, that was just
as troubling as the creature itself, a monster that was
not native to this planet. The *oomans* had seen the
yautja. The *oomans* had killed one of their number.
How? Lar'nix'va, though he struggled hard not to
show it, was clearly troubled. Bakuub had heard tales
of the female *ooman* Dahdtoudie, whom Lar'nix'va
had fought with. Surely this was not the same one. . . .

Bakuub had wanted to do some kind of detailed
exploration of transmissions and emanations from
that settlement, utilizing what little of that sort of
equipment they owned. The other packs Hunting now
on this world had been notified, but they did not seem
as concerned as he. And he, alas, was not the Leader
here. Lar'nix'va was the Leader, and Lar'nix'va was a
fool.

Bakuub could see straight through the *tarei'hsan*
offal. A yautja like Lar'nix'va did not have the best intentions of his people at heart. A yautja like Lar'nix'va
cared not for True Glory, merely for his own stupid
ambitions. Normally this would not be troublesome,
for fools such as he were eventually found out and
dealt with, hoisted on their own petards. But in this
ticklish situation, with much at stake, leadership by
such a fool could be dangerous for the yautja's cause.

Bakuub would have to monitor the situation carefully. True, tendencies toward personal ambition were
rife among the yautja. That, after all, was a part of
their nature. Ego was a genetic as well as a cultural
development in the True Dominators. Ambitious fools
tended to get themselves killed at an early stage of

warriorhood; however, an occasional hothead would advance to Leadership and make a mulch of things—a situation not considered particularly bad, but, rather, a challenge—part of the OverPath's progress. But at a ticklish time like this, such Leadership was not opportune and could cause a great deal of trouble.

Below, Bakuub could smell the terror and urine of the prey mammal as it cowered. The Hard Meat slunk forward, lizard-insect evil in its every smooth movement. The acid smell rose from below, amid the offal and straw scents. Soon it would mix with the harsh copper smell of mammalian blood.

Bakuub had personally seen that the others of the flotilla were alerted to the potential problem. The Leaders of the other packs had all shown concern and stated that they would join them in their efforts if needed. However, they were presently in the midst of their own particular Hunts, be they sport or blooding rites, and had to see to that.

Yes, Bakuub thought. But this was much more of a problem than anyone else realized. When Ki'vik'non had been killed by a weapon-holding *kainde amedha*, that had been bad enough. The implications were enormous. That such a creature existed meant a new and dangerous enemy for the People. Challenges were challenges, and to be cherished—however, just as the arrival of the Soft Meat amid the stars was more than a mere challenge, so was the advent of this super Hard Meat.

It was a threat.

Suddenly a wave of hatred passed through Bakuub.

For the Soft Meat, certainly.

But also for the Hard Meat.

Hatred was not unusual in a yautja, but generally reserved for another of their species. Hatred for the Hunted usually meant fear.

Hatred flowed through Bakuub's veins.

The Hard Meat's secondary jaws were extending.

Its claws and extensors held the *bisor* firmly. The progress of the creature's dinner was painstaking and deadly.

Bakuub reached forward, hit a button. The entry lid of the cage slipped back. Even as it did, Bakuub reached behind his back, pulled out his spear, aimed.

With one swift motion of his trained arm, Bakuub sent the javelin downward with blinding speed. The razor tip met with the back of the *kainde amedha*'s head, driving down with such force that the upper carapace was pierced as well.

Bakuub had judged well. It was for good reason that he had taken pains to study the anatomy of the Hard Meat. He had judged his blow not only so that the nexus of nerves in the thing's helmetlike head would be destroyed, but also so that there would be a minimum of its acid blood spilled.

The Hard Meat let go its prey. Shrieking, it reached back for the spear, but it was far too late for that. The angle had been perfect, an angle that was never presented in normal combat, and the blow had been swift and sure.

The creature shuddered and staggered.

Its limbs twisted and shivered like dying snakes.

With a final horrible scream the *kainde amedha* flopped to the floor of the holding pen, writhing out the last of its life in hisses.

Stillness descended upon the holding pen. Bakuub reached out and thumbed another button.

The outer door opened and a small ramp extended. A breath of outside sailed in, rich with green life and sunshine.

"Go now," said Bakuub to the *bisor*. "Live. And the life you have now will be the purer and more cherished for your terror here."

The *bisor* paused for only a moment. Then it inched around the side, eyeing the fallen Hard Meat as though it expected the creature to rise at any moment, and ran down the ramp to the outside.

Bakuub closed the door. Just as well. The Hard Meat would pose a distraction, anyway, to the true task at hand. He would tell Lar'nix'va that the thing had attempted escape. And if the fool challenged him—well, then, the fool would die that much sooner, and all to the good.

14

Tell me again why we had to leave the omniterrain bus," said Attila, looking around warily, his sensors doubtless high.

"This is a *maneuver*, chum," said Dick Daniels, his gun tilted slightly toward the ground, but obviously ready. "We're just lookin' over territory. I don't think we're going to run into anything much."

"This *is* the place where the sporting safari ran into the Hunters," said Machiko. "We're just having a look, checking out the lie of the land. And operating as a unit for the first time. Which reminds me." She clicked on her wrist radio. "Unit? How are we doing?"

The answers ticked off one by one from the twenty-member team. They'd spread out in a wing formation, covering this open area of ground. Machiko could see them all, but she figured that as long as you

146

had technology, you should use it. Besides, she wanted to make sure the stuff still worked.

The sun had just lifted off the horizon, and mists were rising up like moody chromatic wraiths from vines and the *yanga* trees. The air smelled ripe and yeasty with a damp chill soon to be burned off by the sun, but enough to give early risers a shiver or two. Machiko still had the taste of good coffee in her mouth. She savored it, as did the rest of the men. As Daniels had said, "At least the food and the drink are good on this gig."

Food, in fact, seemed to be on everyone's mind.

"So what's for lunch?" said Lou MacCraken, still yammering away as usual.

"Shit on a shingle," snarled Truck Tankerslee, a grotty short toad of a man with a foul mouth, a foul mind, but the record for the most bugs obliterated of the lot of them.

"Yeah," said Nick Gillespie. "Question is, is it *good* shit?"

"I don't know," said Machiko, trying to keep in the jocular mood of the bunch. "You want me to call back to the bus and check?"

"Good idea," said Marino, squinting into the dark below the mists. "I got a feeling that looking forward to something's a good idea on this particular mission."

Machiko shrugged and looked over to Sanchez, on her right side. "What do you think, Ned?"

He smiled at her. "Better to think about beans 'n' franks than lurking Death. I say go for it."

"Yeah," said Daniels. "We got guys back on the bus. Might as well have 'em do something other than sit around with their thumbs up their butts."

"Well, I should hope they're not preparing the food," sniffed Attila.

"Right. And I should hope that it's something better than beans or creamed chipped beef," grumbled Daniels.

"Let's check." She tapped out the numbers, spoke into the radio node sticking in front of her face.

"Yo. Michaels?"

A bit of static in her ear. Then: "Got you."

"How's it look there on the bus?"

"Still all bozos here." Pause. " 'Bout the same as before. You guys just left minutes ago."

"Well, you know the saying. An army travels on its stomach. So we were just wondering here—what's for lunch?"

Lane Michaels laughed. "You mean that big ice chest they sent with us? I been wondering about that myself. Maybe I better get that lawyer in to work on it."

Machiko laughed. "You do that. Get him to do *something* other than cower in the back."

Abner Brookings was turning out to be something less than the Great White Hunter he fancied himself. He hadn't wanted to come along on this mission, but Evanston had ordered him to, so he could pinpoint for the group the exact location. Brookings at least had the gift of a quick and smooth tongue, and he'd persuaded Machiko to allow him to hang back as consultant rather than directly participate in the maneuvers. His "inexperience," he claimed, might hamper the operation. But, please, don't tell old man Evanston. In return he promised to "have another look" at Machiko's contract and "provide her with free legal help." The ashen pallor of his face informed her that this was no act. Although he had a gun, it was clear that his enthusiasm for weapons had waned somewhat.

Just as well, really. Amateurs and guns generally didn't mix.

"I am not cowering at all," declared Brookings's voice abruptly. "I am available for consultation. And I am performing valuable help in guarding your means of transportation back."

There wasn't a trace of irony in the man's voice, which ingratiated him to her not a wit. "That's very kind of you. We do appreciate that effort. . . . Now, could you both check that storage box?"

There was a moment of silence, followed by thumping and opening sounds.

Michaels came back on-line. "Hmmm. Lots of cheese. Fruit. A nice ham. Crusty bread. Looks mighty tasty. I think I'll make myself a sandwich right now."

"I think you'd better consult with Mr. Lawyer there on the legal implications before you do that," said Machiko, laughing. "But I think you'll have a few disgruntled comrades as well."

"Oh. Yeah. Guess that wouldn't go down too well." Dumb voice, with fake realization.

"Right. Just stay on call, both of you. We're getting into the area where you said you were attacked, Brookings."

. "Good. Keep your line open. I'll do what I can from here."

Just because she was actually glad he hadn't come along didn't mean she couldn't rib him about the subject. Besides, the other guys were in on the joke. It kept things light in the face of some pretty heavy-duty danger.

In fact, they were entering some heavier growth, just as Brookings had described. Without focusing Machiko could almost imagine herself on some African veld, approaching forest. However, there were no earthly leaves that looked quite like the ones that dangled in the breeze, glistening with jewellike dew.

"Anything, Til?"

"Nope. No signs of bodies."

She didn't really expect any. When working covertly like this, the yautja tended to take their grisly trophies and dispose of the bodies cleanly. Still, you never knew, and she actually approved of Evanston's suggestion. She wasn't thrilled with the idea of coming up against a pack of the Hunters so soon, but she honestly didn't expect any such contact.

Too, it was good to work with these people. On the way out they had been an unruly lot, joking and cursing and laughing. Now, though, they were falling into line like a practiced crack unit. Zorski had chosen well.

"Just a minute," said Attila. "I'm picking up something. . . ."

Machiko's stomach lurched a moment, that familiar surge of fear. However, the adrenaline kick that followed evened her out, even thrilled her. This was what she'd been seeking—this moment of on-edge *aliveness*.

"Anything specific?"

"Odd. It's about sixty yards over there, among the bush. Residual traces of burning . . . carbon ash . . . acid . . . biologic residue."

"We'd better go check it out then, eh?"

"Yeah. That would be a good idea," said Daniels. "Ned and I will take point, if you like."

"No, just back us up. Attila knows how to use the sensor unit." The android had an instrument sensor pack to account for his talents, but in truth he was relying mostly upon his internal nodes.

"Sure. Go ahead. Ned, you'd better go with them, though."

"Right." The dark eyes remained expressionless, absolutely free of fear or nervousness. There was, however, a flicker of something in them now, a crinkle of a smile, as though Sanchez was grateful to help out.

Machiko felt an unfamiliar warmth in her heart at the sign. The guy liked her, wanted to watch out for her. An instinctual man-woman thing. Not that she needed it; she'd watched her own ass for a long time, but it warmed her cockles. Maybe, just *maybe*, she wouldn't mind warming his.

There might be some *other* perks to this job.

"All right," she said. "Let's do it."

The three of them, weapons at the ready, moved ahead into the area that Attila had indicated. They walked through weeds and brush, and the sweet smell of bright flowers. The mist was gone now, and the sun was fully launched, chasing away most of the shadows. They passed through a stand of trees into another clearing, cautiously. Immediately Machiko's nostrils flared; a harsh acrid smell assaulted them.

"Damn. No wonder your sensors beeped. What *is* that?"

Burned shell?

Burned insulation?

Burned blood?

All of them.

"Over there," said Attila.

"Right. I can see it," said Sanchez.

Machiko could see it too, poking above a clump of grass. Some kind of greasy, blackened pile.

"Something dead," she said.

"Yeah, but no flies," said Sanchez.

"Correct. Presumably this planet has other decompositional agents."

"I don't know. Even a bacterium couldn't grow in *that*," said Sanchez.

Machiko stepped up to it. At first it looked like the remains of some kind of garbage-heap fire, but then she started to discern identifying details.

"Looks like the burned remains of a bug. That would explain the acrid odor. Burned acid."

Machiko found a stick and poked around.

"I detect metal and plastic and glass as well—" said Attila.

Machiko poked some more. Overturned fused glass and blackened circuitry.

"Analysis?"

"Too far gone to tell," said Attila.

"Looks like somebody threw some equipment on

top of a bug body, doused it with incendiary chemicals, and then torched it," said Sanchez. "But why?"

"Some sort of cover-up?"

"What—by the alien Hunters? To hide their presence?" said Attila.

"That must be it."

"On top of a bug and equipment?"

"I don't know. Maybe they were hiding the equipment too. Maybe it was just convenient. Maybe we should take back a specimen—"

A yelp over the radio, echoed by a real-life vocalization beyond the tree.

Then:

"Noguchi. You'd better get back here." Daniels's voice.

"Right. Come on, guys."

It could be the Predators. She steeled herself. She wasn't particularly ready for them today.

But, then, was *anyone* ever ready for them?

They ran back. She expected to hear the sounds of battle at any second, the sizzle of blasters through the air, the booms of explosions.

Instead she saw merely that the party had moved closer together, and weapons aimed toward a clump of bush.

She ran up to Daniels.

"What's going on?"

"Something's in there."

"Could be some kind of animal."

The bushes shook. Something stood up, staggered out.

Weapons raised.

"No. Hold your fire."

The figure stumbled into a clearing. Blood. Torn clothing.

A woman.

She gripped a gun but made no effort to use it. She just staggered forward.

"Stay back," said Machiko.

The woman stopped. Fell to her knees.

"Thank God," she said. "Thank God you've come for me."

"It's one of the damned guests," said Daniels. "She's survived somehow."

"How come you didn't go back?"

The woman shook her head dizzily. "Don't . . . know . . . unconscious . . ."

"Well, don't just sit around gawking," said Machiko. "Give the lady some water. She's probably dehydrated."

Water was administered, and then a name was obtained.

"Petra Piezki," said Machiko over the radio. "Ring any bells, Brookings?"

"I don't believe it. . . . I thought she was dead. There was this—"

"Whatever. We're bringing her in. She needs medical attention. You want to break out the first-aid kit?"

"Of course."

Piezki drank some water. With the help of a man to either side of her, she was able to walk.

"Piezki. What did you see out there?" Machiko asked her.

"Monsters. Killers." Then her head slumped, eyes dimming, as though to escape.

"Let's get her some help. And then we'll think about looking around some more."

Actually, Machiko had pretty much found what she wanted to find. She'd tested the mettle of her people and was satisfied that she had a crack troop.

Anything else would be pushing things too far.

They'd probably stretched their luck far enough, and when you dealt with the Predators, luck was a commodity you didn't play games with.

15

You bastard. You left me!"

"Piezki! I thought you were dead."

"That's a lie! You left me out there to die!"

Before Machiko could do anything to prevent it, the seemingly weak Piezki lurched from her slumped position at the campsite and lunged across toward Abner Brookings. Her thick hands clamped around Brookings's neck, and she began to throttle the lawyer, shaking him violently.

"You left me! You left me!"

Brookings's eyes bugged. The surprise of the attack had caught him off guard, but he was not a defenseless or weak man. With one great heave he pulled Petra Piezki off her feet and then slammed her into the metal side of the ground crawler.

Piezki's hands lost their grip. Her eyes rolled up. She slid down the side of the bus, unconscious.

"Oh, great," said Machiko. "She's going to tell us all about what she saw now."

Brookings loosened his collar. He was gasping. "You saw it. Self-defense. She was trying to kill me!"

"Apparently with good reason, if you left her to die!"

"I swear, we were both running. . . . I thought she was a goner. If I thought I could have helped, I would have."

"She's all right," reported Sanchez, looking up from the unconscious body.

"Save the real story for later," said Machiko. "Let's get her back to Evanston. We've got a report to make."

Machiko sat down beside Sanchez. Their vehicle was bumping its way back home, and the man's dark eyes were directed toward the passing landscape.

"Nice planet," said Machiko.

"I've seen more beautiful, I've seen more danger-ous, I've seen not-nice planets I liked better," he said, not looking at her.

"I get the feeling you've been on your share."

He shrugged. "After you fight the bugs awhile, you get sort of empty inside. You need to go away for a while, or you just get a bad case of interior rot."

"So why are you back in the bug-battle saddle?"

He looked at her. "Money."

"A guy like you could earn money other ways."

"I did. Not enough. Let's just say this was an offer I could have refused but would have been an idiot to."

"I think I know what you mean. But there's more to you than just money, isn't there, Sanchez?"

He looked at her. "Is there?"

"You fight bugs for a while, you get a sense of nobility, don't you? Like you're doing something important. I bet you haven't been doing anything really important for a while."

"Combating an intergalactic blight. Yeah, I guess it makes you feel like something more than a pile of shit."

For the first time something tremulous and deep crept into his intonation, something beyond sardonic monotone.

She thought about this for a moment.

"We may have more in common than our brilliant and wonderful personalities," Machiko said finally. "Maybe I should buy you a beer tonight and we can talk about it."

He looked at her.

"Sure. Can't hurt."

"A nice beer generally helps." She looked up and saw that they were approaching Evanstonville. "And something tells me after today we're both going to need one ... even though I generally don't drink the stuff."

"Ms. Piezki. How are you feeling?"

"Better."

"Ms. Piezki, I can't tell you how sorry we are about what happened," said Livermore Evanston in his most charming and millifluous tones. "Nonetheless, you were aware of the danger involved. It was in your contract with us. And you are an employee."

Piezki eyed them, daggers gleaming in her eyes. She said nothing, but the threat was there: I'm going to nail you if I can.

Lawyers, thought Machiko Noguchi.

What a lovely, lovely bunch.

Take Brookings, for example. The bastard was sulking in a corner, clearly not wanting to be there, but waiting for the debriefing.

Chet Zorski was there, looking awake and aware and concerned, leaning on her chair and studying the patient, clearly taking mental notes.

And, of course, there was old Evanston himself, solid but hovering. He'd come immediately to this treatment room when he'd heard there'd been another adviser located.

"May I suggest you settle that matter later?" said Machiko. "What we need now is information. Ms. Piezki, we've pretty much heard your colleague's story about what happened on that safari. Would you care to give your version?"

Piezki coughed.

"Are you all right?" asked the medtech who'd cleaned the woman's cuts and applied the bandages.

"Yeah. Little pain in the chest. Catch in the throat. Glass of water." The medtech got her one, and Piezki drank it all down. "Yeah. Better. Thanks."

She told her story.

It was almost exactly the same story that Brookings had told, save for one significant strand of facts.

The hunt. The hunters. The quarry. The invisible hunters. Massacre. The run . . . loss of memory . . .

The change of detail was that Brookings's valor had not quite been as much in evidence as he'd claimed.

"What happened when you tripped?"

"Can't remember," she said, shaking her head. "Something dark. I remember screaming and hearing my own muffled screams . . . and that was it." She put her hand to her chest. "Nurse, do you have something that will settle my stomach? I seem to have developed a really terrible case of heartburn."

The woman looked uncomfortable, but nothing that made Machiko immediately alarmed.

Something bothered her, though.

"And you were in the same location for about a day and a half—most of it unconscious."

"I remember bashing about in the brush, but that was it. I'm just glad I'm"—she accepted a glass of fizzing stuff with a thank-you—"alive." Drank.

"They let her live," said Evanston. "How curious."

"Perhaps they didn't know about her," suggested Zorski. "If she was out in the bushes, they just must have moved on."

A possibility. If she'd run far enough away, they wouldn't have detected her heat-image, thought Machiko.

Then again, there were bugs in the area ... and that was what bothered her.

"Brookings. Did you see anything attack this woman?" she demanded suddenly.

Brookings shook his head. "No. Like I said, I thought that she'd been killed. Truly."

Muffled screams? Something over her head? Why hadn't she thought about this before?

"Brookings, this is very important. Is that the absolute truth? Because if it's not, this woman could be in danger from—"

"Absolute truth," said Brookings, looking as though butter wouldn't melt in his mouth.

Suddenly a surprised look came over Piezki's face. Her face twisted.

"Ms. Piezki," said the tech. "Are you all right?"

Piezki belched.

She took a breath and smiled. . . . "Oh. That's much better." Relief was obvious on the woman's face.

Machiko relaxed.

Piezki fell off her chair.

She writhed and screamed, and a sudden bubble bloomed on her chest.

"Get back!" cried Machiko.

Too late.

Before any of them, frozen with surprise, could do a thing, the bubble burst. Like a gory jack-in-the-box, flaps of bone and flesh lifted off, and suddenly a wormlike thing stood up in the middle of Piezki's chest. Blood sprayed around the room like a crazy water sprinkler.

They were all splattered with it.

Petra Piezki got one look at the creature she'd given crimson breech birth to, and then her head fell back, holding Death in its eyes.

The wormthing chittered at them and started sliding out.

"Stand back!" cried Machiko. She pulled out her gun from its holster and fired at the creature.

It slapped off to one side and skittered away.

The two slugs slammed into Piezki's body, kicking up divots of shattered ribs and gouts of flesh and blood.

Machiko tracked the running, slithering thing. No question. Bug-larvae time.

If she knew one thing, she knew she had to clip its wings before it flew into ductwork or down the hall to hide in some broom closet. She was grateful she'd had pistol practice.

Now, though, she'd have to prove she could use it in the clinch.

The thing was at the door. Closed. It slithered quickly toward shadow.

Machiko squeezed off three shots.

The first missed.

The second bit off a chunk of flesh on the tail.

The third rammed directly into the head, exploding the ugly, bloody mass into an uglier, bloodier mass. The thing flipped over and commenced spasming, somehow still straining for escape.

Machiko calmly walked over and put another bullet in it.

The acid blood smoked as it ate away at the floor.

"Better get some neutralizing agents in here, Zorski."

Zorski got on the phone.

Machiko put her gun back in her holster.

Too bad Attila couldn't have seen that. He would have been proud of her.

She turned and walked over to where Abner Brookings stood, bloodied and horrified.

She tapped his chest. "Hello. Hello. Anyone in there?"

"No. No, I wasn't infected. Don't cut me open. . . . I swear."

She looked at him in disgust. "I was talking about your heart."

Recovering, Evanston had somehow found a towel and was wiping off the blood. "Nurse. Have that body taken out of here and destroyed immediately."

"The problem hits a little closer to home, Evanston."

Evanston nodded. "Yes. That's why I hired you and the others."

"An excellent choice, all of us."

"You worked well this morning?" His words were strained.

"Very well."

"Good. I'm sure you're going to be busy very soon."

"Fine. That's what we're here for." She found a towel herself and began to get rid of some of the blood. Funny, it didn't really bother her. After the business on Ryushi, after her time with the pack, after helping those miners, she'd experienced plenty of blood, much of it hers.

A detail.

"That tour of the genetic biolab," said Machiko. "I really should have a look. There may be infection—"

Evanston shook his head. "I can't—I'm in no state now for any kind of silly tour."

"This evening, then?"

"No. No, I'm sorry."

"Well, tomorrow."

"Tomorrow I want you to go out again and do what

I hired you to do, Noguchi." His voice was firm. "I will advise my scientists and workers to look for infiltration into their systems. When things are down to a mild roar here, I'll be happy to show you the place myself."

"Surely someone else can—"

"Have you forgotten? I am your employer. I make the rules. Now leave me be. I have"—he shook his head sadly—"to take a shower and start coordinating precautions against these things." He put a chubby hand on her shoulder. "Thanks for the good work here, though. And the quick thinking."

"Good thing you let me wear a sidearm," she said. "Better if you'd let me see that biolab."

"No," he said firmly, and began walking away. "That's impossible."

She looked down at the body of Petra Piezki, eyes wide-open and face frozen in a rictus of terror.

She could sense it now.

Something was very wrong here, and it wasn't just the yautja, it wasn't just the *kainde amedha*.

16

They were having that beer.

"Too bad about Piezki," said Sanchez.

"Yeah." She took a long, hard gulp. Grimaced. She didn't particularly like it, but sharing a beer with someone seemed important now. "I should have called it."

"Me too."

"We can't get everything right."

He drank again and there was silence.

"I guess there have been times with both of us when everything has been wrong, hasn't there?" said Machiko.

"You know, Noguchi, you're just too damn perceptive for your own good."

"That beer looks gone. You want another one?"

"Helps limber the tongue, doesn't it?"

"Sometimes."

She went and got two fresh brews. Opened his. Set it before him.

The beer was good and cold, a dark, yeasty ale. No label. Brewed here.

They sipped in silence for a moment.

"You know," the man said after a while, "back where I come from, when a woman takes a fella back to her room, orders the assistant out, pours him a couple beers, and starts talking personal stuff, the man might think she was trying to seduce him."

"So what do you think, Ned Sanchez?"

He shrugged. "I'd say you're not the most feminine creature that's crossed my path. But, you know, you're probably one that I could respect in the morning—so to speak."

She smiled tartly. "Bullshit. I can tell when a man fancies me, Sanchez."

"Sounds like you can tell when you fancy a man, too."

"The hard head takes a little cracking—" She looked away. "I'm sorry. It's just been a while since I've felt that way, I guess. Never mind. Sorry to be so forward. Probably turns you off."

His hand suddenly took hers. Although it was a rough hand, it was warm, and it had a firmness and a purpose to it.

"No. Not at all. I guess I'm just used to being the pursuer."

"Want to start over?"

"No. I'm fine with the way it is." He took another drink.

He slowly and solidly got up.

Pulled her to her feet.

Brought himself up against her.

She could feel herself melting against him. His arms went around her, and for once her mind could just drift away into nothingness and release. The next thing she knew she was kissing him, and it was warm and right.

When they came up for breath, he said, "I take it back."

"Take what back?"

"The crack about your not being feminine. You're entirely female."

"I'd hardly get respect bug-killing in a dress."

"No."

"We might both be dead tomorrow."

"But we're not dead now."

Later, in the afterglow of a particularly satisfactory biological act, coated with an intriguing amount of pheromones and a kind of odd connection she'd never quite felt before, Machiko found herself speechless.

"You know, I guess I should count my lucky perks," Ned Sanchez said finally.

She put a finger to his lips. "Shh. Let me savor this."

"It's been a long time since you've had a man."

"No. It's been a long time since there's been any feeling involved."

"Ah. I think I'll need some silence to think about that one."

He took it.

She closed her eyes and just lay there a moment. God knew what was ahead of her, but she knew what was here now, and she accepted it gratefully.

Eventually, he spoke.

"Maybe I should tell you something, Machiko."

"Maybe you shouldn't."

"No, I think it would be a good idea."

"If you like. I'm not digging anything out of you."

"No. And that's why I'm telling." He closed his eyes,

took a breath. "What I said about quitting the bug-killing business?"

"Yes."

"It wasn't really the total truth. You see, I had this buddy. Let's call him Joe. Joe and me . . . well, we killed a lot of bugs."

She was going to say something smart-ass but realized it wasn't the time or the place. She smelled an intensity, a seriousness about him now. The only appropriate response seemed to be just to listen.

After a moment to put the story together right, Ned Sanchez said, "You know, I could tell you a long, long story."

"If you like."

"No. I'm going to make it short."

"Fine."

"Joe and me, we went into a hive. We made a couple of mistakes, some big mistakes. Joe didn't come out. I did. Sometimes I think it should have been the other way around."

"I understand."

"Do you? Do you really?" He snorted. "Well, maybe you can tell me, but when I heard about another chance to prove myself, I guess I was just fed up with all the guilt that had been building up inside me. So I signed on."

"It wasn't just for the money, then."

"No, I guess not."

She nodded. "I can relate. I felt that in you, Ned. Maybe that's why I was attracted to you."

"Hmm? What—you've got a story, too?"

She told him about her father. About the family shame. About how she was trying, in her own small way, to alleviate that shame.

She told him about Ryushi, her first colony world, and how she had failed it. People had survived, and she was responsible for that; but the colony was gone.

All in simple, concise terms.

"What say we promise each other something, okay, Machiko?" he said, cupping her face in his hands.

"What's that?"

"Let's live long enough to tell the long version of our stories."

"That's going to take a long time."

"Then we're going to have to live a long time, aren't we?"

He kissed her, and that was the only reply that was necessary.

"You slept with him, didn't you?" said Attila the Hun.

She was changing her clothes. Ned had gone to eat dinner with the rest of the men, but she couldn't bring herself to go with him. Superstition or something. Maybe they'd be able to smell the sex or something. Anyway, for some reason she had no appetite.

"I did," she said.

Attila plopped down in a chair, folded his arms. "Great. Just great. Now when you dump him, we're going to have a heartbroken soldier on our hands."

"What did Lao Tzu say about heartbroken soldiers?"

"Unreliable." He sniffed affectedly.

"I didn't say I was going to dump him."

He gave her a surprised look. "Well, did you ask him to help us break into the biolab and have that look you so desperately and foolishly want?"

"No."

"No? Why not?"

Looked at him. "I just didn't."

"Look, I thought the whole idea of getting to know this guy was that if he liked you, he'd help us."

"No. That wasn't the whole idea."

"Okay, okay," Attila said peevishly. "You had the hots for him."

"I liked him. I saw something there. And you know what, Til? It *is* there."

"Wonderful. I'm happy for you. There's a there there. But you didn't ask him to help us."

"Look. It's our suspicion. It's our problem."

"He's a hireling, too. It's *his* problem if we find anything we don't want to find. Which makes me wonder now if we should even bother. I mean, clearly you're not that concerned."

"Look, Til. I'm sorry I've upset you. Are you jealous?"

"What! Nothing of the sort. I hope you had a very good time. May you both be very happy together. Et cetera, et cetera."

"I just don't want Ned to get involved at this point. . . . Okay, okay, I don't want him to get into trouble. *We* get into trouble, that's different. We're at a higher level. We're more likely to take the heat without a burn. Sanchez, though—they can boot his ass out of here, no money, no nothing."

"Okay. It's your decision. Maybe it's for the best."

She nodded. "Thank you." She put her dinner plate to one side. "So, Attila. Your little recon—how did it go? Are we even going to be able to take a stab at this crazy mission?"

He finally smiled.

"While you were so amorously whiling away your time, ducks, I simply waltzed into the biolab factory."

Her mouth dropped. "So then we don't even have to break in! You've done it."

"Hardly. I certainly wish. No, the truth is that apparently much of the factory is under very loose security. And why not? This is a small settlement. There is no crime here."

"So how did you get in?"

"I just walked in, saying I wanted to look around.

They said fine, sir—there are just certain areas that are off limits. Certainly, I said. I understand completely. I took a little tour."

"And?"

"And it seems to be just what Evanston claims it is—a biolab. Cloning factory. Lions and tigers and bears. Exotic alien animals. Simple enough."

"But."

"I'm glad you inserted your but there. It's a big but."

"Hey. I like it."

He smiled. "But a cute one, as Mr. Sanchez will no doubt attest. No, Machiko, there are large areas simply off limits—and I saw most of what was necessary to be a fully functioning biolab."

"So the question is, what else is there?"

"Precisely."

"Any sensor input?"

"Nothing much. I need to get closer."

"So how do we get in tonight? How do we get closer when we do get in?"

"To the first question"—he pulled two badges from his pocket and put them on the table—"I stole these and altered them, complete with fake retinal and DNA patterns. These will get us in. As for the rest—well, with my sensors and a good laser toolbox—"

"Good job."

"You didn't even ask this Sanchez guy if he'd ever been a burglar."

She frowned at him. "That subject is closed, Attila."

"Okay, okay."

"And you had no problem? They didn't ask you what you were doing there?" she said, looking for potential foul-ups.

"No. Security seemed amazingly lax on the outside. I daresay that Evanston and company are worried about other things. However, beyond the main part of the lab—behind those closed doors . . . they are definitely hiding something that they don't want us to see."

"Well, that just makes me want to see it all the more."

"I confess, despite my less-than-warriorlike attitude for this entire adventure, I too would like to have a look."

"Tonight, then, a little private exercise of our own," said Machiko.

17

Attila had done his job well.

Not only had he counterfeited those badges, but he'd managed to sneak into a supply closet and procure two of the biolab uniforms. They actually fit well, too.

"The deal is this," said Machiko Noguchi as they strode past the open outer gates of the factory, past security operatives, the setting sun of Norn at their backs, the brisk cool smell of evening settling down on the still lushness of this cultivated frontier settlement. "We get caught inside the perimeter, we tell them we're authorized by Evanston."

"And if we make it through to the other part, but get caught then?"

"We run. We go back to the barracks and grab beer

cans. I didn't want to involve Ned in this actual operation—but I don't feel bad having him back us up."

"I suggest that we just not get caught. And most certainly not use weapons."

"I like to have one on hand, if possible. They let me wear one here, and it put me in good stead with that bug this morning."

Attila had prepared tiny stasis generators to cancel out any weapons-detection device, and again Machiko was impressed and grateful for his varied talents hidden in that plain-looking shell.

For all her martial-arts abilities, Machiko felt far more comfortable with a sidearm. The news that she'd be able to wear one on this mission was certainly welcome.

They walked past the posted guard with just a flash of their fake IDs. Security officers were not as numerous as Machiko had expected. Much of the security was automated. Shifts were apparently changing, and stragglers from the midshift were just making their way home. They appeared to be normal workers, looking forward to dinner and a beer. The shift that they were infiltrating, on the other hand, had far fewer workers, who were clearly far less industrious. The few people they encountered did not seem at all upset about the pair of new employees in their ranks. The departments in the biolab were diverse enough that they probably assumed Machiko and Attila were headed for sections other than theirs.

And of course, they were totally correct.

Attila had briefed her on the layout of the biofactory in descriptive enough terms that Machiko was able to wend her way knowledgeably through it, acting as though she had a definite mission, not goggling about like the first-timer she was. Nonetheless, she allowed Attila to lead slightly and used her peripheral vision to take note of the stations and activity around her.

Tanks.

There were tanks of stainless steel and glass, connected by tubing all around, with conduits and flanges and wheels. There were lab stations and racks of chemicals and equipment—the usual panoply of functioning scientific research and production. The smell of flame and harsh elements clung to the air, wafting in currents of warm and cold. Wisps of steam and frost escaped from doors and hatches opening and closing, and altogether the effect was of some well-scrubbed, sterile satanic kitchen.

Walking by one of the glass-enclosed tanks, Machiko caught a glimpse of something through the glass paneling—something caught in milky liquid.

A half-formed beast with great claws and sharp teeth, slowly forming in a nutrient bath.

A lion? Some alien critter. A Hunter being aborn for Hunting? Hard to say, but it certainly was pretty much as Evanston had described it, at least so far.

"There's a whole wing over there," whispered Attila, discreetly pointing toward the north, "devoted to cages, many of them empty so far."

"The beasts to be set free and hunted."

"Precisely."

"Nothing here to cause alarm to my perspective," she said as they went to a drink dispenser and pretended to fish for credit vouchers.

"That's just it. According to my data catalog, these vast rooms have got everything they need for a fully functioning biolab factory."

"So?"

"So much of the operations of such are patented secrets and usually kept secreted away. However, they're out here for all to see."

"Which means—?"

"Think about it."

It didn't take long.

"Which means *what* the hell have they got locked away, if they're allowing most people to see all of *this*?"

"Exactly."

She looked around again. She heard the murmurings and burblings of bubbling beakers, the slurpings and drippings of liquid, the tapping of retreating footsteps. It all smelled mysterious and acrid, like the entranceway to some chemical amusement-park ride.

Only they had no ticket for the next part.

"So, what now?"

"Down this hallway here."

They waited until there was no one around.

This time there was no pretense of who was leading and who was following.

Attila went first.

They moved down a corridor that eventually bent to the south. Doors lined either side.

"Storage rooms," Attila explained.

"Open and innocuous."

"As far as I can tell." The hallway was totally deserted. "This, though, was what I was telling you about—down here at the end of the hall."

Another slant to the hall, and they were there.

Machiko was taken aback.

At the end of the hall was a round, vaultlike door of hard, shiny alloy. It was more than apparently *extremely* locked.

"What—is this the *gold* supply here?"

"Looks like it, doesn't it?"

"What do your sensors perceive?"

"It's an alloy they can't get past."

"Hmmm. But you think we can pick this lock?"

"Oh, yes. It's an electronic locking device, and I made sure to bring a probe." He held up a long metal device.

"Looks like a coat hanger."

"I'm sure it could be used as such. In any case, by inserting it into this aperture here"—he did just that—"I can change polarities and reroute electrical flows in such a way as to cancel out the necessity for codes and thus gain access."

"In other words, we can get through."

"Precisely."

She looked around. "Nobody coming?"

"No."

"Problem is, there could be someone inside."

"True—however, shifts are changing, and an entry would be presumed to be authorized. We can take a quick look. I can store data through visual and auditory means, as well as my usual sensory panoply. Thus we can nip in and then duck out, without causing undue notice."

"Sounds good to me."

She was happy there wasn't much security there; but then again, why should there be? It wasn't as though an intelligence agency was necessary in Livermoreland; it was much too far removed from anything. The security forces seemed more interested in their war re-creations than in actually patrolling the colony. Evanston's people must have reasoned that these simple precautions would do.

For Machiko they would have done quite nicely.

However, they hadn't reckoned on having a talented android picking their locks.

Attila did his stuff, slipping his device in. Machiko heard a few clicks and whirs and then watched Attila's concerned expression change to one of relief.

"There we go. That should be it."

He stood and pulled a latch.

The door opened.

Machiko leaped to action, helping Attila pull the hatchway open with the minimum of noise. It eased back as though it had just been oiled.

Machiko peered into the next room.

It was a large chamber that stretched off into the distance. Along its upper sides were catwalks and pulleys and waldos. Racks of laboratory equipment hung below these. The lighting was quite low, the dominant colors being deep reds and lambent yellows.

Burblings.

The acrid smell was even heavier here, and there was a new scent to the air: something dreadful, something familiar, and yet Machiko could not precisely place it.

In the distance was the quiet sound of voices, yet this part of the long chamber seemed absolutely deserted.

Ahead of them were the familiar tanks, only these seemed noticeably larger. From the two intruders' angle, however, there seemed to be no viewports into the contents.

Machiko quietly pointed this out. "Could be that what they're brewing in there, they don't want us to know about."

"I was thinking the exact same thing. Just a moment here." Attila placed a small piece of metal between door and doorjamb. "This way we can exit quickly, I think, which may prove most fortuitous."

Machiko was in a hurry, but she took the precaution of moving as quietly and warily as possible, as they made their way around the tank.

There *was* a porthole on the other side, and she was able to peer through the murky liquid, and into the contents.

"Oh, my God," Machiko said, and though she was not particularly religious, it was as close to a prayer as she ever got.

18

Back in Boring-World, with so much time on her hands, Machiko Noguchi had done a great deal of reading. Fortunately, the Company had been considerate enough to vest its mining world with an excellent library of varied files on their Comp-Access.

One of the books she'd read was a large picture book concerning the history of human freaks, and there had been some horrifying anomalies indeed, from Siamese twins and pinheads, to geeks and other abnormalities of human and bestial natures.

However, nothing in the book could match the horror of what Machiko stared at now through the glass, through the milky nutrient bath.

At first it just seemed another beast, some hapless genetic code from some far-flung alien clime that had been appropriated for hunting purposes by Evanston's henchmen.

Claws.

Teeth.

Mandibles.

However, as she looked closer, she saw other things in the brew.

A shell that would become chitin.

Legs.

Arms.

And at the ends of those arms, digits.

Digits with opposable thumbs.

The result was obscene beyond belief. A combination with aesthetics from hell, but doubtless incredibly deadly.

Machiko took a sharp intake of breath.

"What is it?" asked Attila. "Besides really, really ugly."

"You can't tell?"

Of course he couldn't, she immediately told herself.

He hadn't had experience of the things. He hadn't gone through what she'd gone through. He wouldn't appreciate either species, much less the juxtaposition.

And then the realization hit her, so hard that she was stunned.

She would have invoked a deity's name again, only something had stopped her vocal cords.

"Well? Communication would be helpful," he said sharply.

"It's ... it's the most incredible warrior ever designed ... and Jesus, Attila ..." She pointed. "Look ... behind the neck there. Is that what I think it is?"

He peered closer. "My goodness. It does look like some sort of electrical neurotransmitter link-ups."

"As in cyborgs ..."

"As in cyborgs, precisely."

She tapped the window, pointing. "Attila. What you're looking at is ... well, apparently, and I don't know how—but these crazies have been able to warp the genetic code of the bugs . . . and add their own twists."

"What—to create some kind of ultimate target for guests to hunt?"

She shook her head vehemently. "No, that couldn't be. One of these . . . linked up to Buddha knows what . . . could tear apart a bunch of hunters. It could outhunt, outkill anything. . . . Hard Meat with brains and weapons!"

"Some sort of bug/yautja hybrid?"

"Thank God, *no*. Just an *improvement* on the bugs." She snapped her fingers. "What's the root of any army, Attila?"

"Warriors, of course. Soldiers."

"Smart bugs. Incredible, resilient . . . well, put some of these down and breed them on a world and you'd—"

"Why, you'd dominate the world!"

"Yes, and through the computer interface of cyborg connection . . ."

"Of course. You'd be able to *control* those warriors!"

They stood for a moment in silence, staring at the oxygen bubbles forming around the growing creatures and then floating up to the surface. A mad mélange.

"But *why*?" she murmured.

"Power, presumably," said Attila. "Why else? Evanston doesn't want just a world. He wants *worlds*."

"*That* was what we saw out there—one of these creatures. It wasn't a pile of different creatures and some machinery. It was a *single* creature . . . somehow on the loose. That had somehow been killed."

"By the yautja?"

"I guess so. That would make sense . . . but who knows?"

Thoughts were twisting and turning inside her

head. She wasn't sure what she had expected to find inside this part of the biolab factory ... but it certainly hadn't been this.

"What now?"

"Are you taking all this in?"

"Yes."

"Sufficient data?"

"Yes."

"Then now we get the hell out of here and figure out the next step. Now we—"

Inside the tank the creature's eyes opened.

A bug with eyes!

The head of the thing was a terrible and ungainly amalgam of the banana-insect helmet of a bug and the chromium sheen of complex cyborg implants. But the eyes looked just as sharp and intelligent as any that Machiko had ever seen in a warrior's head.

Despite herself, she jumped.

"Damn. It's looking at us."

Attila said, "Time to depart, indeed. In fact, I hope it's not too—"

A siren started to sound.

"Late."

"Go! Go!"

They tore away, heading back toward the vault door they had entered. They were just pulling it open when the security men rounded the corner about thirty yards away.

"Halt!"

Yeah, right, thought Machiko. *Or you'll shoot.*

They didn't halt, of course. They dived through the opening and began running, Machiko hoping against hope that they hadn't been recognized. This would certainly take some explaining. . . . Well, Mr. Evanston . . . I was just looking for the ladies' room. . . .

They were out into the main section of the biolab and still running when the other troop of security came around the other corner, cutting them off.

They dived behind another tank, not pausing for a moment, but scurrying away like pursued rats in a maze.

"Alternative exit?" said Machiko.

"Yes. Follow me."

Attila ran down another aisle, the end of which was a door. With absolutely no ceremony or precaution, he banged against that door, pushing on the latch simultaneously . . . hurling himself into the outside.

Machiko followed.

They were out on permacrete now, in some sort of empty parking lot. Beyond was a perimeter fence, and beyond that a gate yawned open invitingly.

They ran for it.

"Stop," screamed someone from behind them.

"Run ahead of me," said Attila, positioning himself between her and their pursuers. "I can take bullets a lot better than you can."

"Thanks," she puffed.

There were explosions behind them, and the whizzing of fired ammunition to their sides and over their heads.

Something blasted to the left. An incendiary impact nearly tore them off their feet.

"What the hell are they shooting at us?" said Machiko.

"Nothing good, I promise you. Hurry, we're almost through the gate."

She put on a burst of speed, her attention fixed on her goal.

Another explosion, immediately behind her.

This time she was lifted off her feet. With a combination of instinct and training, she rolled with it, coming to rest with a minimum of scrapes and bounces.

"Come on," she called to Attila. "Let's go—"

"That would be very hard," said Attila, ahead of her.

She looked around.

Attila's headless body lay behind her, front down, back and chest section a burnt mangle, oozing fluid.

Some kind of bazooka shell had hit him, exploded, and now the android was in tatters.

"Til!" she cried. *"Til!"*

"Quiet! Over here!"

Still in front of her.

She looked toward where the voice originated from, astonished. There, lying in the gutter, upended, was Attila the Hun's head.

Mouth moving.

"Well don't just stand there, Machiko. Pick me up and let's get the hell *out* of here!"

She got past her astonishment.

Her reflexes went to work.

She dodged over, picked up the head, tucked it under her arm, and started to run.

Another spray of bullets swept past her.

"Over there—that car. That's our only hope," said Attila.

She raced over. It was a four-wheeler, open.

She hopped in. There was no key, and no time to hot-wire it.

"Stick me up to the ignition," said the head.

Not thinking, just obeying, Machiko did just that.

Something whipped from Attila's head, slotting into the ignition.

The car kicked to life.

"Now go," said Attila. "Go!"

She put the car into gear. Bullets whanged into the side.

She pushed on the accelerator and got the hell out of there, Attila's head hanging like a bizarre key chain from the ignition.

She zoomed off into the night, headlights flicking on.

Off and away, escaping.

But to where? crashed the thought inside her head. To *where?*

19

Dawn crept up warily on the horizon.

By its new, thin light Machiko Noguchi cupped her hand and dipped it into the river.

She drank.

The water was cool and sweet.

She'd tasted it early, by the light of two moons, and it had tasted even better then.

She looked up into the sky, as though expecting company at any moment. Nothing. No thropters or skimmers or any of the other number of airborne vehicles that could be pursuing them.

She sighed and stood up. Her back was stiff, but otherwise the couple hours' rest had been fine. She walked back up to where the four-wheel-drive vehicle was sequestered, in a bowerlike assemblage of river-

side and trees. Here it was neatly hidden from sight
... but, then, who knew if there were other ways of
detecting it?

With no other place to go, she headed out to the
wilderness.

She couldn't exactly hop on a starship and race off
for the safety of light-years-distant planets. She
couldn't barge into the barracks and holler for help
from men who didn't really know her from Eve and
who were being paid royally for their loyalty. The
thought that she should somehow contact Ned
Sanchez crossed her mind; however, she nixed it immediately. No way would that work now.

No. She had just one hope.

With what she knew now, there was another
chance.

With her added understanding it was a slim possibility but one that she had to take. Oh, she supposed
she could have simply allowed herself to be caught.
Evanston most likely would not indulge in simple
Death; her talents and abilities were too valuable. No,
most likely he'd just do a selective mem-wipe. Of
course, some of her personality might get pulled up
by the roots in the process, but hey, that was too bad.
Make her a little more docile and less likely to poke
her nose where it didn't belong.

She went back to the car.

In the passenger seat was the head.

"How ya doin', short stuff?"

"S'all right."

Attila winked at her.

She remembered her shock and grief at his seeming
demise.

However, as interesting and valuable as the android's body was, it would seem that his actual consciousness circuits were in his head, and apparently
capable of operation for quite a while on their own

batteries. For his part Attila seemed oddly resigned to his new state, merely glad to be still in existence.

"What do you think? Shall we keep going in this thing?"

"If speed is what you want, then we should. However, it would be risky."

"Yeah. They're bound to have copters out looking for us now."

"Not necessarily. Wouldn't that be admitting that there was some secret they were keeping?"

"No. All Evanston has to do is claim we were snoopers for some rival company. I'm sure he's well within legal rights to seek us out and kill us."

"Or he can cover up."

"So the question remains."

She thought about the issue for a moment.

Decided.

"They must be watching. They know we're here." She looked ahead. "That clearing there. That will do."

"And if it doesn't?"

"Then we'll get back in the car and raise such a ruckus, they'll find us."

"I'm glad you know what we're doing. I certainly don't. But I'll be glad to back you up."

"All I can say is that I'm just glad you're still around, Attila—in whatever form."

His mouth managed to form a smile. "Thanks."

She put on the backpack she'd found in the car, and then she tucked Attila under her arm and set off.

"Looks like it's going to be a nice day," said Attila.

"Yes," she said.

She marched.

It took ten minutes to get to the clearing. She strode across it, toward the trees that ridged the other side.

"What now?" said Attila.

"Watch. Listen."

She set him on a nearby rock with a good vantage point.

She placed herself into a stance.

She raised her hands to her mouth.

She made the Call.

A high ululation carried over the trees, punctuated by a gruff, low-pitched snarl.

She let it unwind for a full ten seconds, then allowed its echo to settle into the leaves.

"You learned that from the Hunters?" said Attila.

"Yes. Now, be quiet. This is going to be very delicate."

"If it happens at all."

"Yes."

She waited some minutes, listening.

There was no direct answer. However, her honed instincts detected something in the distance.

Something coming.

She felt her adrenaline rising. She felt the old machinery clicking into place. Machiko Noguchi let loose again the *ka'rik'na*, the summoning, and the *mesh'in'ga*, the battle-dreamtime, folded over her. She was able to access areas of her mind that had been retreating from her human state.

Yes.

They *were* coming.

The question was, would she have time to explain what had happened? Would these creatures remember her betrayal? If so, then she had just one slim chance, and she inwardly prepared herself to take advantage of that chance.

One moment the glade in which they stood was empty save for them.

The next, a warrior materialized, shutting off his invisibility device.

She did not recognize him. She spoke immediately, using a few simple phrases she remembered from the abrupt, barking language of the yautja.

"I am one with you. I come to fight with you. I am a Blooded One."

She had made sure before that her locks were well pulled away from the singed marking on her forehead, the marking that Broken Tusk had given her, the marking of bug acid mixed with yautja blood. This had saved her before and would give them pause now.

The warrior was dressed in armor and helmet and stood in a battle-crouch.

He advanced slightly, to have a look.

Grunted with surprise.

Called back to companions as yet not visible.

Seeing she was not armed, he stood up and addressed her.

"Prepare to die."

She had warned Attila to expect this, and when it happened, to keep quiet, no matter what. Even though he wouldn't understand the word, he would doubtless distinguish the doom in the intonation.

However, this was to be expected. It was a kind of rough greeting as well as a challenge. A test, if you will, and easy enough to pass.

"Should I die, it will be in battle. I have many trophies. My honor will last while my bones last."

The Predator grunted.

He approached her.

He was a regular-sized creature, which is to say much taller, much bigger than she. Although with one swipe of the blades on his wrist he could cut her down at any time, she stood stock-still. One hint of fear, one tremble, could be her undoing. She stood, chin outthrust in a stance of honor as he walked around her.

With a sudden clang the blade erupted.

The creature jabbed.

The alien steel stopped just inches from her eyes.

He said something quickly, only snatches of which she understood.

". . . death . . . dismemberment . . . skull . . . wall . . . treachery . . ."

It didn't sound good.

She said three words.

Honor.

Courage.

Danger to the megapack (or words to that effect).

The blades lowered.

"Danger?"

"Hard Meat. Soft Meat take Hard Meat." She tapped her cranium, indicating her brain. "Dangerous warrior now."

The creature shook his dreadlocks with a great moaning growl.

"We must stop," said Machiko.

The Hunter stepped back.

"Trick," he snarled.

However, if he really believed this was a trick, then her guts would be hanging from the trees now, and her white, shining skull would be inside the guy's net bag.

"No," she said.

An easy word, even in yautja parlay.

The Hunter growled up some word from the back of his throat, spat it out. He backed up, bristling. From a belt he drew a knife. He raised it to the skies, and a call ripped through the air.

Machiko, however, was not afraid.

Machiko knew the meaning of the gesture, if not the precise meaning of the word.

It was a summons.

The bushes ridging the glade rustled as though some sudden selective wind had passed through them.

Like some sort of photographic special effects in a 3-D movie, spectral figures began to take shape, walking from the bushes, fading into reality.

Ten of them.

From a blur to solid, fierce reality.

The pack.

They stood, some holding spears, others holding burners. The fact that they had more than just spears and knives meant that they were now involved in more than just a Hunt.

They stood as a unit, staring at Machiko, their eyes burning into her soul.

She stared back, defiantly, proudly. It was as though she could feel the sign on her brow pulsing, its burning flame a signal to them.

This one is Worthy.

She is a Hunter.

She has been Blooded.

She stood her ground and called a greeting of comrades.

"I need your help in a great battle," she said. "I have come to tell you of something you should know."

Suddenly, though, another wavering, and another smaller spectral figure emerged from the bushes.

Took form.

Became.

"We know," said the new arrival. "You are Traitor."

Machiko's heart froze.

Lar'nix'va.

The Hunter she had come to call Shorty.

20

Shorty.

Lar'nix'va.

No question about it, even though he wore his armor and a helmet, she recognized the diminutive form.

He was no longer the youth he had been; he had grown in muscle if not in height. There was a Napoleonic swagger to his step, and arrogance to his stance.

Not only was it Shorty, but from all signs he seemed to be the Leader of this group.

"No," she said. "No traitor. Warrior!"

Damn!

In this kind of situation she wished she had more than just a few words, a few honor-filled postures to use. She could explain everything in detail. Instead, she just had to rely on imperatives and single emphatic words to get her meaning across.

"Kill her," said Shorty.

There was no time, it would seem, even if she had the words she needed.

She had one slim glimmer of hope, one trump card, and even as weapons were raised, she took a step forward and held up a hand.

"No. I *challenge*. I defend honor. Battle."

This caused a great commotion among the yautja. They jabbered among themselves for a moment and then stepped back as one, away from their Leader.

Shorty grunted.

He raised his spear.

Threw it.

The thing throbbed to a halt in the dirt at Machiko's feet. Without hesitation Machiko picked it up. Brandished it.

Shorty called to a second, and immediately there was a spear in his hand.

He took a significant step forward.

The duel was on.

Machiko had gambled on this. She knew that if she threw down the gauntlet, it would have to be picked up. Such was the code of yautja. Honor was all. Courage had to be met with courage, and life itself was not so important as the valiant and brave departure of life.

If she could best the Leader of this pack, then she could get them to listen. And she felt that if she could get them to listen, *really* listen, then she could get them to join with her in an assault; then possibly this horror being perpetrated by this rich maniac might be prevented, curtailed, stopped.

First, though, she had to defeat her old nemesis, the Hunter she called Shorty.

And defeating a Hunter in this kind of situation meant one thing.

A fight to the death.

Shorty feinted, then stepped back two steps.

He made a series of snorting sounds that was the equivalent of yautja laughter. Did a little shuffling dance, then mimed her usual initial attack moves.

Damn!

He'd seen her fight, of course. He knew that she knew some fancy steps, knew some sort of odd physical/mental laws generally dubbed "martial arts."

If she tried anything ordinary on him, this genius of combat, this Predator would know exactly what was going to happen and would be a couple of steps ahead of her.

Besides that, all she had in terms of weapons was this short spear. Shorty had his spear, along with his personal arsenal, to say nothing of his armor and helmet.

The Hunter concept of "even-steven" was rough indeed.

Shit.

"Well, you bastard," she said. "Thank God I've got some new moves."

She attacked.

If anything, she was in better shape now, more limber and agile, and she put it all to the test in just under two seconds. She feinted, flipped, rolled, jabbed, retreated, rolled, ran, fell, and then thrust upward toward the place she knew was the most vulnerable.

The moves clearly surprised Shorty.

Nonetheless, he wasn't quite in the spot where he was supposed to be, so the point of her spear only glanced off the side of his armor.

With a snort he brought his own spear down toward her.

Mistake.

She dodged the thrust, grasped the shaft by its base, and twisted the torque of her body in such a way as to capitalize on the momentum he had generated.

Her legs went up, and she executed a perfect flip.

The force of his fall on his back broke his grasp on his spear, and suddenly she had two weapons.

She used her original immediately, trying to push the head under the armpit of the armor.

Shorty wrenched away.

His wrist knives flipped out as he rolled to another fighting stance. He crouched and regarded her, doubtless with more caution and respect now.

"Bitch," he snarled. Or a word to that effect.

Well, maybe not respect.

She bounced on the balls of her feet, agile and ready, warming up and prepared for the next onslaught, the next maneuver.

They circled each other warily. She could hear him breathing harshly behind his mask. She could hear his mandibles working with hate and frustration. Shorty had despised her. Now he loathed her even more, and he had the chance to finish this particular warrior's tale. Oh, how much the little bastard longed to rip her spine out. Oh, how proudly would he display her bleached Soft Meat skull, finally removed of the counterfeit blooding scar that had tormented him so!

Yeah, buddy, she thought.

Come and get it, you asshole.

Two spears were not the ideal pairing of instruments.

In fact, she would have preferred a good hard knife. However, Machiko knew she had to make do with what she had. Although a thought occurred to her. . . .

The spear shafts were made of wood. She dropped the blade of one quickly to the ground, then stepped down, hard, upon it.

Snap.

She now had a knife.

She picked it up just as Shorty lunged.

With no wasted motion she leaped, rolled, and came up several feet clear of his attack. Seeing an opening, she whacked him across his buttocks with the broad side of the spear.

No damage, but doubtless it hurt his pride.

She laughed and called him the Hunter equivalent of "jackass."

He roared around and came for her. The move was expected, but it was so fast that she had to meet him head-on. She narrowly avoided the slash of his blades as she sidestepped him. She thumped the knife against the back of his head.

When she came away, she saw the blood on it. A nasty yellow-green.

She displayed it for the others.

"First blood!" she called.

Anything to put this killing machine off balance.

Maybe too off balance. Before she could recover from his last lunge, he lunged again.

This time she didn't have time to dance away.

Shorty whacked into her, and suddenly they were rolling around on the ground. Not exactly the optimum position in which to exercise her knowledge of martial arts.

Now it wasn't even street fighting.

It was dirt struggle.

Had he been a normal-sized Hunter, surely his strength would have overwhelmed her immediately. Fortunately, he was not, and she was able to keep those deadly razor-sharp blades away. Nonetheless, when they finished their roll, he was on top, bearing down, albeit without his mask, which had somehow gotten loosed in the ruckus.

His eyes glared evilly, and his mandibles crawled like crab spiders descending upon their prey. His blood seeped from behind his head, dripping at her.

"Know that I have killed you." He said the ritual

words and brought the blade down toward her neck, struggling against the grip of her right hand.

It was like an unfair arm-wrestling match. Shorty had the right angle for all the power. Sweat popped out on her brow.

Her other hand. It had the knife. If she could just have a moment, she might be able to use it, now that the helmet was gone.

The clicking mandibles came down.

The burning eyes . . .

The blades . . .

Inches from her eyes and—

There was a hissing sound.

A wisp of smoke.

Machiko watched, astonished, as a tiny hole was punched in the side of Shorty's temple.

His force bearing down on her was abruptly diminished, and she did not wait around to question her opportunity but pulled the spearhead up, around, and stabbed with all her might at this oblique angle.

The edge of the spearhead thrust up into the soft juncture of chin and neck, below the mandibles.

Up, *hard* up, through arteries and brain tissue.

Shorty's eyes flamed and looked down with surprise at the warrior he thought he had bested.

Blood spurted from his neck.

The lights in the eyes struggled to stay lit. They went out, hatred still glaring, denying that Death was coming.

The muscles relaxed, and the Leader of the Hunters dropped upon her.

She pushed him off.

Got to her feet.

Pulled the makeshift knife from his throat, ripping out corded vein and artery and muscle in a swift coup de grâce.

Not necessary, but an effective touch.

She brandished the gory weapon, the defeated's

blood runneling down the blade onto her hand and her shirt.

"Victor! To me, glory!"

She didn't know many phrases in the yautja language, but she knew the most effective and necessary ones.

The Hunters raised their own weapons. Not to retaliate, but as a gesture of acceptance and respect.

She stood there a moment, taking her due for the victory, a foot squarely on top of the defeated Shorty.

Well, you bastard, she thought. *Payback time.*

However, most of her mind was preoccupied with trying to figure out what had happened. The other Hunters clearly hadn't noticed the hole burning into their Leader.

The question was, Where had it come from?

She calculated its direction of origin.

Took a quick look.

And was astonished.

There, looking out at her from the open bag in which he had been transported, was Attila the Hun.

The android winked at her.

What the hell was going on?

21

Livermore Evanston watched the creature through the thick glass wall. No matter how long he stared at the things, he could never get enough of them. His geneticists told him the same thing was true about the study of their genetic code, and they had similar adjectives to employ.

Fiendishly clever.

The bug had been drugged by a gas, and the mist of the stuff still clung to the chitin of its ventral section. This one happened to be a genetic parent to the altered replicants down in the tanks. There had been another bug, another batch, but for some reason those had not worked out so well. In fact, one had managed to escape with a gun, of all things. It had long since disappeared, but Evanston had been gratified to learn of its discovery. Apparently the other mysterious alien life-form that visited this planet had killed it, which was just as well.

The bug's helmetlike head stirred. It's secondary jaws were extended, and Evanston marveled at the hard black of its teeth and jaws. The creatures, his scientists had reported, had the approximate intelligence of dogs. Alas, however, unlike dogs, they could not be trained. When Evanston had bought his first bug, obtained on Ryushi after the calamitous infection there, he'd seen its potential immediately, but the genetic work on it had taken years and an incredible amount of money. Evanston had seen immediately that this work could not be done with the Company's knowledge. Evanstonville was already in the works, and so it was a natural choice to establish his bug project there.

He'd searched for a cornerstone of Conquest, and these cybernetic warriors, surely, were it.

Cybernetics: that was the key, and Livermore Evanston had seen possibilities, if not the actual bio-technical details, immediately. Breed the things for higher intelligence, to be connected to hyperneural-tech transducers and synaptic shunts. Stick on machines, wire up the correct programs for radio control, design armor and weapons.

Result: efficient, almost unstoppable warriors of the future.

An army with which to conquer worlds.

In school was where Livermore Evanston had dreamed of conquest. Not military school, but business school. It had been his hobby. He'd played computer war-games. He'd fought all the great battles, from Waterloo to Gettysburg, from the Battle of the Bulge to the Battle of the Millennium. And as his ties with the Company grew, he began to see the potential for his dreams of absolutely boundless power.

The Company had little vision. They were bean counters. Evanston, however, saw the potential. Economic might was just the springboard. With the energy of scientific breakthroughs, all the way from faster starships to this marvelous genetic razzle-dazzle, the proper kind of mind could unlock the keys to the universe.

Livermore Evanston knew human history.

Humankind was destined for this kind of conquest.

If he didn't spearhead this effort through the means at hand, then surely some other great mind would. If not this century, then next. The stars were in reach, but the stars had to be *grasped*.

The history books were open and there was a gaping blank there.

If he didn't write "Livermore Evanston" in them, large, then someone else would.

And maybe too late.

These new races . . . they were frightening, and they had to be nipped in the bud: get them before they got humanity.

What better way to kill them—and use the best, most terrifying qualities of one of them in the process—than to combine them into one easily controlled being?

It had been a stroke of genius that had been his genetic engineers', not his, but he'd hopped onto it quickly and immediately implemented it into the growth of Evanstonville.

He thought, however, that he'd have more *time*.

Oh, well. He was not a stupid man. From the time he was a little boy, under the tutelage of robots and virtually ignored by his parents, he'd seen life as a playing field of diverging possibilities.

If something went wrong, you tried another tactic.

It was unfortunate about Noguchi. His hope for her had been that she would not only command his mercenaries in their efforts to control escaped bugs, but that she'd seek out and destroy this other race that had visited Livermoreland. It had been with his discovery of oddments of alien armor and clothing upon settling this planet that he'd realized that Evanstonville would need a significant security force, proper fences, and armament. He knew on a gut level that she'd dealt with the monsters before and had betrayed them. After a few years of employ he would gradually introduce the Augmented Warriors, and she would train them, and finally, perhaps, she would even become one of his right-hand generals.

Alas, it was not to be.

She was out in the wild, probably doomed. If the bugs didn't get her, then the things she'd betrayed surely would. She didn't have her android buddy to help her now, either. The idiot's body was off on one of the scientists' tables. He'd have it dissected and analyzed later. Right now there were other things to deal with.

As Evanston looked at the creature behind the glass, a recurring vision suddenly rose before him. He saw himself in a proud battleship in space, commanding a flotilla of vessels. From planet to planet would these vessels step, and upon each one, should it not surrender, should he need ground troops, he had only to let loose these creatures, controlled from afar—

Let loose the Dogs of War.

And then he could remake human civilization according to the ideas he knew were correct.

His personal comm button sounded. He sighed. There were many things to deal with before that time, but oh, when it came, it would be glorious; it would put all other human visions of conquest to shame.

Suddenly, without warning, as he was about to answer the comm, the bug leaped.

Leaped at Evanston.

It smashed into the reinforced glass, snarling and shrieking. It was as though it knew the purposes for which its species was being used.

Evanston flinched, but he did not move. He pressed a button that would summon more gas down upon it and quiet the thing.

Then he answered his comm.

22

Whathat the hell is going on?" Machiko demanded.

"I mentioned before that I was equipped with other 'gifts.' I merely placed some new programming into effect, accessing new weapons," said the head. "I should explore my circuitry. It really is something that I should analyze."

"Would you do that? It's not that I'm ungrateful. It's just that *I really would like to know what the hell is going on!*"

She spoke the words in a terse, urgent voice.

This android—what the hell was he? Truly?

She needed to know, and she needed to know right away. There was nothing in the manual about laser-beam support, that was for sure. But, then, he could project holographs. Why not deadlier light?

They were off by a tree. She had taken the break while the Hunters were conferring among themselves. Clearly, she had bought her life by defeating Shorty. She'd tried, as best she could, with the few words she knew, with gestures and mime, to present them with the facts. They did not seem to understand entirely, but they were picking up something of what she was trying to communicate.

Now a representative was coming out.

He was much bigger than Shorty; she just hoped that she didn't have to fight him.

"You are accepted," she thought the creature said. "However, we do not understand what you are trying to say."

Or something like that.

A few more words.

The Hunt.

A state of Oddness.

Bad Hard Meat.

Well, at least they accepted the fact that indeed something was rotten in Blior. Nonetheless, there was still the same uneasiness with them that she'd felt at the beginning of her jaunt with that other pack. Despite her blooding from Broken Tusk, from Dachande, she was still an alien to these creatures and likely would always be.

Nonetheless, she was reasonably safe now.

She had allies.

Her whole life, in falling apart, had tilted onto the edge again. . . .

And that, she found now as she looked on these creatures and this world with new eyes, was where she liked it.

"Machiko," said the head, still within the confines of its carrying bag, "I believe I've come up with something."

"Look, Til. I appreciate your help, I really do. But *I'm* the one who's going to have to deal with these guys, okay? Maybe you'd better let me muddle through it on my own."

"They don't seem to be thoroughly accepting."

"That's something that I've had to deal with before ... and something I'm going to work on now."

"I hate to tell you this, Machiko. I can understand them, and they're giving you about two hours before they decide to kill you again."

She did a double take. "What ... ? You *understand* them?" She was flabbergasted. "Some newfound program?" Disbelief. Sarcasm.

"Yes," said Attila.

"A program that allows us to speak in the Hunter language?"

"Yes."

"Where the hell did you get that? Why didn't you *tell* me about it?"

"I didn't know. I was not programmed to explore programs, and you never asked me to. You see, in many ways I *am* merely a machine. Actually, the program seems to be some sort of Universal Translator. From the information you've given me and what I picked up from listening in on the Hunters as they've spoken, I've been able to pick up deep structure and words. These are not complex creatures, I think. Their language is not complicated."

"No. I mean, yes. I mean ... Attila, anything *else* you're going to spring on me?"

"I don't know. Perhaps you'd better bring me over to them?"

"A head? Oh, they're going to like that a lot. A talking head."

"Just call me exactly what I am. Your assistant. A kind of robotic Swiss Army knife."

The Hunters had stopped talking.

They were now staring over at them.

She had to do *something*, that was for sure.

"Okay, okay. Let me introduce you to the crew."

She grabbed him up and took him over.

She pointed at him and said simply, "Attila."

"Attila," barked back one of the Hunters, his expression unreadable.

"Yes. Attila." She held him up. "Okay, Attila. Do your stuff."

Immediately the android began speaking slowly but clearly. Machiko understood some of the words, but the way they were connected was different.

The yautja, however, listened with obviously surprised attention.

Well into the explanation, though, she could see they were increasingly reacting with gestures of rage and challenge. Not toward her or Attila. Clearly to the information they were being presented.

Finally, after a pause, Attila asked them a simple question that Machiko understood clearly:

"Do you know how this could have happened?"

The Hunters conferred among themselves.

A spokesman stepped forward eventually and said, "Yes."

Then he told them his tale.

Machiko listened to it later from Attila as she sat down by a tree, eating the cooked Meat and drinking the water that the Hunters had given her.

It was like old times. The rancid smells of the creatures, the ripe, yeasty taste of their favored meat, the sound of their harsh, grating, challenging language.

One big difference.

She had herself a translator now.

Only what *else* did she have on her hands, buried inside that inscrutable lump of circuitry that was Attila the Hun's head?

Only time would tell. She was paying damned close attention.

"It does tie together," said Attila. The android head

was propped on a rock with a view of everything, and an ear cocked toward the conversations of the Hunters, in order to pick up new odds and ends of language to communicate better later. "The oddments of Predator uniform we discovered on Evanston's ship—"

"Yes, of course. That figures in with the knowledge they have of the yautja. I'm not sure how that ties in with augmented *kainde amedha*. Question is, Where did they get them?"

"The answer is simple enough. Something we should probably have realized from the outset."

"Okay. I'm all ears."

"This planet has been in use by the Predators for a long time. For Hunting purposes. Not just bugs, either, but other beasts. And apparently there haven't been the slipups that would have created a bug world either. . . ."

"But the bugs are no strangers here."

"Precisely. As for the Hunters, though—apparently, some years before Evanston and company arrived, the Hunters crashed a ship here. All aboard were killed, and the ship was considered a monument to their lives. The Hunters left for a while, as is their wont. When they returned to this world, they discovered an entirely new situation. This continent had been settled. And the monument to their dead had been plundered and taken apart. Alas, there were apparently preserved bodies of bugs there too.

"The Hunters bided their time. They watched and waited—and, of course, Hunted. Eventually, they came to realize what we'd speculated. They realized that Evanston was turning this into a hunters' planet: a perfect place for them, an ideal situation in which to operate. They could prey on hunters, their favorite source of amusement, a perfect way to derive honor and excitement from kills."

"And they killed that augmented bug we found?"

"Yes. But not before it killed their leader with a gun. Seems to have been an escapee. Crazy and out of control.

"So we can assume that this brand of bugs—let's call them the 'Buggers'—is not quite perfected yet. The Hunters spoke in rather intuitive terms—no concrete evidence."

"However, they did not take this news well."

"No. They are incensed. They spoke of revenge, destruction, terror—trophies. They see great honor in store for themselves here. . . ."

"And the eradication of a threat to the galaxy," Machiko added.

"Yes. They see themselves as the biggest threat to the galaxy, and that's apparently the way they want to keep it."

She nodded. "Yes. The yautja, the way I know and love them. The biggest badasses on the galactic block."

"No great intellect here," Attila observed. "However, I didn't care to point that out."

"And they've agreed to help us."

"Yes. We need to formulate a plan that we can present to them."

"We'll get to that in one moment," Machiko said. "What we need to talk about now, though, old chum, is this progressive improvement in your abilities."

"I thought we'd get around to that."

"When I purchased you, you were guaranteed to have been wiped and then programmed to my specifications. Apparently this is not the case. The question is—who are you, Attila? And are you my friend, still . . . or an enemy?"

A chagrined look passed over the face of the android. "A friend. A dear friend, of course, Machiko."

"An enemy would say the same. What was it your beloved *Art of War* author said about spies being the most important part of winning a war? It would seem that you, my friend, are the spy. The question is, what war am I in?"

"You must realize, this is all new to me. This programming has just kicked in. However, I will try to explain." He sighed, an odd affectation for a creature without lungs. "There is more to human civilization than the Company. . . ."

"Yes. Of course. Like Evanston."

"Evanston? Livermore Evanston has deep ties to the Company. Who do you think has allowed him to grow and prosper? He is not independent. He is a puppet. And, in an ancillary sense, so is the program."

"The Hunter's World?"

"Masquerading the preparation of new warriors to confront threats, to destroy civilizations that stand in the way of the Company's galactic conquest. Why do you think it was so easy for Evanston to get you out of your contract? Because the Company felt you were needed here."

"Okay. Assuming all this is true—where the hell did you come from?"

"Machiko, when you returned from your lark with the Hunter Pack, do you think that your work for the miners on that world was not noted?" Attila asked.

"Of course it was noted. That's what saved my butt. Otherwise the Company would have crucified me."

"As I was saying, there is more to present-day human civilization than just the Company. There are people, groups of independent thinkers within the Company itself—and without, of course—who do not agree with its policies and philosophies for the future of humankind."

"Subversive groups?"

"Yes. And there is a selective group, linking these loose and very different people. . . . I will not burden you with their true name. Call them X Group."

"Okay. X Group. Now what the hell does X Group want with Machiko Noguchi?"

"Your maverick tendencies were noted, as well as your loyalty to the human race. More important, your ties with this mysterious race of Hunters were noted. X Group realized that you had been noted by the Company as well—or at least by significant members therein. When you made inquiries concerning a training assistant, an android companion, that information was noted—and one was especially programmed for you."

"Namely you."

"Programmed to help you should just this kind of situation become reality. But also, ultimately, to contact you and induct you into its cause."

"Wonderful. And I'm supposed to believe this garbage?" Machiko asked.

"Believe what you like. Right now I have sourced all my latent abilities and am here to help you do what you know in your heart is right: Stop this awful menace to humanity, to civilizations everywhere."

"The Buggers, you mean," she said, mulling the notion over. "Yes, you know, Attila, I must admit: I can't think of something more worth stopping. And as much as I hate working for some secret subversive group ... the present cause seems just and right ... and about my only recourse now."

"So you trust me, then?"

"You've really given me no cause not to, have you? Except perhaps hiding oodles of information from me."

"That information was hidden from me as well," Attila pointed out.

"Yeah. So you say." Machiko looked back at the group of Predators. "What other resources do we have besides these boys?"

"This is not the only group. All told, they say they number fifty."

"Hmm. Still not a whole lot. There are only fifteen mercenaries, true, but there are hundreds of armed security forces in Evanstonville. And I'm certain that now that they know I know what's happening there, they are going to be on the cautious side."

"They haven't searched for you."

"No. And probably wisely," Machiko said. "Where am I going to go? No place but back, eventually. The question is, When? The sooner the better." She shook her head. "The damnable thing is, some of the other mercenaries, if they knew what was going on, would help me."

"Like dearest Ned?"

"Ah, that personality of yours remains sparkling, despite the new programs."

"Twinkle twinkle."

"Yes. Ned Sanchez would help."

"He's in this for the money, just like the others."

"Yes, but there's more to it, too. You can only take cynicism so far."

"You're absolutely sure about this?"

"Yes." She shook her head. "How can I communicate with him, though?"

"If you could communicate with Sanchez, do you really think he'd help us? Because, believe me, we need all the help we can get, brilliant warriors or no. I've got the feeling that even as we speak, Evanston and Zorski are putting all their trumps in a row, just in case."

"Yes. Yes, I'm certain."

The android head said, "Fine. Because we have a trick up our sleeve as well. And I can play it tonight."

"Is it a trump?"

The head smiled. "Oh, and more. That is, if it works."

23

*L*eader!

Bakuub was the Leader now.

As he stood in the stark control room of his ship, he gloried in his new position exactly one second, allowing the pride and thrill to swell in his chest.

Enough.

There was important work to be done.

Bakuub turned to the communications controller.

"Open the lines to all fellows in the vicinity. Be sure it is on a wavelength not monitored by the *oomans*."

"Yes, Leader."

Leader!

There were moments of static, and then slowly the acknowledgments of contact began to come in.

Finally, when full communication was engaged, Bakuub began.

"Lar'nix'va is dead. I am the new Leader of this pack." He paused for that information to be assimilated. "The *oomans* in the settlement have begun a dangerous program transforming Hard Meat into warriors. It must be destroyed. We shall need to join together for a ground assault upon their program, under my direction."

Questions poured in. Defiance. Disbelief. Tactical advice.

"The evidence was presented earlier. We cannot utilize our ships. The airways above the settlement are secured by weapons we cannot match. However, we have allies within the compound." He paused for a moment and his mandibles clicked dramatically, like the clashing of daggers. "It shall be a Hunt of Great Honor, Great Glory, I promise you."

Growls and snarls of enthusiasm.

This was language that the yautja packs understood.

24

The sun set.

All day long Machiko Noguchi, expecting some sort of attack at any moment, had watched it rise in the sky, then slip down through the afternoon. She requested a scout be set up. The yautja had assented. Silent and inconspicuous surveillance, after all, was one of their specialties.

However, there was no sign of active pursuit.

According to the relay of information, another scout had seen a couple of copters trolling through the air, but this was absolutely casual compared to the kind of military manuevers that she was expecting.

There was nothing more, though, and it made her a little nervous.

When the last of the sunlight slipped down over the

edge of this beautiful world, the new Leader of the yautja, the warrior named Bakuub, came to them. He informed them that the warriors were ready and that they would prefer to do battle as soon as possible.

"Please, Attila. Explain to him that the preparations are not quite ready."

Attila had acquired a much larger vocabulary that day, and by now he was able to speak with greater facility and diplomacy. Nonetheless, it did not take much understanding of his language to realize that Bakuub was not happy at the news.

The warriors were straining at the bit. They hungered for action. They longed to avenge this slight upon the sanctity of their place in the universe.

Eventually, Bakuub went away, but only after a great deal of reassurance that soon they'd be on their way to scoop up many trophies.

They had collected, all told, fifty Predators for the attack. This was not as many as Machiko would have liked, but at least it represented several packs. Against this kind of opposition, they certainly would need more than a pack, no matter how excellent their battle skills were.

"Look, I don't know how long we're going to be able to stall these guys," said Machiko. "What's going on back at Evanstonville?"

Even though she'd had some sleep during the day, she felt tired. Unusually tired and ill at ease, and eager to get at this thing herself. They'd spent half the night planning it with the help of Ned Sanchez and the three others he had corralled to take part in the rebellion. She'd been surprised that he'd been able to get so many. Dick Daniels hadn't been difficult. From the very beginning the man had not liked this particular setup. "Fishy to the extreme" were the words he'd used. It was Daniels, though, who'd seen the opportunistic value of a rebellion such as this. "Shit. You knock out this crappy genetic-lab operation, you whack the bosses—you're in charge. You got the spaceships, you got the whole friggin' world. I've *always* wanted a world to myself."

Machiko had pointed out that this was not at all their goal—that they simply wanted to stop the obscene and dangerous genetic engineering. She hadn't mentioned the Company subversives. They had a big hump to get over. If they got over it, they'd figure out the rest later. However, it was the "even more riches" line that Daniels used on MacCraken and Marino, and Machiko was glad he had, because it worked. Not that Lou and Jim were not appalled at the truth of what was happening here—they were simply mercenaries, with a taste for loot and adventure. It had taken a very long time, through the medium of Attila's burned body, to explain the situation, to convince them. Finally, what it came down to was cold, hard cash. Nonetheless, their roles in the rebellion could be minimal, though vital. She and Sanchez, along with the horde of yautja, could deal with the principal part of the operation. But they were going to need some serious help in getting to that point alive.

"What's going on back in Evanstonville?" said the head of Attila the Hun. "Just about the same thing as when you asked ten minutes ago."

"Yes, but when do you think we can be ready?"

"You're going to have to ask Sanchez yourself, because I certainly don't know."

"But where *is* Sanchez?"

"Out getting ready, I suppose—"

"Look, I know it takes a great deal of effort, but could you please tune back in and see if he's gotten back to Operations Headquarters?"

"Operations Headquarters" was a tool shack behind the garage which they were using for a base.

"All right, all right. Hold your horses."

The light in Attila's eyes momentarily dimmed as he made the necessary interneural connections.

They brightened again.

"There. I'm through. You can speak," said the android.

"He's back?"

"Yes."

Machiko leaned closer to Attila's head, which served as her microphone in these communications.

"Sanchez?"

"Yes, Machiko." His voice sounded weary.

"How's it going?"

"Well."

"Good. What time tonight can we make the raid?"

There was a pause. "Look, Machiko. I'm not so sure that tonight's the right time."

"What! Why not?"

"Zorski called in all the troops. They're patrolling. Armed to the teeth. It's like they're expecting you or something. It's hard to coordinate this because they've got us out there too."

"You mean it's impossible."

"I didn't say that. It's just that—well, we were up most of last night, and we're pretty damned tired."

She thought about this. Not good. On the other hand, she had the pack of Preds in fighting trim and ready to go. Nothing worse than a huffy, impatient pack—and there were numerous packs here. Hell, they'd start fighting with each other!

"Look, I can sympathize. I'm tired, you're tired. But you've got stims, right?"

"Sure."

She sighed. "Then you're going to have to use them, because it's gotta be tonight."

Another pause.

"Okay. You're the boss here. I guess I'm going to have to go with what you say, Noguchi."

"When can you have the setup ready?"

"No earlier than midnight."

"Midnight's a little too dead-on. Let's make it a half hour later."

"You got it."

She was half expecting more complaints. When she got a positive answer, she was taken aback, but relieved.

"As planned?"

"As planned."

"Fine. We'll count on you. And you know what to do if there's any problem."

"Twist this body's right hand off."

"Yes, but only in an emergency. I think it's going to be as hard to get back on as the head."

She switched off.

"You *had* to remind me," said Attila.

"Look, pal. You had better hope we get you and your erstwhile body into the same room together eventually," said Machiko.

"Oh, that's all right. I've always been rather cerebral anyway."

"Attila?"

"Yes."

"Heads up."

She tossed him in the air like a basketball, caught him on the way down.

"You're the kind of gal who tries a poor android's soul, Machiko."

She grinned, feeling a little better.

"Thanks. I'm starting to appreciate better that you've got a pretty special one, Attila."

"One favor, then, Machiko—that is, if we get through all this?"

"Yes?"

"Can I get a new name? I think I'm going to want to disassociate myself totally from this war business."

She looked over at the group of yautja, fencing and sparring and exercising in the glow of their lanterns beneath the cover of their bower.

She took a deep breath.

"I think I know exactly what you mean," said Machiko Noguchi.

At midnight they met at the base behind the garage.

Sanchez.

Daniels.

MacCraken.

Marino.

Ostensibly, they had turned in for the night in their rooms at the barracks, pleading exhaustion after a long day's work. As mercenaries, they were not under any particularly strict military pattern, cut off from the rest of the security forces, especially now that their leader had gone rogue. However, Sanchez had figured that it would be best for the operation if anyone in even vague authority believed that they were presently visiting slumberland and not planning outright and total mutiny.

Sanchez drew in a lungful of smoke from his cigarette. "All right," he said. "Are we all clear on our orders? Have we all got the equipment we need?"

"You bet," said Lou MacCraken, holding up his compact but quite effective incendiary device. It had been programmed personally by Sanchez for maximum pyrotechnics, maximum noise. "Gee, I always wanted to blow something up."

"You want mine, too?" said Marino, looking down with extreme misgivings at his own device.

Since Sanchez doubted these two soldiers' abilities the most, he'd given them the simplest things to do.

All they had to accomplish was a simple jaunt to an area on the southern perimeter of the settlement, farthest from the biogenetics lab. Here they would set their bombs by the force-field emplacements. They would blast away the perimeter barrier with maximum effect, leaving a gaping hole in the preliminary defenses.

Many troops would then disperse to meet with presumed attackers.

However, they would find nothing.

Meantime, Sanchez and Daniels would go to the appropriate section of the perimeter fence itself and turn that off quietly and discreetly. Fortunately, Dick Daniels had the circflow experience to accomplish this, without a great deal of trouble. "You just gotta know which fuse to fry," he'd explained. Even Attila had agreed this was the proper tactic.

At that point Machiko would lead the Predators to the lab.

The rest would come naturally.

She'd instructed them as to the lab's layout. They'd be equipped with plasma blasters, not just sharp weapons.

It seemed to Sanchez a bit of a suicide mission on the part of the aliens. He just knew they couldn't accomplish this on their own.

"You haven't seen these guys working as a group before," Machiko had said, adding that it would probably be best if all four just stayed out of the way and came to clean things up when it was over.

All four seemed to think this was a marvelous notion.

"What about the other guys?" said Lou.

"They're getting paid for fighting. They're going to earn their money," said Dick Daniels. "If all goes well, they'll survive, and Evanston and the others won't—or will be taken prisoner. At which point we'll be the ones who will offer the fighters money. And they'll be our mercenaries."

"Which means, as our own bosses, we're just going to have to pay ourselves double, right?" said Marino cheerfully.

"Hey. Just don't fry your goddamn chickens till they're hatched," Daniels said.

"Yeah, something like that." Ned Sanchez got up. He started to distribute the weapons and ammo and equipment he'd swiped from the nearby magazine.

"Everybody know what they've got to do?"

They all knew.

"Everybody got your comms on the prearranged frequency?"

Namely, one that Zorski's men would be able to pick up, accidentally or on purpose. Daniels had done the handiwork on that one, the sly fellow.

"Good," said Sanchez. "We've got a new job to do, and I'm here to tell you it feels a lot better than the one we were stuck in before. Now, let's go do it and live to tell the story over some beers."

They charged out into the night.

25

T ime?"

"One half hour after midnight."

Machiko Noguchi looked around at the Hunters gathered impatiently behind the car. They looked startling in the dim moonlight, like primitive gods sprung up from ashes of past bonfires, wild and slavering for revenge. The night smelled of blood and horror, and her heart beat with adrenaline and with purpose.

"Bakuub?"

She gestured in a questioning challenge method, a kind of stirring motion meant to bring up a fellow's blood, charge him with kinship and all the finer points of bonded honor.

"We hunger for it!" proclaimed the Leader of the Predators, his snarling voice muffled through his mask. He pounded his hand blaster on his armor. A stream of words came out that Machiko did not quite recognize.

"Destruction to the outrage and the perpetrators of this abomination," Attila interpreted.

"My sentiments exactly," returned Machiko.

She thumbed a switch on the car's control panel. The motor throbbed to life. Her senses were so keen now, she instantly smelled the engine discharge.

"All right," she said. "All we have to do now is wait for the diversion."

They waited.

This waiting seemed to be a bit of a strain upon the Predators. They had ceased their warming maneuvers and now stood tall and still against the night, ready for the Hunt, but Machiko could sense their impatience, their bloodlust. They would as soon charge the settlement now, diversion or no diversion, but their patience and obedience to their new Leader held them in check.

The same patience of lions, hanging back in the bushes, waiting for the proper time to lunge and give chase to a herd of antelope.

Problem was, this time the herd of antelope was heavily armed!

"What time is it?"

"Two and a half minutes late," answered Attila.

"What the hell is taking them?"

"There's no way to tell. They're all out—I hope doing their jobs."

Another moment passed.

"Dammit," said Machiko. "This is what we get for using a damned body as a radio. There's no way to carry it around with you."

"A relay system could have been concocted, but it would have been difficult to regulate. No, Machiko. Have confidence. You have chosen your allies well. They are good soldiers."

Machiko looked yearningly toward the settlement.

Its taller buildings were in its center, and they gleamed in the moonlight, the smaller outlying buildings huddled around them like children gathered around parents. The genetic factory was one of the farther buildings to the northwest, but it was to the west that the attack party was skulking; this was the portion of the fence that Daniels claimed could be most easily deactivated.

Then, as though in answer to her mental commands, the diversion began.

The bright flare of an incredibly incandescent explosion leaped up from the far side of the settlement, like a knife in the sky.

Moments later another separate explosion of radiance, slightly more amber and jagged, shot up—a rocket flare, without the rocket.

Yes!

Machiko called out, "Advance!" raising her hand at the same time: the agreed-upon semaphore.

They moved out.

"Oh, ye of little faith," said Attila.

As though in agreement the thunderous sound of the initial explosion finally reached them. The second echoed soon after, even louder.

"Ah!" said Machiko. "That should get their attention. That should bring their forces to that side. Meanwhile, we go in through the side closer to the factory."

There were two Predators lying on top of the roof riding shotgun, and the added weight slowed the vehicle down somewhat. However, as fast as the Predators were, they still clearly struggled to keep up. They did not complain. The fighting frenzy was upon them, and they had plenty of strength and energy to draw upon.

Less than a kilometer separated the fence and the factory.

When they reached the perimeter, Machiko noticed a shimmer.

Her heart leaped into her throat.

What—were the force fences still up?

What had happened to Sanchez, goddammit?

However, as they got closer, she could see that a section of the fence was down, and two figures were gesturing at them.

Sanchez and Daniels, waving guns.

"Come on, come on!" Daniels yelled. "There's a damned good chance, diversion or no diversion, they've spotted you on sensors."

"I thought you took care of that," said Machiko.

"I did. You just never know."

The two opened the back door and hopped into the backseat while the car was still moving.

"Hey! I thought you two were going to stay out of this part. I thought that was the agreement."

"Hell with it," said Sanchez. "You go, we go."

"Yeah," said Daniels. "Anyway, I want to see what they've got in there before you and your weird aliens blow it all up."

Machiko had about one moment of consternation and concern, which instantly changed to appreciation and a kind of hard, flinty, steely love. A comradely love born of brethren in arms.

"Okay, it's your butts. Off we go—"

"The Alien Mobile!" said Daniels.

Sanchez said nothing. He just got his gun out as Machiko hauled ass toward the factory.

"So there you are," said Daniels, leaning his brawny visage over the seat and regarding Attila's head, snuggly fitted between two boxes so that it wouldn't roll around. "I must say, it's been damned strange working with that headless body of yours, buddy."

"You think it's been strange for you? You're not the one who's counting on Machiko Noguchi for transportation. I am *not* the dependent sort."

"You've been a godsend, I'll tell you that. What else can this android body of yours do?"

"That's something that I am finding constantly surprising," answered the android head.

"Well, for the record, in contrast to these hunting behemoths I find myself surrounded by, you're Mr. Normal." Daniels looked around. "Hey! Where the hell'd they go?"

"They've put their invisibility devices on. If you look at them peripherally, you'll notice a blurring of their form as the light bends around them."

"Jeez. Yeah. You're right. These are some high-tech whizzes for such barbarian-brains."

"Who knows where they got it?" said Machiko, shrugging. "Maybe they stole it. Maybe they have scientists."

"Heads up," said Ned Sanchez. "Factory dead ahead—and it looks like, for all our efforts, they still have a welcoming party."

Livermore Evanston was expecting something like this.

Nonetheless, when it came, it came more spectacularly than he'd expected. . . .

And from *inside* the compound.

His instruments told him that.

He'd anticipated an attack sometime this evening, and so, after taking a long nap, enjoying a steam bath and a first-rate therapeutic message, he'd camped out here, in his state-of-the art war room.

Even though Blior was situated in the middle of nowhere, he'd always been aware of its military future, and so one of the first things he'd constructed, in the basement of his central fortress, was a personal bunker, linked to the topside world by the most sophisticated sensor and communication system possible. Here he was safe and snug from any kind of attack, shielded behind firm layers of permacrete and steel. At his fingertips was a wealth of weapons.

Still, for all its shimmering completeness, Livermore Evanston hadn't expected to be using it this soon.

Nervously, he snacked on his own special blend of spiced, salted nuts for the energy and stamina he felt he was going to need, even though he'd packed in a full dinner that night, supplemented by vitamins and tonics, minus his usual doses of alcohol. Cigar fumes hung about him now as he stared out his screen, watching as the light of the explosions reached for the nighttime sky.

"Damn," he said. "They're breaking into the south perimeter."

"We're dispatching forces to deal with it, sir," said Zorski, via radio.

"Yes, of course. But watch out," said Evanston after the computer analysis floated up on the screen. "Those blasts came from within the fence."

"Saboteurs?"

"Got to be."

"Damn."

"Look," Evanston said, "there's no reason to leave the principal thing we're worried about unguarded. Just put out an exploratory force to see if there's really anything coming in. It can always be reinforced if necessary."

"Evanston. We've got people out here—civilians. Guests."

"Give them guns. Tell them it's a part of the show we're experimenting with—and just might get out of hand. If they're not security, just have them shoot at anything that looks like a monster or Machiko Noguchi from the window."

"Yes, sir," said Zorski. "But don't you think you're being a little too glib?"

"I wouldn't be glib, Zorski, if I didn't think that this wasn't something we could deal with."

"That's a fine thing to say when you're tucked in safe and tight where you are."

"Ah—do I detect a hint of insubordination? May I remind you, Zorski, that you're one of the architects of this great plan, and every bit as enmeshed as I?"

"Frankly, I wish I was enmeshed down there with you right now."

"Zorski, Zorski." He might have been saying "Tsk, tsk." "Rewards demand risks. This has never been a sure or safe enterprise. And yet its rewards will be astronomical."

Zorski sighed. "Right. No time to bicker."

"Time to fight. Time to solve problems. I'll be here, the voice of experience, monitoring, controlling the vital elements that need controlling. And believe you me, Zorski. If worst comes to worst, I'll be out there with a blaster pack strapped to my back."

"Yeah. Right. I'll believe that when I see it."

Communication ceased.

Evanston turned back to his equipment, glittering and shining competently.

He just wished he actually felt as confident as he sounded.

Anyway, there were far more effective measures that could be taken than strapping a weapon on himself.

The thought made him smile.

He almost hoped it would come to those measures. The results could solve a great deal of testing.

Humming an aria to himself, his hands began to tap emphatically across controls.

26

Lights.

They blazed on with unexpected brilliance.

It was as though a batch of stars had suddenly settled down upon the sides and top of the building that held the biolab factory and then blazed their light in shafts toward the approaching troops.

Machiko Noguchi had been in raiding parties before with the yautja, of course, but she'd never been in an actual planned military maneuver against an armed opponent.

She was running this one by the seat of her pants.

So she was surprised that the exactly correct thing sprang to her lips, even as fire began to rip through the newly brightened night.

She pointed. "Kill lights!"

The result was immediate, and shockingly effective.

The alien rifles went off almost as one, hurling plasma and laser beams with pinpoint accuracy. Most of the lights were eliminated. Crash of plasglass. Trickle-tinkle down the sloping sides of the factory.

"Okay, we're out of here," said Daniels.

"You know what to do," said Sanchez to Machiko. "You bet."

The two mercenaries leaped from the car and began to fire at the gaggle of security forces.

A couple of them went down immediately.

The rest returned fire, but it was clear that they were not highly trained. They should have had some sort of cover—instead they were out in the open, behaving like total idiots.

Machiko wasn't really surprised at this. It was Attila who had pointed out that there hadn't been any military operations on Blior in decades, and many soldiers simply were not trained in the basics. It certainly wasn't just a matter of standing in the open, firing at the attacker.

Machiko didn't complain, though.

Certainly, she was also surprised at the Predators. They behaved like a crack unit, working together seamlessly. Like a bunch of well-trained Trojans. These guys had a military background, no question. It wasn't just Hunting. Was it in their traditions, their training—or their genes?

Her job, however, was not to dawdle about and gawk.

As driver of the car, she had specific goals.

She watched as the intense fire of the attackers cut a swath through the defenders. The security forces wisely beat a retreat, leaving an opening just the right size for her.

She checked her safety harness, then grabbed Attila and stuffed him tightly between her legs.

"I suppose I should get a thrill out of this," said his muffled voice from between her thighs.

"Just get set for a different kind of thrill," she said.

She gunned the accelerator.

The skimmer skipped ahead with the last reserves of its power. Machiko kept low, and it was a good thing. Bullets splattered through the side windows, raining her with glass.

She kept on, though, aiming for her objective.

When she and Attila had run their reconnaissance, the first thing they'd done was to scope out the exterior of the building. From her memory of that survey, Machiko had calculated which of the doors into the main hall would be the weakest.

It was toward that door that she streaked now.

She guided the car as best she could, angling it just so—and then braced for the crash.

It came, just as expected, but with a fury and violence that could never be prepared for.

Upon impact the crashfoam grew, and just in time.

The windshield shattered, and the front of the skimmer crumpled.

So did the door ahead of her.

This portion of the factory had not been built to withstand assault and was not reinforced. The four-wheeler smashed through. One door was torn off its hinges. The other smashed down onto the ground beyond.

Braking was not necessary.

The skimmer smashed into a cement stanchion-and-girder arrangement a few yards in, bringing it to a halt.

"Damned good job if I say so myself," said Machiko.

She grabbed Attila's head by its hair in one hand, and with her gun in the other, kicked open the door and hopped out.

Next stop: those tanks, and their hellish contents.

*   *   *

Livermore Evanston watched on his screen as Machiko Noguchi's car smashed through the door into the main portion of the biolab factory.

Livermore Evanston was not eating.

"More troops," he said. "Get me some more troops into this breach," he shouted.

"I'm working on it," said Zorski. Her voice seemed to have lost its composure.

Breaking into the factory was not difficult, and was expected.

However, the suddenness of the breakthrough was *not* expected.

There had been no time to maneuver more troops around.

Noguchi and this strange army were acting like kamikazes, not soldiers. They seemed to have absolutely no regard for their own lives, which was not something that Evanston had anticipated. It broke all the rules he knew of common sense, all he'd studied about war in school.

Livermore Evanston swiveled in his chair.

He examined his options.

"Surround the building with any available troops, Zorski. But don't go inside. I've got other options available."

Eyes canting up to take in the action as the hordes of invisible Predators swarmed through the opening that the skimmer had just bashed into the factory, Evanston bided his time above the proper controls. He could see the disturbances their devices made in the air, some imprints in the ground vaguely determining their numbers.

He bided his time until the alien warriors would be unable to escape.

And if, for some reason, they could—

Well, the rest of his soldiers would be waiting out there for them.

No.

Things were not that bad at all!

Machiko watched as the horde moved in, cleanly and efficiently, weapons cocked and ready for action.

Bakuub stepped up to her.

"That's the entrance, down at the other end of the building," she said, pointing.

Bakuub got the gist of the message and gestured accordingly toward his companions.

They started advancing upon their objective.

"This is most satisfying," said Attila amid the sound and fury coming from outside.

"I don't know," said Machiko. "It's almost too easy."

"Nothing is easy in war. You take your victories where you find them."

"Did you warn them about possible traps?"

"They already anticipate such. According to Bakuub their motto is something like 'Take things as they come.'"

"Yes," said Machiko. "I know that all too well. Well, come on. We might as well get into the action."

She stuffed the head into the strap pocket that she'd prepared especially for him, cocked her gun, and then began to advance warily.

Attila's head swung on her side like some bizarre baby.

A voice called out from behind her. "Machiko."

She turned around.

It was Sanchez.

"Sanchez. What's the situation outside?"

"Glad you're okay."

"Oh, I used to wreck my cars all the time. I'm real good at it. Too bad I don't have insurance now, though."

"I don't think anyone's going to sue. Daniels is out there guarding the back, and a good thing. I'm going to have to join him soon. All the Hunters seem to feel the party's in here."

"Yeah. They tend to be like that."

"No complaint. They seem to know their stuff. Better than the security forces. They've made like pea soup and split."

"Now you get talkative!"

"It's the excitement."

"Okay, they're probably just regrouping. I want you and Daniels to get in here and guard our backs. What about MacCraken and Marino?"

"On the lam after the fireworks."

"Fine. No reason to stick their heads in where they might get them blown off. They've done their jobs, even though a little late." She patted him on the butt. "Go on out there, hero. It's good to fight with you."

"Thanks." He skipped on out, calling for Daniels.

"How touching," said Attila.

"Give me a different time, a different place, peace, and a bed, and you'll see some touchy-feely."

"Please, don't subject me."

"Then be nice." She turned around to see what kind of progress the Predators were making.

They had slowed a good deal, cautiously making their way toward the entrance of the sealed-off lab that Machiko had pointed out.

Suddenly a booming voice blasted from ceiling speakers.

"Welcome, marauders," proclaimed the amplified tones of Livermore Evanston. "Welcome, Machiko Noguchi. Welcome to a lovely trap!"

27

The yautja stopped. Raised their weapons as though to blast at the voice. They restrained themselves, however.

And then continued on their way.

"I would sincerely advise against that action!" suggested the voice imperiously.

The Predators ignored him, heading for the door.

"Noguchi! Warn them. They must stop, or they will be sorry!"

"I don't think that these folks have that particular word in their vocabulary, Evanston."

"You know, darling, you never even gave us the time to talk. I could have explained a great deal, and we could have had an even more mutually beneficial alliance."

"Gee, you know, that might have been a real

possibility—if you hadn't blown up my partner and tried to kill me!"

"That wasn't me. That was my security system, which you should have known would be in place and programmed to take defensive measures." Evanston's voice reeked with self-righteousness.

"I don't think, you lying monster, we would have had much to talk about, anyway."

"You may have made too many assumptions about my program, Machiko. It is for the best interests of humanity! You want to stop us from achieving our destiny?"

"If it's doing something stupid and dangerous and plain insane like what you're doing in there—then yes!"

"You are a traitor!"

"Okay, so arrest me. Lynch me. Whatever you want, Evanston—but first you have to get through my friends here."

The Predators were already pounding and blasting at the entrance doors to the secret lab.

As they worked, a green mist began to plume from the doors, folding in upon them and through the chamber.

Laughter drifted and echoed down from the speakers.

"You're a fool, Noguchi. You'll soon be surrounded by the well-trained security forces you managed to divert. What do you hope to accomplish?"

"Destroy this abomination!"

"Well, haven't we become the torch-bearing villager approaching the castle of Frankenstein? Perhaps if you'd attempted this a month ago, you might have had more success. Unfortunately for you, what you saw in the lab is only the process."

The sound of gears.

The sound of doors opening.

"We've had plenty of excellent results."

The sound of boots clopping toward them from the other side of the chamber.

Figures moved through the mist.

Emerged.

Machiko gasped.

"Oh, dear," said Attila, peering out of his little hammock.

"May I introduce you to our new warriors," said the voice of Livermore Evanston. "We have twenty up and on-line. I think they'll do very nicely. Aren't they stunning? They'll do humanity proud."

A clank.

A creak of chitin and armor and equipment.

The familiar, stomach-wrenching smell of acid.

"And now we shall deal with invading vermin, eh?" said Evanston.

The new arrivals attacked.

There was a booming of speakers and voices inside, but Ned Sanchez couldn't make out much from where he and Dick Daniels were entrenched behind a permacrete outbuilding, guarding the flanks of the operation.

"They're not coming in," said Daniels. "The bastards are just forming up out there, waiting for something."

There had been a few who'd rushed in, but Sanchez and Daniels had toasted them properly, and they'd scurried back to douse their tails in buckets of water or whatever.

Otherwise, they weren't doing anything.

"They're not shelling 'cause they don't want to hurt the building, if they can avoid it."

"Or what's *in* the building."

"I don't like the looks of it. We should be in there and out by now. It's going to take a lot to get through those guys!"

"We got in because we've got some pretty fierce fighters on our side. Take my word for it. Machiko knows her stuff."

"She was one of the survivors on Ryushi. I just hope that's not the case here," said Daniels.

"What? You want to have your cake and eat it?"

"You bet."

"Me too."

There was some sort of commotion within.

A seepage of mist.

"Somethin' sure as hell stinks in there," said Daniels. He made a face. "Literally."

"Yeah." Sanchez glanced uneasily toward the security forces, hunkered behind their vehicles.

"Look, you better get your butt in there and see what the hell is going on," said Daniels. "I'll keep the army guessing."

Another clatter. The sounds of blasting from within.

"Yeah. Right. Thanks."

Sanchez patted his fellow on the arm and then made a quick dash for the opening of the building.

No one shot at him.

As he entered, he immediately felt a raw blast of intuition.

Something was very wrong.

He saw, first, Machiko Noguchi, standing tall but with a somewhat cowed expression on her face. The face dangling below her—Attila's—appeared equally upset.

He turned in the direction of what they were facing, and saw the problem immediately.

"Jesus!" he said.

Though there was absolutely nothing holy about what he was looking at.

"Exactly," spat Machiko.

A trapdoor had opened in her chest, and her heart had fallen through.

"We've got more than we bargained for, I think," said Attila. "I just hope your boys are as good as you say."

What they had witnessed growing in that bubbling nutrient tank only hinted at the true monstrosities that glowered over them now, outfitted fully for killing and destruction.

They were the Buggers.

Bigger than normal bugs, they towered over the Predators, armored and outfitted with cyborg exoskeletons and extensions, with several arms, all holding weapons of various kinds, from blasters to spears and knives.

Nor were they all identical.

Some leaned more toward Queenhood, drool dripping down from their razor-sharp fangs, claws curiously tangled with weapons in awkward grips.

Some looked almost exactly like normal Hard Meat, from claws to shells to fang-ended head-tubings. However, metallic extensions wrapped around these: focusing oculars.

These Bugs could *see*.

All, however, moved stiffly, without the fluidity of their counterparts.

These were not tested models, Machiko realized.

These were creatures that had just been put on duty today, and hastily at that.

This was their first testing.

And *that* was their one hope.

With this realization Machiko called out to Bakuub.

The Predator immediately began to strike back toward them.

Machiko communicated her perceptions quickly to Attila.

"Tell him. Tell him there's hope—but his people must fight quickly and agilely."

Attila did so immediately and fluidly, also adding his own particular strategic insights.

The Predator traipsed back to his crew, speaking rapidly and gesturing.

The group split up.

"Thank you, Evanston," cried out Machiko Noguchi. "We don't have to go in there to destroy them now!"

She lifted her blaster and fired at the closest one.

It was a good shot.

She hadn't fired to kill. She had a good angle on what appeared to be an opening: an uncovered portion of the frontmost monster's leg.

The blast caught the thing in the knee joint. It emitted a high-pitched squawking and tumbled in the path of the others in a squabble of limbs and armor.

Like formation fighters, the Predators split and began to attack.

The monsters seemed taken by surprise at the fall of the foremost. Nonetheless, they aimed their guns and began to fire as well.

A Predator was caught full in the chest and bashed across a table like a toy, crashing out of sight. However, a moment later it popped back up like a burned jack-in-the-box and charged again, firing at its adversary.

The Buggers were more impressive physically than kinetically; however, they were not without power and cunning in battle. Nonetheless, there was a feeling of inexperience and confusion to their monstrous visages, a tentativeness to the movements.

And why not? They were, after all, fresh out of the vat, so to speak, armed with artificial memory and directed from afar.

The Hunter in Machiko sensed this.

She intuited that the Predators sensed this as well. She could see hand motions and clipped commands. Clumps of them broke apart, re-formed differently.

The fallen Bugger rolled away, and the others hurled past, eager to tear apart their prey. They were met with cross blasts from unexpected angles. For a moment their ranks held, but then, when two of their number literally blew up under the blaster onslaught, they retreated. These close quarters were not what they were programmed to fight in. And whoever was commanding them wasn't doing the proper job.

Nonetheless, it was a bloody, nasty melee.

Inexperienced though they might be, the Buggers were still fighting machines, and they fought with a fearsome coldness that held the worst and the deadliest of both races.

Nonetheless, the Predators were fighting machines as well, and fighting machines that now, in a contest not just for honor but for survival, fought with a single will and absolutely incandescent genius.

Machiko had never seen the like.

Nor, apparently, had Ned Sanchez.

He stood there, gawking.

"Get down," order Machiko, taking her own advice and parking herself behind a high-backed lab table.

"Shouldn't we help?"

"We'll just get ourselves killed now."

Anyway, Sanchez would. She'd run with a pack before and could probably meld her instincts into the group mix. Sanchez couldn't; he would probably get caught in the buzz saw of action and get ripped to pieces.

He got down as well, though he peered out at the action with great interest.

"My God, I've never seen anything like this. Talk about berserkers."

The Predators were fighting with a grace and precision that bordered on ballet. They somehow knew just the right moments to dodge, just the right moments to fire, just the right moments to advance.

They were defeating the enemy, an enemy programmed only for victory.

"Evanston bungled *this* project," said Machiko. "He

didn't realize how *stupid* the bugs are, and that's programmed into these creatures as well."

"What—you're saying they were no threat?" said Sanchez. "That we're doing this for nothing?"

"Oh, no. He could certainly make refinements, I'm sure. Nonetheless, fearsome and nasty as they are, they don't have the thousands of years of practice that the yautja have."

"Would someone please tell me what's happening?" said Attila.

"We're winning," said Machiko. "As far as I can tell."

From the looks of things, there were five of the twenty hybrids down, and only a couple of Predators. The Buggers were backing up toward the exit they had come from.

This retreat could not have come from their genetic programming. Retreat was a human notion. Evanston must be backing them away, hoping to re-form.

And then something odd happened.

"Dammit!" said Evanston.

Sweat was dripping from his brow.

Frantically, he engaged override programs for the team of xenos he'd sent in to kill the marauders. They had to retreat, re-form, and then attack again.

They would defeat these bastards. They had to. The computer had predicted a 95 percent probability of victory for just these conditions. He was going to have to run strategy variations and then—

A blue arc of electricity snapped from the panel.

Static power frizzled through his hair, making it stand on end.

The screens blacked out for a moment, then zapped back to normal.

What they showed on the screen, though, wasn't normal.

His creations were moving of their own volition.

Those that remained operational were not merely retreating, but scattering in all directions at a speed that he had not anticipated.

Evanston hit the control override button.

There was no response.

The control signals had shorted out. This was all happening too soon. There had been inadequate preparation time, dammit!

The things were free!

He snapped on the troop-radio comm-link.

"Zorski."

"Yes, sir."

"Red alert. There's a problem here at central. I've lost control of the creatures."

"Which creatures, sir. The bugs? These Hunter things? You want to settle down and stop shouting?"

"No, Zorski. The goddamn project. I've lost control of the project."

"That's just peachy keen."

"We've no choice. We're going to have to abort. Destroy everything. Get away from the lab. I'll give you thirty seconds, then I'm going to blow the whole thing," said Evanston.

"Yes, sir," said Zorski.

Livermore Evanston knew exactly what his creatures would do.

Rampage and destroy.

Indiscriminately.

At this point Livermore Evanston realized he had little reason to feel as confident as he had about the future of this project.

He'd have to scrap it and start over.

Fortunately, he'd be able to eliminate a number of his problems with it.

His fierce little smile returned as he groped for the keyboards and began to tap in the code for the program he would need.

28

At the top of the Buggers' shoulders sprouted the metallic squibs and squiggles that constituted the upward portion of their cyborg attachments.

A shiver of sparks and power spouted from these, like fairy dust spraying over their heads. They spasmed for a moment—and then they bolted.

"Dammit!" cried Sanchez. "One of those big bastards is heading this way."

Machiko had noticed, and she was up and ready.

Because the retreat had been so regulated before, despite their quick reflexes, the change in the Buggers surprised the Hunters. Several of the Buggers simply whipped through one flank, managing to injure one of the smaller warriors in the process. They were moving with a speed that Machiko had never before wit-

nessed in another species. There was a frenzy, an
insanity to their movements that was unnatural.

She could feel it in the air.

"They're *nuts*!" said Sanchez. He readied his gun to
fire, drawing bead.

"He's lost control," said Machiko. "Totally lost control!"

She suddenly realized something else.

"No," she said. "Don't—"

"What?"

Before he could fire, Machiko jumped on him. She
pushed his blaster rifle away, pushed him down behind a lab cabinet.

"What the hell—"

"Let it pass," she said. "It's not after you. It just
wants to get out of here."

Even as she spoke, the creature hurled itself past,
all aclatter, toward the door.

Machiko looked up.

All the Buggers were thundering away, not interested, it would seem, in fighting the yautja—except if
one got in the way. In that case it was the Predator
who was in trouble.

The Predators seemed as surprised as Machiko,
and for the most part allowed the Buggers to race out
into the night.

"We've got to get out of here!" said Machiko.

"Why?"

"What—do you think it's a trap?" said Attila.

"That's a definite possibility—what I think, though,
is that Evanston has lost control and he's panicking
right now—and he's going to just cut his losses and
try to cut us in the process."

"How?"

"Blow this whole place up." She didn't wait to explain more. "Attila, I want you to tell the Hunters in
no uncertain terms to *get out* of here. Right away."

Attila did not quibble.

Machiko lifted his head, and in a loud, command-ing voice he made the announcement in the Predator language.

The Hunters turned to Bakuub for confirmation.

Bakuub made a definite gesture.

Out of here!

Machiko and Sanchez ran.

They ran through the door, out to where Daniels was stationed.

"What the devil is going on? Those monsters—" said the man, still behind cover. "Look!"

He pointed.

The Buggers had run straight for the security troops.

They were tearing them apart wildly, savagely, pausing in their flight to rend and mutilate. Splatters and mists of blood rose, and blasters churned with bright fire, limning the beasts in mad berserker car-nage.

The Hunters started to stream out of the place.

"Trust me," said Sanchez, grabbing Daniels by the arm. "We've got to make a run for it. Now."

Daniels nodded. Unquestioningly, he followed as Machiko raced ahead, guiding them to the safe side of the insanity.

She could feel the urgency boring down upon her.

Got to get away from here.

Away.

Her breath was strained and heavy in her lungs. She could feel the deadliness in the atmosphere—

Livermore Evanston groped, found the button.

Pressed it.

Spoke the voice commands, modulated on his tones alone.

Better luck next time, he thought.

*   *   *

The biofactory exploded.

The blast emerged from the very center, like a vortex of pure energy, ripping apart every board and girder in its flash-quick pathway.

The force of the explosion slapped across Machiko's back like a hard hand, picking her up and throwing her a full two meters, trying to pluck Attila's head from her grasp.

She held on.

She held on and hit the ground, rolling and clinging to her consciousness.

Around her she could see, peripherally, the equally devastating effect that it had on the others. Several Predators who had not quite gotten out of the building were just pieces of flesh and bone and armor now, spread in clumps of gore. The others had been tossed a greater distance than Machiko had, some into unconsciousness.

Most, however, survived.

Most got to their feet immediately.

She could see them now, taking stock of things as a great wave of fire ripped and tore through what little remained of the factory.

The force of the blast had knocked over the security soldiers. Some were running for their lives now. Some were being wasted by the hybrids, who were buzzing through them like bloody chain saws, senseless slaughtering.

"Attila?" she called.

"Still here. Getting used to this."

"Sanchez? Daniels?"

" 'Fraid Dick got himself pretty well konked out. But I'm still here," Sanchez said.

"He'll be all right. Leave him for now. Probably he'll be safer there."

She could see Bakuub rallying his troops.

"They sure haven't quit. They're going after the hybrids."

"More power to them."

Even as he spoke, blaster fire began again, faded in the light from the fire.

"What do we do?"

"We take advantage of the chaos," said Machiko, "and we find the people who are responsible for this carnage. That might be the only way to stop it."

She pulled on his sleeve and then headed for the control headquarters, leaving behind the screams and the heat.

29

They found Chet Zorski in the main headquarters.

She'd had security guards around the building, but it took only a show of the firepower of Machiko's team and an explanation of what they were about ("We've got to stop these monsters—help us and we all might survive") for the security force to capitulate.

As for Zorski, she folded like a bad poker hand.

"It's out of control." She addressed Machiko calmly, but with her eyes wide with fear as she left her office. "We need your help to stop it. Have you got command of the Predators?"

"No, but we can work with them."

"We can establish some kind of truce and understanding?"

"Yes. But they'll want those superbug creatures destroyed."

"It's a bargain. They've gone nuts. I told Evanston it was too soon to use them."

"Where *is* Evanston?"

"He's got a control bunker. Down in the basement."

"Take us there."

"That's a bit difficult. He's got it pretty well sealed off. I don't think he's liking what he's seeing on his monitors."

"You've seen it?"

"You bet I've seen it. Between the bugs and the genetic progeny that we concocted, this settlement is going to get sliced up pretty badly."

"It doesn't have to be that way. Let me talk to him," said Machiko. "That is, if there's still a communication line down to him."

"Oh, yes, there certainly is. And it's glowing cherry-red now, believe me."

The group was quickly conducted into the room.

The monitors hanging from the wall depicted different scenes from the settlement, all showing a similar theme:

Violence.

Explosions against the night sky limned the struggle of man versus alien . . . versus beast.

The technicians all stayed in their seats, their hands on their heads without that gesture of surrender being requested. They, like most of the people there (with the exception of the mercenaries) looked as though they'd never had any experience with this kind of thing, much less the proper training. They were just colonists. Soft, noted Machiko, like most colonists.

Well, with what was coming out from under galactic stones lately, they were all going to have to get hard, fast.

That, of course, was why Evanston—and doubtless

the Company he was associated with—wanted creatures like those they were breeding.

Humanity, in its present stage, just didn't have the
hard edge to spearhead deep into the heart of the
stars.

Now, though, they were discovering that it took a
lot more than a genetic mix to deal with the Unknown.

The Unknown was buried deep in the heart of that
very mix.

"Punch me through to Evanston—immediately."

"Sure."

Zorski reached over for a comm-mike, handed it to
Machiko, then caught sight of what she was carrying
in her bag.

"God. It's the android," she said with an audible
gulp.

"Hello, there!" said Attila.

"Just keep them covered, Ned," Machiko said, and
clicked on the mike. "Evanston. Livermore Evanston.
Do you read me? I need to talk to you, man. I need to
talk to you *now*."

Silence.

She turned to Zorski. "Are you sure this line is
open?"

Zorski leaned over and punched a button. Con-
sulted a readout. "Yes."

"Evanston. Talk to me, dammit. You've got people
out there getting killed!"

A voice, slightly shaking with stress, broke through
the speakers.

"Yes, and who's killing them? Those damned creatures that you've led here. It's you, Noguchi! *You!*"

"Let's take a step into reality, you bastard. You
know what's gone wrong. Don't deny it. There's no
time for that now. No time for philosophizing."

"What do you want?"

"Something went wrong with the control on those things."

"Yes."

"There's got to be an override on them—right? A button you can push. You're no dummy, Evanston. You foresaw the possibility that you might not be able to control them. You had to have foreseen the need to destroy the things. Individually."

"What if there is?"

"Use it. Kill them, and we can make a truce. I can talk to my alien companions. You and your settlement will be spared. They just want the creatures destroyed. They are an insult to their sense of honor!"

"No! They are *mine*, and they contain the work and wisdom of decades! This eventuality *was* foreseen—there are independent programs in the creatures that will make them seek shelter. That's what they are going for now—shelter. When they are safe, they will turn off and be malleable—to the proper parties, of course."

"Bullshit. You'll blow them now, you bastard!"

"No. Plain and simple, no, Noguchi—and there's no way you can make me. I'm sitting tight here. Don't worry—everything's going to work out fine for me. For you, though—I honestly don't think so. . . ."

"Machiko!" cried Sanchez.

The mercenary pushed her aside, bringing his gun around. A flash of energy ripped into his side, knocking him back and into her gun arm.

The smell of singed flesh.

A yell.

Sanchez was down.

Standing just meters away was Zorski, holding a gun.

She looked terrified, but triumphant.

"Okay, you bitch. The ball's in *our* court now!"

30

Machiko did not even think; she just acted automatically.

The smoking, unconscious body of Ned Sanchez had fallen upon her own gun, but she had access to the sling that held the head of Attila the Hun. She allowed it to roll away to the side.

"Don't shoot!" she said.

"Oh, don't worry," said Zorski, still looking terrified, but a little more under control. "I think that Evanston has other plans for you."

"Good job, Zorski. That's why I was talking to her, to distract them," came Evanston's sneering voice. "Now I think we might be able to accomplish a few things."

"How many of your Hunter friends were still alive

after the blast?" Zorski demanded. "We need to know—ungh."

The grunt was due to the pencil-thin beam of light that streamed from the floor, connected with Zorski's forehead, and drilled a neat hole through her brain.

A wisp of smoke flew up from the cauterized wound.

Zorksi's gun dropped with a clatter.

Zorski dropped.

Dead.

Machiko was up in a moment, covering the technicians.

"One wrong move, and you're all on the floor." She looked over at Attila's head. His forehead still had the laser device peeking through. "Good job, Til."

"Ready for anything. Good placement. Excellent tactic."

She checked Ned. Still breathing. Burned some, but he'd make it.

She grabbed the mike.

"You heard that, you saw it," she wailed. "Now, Evanston, get your fat ass up here before we have to *blow* it up here!"

There was no reply.

There was no reply in the main headquarters from the lower bunker, because that bunker had been abandoned.

Plan B was in effect.

No sooner had he seen Zorski go down, his last hope, than Livermore Evanston grabbed his own gun and pack of necessary supplies, jumped, and lit out the emergency-exit tube, stuffing a handgun into his belt, just in case.

He'd foreseen the possibility of having to get out of his bunker. That was a little military lesson that the luminary Adolf Hitler had neglected in planning his escape, and since Evanston had studied all the great leaders, it was natural that he'd wanted to avoid their mistakes.

He'd made enough of his own.

After slipping his rotund self inside and strapping in, he pulled the glass top of the car down, pressed the release button. The car pneumatically responded, rocketing down the tube. The rush was amusement-park-ride quick, zooming through the darkness, zooming under the complex, and then suddenly rising at a rate that pushed him back in the seat with G-force.

Then he hit.

Springs and belts cushioned the impact, but still Evanston almost lost his breath.

The door whooshed open.

No time to waste.

There was but one hope for escape, and it was beyond that door. He struggled up and hurried there, grabbing the handle and pulling it open.

Night air rushed in, smelling of burned flesh and other less savory things.

Evanston didn't notice. His attention was on the sleek vehicle below the ramp above which he was now perched. The limo. And there was a figure inside, slouched down so as not to draw any attention from anything that might emerge from the violence that flamed just a few hundred meters away.

Evanston puffed down toward it.

The light of flames streaked across the door as he opened it.

"Good job."

"Thank heavens it's you," said Abner Brookings. "We're getting out of here."

"Yes. For now." Evanston got in, slammed the door, and motioned for the lawyer to get away from there. "My ship. We'll get out of here for now. But when I get back—there's going to be payback. Believe me."

The limo rushed through the night.

*   *   *

"Where's he going?" said Machiko. Not fooling around: Her gun was pointed right under the nostril of the chief technician.

A drop of sweat slipped down the man's smooth brow. "There's an escape tube from the bunker. He'll have a car waiting. I'd say he's given up. He's always got his spaceyacht ready. He's capable of piloting it himself. He's out of here."

She looked down at the head of Attila.

"Any thoughts on this?"

The thing lumbered out of the night.

"Jesus," said Brookings.

Evanston recognized it. It was too fast. It would catch them. The silhouette of his spaceyacht loomed just a hundred meters distant. So close. . . . How had the thing stumbled out this *far*?

He couldn't take a chance.

The limo was rocketing along, but the hybrid would catch them. Evanston leaned over and jerked the steering wheel, sending the limo careering off at a different angle entirely.

"Evanston! What are you *doing*!"

The limo hit the hybrid so hard it buckled its legs. Its body crashed through the windshield. It shrieked, its hands and claws scrabbling.

Evanston didn't wait to see what would happen next. With the car slowing to a stop, he pushed open the passenger door and jumped out, a peripheral glimpse of jaws closing around the right shoulder of Abner Brookings, Esquire.

Brookings screamed.

Evanston ran.

He ran for all he was worth, and he pulled his wrist up as he did so, hitting a radio stub, already attuned to the proper frequency. When he ran up the ramp, the door would be open on its other end, and the instruments ready and activated. There would be a minimum of preparation for takeoff.

His breath burned in his lungs. He could hear Brookings' cries suddenly cut off. The hybrid wouldn't be able to follow him, though. He'd snapped the creature's legs.

At long last the ship reared before him, beautiful and shiny in the moonlight. He raced up the ramp and sailed gleefully through the door, open as expected.

He cycled it closed.

Safe! Truly safe at last! All he had to do now was run up to the bridge and tap the codes for automatic takeoff! A force field had automatically erected outside the ship, and no one, not Bug nor Predator, not Machiko Noguchi nor the genetic hybrids, could *touch* him. He would take off, return to the center of his true power. Regroup. Recoup. Talk to the Company. Bring in the Marines and wipe these traitors from the face of *his* world. The determination and anger gave him the additional power to climb the steps to the bridge. He stumped through with a happy sigh.

A sigh that changed into a shriek as a form rose from the pilot's chair.

A form without a head.

It finished tapping out its final work on the computer bank and then stood up. "I suggest you not move," said the headless android body. "There will be parties here soon that will bring you back." The voice of Attila.

"No," cried Evanston, frustration replacing his fear. "No, you can't *do* this!"

He pulled out his gun and fired at the android torso. The bullet smashed the chest, pushed back the body. But it did not bring the robot down.

"I suggest you put that weapon down." Machiko's voice. "We've gotten the door open below. There will be a party there very soon to pick you up and take you back."

"Can't we talk about this, Noguchi?" said the man, his voice quavering.

"We certainly can, Evanston. Once you get back here. Once we get things back on-line. Now, I suggest you tell us what we need to know, or you're going to be in deep trouble."

Evanston considered. But not for long.

He told them.

"Thanks," said Noguchi. "See you soon."

Evanston took a deep breath. He sighed. There was nothing more to do. But if he could just stay alive, there would be hope.

He heard the pound of feet in the hold.

Looked up.

One of the Predators strode in. Evanston could smell musk and blood and hate. The thing took off its mask, and bright red eyes burned.

Gore dripped freely from its wounds and from the long knives attached to its wrists.

"Machiko," called Evanston. "Machiko!"

The android's headless body had, however, slumped back into the pilot's chair.

EPILOGUE

On my mark!" said Machiko Noguchi.

Technician hands hovered over controls.

"Now!"

Fingers flicked switches.

Machiko watched the monitors. On the screen closest to her, one of the Buggers was tearing through a doorway to get at men who had taken shelter.

Its cyborg portion simply blew up, rendering its bizarre body into tatters.

On ten other screens similar bloody and explosive fates met other Buggers.

When the last of the blood and bone drifted down, Machiko got on the all-comm.

"'That was to save your miserable carcasses as well as ours," she said. "The rule of the particular tyrant

256

here has ended. Lay down your arms. The yautja will not harm you if you are not armed! An immediate truce has been called. Headquarters has been captured and Livermore Evanston is being incarcerated. This is Machiko Noguchi. All will be explained in the fullness of time. Call in and report."

"Pretty authoritative," said a voice from behind her.

She turned and saw that Ned Sanchez was standing. He hobbled over and slouched into a chair.

"Ned." She went to him.

"Go back to work. I'll be fine."

"You need something for those burns."

"Yes, I do, but I'm sure that one of these technicians can fetch me something appropriate."

She snapped her fingers, and one of the techies went to a cabinet, pulled out a first-aid kit. As the guy attended to Sanchez's wound, the reports began to come in.

It took a few minutes, but everyone seemed to be willing to throw in the towel.

MacCraken and Marino called in, still hale and hearty, and were given assignments to help take care of the wounded.

"Hey, you sons of bitches. You left me out here to rot!" called the friendly voice of Dick Daniels.

"Hey," said Machiko. "You're alive. You should be grateful for that."

"I seem to have missed most of the fun."

"You okay?"

"Yeah, sure, nothing that a couple of beers won't take care of. Hope you're buying."

"You got a case coming, soldier. Now, get yourself to HQ and we'll put you to work."

"The only ones not to report in are the Hunters."

"I see 'em forming ranks on the vids," said Machiko. "Attila, have you still got that contact with Bakuub?"

The eyes in Attila's head dimmed a moment, then

brightened. "Yes. They're on their way in to talk about what happens next."

"Well, that about wraps it up," said Machiko.

"So to speak," said Sanchez, holding up his newly dressed arm. "What happens next, kiddo?"

"We let the Hunters hunt. We stay out of their way—and put down the guns here. Like I said, these guys will only kill those who kill. It's a part of their honor system, as that system is stronger, believe me, than the high-tech armor they wear."

"What about the settlement?"

She turned to Attila. "I guess we're going to have to ask Mr. Subversive about that."

"I know the correct parties to contact. We shall receive the necessary supplies and armament. This can be a free planet, independent of the Company—free to trade with whom we please. Free to accept the colonies we please."

"You think the Hunters will want to help us?"

Machiko shrugged. "I think the Hunters will do what they want. What I *hope* is that they don't stick around too long."

"After a good look at you, I don't blame you."

"We humans are lucky. We can change." She shook her head. "I don't think they can. I think they like themselves exactly the way they are. And that's why they are the way they are, and have been for a long, long time."

"No interest in psychoanalysts from the Predators?"

"Sure. Give some shrinks guns and send 'em running, and you'll get a lot of interest."

"Monitors are showing the arrival of a Predator party," said a technician. "Can't see them too well."

"Let them in, if you please," requested Machiko.

Appropriate controls were touched, and within moments they heard heavy footsteps outside.

"I believe the next thing to do is let them in," said Machiko.

The appropriate technician looked reluctant, but one proper glare from Machiko solved the problem.

Within moments the big aliens shouldered their way into the room. Attila made the proper greeting noises.

Bakuub stepped forward.

Machiko stepped toward him.

They made a gesture of mutual respect.

"Where's old Evanston?" asked Sanchez.

Machiko could handle that question, and so she asked.

Bakuub gestured to a member of his pack.

A warrior stepped forward.

Held out his hand.

From the hand dangled a net sack, holding a skull with only the spinal column, some flecks of brain, and a dangling eyeball to testify for its freshness.

"Trophy," said Bakuub.

One of the technicians gagged and then was sick beside his station.

"Alas, poor Yorick," said Attila.

"Straight from the horse's mouth," said Machiko.

"We rest now. We talk tomorrow."

Machiko nodded, and the Predators turned and left.

There was a moment of silence as Machiko looked at the blood of Livermore Evanston that had pooled on the floor.

Ned Sanchez looked at her with a different cast to his eye. "Well, Machiko. Looks like you've got yourself a world. What are you going to do with it?"

"Uh-uh, guy. *We've* got *ourselves* a world. And what are we going to do with it." She smiled. "Well, we're going to make it the best world in the universe." She raised her blaster. "Any objections to that?"

"Sounds great to me!" said one of the technicians.

"Me, too," said another.

She grunted. "Good." She poked a free finger at Attila. "In that case I'd like you to meet your new Head of State." She stepped forward, picked up the severed head, and placed it in a chair. "And what, O Head, is our first order of business?"

The eyes traveled around the room.

"I think our first project is exactly what Bakuub is going to be talking to us about tomorrow."

"Which is?" said Machiko.

"Have you forgotten the reason you're here? There are bugs on this planet. And unless I miss my guess, while we've been warring with ourselves, they've been increasing exponentially, as is their wont."

"Right. That's what we'll do. First, though, I think we could use a bit of a rest."

"Oh, and one more personal request," said Attila.

Machiko bowed. "Yes, Your Majesty."

"I really would like to reunite with a certain large part of my physical anatomy."

Machiko nodded. "We'll give it a try. I can't guarantee you anything, my dear friend." She scratched his scalp affectionately. "We'll try."